# IN THE GLORIOUS FIELDS

## EMILY HAYSE

# CONTENTS


The People     1

1. Pike     5
2. Selby     8
3. Thatcher     11
4. Carnegie     15
5. Thatcher     22
6. Irene     26
7. Rosamund     34
8. Alan     38
9. Gable     42
10. Selby     46
11. Gable     52
12. Irene     57
13. Carnegie     63
14. Gable     67
15. Thatcher     72
16. Alan     77
17. Newton     82
18. Selby     89
19. Irene     92
20. Thatcher     96
21. Newton     99
22. Pike     108
23. Sikes     111
24. Alan     115
25. Carnegie     118
26. Sikes     123
27. Pike     125
28. Alan     127
29. Gable     132

30. Jem     136
31. Rosamund     143
32. Newton     147
33. Jem     150
34. Thatcher     155
35. Carnegie     159
36. Gable     166
37. Selby     169
38. Jem     181
39. Thatcher     190
40. Carnegie     199
41. Newton     202
42. Selby     208
43. Thatcher     214
44. Gable     222
45. Newton     228
46. Irene     233
47. Rosamund     239
48. Pike     244
49. Alan     248
50. Thatcher     252
51. Newton     257
52. Rosamund     266
53. Irene     269
54. Selby     276
55. Newton     279
56. Irene     286
57. Carnegie     294
58. Pike     299
59. Carnegie     301
60. Rosamund     305
61. Newton     317
62. Carnegie     320
63. Rosamund     325
64. Thatcher     332

65. Rosamund                336

66. Alan                    345

67. Newton                  348

68. Rosamund                353

69. Thatcher                364

70. Gable                   368

71. Rosamund                374

72. Thatcher                382

73. Pike                    386

74. Newton                  391

75. Selby                   394

76. Alan                    401

77. Selby                   407

78. Thatcher                411

79. Rosamund                415

80. Selby                   422

81. Newton                  425

82. Carnegie                429

83. Pike                    435

84. Thatcher                438

85. Gable                   442

86. Carnegie                450

87. Archer                  454

88. Pike                    458

89. Archer                  462

90. Newton                  466

91. Carnegie                471

92. Rosamund                474

93. Thatcher                477

94. Carnegie                481

95. Selby                   486

96. Newton                  490

97. Thatcher                493

98. Peter                   495

*Acknowledgments*                499

*About the Author*               501

*Also by Emily Hayse*            503

*When I was a little girl, the West symbolized freedom to me. When I was sad or lonely, I imagined myself going West. This book is dedicated to those glorious fields, mountains, mesas, and pine forests that comforted my soul and fired my imagination.*

# THE PEOPLE

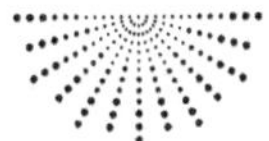

Doctor Sikes: Old as the hills with as many secrets. He set Archer Scott's life on its course and continues to watch him from afar.

Archer Scott: Governor of the Western Territory. Trying to keep his head above water as the territory expands and the demands from out East increase.

Rosamund Scott: Thriving in her role as the wife of the Governor of the Western Territory, Rosamund is eager to begin her family and build her dream.

Raymond Lacey: Marshal of the Western Territory and brother to the governor's wife, Raymond is ready to begin his life as a husband and rancher on top of his duties as marshal.

Jesse Thatcher: A rancher at heart, his loyalty to his cousin Archer lands him in trouble more often than not.

Lesley Gable: Glory Mesa's surveyor, desperate to recover the honor he believes he's lost in the eyes of his wife.

Edith Gable: Remorseful over her fight with her husband, she fears he will die trying to restore his honor.

Kate Carnegie: Formerly employed at Carson's saloon, she is determined to make good on her opportunity as a newly sworn-in Deputy Marshal of the Western Territory.

Irene Sandler: After making the journey West to escape the suffocating atmosphere of high society back East, she is now engaged to Raymond Lacey and eager to begin the next chapter in her life.

Cristobal Newton: One of the wealthiest men in the West, he wants nothing more than to stay home and work his ranch.

Maria Pike: After fleeing Glory Mesa, she hides in the wild hills and plans her revenge.

Peter: No-one's boy who cleans at the saloon and runs errands.

The Swift Brothers: Laughing blond fellows, hard to tell apart and settled on a large spread. One-quarter Auki on their mother's side.

Jack Selby: Rifleman, paid to guard sheep from the predators of the range. His shy demeanor and love of poetry belie his skill at tracking and killing.

Harrison Terhune: Still fighting to regain his place in society after his unfortunate relationship with Maria Pike, he faces new challenges due to widespread drought and personal controversy.

Blue Harding: Former leader of the largest outlaw band since Mortimer's downfall, he now rides under the tin badge of a deputy marshal.

Tagweiah: A member of the Auki nation and cousin to the Swifts, he frequently rides over the border to visit his cousins and his friend, Archer Scott.

Hannah Milton: Having no family ties, she comes West as a mail-order bride and finds it more than she bargained for.

Holt: A former henchman of Mortimer's, he is now a drifting troublemaker and gun for hire.

1

# PIKE

I STAND ON THE EDGE OF THE CLIFF, SO NEAR THAT I feel the pulse of the wind rising below me, and drink in the warm light of the rising sun. All my life I have been misunderstood. Any fool can say that, of course—but in my case, it is true.

My men consider it a blow that we have been forced to flee. They do not know that now I am unfettered. No time shall be wasted in pleasantries and my old ladders to fame.

Now all I have is a broad, strong path forward and no one here to stop me. I came to this land twenty years ago with nothing but a husband and raw ambition. I lived through the wildest days; I cleaned my share of wounds, held my share of dying men's hands. My hands helped build Glory Mesa, and though younger, softer hands have pried it from my grasp, they will not keep it from me long.

I am a woman who knows what it takes—the only one

who truly knows. These women, even these men, will find their limit, but I will remain like the desert sun, relentless and powerful.

Inescapable.

Because if the thing you love most is threatened, you will abandon all else to protect it. And I love nothing more than this territory and the reins of power that will soon lie slack in these men's grasps.

"Mrs. Pike," comes a deep, rough voice behind me.

I have no love for Holt. He is uncouth and a coward at heart. But he's a fighter, and he fights dirty; and men like that are useful to me right now.

I turn to him. "What do you want?"

"What's your answer? If I'm to ride, I should have done it before dawn."

"Ridiculous. You're not a greenhorn. You can make up the time. Stop whining and have some patience."

This silences him.

I turn away and finger the thin gold necklace around my throat. "Go to him. Guard his water holes. Do what he says and don't turn on him, or I'll have you shot next time you're riding out on some lonely stretch, you hear?"

"Begging your pardon, ma'am, I'm the one who does that sort of work, not t'other way round."

"I have others besides you. Your type's great weakness is that gold will buy anything from you."

He grunts, displeased.

"Do you need anything else?"

"No, ma'am."

"Good. Give Stanton my regards and—don't mention anything about my leaving Glory Mesa." I turn to him with an easy smile. "I will have more work for you before long, I assure you. With gold, of course."

"Where does all your gold come from?" he asks.

What a fool. I give a little laugh. "Keep your mouth shut and you'll see more of it. Open your mouth, and it dries up." I snap my fingers. "Safe journey."

I hear the rocks dislodged by his rough boots as he leaves. He's such a bull about everything, no delicacy about him.

I turn my gaze back out over the wild land, caught in rich light and hard shadow.

Far below me, between the hills and the horizon, moves the thread-thin train, heading westward toward Glory Mesa.

I pull my shawl tighter about my shoulders, against the wind, against the world.

What a beautiful morning this is.

## 2

## SELBY

A ROAR OF RUSHING WINGS WAKES ME, FILLING THE darkness. I struggle up, fumbling for my rifle, raising myself to a crouch.

The stars cut in and out as dozens of *isarks* flash across the sky. Their deep, throaty cries rip the cool night.

The sheep are scattering, noisy, some scrambling over each other to reach the rocky overhang beside the shepherds' camp, cramming themselves against the rock walls, crushing each other in their frenzy to escape the predators.

I've never seen anything like this in all my days, even on the battlefield. *Isarks* rarely fly by night, let alone swarm.

Something is wrong.

By some miracle, one of the shepherds finds me in the dark. He seizes my arm. "What do we do? Can't you shoot them?"

"Not this many. Not in the dark."

"It's bad," he whispers. "It's very bad."

"Sure is." One of the beasts swoops too close; the air from its leathery wings whips against my shirt. I raise my rifle.

Next one that comes too close is going to get it.

"You don't understand. They say the *isarks* will swarm when the curse is coming upon us."

"Do they, now? Who, the Far Hill clan?"

"Yes. And the Red Tree. The Auki too, maybe. I am not sure."

"So it's the end of the world."

"Not yet." I feel the warmth of his breath as he draws close to me in his fear, closer than any of the shepherds have dared in all the time I've traveled with them. Compared to two hundred swarming *isarks*, I guess I don't seem so dangerous.

Another swoops close and I fire. It crumples to the earth, swiping us both to the ground with a shuddering wing.

I pick myself up off the rocky ground, my head throbbing. I feel around for the other man and find his arm. "You all right?"

"Yes," he grunts.

"Hurt?"

"Not bad." His boots scrape audibly against the hard ground as he pulls himself up.

The swarm has passed us over.

The other shepherds are gathered a little below us, most huddled together in the dim gray of approaching morning, a few brave souls trying to pen up the terrified sheep and sort the living from the dead.

They'll probably be collecting them for days.

"You're bleeding," one of them observes without emotion. He lets go of his staff long enough to gesture to my right arm.

"So I am." I dig a spare handkerchief out of my vest pocket and rip my torn sleeve further to get at the wound.

It's not deep.

"Is my horse still here?"

One of them nods to the cave where the sensible animal stands, remarkably calm in the face of panic and carnage.

I saddle him up and find my canteen, pouring a little water over the bloody cut. I hang the canteen back on the saddle and reach down to check the cinch.

"Where are you going?"

I knot the handkerchief around the wound with my teeth and my left hand. "Glory Mesa."

I heave my pack up behind the saddle and shove my rifle into its sheath. Then I draw my pistol, checking the chambers and reloading the empty ones.

"Are you coming back?"

I swing into the saddle and lean low, my eyes searching the sky overhead for wings. I'll have to ride out of here like quicksilver.

I glance back at the ravaged camp. "Back to what?"

I clap spurs to my horse and we're gone into the pale morning.

3

# THATCHER

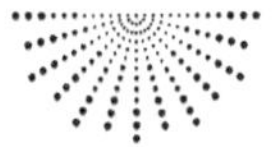

I STAND ON THE TRAIN PLATFORM UNDER A SIGN THAT declares the Glory Mesa stop in bold golden letters.

The sign's not strictly necessary, since there's no stop beyond us but the stockyard. Gable tells me the railroad'll eventually run south to the border and westward to far-out places beyond this territory, but for now, it's just us at the end of this lonely, dust-swept track.

Archer stands beside me, hands thrust in his pockets, eager at the sight of smoke on the horizon. Beyond him stands Raymond, quietly checking his pocket watch. He reaches up and absently smooths down his mustache.

Folks in Glory Mesa are used to seeing them around, but the quick hum of voices still starts when they're spotted. Women whispering behind hands, men staring, children turning around to look even as they're scolded by their mothers.

I'm not sure why I agreed to be part of this circus. I didn't come to be stared at, nor do I have any interest in seeing a flurry of womenfolk get off the train.

"What's the matter, Jesse?" Archer raises an eyebrow. His concern is cheap. He's looking at my scowl with amusement.

"It's too hot," I grumble, pulling at my collar.

"Is it?" He whistles sympathetically. "Even in the shade."

Raymond chuckles low in his throat, but there's understanding in his eyes. He knows exactly what I'm feeling.

A shrill blast sounds down the track and the engine belches smoke. The platform is filling with people.

Raymond straightens his vest.

The train gives one more shriek as it thunders in, grinding slowly to a halt and releasing a long hiss of steam.

The doors open and the passengers flood out. A few are newcomers, staring and whispering. The rest rush on their way with a speed that never ceases to amaze me.

And then I see the familiar faces. Rosamund descends with all the grace of a queen, her eyes bright, her wide smile like sunshine, not caring that there are a dozen onlookers. She goes straight to Archer, who sweeps her into his arms.

"Did you miss me?" she asks.

"It felt like a whole week," he replies. "How's the child?"

"Just fine." She closes her mouth in a demure, curving smile. Their baby is due soon, a month or so now, but you wouldn't know it to look at her.

It's not my baby, I know. But there hasn't been a child in the family since me, and since Archer's practically my brother, I figure it's only natural I take an interest.

"Jesse." Rosamund turns to me. "Look at you."

I look down and spread my arms sheepishly. I look like an unwashed rancher.

She clasps my hand in both of hers. "You look so well. I do hope you'll stay awhile after the wedding."

"If the ranch cooperates," I promise.

Irene Sandler is descending, her arms loaded with packages, followed by Edith Gable and a couple train attendants.

"Let me take those for you." Raymond somehow manages to take them all and still has room to offer his arm.

Irene takes it, clasping one of her hands over the other and looking up adoringly into his face. "I hope you won't be displeased...there was ever so much of a to-do over us in Square's Run. The press too. They were horrible."

"Nothing we can't handle," he says mildly.

"Hello, Jesse," Irene greets me. "You are in town again!"

"Wouldn't miss this," I grin.

"It means a great deal to Raymond that you've come, so it means a great deal to me as well." She smiles so sincerely that I think she must really mean it.

"We should get these back to the house." Raymond nods in farewell, and they head for the team and wagon waiting on the other side of the platform.

That leaves me with Archer and Rosamund, who are talking in undertones, laughing.

"Jesse." Rosamund looks up at me, her eyes dancing. "When are you going to get married?"

"What? Me?"

"Look how happy your cousin is." She smiles up at Archer.

"Ain't no woman's putting her lariat around me." I stiffen as if there's one ready to jump out of the shadows.

Rosamund studies me, her lips parted in the beginnings of a smile. "Just you wait, Jesse Thatcher. A good thing's bound to come your way eventually."

As they pass me by, Archer catches my eye with a little smile that says, clear as day, *You know she's right.*

"What do you call my ranch, then?" I call after them.

4

CARNEGIE

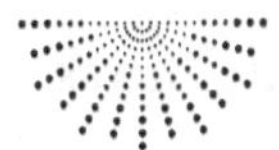

THE DESERT STRETCHES OUT SHIMMERING BEFORE ME. I uncork my canteen and take a warm sip.

Some days I do miss the way water rushes cold from the ground out of a pump, but I sure don't miss the view from the porch of Carson's saloon.

I give the horse a drink too. It's not much, but it'll hold us until we reach Pecos Springs, a few miles north of here.

I tie the canteen to the saddle again and take off my hat to wipe the sweat from my forehead.

That's when I see him coming across the desert: a lone figure on a dun horse, his tattered coat whipping in the hot wind.

He's riding from the east, slow and easy, but he and his horse both look to be in rough shape.

I swing up into the saddle and ride to meet him. The

figure halts as I approach, and his horse shifts nervously. I'm careful to keep my hand away from my gun as I ride up and rein in.

It's Jack Selby. Dusty, a bit bloodied, but Selby all the same, and studying me intently.

He touches his brim with a bloody-knuckled hand.

"Kate Carnegie, isn't it?" he asks in his soft voice.

"Yes, it is. You look rough. Your horse does too."

"We ran into some trouble out on the grazing ground east of here. The *isarks* are swarming. I've never seen the like."

I've never before heard Selby admit he's never seen the like of anything, and I daresay there isn't much he hasn't seen.

"I'm headed Glory Mesa way," he says wearily.

"Not in that condition, I hope."

He just smiles, ever so faintly.

"Let me ride with you up to the springs, Jack. We'll camp and you can eat and clean out those wounds on you and your horse. They don't look good."

He gives in with a nod. I turn my horse around and we head north together.


THE SPRINGS ARE a nice little spot in the middle of otherwise unforgiving territory. Water, some trees and grass—it's a good place to camp, or, if you're lucky, to rest awhile during the heat of the day.

We build the fire together, and I set water to boiling. We'll eat first and then I'll see to him and his horse, if he'll let me.

He offers beans to add to the pot, and since I'm fresh up from Laramie station, I've got a side of bacon. I make a quick batch of pan bread to go with it.

"Smells good." He sounds shy.

"Should be." I take a taste from the end of the spoon. "I had to cook a mess like this every day for four years."

"I remember."

"It's ready." I sit back on my heels and hold out my hand for his plate.

He's kept it scrupulously clean, something I can't say for most men around here who carry their own kits.

I plate the food up and we eat hearty. He's quiet through the first plate, and by the second, he seems more relaxed.

"It's none of my business," he says at last, "but may I ask what you are doing all the way out here?"

"I work for Marshal Lacey now." My heart still warms at the words. "I ride this trail from Glory Mesa all the way to Santos Flores."

"Have you had any trouble?"

"Some, but not much. I try not to get into scraps, just be eyes and ears. If folks know the marshal's got someone on the watch, they're less apt to make trouble."

"I meant—on account of you being a woman." There's a gently troubled look in his eyes.

"Sometimes," I admit. I've never admitted it before. "But I try not to expect it. That helps."

"I'm sure it does." He scrapes his beans together and takes a last bite.

"I've got hot water for you here, and the poultice," I say as he sets the plate aside. "Would you let me help you?"

"I'll let you know if I need it." He unwraps a blood-stained handkerchief from his hand. He goes to his saddle and pulls out an extra shirt that's in tatters. "I don't suppose you have any spirits?"

"Sorry, no."

"We'll make do." He tears the shirt into strips and carries the hot water over to his horse. He hums and talks to the animal in a low voice as he wets the strips and washes the scabbed scrapes and gashes.

The horse trusts him entirely. It flinches and shifts at the sting, but it doesn't step away.

"That's a good horse."

"He's seen me through just about everything," Selby replies, warmth entering his tone.

By the time he's done with the horse, the next pot of water has been long ready and the light's fading. He starts with his hand, dabbing it out carefully with the end of a clean handkerchief.

"Will he be all right?" I nod toward the horse.

"He should be. The scars will fade. I wrapped him with my slicker and strapped a blanket around his neck when we made a run for it. There wasn't much left of the flock, and I didn't want to lose him too."

He sighs softly. He's seeing it over again in his mind.

"You've been with those herds a long time."

He shakes his head slightly. "There's nothing I could have done against *isarks* in those numbers. And I figured the governor ought to know what's happening."

"You mean they might come our way?"

"No telling," he grunts, fastening the handkerchief around his hand again.

He rolls up his sleeves next. Bruises and bloody scratches of all sizes run across his forearms and down his shoulders.

I wince a little. "Was that all from the *isarks?*"

"No, only the bruises. It's lucky I tangled with a smaller one. A larger one could have broken my arms. The scratches are from thorn brush later on, trying to lose them."

"Ah."

As he reaches for the hot water, I see an old brand on his arm, initials of some sort, obscured by the bruises.

Slowly he cleans both arms.

"I have a couple I can't reach." He hitches one shoulder. "Do you mind?"

"Of course not."

He turns his back to the fire and hikes his shirt up over his shoulders.

His back and shoulders are covered with old scars. Some run parallel like claw marks. One looks like the exit of a bullet wound. A fresh laceration runs from one shoulder blade across his back, and another, deeper, runs half the length of his spine.

"Were those the claws or teeth?" I dip a strip of cloth into the hot water and wring it out.

"Claws. They catch with their claws if they can and make the kill with their beaks."

He talks of it so easily.

The wounds are slightly infected, but not dangerously so. If it hurts, he doesn't show it; he's perfectly still and doesn't catch his breath once. But his skin feels abnormally hot.

"These should really be bandaged," I sigh, leaning back on my heels. "Your shirt isn't that clean."

"We'll be in Glory Mesa soon enough." He reaches up and pulls his shirt down, tucking it in, adjusting the collar as if he were a fine man used to the proper way of things.

The firelight plays on his long, sun-weathered face, on his sensitive features, on his chestnut brown hair. I suddenly see the boy he must have been and wonder how far he is from home.

"Thank you." He gets to his feet and dusts himself off gingerly. "I'd like to start early tomorrow. You may want to get some sleep."

I stay on the ground beside the fire, watching as he pulls his rifle out of its sheath. "I can watch. You should be the one sleeping."

"I don't sleep," he says gently. He settles beside the fire with his rifle over his knees.

"Wake me up anyway."

I stand up and go to my saddle, unfastening the bedroll.

"Here, I've got an extra blanket."

I toss it across to him and he catches it with one hand, quick as a cat. "You wake me up, Jack. Hear?"

5

## THATCHER

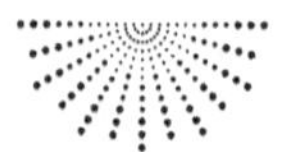

I glance out the window of Archer's office and see Doctor Sikes walking down the street, out toward the south end of town.

Alone.

Sikes usually takes his mule with him if he's going to the hills.

Archer looks up from his desk. "What is it, Jesse?"

The scratching of his assistant's pen stops. The assistant is little more than a boy—more than twenty, maybe, but reedy and nearsighted and talks softly.

I think my cousin took him in out of charity.

"I dunno. Sikes is walking south down Main Street."

"Well, as long as some jasper doesn't ride him down, I don't see why that's cause for concern."

I shake my head. "It just ain't normal. I can tell." I pull my hands out of my pockets and move toward the door.

"Look, you get Raymond if there's trouble," Archer says. I think he still hasn't forgiven me for almost getting myself killed by an old mountain man.

"And get him shot right before his wedding?" I grin. "Nah, I'll take my chances."

"Get a move on, then."

I swing the door wide and step out onto the dusty porch. That little assistant needs to come sweep it off again.

I mount up on my bay and head out into the street.

Doctor Sikes may be as old as the hills, but he moves fast. I've almost lost him by the time I've dodged a kid on a pony, a lady's buggy, and a stray dog.

Since when did Glory Mesa get big enough to support scrounging stray dogs?

Sikes stops in the road, a stone's throw beyond the town limits, as if waiting for something. As I near the edge of town myself, I see two riders on the horizon.

I wonder if he has been watching for them or if he knew they were coming. It's not likely he could have spotted them from his porch, and even if he did, he would have needed a mighty good pair of field glasses to know who they were.

As soon as they're close enough, I recognize one of them.

I raised that little pinto of Kate's from a foal, and I'd know the dark splash across her chest anywhere. Any thief would have to be an artist to hide those markings.

The other rider is a man, dusty and tattered, riding a dun with three white socks and a snip. I've seen that horse before, but I can't place it.

Kate reins in first. She's talking to the doctor as I near them, and as soon as the second rider's head snaps up, I know him.

"Jack Selby!" I spur my horse forward and spring to the ground when I reach the newcomers. "Goodness, man! I didn't know if you were still alive." He just gives me a small smile and swings down, extending a bandaged hand.

From the looks of him, maybe I was right to wonder.

"He has come at last," says Doctor Sikes with finality.

"Who?"

"He has." He holds out his hand to indicate Selby.

"Yes, we can all see that."

Jack glances up, running a scratched hand through his hair. And then I see the look on Sikes's face. It's a grim pride, as if Jack has done something great.

"He needs a couple of those scratches seen to," says Kate pointedly. "Neither of us had anything strong to clean them with."

"I will see to them," says Sikes. He looks out to the north-west. "It cannot be long now," he whispers.

A strange shiver comes over me and I get a powerful feeling that I'm witnessing something beyond me.

"I'll be all right if you just give me some clean bandages," protests Selby softly. "I can find a boarding room and a bottle of hard spirits and clean them myself."

Doctor Sikes snaps back to his usual self. "Is that how you get by? You will do nothing of the sort. Hard spirits, my soul and body."

He takes Jack Selby by the arm and leads him up the street.

"See to my horse," Selby calls over his shoulder. This once, Jack suffers himself to be led. I know no one who willingly picks a fight with that man.

I take his horse's reins and look the animal over. "Looks like you saw some action," I murmur.

"*Isarks*," says Kate, unfazed, and moves past me up the street.

"*Isarks*! Did you see them?"

"No, I didn't."

"Hm." The horse turns his head to look at me and grinds the bit slowly in his teeth.

"Well, you're a sight braver than me," I chuckle, scratching under his dark mane. "Let's get you put up. There's a big weddin' to-do in a couple days and soon there won't be room for a single more piece of horseflesh in this town."

The dun is not impressed.

6

## IRENE

"To the finest gun in the Western Territory." Archer Scott raises his glass and the sunshine streaming in the barn window catches it, setting it alight. "To the man I get to call brother and to the woman I can now call sister—may each year grow sweeter, brighter, happier. Congratulations."

A strong ripple of applause crosses the room. The raised glasses are sipped and laughter breaks out, but only I feel Raymond's hand tighten on mine.

He doesn't need to speak a word for me to know what he thinks—or for my heart to quicken. I lean my head against his shoulder.

I am so blessedly happy.

A chair scrapes and Jesse Thatcher stands up, holding his glass aloft.

"When I first laid eyes on Raymond Lacey, I knew he

was tough as whipcord. Tougher, in fact. I watched him share a horse with Gilchrist all the way from the desert's edge back to Glory Mesa."

A laugh rises and someone slaps Gilchrist on the back.

"But when I got to know him, I realized he's not only tough as whipcord, he's got a heart of gold. There's no man in the world I'd trust more to have my back in a fight. May you both have every happiness in the world."

"Amen to that," says Archer. And the toast is drunk.

Someone lets out a whoop. The music starts, wild and quick.

Raymond drains his glass. With a slow smile, he stands up and holds out his hand.

I hesitate for a moment, unsure if he is teasing me. But when I give him my hand, he takes it and strides out to the dance floor, and the cheers erupt afresh.

The music thrums like the rushing pulse in my ears. His hand goes to my waist. I put my hand on his shoulder.

He winks, just for me, and we're away, whirling across the floor. The crowd is clapping along. I'm moving so fast, breathing so hard, laughing.

The world blurs and he is the only constant, his eyes twinkling.

The music ends suddenly in an upflung chord and the world returns to normal; I'm still panting and laughing. I don't think I've ever been so happy or so dizzy in my life.

"I didn't know you could dance like that!" I straighten

and push my hair out of my face. I've never seen eyes shine the way his are shining now.

"We've danced before."

"Once, and it was slow!"

"Well, I avoided the officers' parties in the army, but I couldn't avoid them altogether."

I laugh. "Can we go again?"

He holds out his hand.


We walk among the guests, greeting them all. We spared no expense for the wedding, and the barn at the end of Main Street is full to bursting with people—townsfolk, Raymond's old army friends, men from outlying homesteads who rode with him last year. Even a handful of reporters from the East have come, uninvited; Rosamund sheltered me from them early in the day, but I saw them in the street, and it will only be a matter of time before I am sure to see them again.

I shake hands, repeat names, smile, all in a blur.

To my slight consternation, Raymond introduces me to Blue Harding, the outlaw.

"Ex-outlaw, ma'am," he corrects, bending to kiss my hand. "Marshal Lacey is a lucky man."

He has shocking blue eyes and his stiff blond hair is combed down neatly.

"Sorry I couldn't invite everybody," Raymond says with a chuckle.

"They're a mite sore about it." Blue grins. "I promised I'd bring them cake."

"I'll send you the rest." Raymond slaps him on the shoulder.

We move on to a slim, sensitive-faced man who stands quickly as we approach. From the way his hands fidget, I think he isn't used to crowds and parties.

"Irene, this is Jack Selby."

"Pleasure." He holds out a bandaged hand and I shake it. "I wish you both joy."

"How are you, Jack?" Raymond asks.

"Feeling a little better, thank you."

"Anything I can say to get you to stay?"

He smiles shyly and shakes his head.

"Well, I'll keep trying."

We stop to greet Kate, who sits at a table near the door. She is wearing a beautiful dress, purple and blue, and her curls are pinned up.

"I am so happy for you both," she says, her face aglow.

Raymond's eyes gleam in response. "Thank you."

She thrusts out her hand to me, warmth and business all at once, and I clasp it tight.

As we near the door, Raymond bends his head close. "Darling, will you do me a favor?"

"Anything."

"The press want a minute. A photograph and a statement, that's all. We'll be brief."

"I don't mind." I look up at his gentle face. At this moment, nothing could make me unhappy.

We head out together into the blinding sun.

"Marshal Lacey!" shouts a man's voice, spotting him, and a clamor ensues until Raymond raises his hand for silence.

"Mrs. Lacey and I are pleased that you fine gentlemen have come out to share our joyous day. This is a proud day for the territory and a glad one for us."

"Is it true that you fell in love after he saved you from outlaws?" demands one voice. Another shouts, "Were they the notorious Red Arms?"

Raymond turns away from them and speaks quietly with one of the deputized gentlemen who have been guarding the door for us.

The deputy walks down among the reporters and selects a man hauling a great deal of equipment on his shoulder and trailed by a boy carrying more.

"Marshal Lacey, this is Ephraim Clarke from the Morning Tribune."

"Pleasure." Raymond extends his hand and shakes the man's sweaty one.

"The pleasure is mine, sir. Thank you for the honor. Where would you like to set up?"

The side of the barn has to do for a backdrop. The deputy fetches a parlor chair and sets it in front of the slats. I sit in it with my hands folded, and Raymond is directed to stand at my shoulder.

We wait as the photographer and his assistant have an animated discussion, gesturing to us all the while.

Mr. Clarke comes over to me, apologetic and mopping his brow. "I'm sorry, ma'am, terribly sorry, but would you mind standing? Your husband's a tall man—"

Raymond starts to chuckle under his breath.

"Not at all." I stand up and we are rearranged to stand together, holding hands.

The photographer is beaming. "This'll be one of the first pictures taken in the territory."

"You don't say." Raymond straightens his coat and returns his hand to mine.

I stand like a statue and it is hard not to smile, my heart is so full. I do not mind that the reporters want part of our day; I do not mind that they want our picture. Raymond is beside me in the sun, his hands in mine, and that's all I need.

"And—" Mr. Clarke steps aside. "That should do it. Marshal Lacey, Mrs. Lacey, thank you so much for the honor."

"Our pleasure." Raymond twines his fingers into mine as we head back toward the front of the barn.

Another photographer stands by the doors, talking to Governor Scott and Jesse Thatcher. When Archer sees us, he waves us over genially.

"Raymond, this gentleman wants a picture of you and I and any other folks who have 'helped bring peace to this wild territory.'" He gives a wry smile. "It'll be like those staff pictures we took during the war."

Raymond looks at me.

"Do it," I urge.

"Raymond, you must!" Rosamund raises her voice, laughing.

"Do it," I whisper. I plant a kiss on his cheek and retreat behind the photographer.

I watch as Jesse brings out Jack Selby, the Swift brothers and Tagweiah, Kate, Clay Carson, Lesley Gable, even Blue.

The photographer sets out a row of chairs and the men begin lining up behind them.

"Come on, gentlemen," he urges. "Some of you move down into those chairs! They're for sitting in, not decoration."

Raymond sits down on the far side and Archer on the other. The chairs begin to fill.

"Peter! Come on," calls Carson, and the boy, twitching with eagerness, joins the picture.

"Hold still, now! There's a lot of you, so don't be the man to ruin the photograph. Begging your pardon, ma'am."

A flicker of amusement runs through Kate's eyes, but her face is marble.

There they stand, a dozen or more, still and proud, staring hard against the sun.

I am proud on Raymond's behalf. Looking at these fine souls who would follow him anywhere, my heart wants to burst.

When it is over, they disperse in a flood of smiles and voices. The youngest Swift chases Peter around the side of the barn; Jesse is talking with Kate. Rosamund hangs on her husband's arm.

And Raymond is in their midst, laughing. Really, truly laughing.

I've never seen happiness like this anywhere else.

We have it hard in the Western Territory, but I swear, when our time comes, we will have lived more than most.

# 7

# ROSAMUND

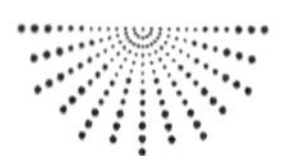

"Two things are bound to turn ugly when not watched," Jesse Thatcher intones lazily, leaning his elbows back against my porch rail in the darkness. "A spark in the dry plains, and men with too much to drink."

Archer laughs appreciatively as he takes a sip. "Those were the days."

"Sounds like they're comin' back." Jesse jerks his head in the direction of the saloon.

It was near dusk when we bade the happy pair farewell. Since then, the rougher sort moved down to the saloon to continue the celebration, not so much for love of Raymond and Irene as for the love of drink.

Over the last hour, the sounds have changed from light and cheery to hard and rowdy.

A gunshot breaks the silence.

Jesse starts up, craning his neck to see down the street, but another shot does not follow.

"Raymond deputized the Swifts and a few others," says Archer. "They'll keep things under control."

Jesse whistles. "I wouldn't be them tonight for all the gold in the Reynolds-Fulcrom mines."

Archer leans back against the slats of the porch swing we share and puts his arm around my shoulders. "And neither would I."

I smile and lean my head against his shoulder.

"To be fair," he continues, "the gold in those mines hasn't brought much happiness to anyone. Both Reynolds and Fulcrom are overworked, miserable men. One because he's decided to be and the other, I think, because of his wife. She married him for that gold, and she makes it clear to everyone."

"The nerve!" Thatcher sits up. "Of all the—"

"Civilization, Jesse. What did you think it was going to look like?"

"Like roads, and more than one mercantile, and no more *darani*?" He throws his arm wide. "I didn't ever say I wanted all the types of humankind running about these hills."

I laugh—I can't help it. He's so aghast and indignant all at once. I want to take him out East to the big cities, watch his rustic idea of crowds and civilization crumble in the face of the bustling metropolis.

"Well, I'd be with you, Jesse, but I'm afraid I've joined them." Archer sets down his glass.

"Now, what'd you go and do a thing like that for?"

I sense something change in Archer. Something tired in the way he breathes suddenly.

"Because I had no other way to protect this land." His hand rubs my arm. "And I'll tell you something, I've felt more alone in a room of a score of men than I ever have riding in the wild country, days from another soul."

"My poor brave darling." I lean over and kiss his cheek, perfectly smooth and cool from the night air.

A low, musing sigh from Jesse interrupts.

I take Archer's hand and bring it to rest on my stomach. "Soon there will be no way to feel alone. There'll be a young one in the house."

He smiles and turns his hand to clasp mine. "Of course," he whispers.

Jesse, seeing the direction things are headed, heaves himself out of his chair with a yawn. "Well, it's late. I better drift."

"Night, Jesse. Watch yourself." Archer gets up, plants a kiss on my forehead, and goes inside to bank the fire and turn down the covers.

"Goodnight, Rosamund." Jesse raises his hat to me in farewell.

"You too. Avoid the street by the saloon."

"I will." He gives a short laugh and pushes his hat back on his head. He steps off the porch and then hesitates.

"Rosamund?"

"What is it?"

He comes back up the step and speaks quietly. "You take care of him, all right? Promise me?"

"Archer?"

He nods. "He needs you worse than he says."

In an instant, he's down the steps again and untying his horse.

I stand in the darkness listening to the retreating sounds of the hooves and to the wild celebration far down the street.

I wonder what he sees that I've missed.

8

ALAN

I feel dawn coming before there's any hint of it in the darkness of the hotel room. Jem is still asleep in the bed above me, and I feel Max's gentle breath on my arm. He's rolled off his bedroll and partly onto mine.

You'd think from his sleeping face he was an angel. It's the only time that kid is ever quiet.

I push aside the blanket and reach for my boots. The wedding celebration went on late into the night, and while we cattlemen are used to keeping long hours, my brothers and I were clean done in by the time things wound down.

This once, they'll probably sleep until after dawn.

I take my gun from the bedpost and buckle it on as I step softly out into the hallway.

Even the hotel is quieter than it would normally be at this hour. I hear the clerk moving papers at the desk downstairs, smell coffee and bacon, but there's no other sign of life.

I descend the stairs on tiptoe and nod to the hotel clerk.

"Breakfast?" he asks.

"In a bit."

On the porch, I pass a lady in good clothes who is waiting, I presume, for a buggy or the stage. The passenger train won't leave until midmorning. Only freight pulls out this early. I put my hat on and pull the brim to her, and she smiles demurely.

I step down into the empty street, enjoying the cool of the dark morning. Every building is shut and quiet, and stars still shine in the sky above. From the far end of town comes the rattle of train cars being loaded.

There's a light on in the livery stable. I open up the big, creaking door and step into the warm smell of hay and horse sweat.

A low nicker greets me, probably Jem's horse. He's usually the first to the feed and the loudest about it.

"Hey, boy." I stop in front of my roan's stall door and he stirs and stretches out his neck. "I brought you a little something."

I hold my hand out, offering a couple pieces of sugar from the hotel's coffee service. He blows on them a moment and then his warm, soft nose presses into my hand.

When the sugar's gone, he licks my hand for good measure.

"We're the early birds, yes?" I reach up and rub behind his ears.

He pushes against me gently, blowing again, nudging me

for more. I love the feel of his hot breath, the tickle of his whiskers and the touch of his lips, soft as a rose petal.

I fork down a pile of hay for him and curry him while he eats. When we've both done our tasks justice, I tack him up and lead him out into the slowly awakening street.

Dawn is just a suggestion of pink over the range beyond Glory Mesa. I throw a leg over his back and we head out into the hills.

THE SUNRISE IS warm and gold by the time we reach the windswept hills. I turn my roan back to face the blowing dust and flatlands around the distant town, still half-shadowed.

He snorts approvingly.

I whistle him up and we head back.

WE'RE ready for breakfast in earnest when we ride back into Glory Mesa, now lit with the rich light of morning under a wide blue sky.

"Good morning." Sikes is leaning against the post of his porch, cleaning out his pipe with the air of a lord.

"Morning." I reach up and touch my hat in greeting.

"A man for the dawn, are you?"

"I reckon it's the Auki in me." I rein in.

"I reckon." A smile haunts his eyes.

I don't know the man much, but he's been in this territory all my life and I've always had the odd impression that he's fond of me.

He wraps his pipe up in a soft cloth and tucks it away in his breast pocket, coming down the steps.

"Good horse," he comments briefly, almost to himself. He steps around the far side of the roan's neck and beckons for me to dismount.

"Son, let me see your face."

I throw my leg over the roan's withers and slip down his shoulder.

Sikes reaches up and turns my face gently toward the light. I have learned that this man is best respected. Strange though he is, he's a legend and always will be.

The wind stirs my horse's mane. It toys with the doctor's hair, blows my own across my eyes and then off my forehead.

"I have never seen your face so closely before," he says softly, after nearly a minute of study.

"I am sorry you have the misfortune now," I chuckle. "My brothers are the handsome ones in the family."

"Their faces are fair to the eye, to be sure," says Sikes. "But your heart is pure."

He lets me go so gently I almost don't feel his fingers leave my jaw.

"Fine lad." He nods slowly. "Goodbye."

He straightens his black coat as if preparing himself for some great task, then walks up his steps and into his office.

"Goodbye," I call after him, raising my hat.

9

GABLE

THE WHISTLE BLASTS. I STAND ON THE DUSTY PORCH OF my office and watch as the train pulls away from the station, pumping steam.

It's a lonely feeling to watch the farewells of a big to-do, to see the final vestiges of a good time slip away. And the marshal's wedding was a big one.

For those two or three weeks, while the town was humming with anticipation, while I was getting a suit fitted and the invitation sat crisp and white on our mantel, things felt almost normal for the first time in a long while.

Things haven't been the same between Edith and me since the day I last rode with Marshal Lacey, and I am afraid they will only become worse now that the territory's truly being settled.

My chance to be someone has slipped through my

42

fingers, along with any chance to win back my honor in Edith's eyes.

She said she was sorry for those words, but that does not erase the truth in them. I let her down and proved myself an incompetent fool. And that's a hard pill for a man to swallow.

I study my fingers, inkstained and soft.

What am I even doing here? Is it really better to be a no one in a glorious place than a someone in an ordinary place where small-town gossip is the most excitement one will ever see?

The wind stirs the dust below me. The hum of voices on the street and the slow tread of hooves return.

"Friend, you're lookin' a mite pensive."

I look over quickly. Reining in his horse beside my hitching rail is Blue Harding, the former outlaw. He pushes back his low-brimmed hat and fixes me with his bright blue eyes.

"Good morning," I say.

"And to you." He rests his hands on his saddle horn and leans forward a little. "Y'know, I always just figured surveyors liked lines and figures and stayin' indoors less'n they had to rough it. But you sure don't fit that."

"Back home, you'd have had us pegged," I answer with a smile. "At least, where I came from. Everything's been surveyed more than once. All farms and small town plots."

Blue chuckles appreciatively. "Sounds like my old home. I swore I'd light out of there soon as I was old enough."

"And did you?"

"Sure did. And look where it got me." He spreads out his arms, gesturing to himself, and I am not sure if he means this as a good thing or a bad thing.

"Well—" I begin, and he bursts into laughter.

"It almost got me a noose around my neck. Though I reckon the war had something to do with that too. Funny how it happens—those men in suits up in their fancy buildings all decide they don't like each other anymore and next thing you know you're picking sides. And when the time came for laying down weapons, I reckon I just liked the feeling of a six-shooter in my hand too dang much to set it down."

I chuckle.

"Let that be a lesson to you," he says. "Live by the gun and the gun'll get you one day."

"Do you think that will be the case for you?"

His lips curve into a slow, ironic smile. "Who knows. I reckon I've learned to live by it a little less, but if my sins come back to roost one day, I'll have asked for it. I do fancy a place of my own one day. Maybe you'd do one of them surveys on it if I found a spot?"

"Sure thing."

"I'll remember that." He picks up his reins with a sigh.

"Are you leaving town?"

"Just headin' out to the Copper River Mines. Half the boys are roosted out there. Some kind of claim dispute." He reaches down and checks the cinch with a couple fingers. "I'd take you with me if you didn't have more important things to do." He straightens and clucks to his horse. "Well, I'll be seeing you around."

I nod to him and he tips the brim of his hat.

I envy these men the ability to simply saddle up and ride away.

10

SELBY

I SIT ON THE EDGE OF THE BED NEXT TO MY SADDLEBAGS, which are packed again with all my sparse worldly belongings.

It does feel good to wear clothes washed with real soap. I've been an article of attention among the charitable women of Glory Mesa, who could not abide the idea of my continuing in rags or dirty clothes. Those shepherds don't know what soap is, and I usually make do for a long time after my cake is gone.

Doctor Sikes's spare room is now meticulously neat and nearly empty; the medicines and bandages are removed, the spare clothes either returned or packed, the tools of the trade boiled and put back in the examination room.

The very last thing, my book of poetry, is on the bedside table. I take it up and rub my thumb fondly over the worn, stained cover.

I open the book to the first page, then turn to the last.

*And when it comes to farewell, my love—farewell let it be, not in showers of regret, but rather gentle sunbeams of content. For we loved well and we lived, and our hopes were not in ourselves, but in Providence.*

"I'll be sorry to see you go." Sikes is suddenly framed in the doorway. "You've been my quietest tenant." I am attuned to every sound, loud or soft, and I did not hear him.

I close the book and wrap my hands over it protectively. Old habit.

"I am glad to hear it. I hated to impose."

"Nonsense. You needed watching, and I was the one to do it. Doctor Everett up the street may be a fine doctor, but I wouldn't think of having you stay anywhere but here."

"I didn't know there was another doctor," I admit. "But I could have taken care of myself."

"My dear boy, you ran a fever for four days after you arrived, and I daresay for however long you were riding from those beasts."

"I've nursed myself through fevers before."

"I won't argue with you, son." Sikes steps in and pulls out a chair, sitting down in front of me. "I am an old man and I have reached the point where I hold my time dear. And I wanted to spend it on you. You will be going far away and it may be that I will not see you again."

"I've barely seen you before," I laugh wryly.

"But I've seen you, and though you think little of yourself, the role you play in this land will be great. I want to see you well before you must shoulder that."

"I'm well enough."

"Well enough to leave me, not enough to leave Glory Mesa. I want to see you once more. A few days from now will do."

"I'm sorry, I am leaving today."

"No," he says matter-of-factly. Regretfully, even. "You're not."

"Are you going to stop me?"

"No."

"Hm."

"Who is she?" he asks, pointing to my book.

Hard shock jolts my body. He couldn't have surprised me more if he had thrown icy water over my head.

"Have you been looking in my things?"

"No. You read that book every night and you gaze long upon the name in the inscription inside the cover. Was she your mother?"

I look at him slowly. Who is this man who puts his finger on my life and reads it like he would my pulse?

"No." I find my tongue at last, unwilling to lie. "My mother died long before I learned to love poetry again."

"Your sister?"

I shake my head.

"Then she must have been special, this woman."

I don't answer.

"I don't suppose you ever talked to her again?"

His voice is kind. I have been spoken to in many ways over the last ten years—respectfully, on occasion, but never with the kindness I hear in this old man's voice. He speaks as if he knows my story.

Perhaps he does, somehow.

I run my fingers gently over the name, written in bold pen that has faded a little with time and use.

"No—she was better off without me."

I thrust the book into my saddlebags and stand up. "Thank you, Doctor Sikes, for your hospitality and your care. If we are not to see each other again, I am sorry for it."

I hold out my hand and he shakes it without a word.

I hoist the saddlebags over my shoulder and head for the livery stable.


"Is my dun here?" I gaze at the half-empty stalls. Most of the out-of-towners left a couple days ago.

"Yes, he is, but I have bad news. He's pulled up lame. Our boy here's been keeping him in good shape, but he noticed a limp this morning after you came by. Nothing serious, I think. It happens now and again after a rough event, and I'm not surprised, knowing what he's been through."

I drape my saddlebags over the stall door and slide the latch.

"Which leg?"

"Back one, left side."

I move in, rubbing his shoulder, then his flank. I feel down the leg. It is a little warm. "How long, do you suppose?"

"We'll go light on the grain, keep him moving a little. Maybe two, three days."

"All right, then."

He thrusts his nose into my shoulder and I push him back gently, rubbing his forehead.

"Good boy."

I'm back on the doctor's porch, knocking firmly. For once, I am bold.

He opens the door, but his face is blank. No surprise, no triumph.

"Did you do something to my horse?"

"My dear boy, I would never touch your horse."

"Did you know he was lame?"

He smiles slowly. "I did not. I suppose you are coming to tell me you will be in town a few more days?"

"Yes." I don't mind being wrong about most things, but this strangeness, this sense of being on a course predestined, unsettles me.

"I cannot give you an answer," he says, as if discerning my thoughts. "But let it comfort you, not frighten you, that there are greater things at work in the world than what can always be understood. I knew you must stay, and so you did."

"Right."

"I'll see you in a day or two."

He closes the door and leaves me on the doorstep in the stillness of the street, feeling empty and alone.

11

# GABLE

When noon comes round, I find myself more and more often at the restaurant at the edge of town near the train station, formerly Maria's. Trasker owns it now—got it cheap from the town of Glory Mesa—but the food hasn't changed.

I'm tying my horse at the hitching rack when a dusty figure rides in over the tracks. There's something familiar about the man, his seat, the way he handles the horse.

Cristobal Newton.

I come around the back end of my horse, shading my eyes to see better. If it's Chris, he's come a far piece. That ranch of his is nowhere near town.

He notices me and throws up his hand in greeting.

"Lesley Gable!" He pushes his hat back and leans on his saddle horn. "I'm glad to see you're still out here. How are you?"

"I've been better," I admit. "But that's neither here nor there. What brings you to Glory Mesa?"

"Bad business, I'm afraid."

"I see."

"Is the governor around?"

"Sure, back at his office. At least, he was a few minutes ago when I rode past."

"Excellent. Good to see you, Gable. You're looking well."

He claps spurs to his mount and lopes up the street.

A great deal of bad business may come and go and never affect a man, but something about this leaves me with a feeling of dread.

I wait and watch as Chris ties up his horse outside the Territorial Governor's office and disappears inside. A minute later the governor himself comes bursting out, trailed by his secretary.

He gestures up the street and the young man takes off in a hurry, heading at an angle for Doctor Sikes's office.

"Archer, what is it?" Jesse Thatcher's voice carries over the noise of the street.

His cousin goes to him and they hold conference for a few tense moments. Archer nods toward his office, then gestures down the street. Jesse seems to oppose him, then relent.

Archer goes back into his office and Jesse comes down in my direction. I step out to catch him.

"What's going on?"

"Cristobal Newton is in town and he has bad news."

"He told me as much."

"Well, he's getting Sikes." Jesse puts his hand on his hip, raising his vest, and gives a sigh. "Which means it's not good."

He turns and looks up the street. The secretary is running back with Doctor Sikes following behind, a gust catching at his long black coat.

I can feel it—the change in the wind.

Jesse looks at me as if determining something in his mind. "Follow me. Archer will have room in the back. We can hear the matter out and stay out of the way."

I glance around. "Are you sure?"

"Of course I'm sure. Come on."

Jesse Thatcher leads me around the back of the office, to a door that stands open to the breeze. He gestures for me to go first and points to a couple chairs sitting along the back wall.

I take a seat, but my leg cannot stop jigging and my hands are sweaty.

We can hear their voices in the front room, see the corner of the table where the governor and Sikes and Newton sit. The secretary takes a seat at a far desk, pulls out a fresh sheet of paper, and dips his pen.

"So what is it?" Sikes demands. "You may as well speak plain. You have not called me in to discuss the progress of the railroad or the petty squabbles of mine shareholders."

"Britt and Buck April are dead. I found them in the wildlands below Mount Spur, mortally injured by a rockslide after killing Tora-Teth. The landscape as I knew it is gone forever. A couple days later, I saw the mountain smoking."

Sikes's voice sounds oddly stiff. "You are sure of that?"

"Yes. It only grew clearer."

"Alas," the doctor whispers. "It has come."

"What is it?" asks Governor Scott. "What has come?"

"The fulfillment of the curse has begun, as I said it would, and by the hands of the April brothers. From this time on, it is no longer a question of *if*. You will break the curse or this land will be destroyed in fire and ash."

"How?" Archer is fighting for words. Beside me, Jesse scowls in a worried, almost boyish way. "How is the curse broken and how...how do we know if it is too late?"

"Go to where the mountain is restless. The end will be known by rivers of silver and gold. Deputize volunteers to go. Send the ones who know this territory best or have hearts of courage and the willingness to die, if they must. The right ones will go."

A sudden thrill, a weight of destiny, hits me strong in the chest.

I will go. I will win back my honor and Edith, by life or by death.

"And what will they do?" asks Chris.

"You will show them the mountain. Those who are worthy will ascend. But there is only one who can stop the long-sleeping guardian. And when the time comes, he will go alone to bring peace to his land."

"And what will I do?" asks Archer. His voice is pained.

"Keep what has been entrusted to you, if you can. The curse must be broken, but the wolves want those who will be left unprotected."

"Sometimes I wish you spoke clearer." Archer laughs, soft and strained.

"I speak how I speak. Some men are made to say a thing outright. You are such a man. I am not. It is not what I was created for."

For a few seconds, everything is silent.

"Gather the men who are willing, before it is too late," Sikes says quietly. "And lead with all your heart."

I glance at Jesse, who is sitting with his fist pressed to his mouth. "Raymond's got to hear about this," he mutters.

"Where is he?"

"Out at his ranch. Enjoying his first week as a married man in peace—not for long."

"Poor fellow."

"Out here, it can't be helped." He looks at me slowly. "I saw your horse outside the restaurant. Did you eat?"

"No. I didn't get the chance, I'm afraid."

"Let's go, right now, the two of us. Whatever comes, we'll face it on a full stomach."

"I thought you didn't like the food there."

"It wasn't the food I didn't like." He gives me a knowing look. "Come on, I've a mind for stew."

12

# IRENE

THE MORNING BREEZE IS COOL AND SWEET, AND THE porch boards are so new I can smell the sharp tang of fresh wood.

But the view is what I love most. The front porch looks out over a wide, green swath of valley that must be some of the most beautiful country I've ever seen.

And Raymond saw it—saw the same beauty in it that I do—and made it ours.

I hear a soft step on the porch behind me and I see Raymond coming out, stretching slowly.

"Morning, darling," I say.

"Morning." He regards the view for a moment with a sort of deep, settled conviction and then comes over and puts his arms around my shoulders from behind.

I reach up and rub his strong hands. "Did you see I made coffee?"

"Smelled it the moment I woke up. You could have left it to me."

"Nonsense, you needed the sleep. Heaven knows when you last had more than three days strung together when you didn't wake up to guns and business and hard riding. The least someone can do for you is make the coffee."

He chuckles under his breath and gives my hands a squeeze before extricating himself and going back inside.

The birds are singing somewhere in the distance and I think I hear the rush of distant water. Raymond said there was a river running through the property somewhere.

His footsteps come again, across the floorboards of the front room and out onto the porch. He hands me a cup of coffee without a word and stands where he is, watching the morning and drinking slowly.

I don't want to speak, to break this beautiful silence. To talk with the one you love is a wonderful thing, but to exist in peaceable quiet together, perfectly happy and content, is an understanding some never achieve.

I wish we could stay out here for good. Two days' distance is too far from town for us to live at present, as Raymond is needed in Glory Mesa nearly every day; but after seeing this, I will never be able to stay away too long.

"What do you say we saddle up a couple horses and see a bit of the land for ourselves?" He takes a sip of the still-steaming coffee.

"I would love that."

A gleam comes into his eyes, and then a twinkle. "Good."

"I should fix us breakfast, then," I say. "I can fry the cold corn porridge left from yesterday."

"Sure." He sniffs and settles himself above the porch steps, all legs. "But let's just sit awhile. No hurry, hm?"

"No hurry." I wrap my hands around my cup and breathe in the sweet air.

RAYMOND IS SLOWLY BUILDING the homestead into a ranch. A couple men already work the place, care for the horses, build more corrals, keep animals for milk and meat and eggs. Soon he'll buy some breeding stock from Jesse Thatcher, but for now, the range is nearly empty.

As we return from our ride, the hands greet us with respectful smiles and waves. They've kept their distance from the house; Raymond goes down and talks business with them sometimes, but I haven't met them beyond a pleasant thank-you when one of them brings milk up from the barn in the mornings.

"Sam and Frank are good men," Raymond says as we ride past. "Honest fellows. If you ever had to stay here without me, they'd watch out for you."

"I'm glad to hear it."

We stop at the corral and he dismounts easily. Looking at him, at the way the muscles gather in his shoulders as he leans briefly on the saddle, at the lightness with which he steps down, I wonder about all the life he had before we met. I wonder what he was like as an officer. His uniform hangs in our closet, but he won't wear it.

He comes over to my horse and gives me a hand down, though we both know I don't really need it. "My lady."

He takes the saddle off my horse and heaves it over the rail. "What did you think of the land?" He goes back to his horse as I lead mine around to the gate.

"I love it with all my heart. How did you ever manage to get to it before someone else?"

"I reckon it was too close to Mortimer's outlaw road, back in the day," he grunts, bent over, pulling the cinch out.

"What were they like, those days?"

"Not much different." He heaves the second saddle over the rail. "They weren't so long ago, you know."

"The way people talk about them, they were."

This makes him chuckle, all the way into the corral. "Well, when hard times are past, people like to talk about them with that shine of glory. It's rarely deserved."

He unbuckles the bridle and slips it off the horse's head.

"Whatever they say," I reply as he shoos the horse away, "I have a good feeling about these times coming up."

He puts his long arms around my shoulder and draws me close.

"I do too, Irene."

The sound of distant hoofbeats reaches our ears.

A rider is coming up over the hills, riding up the dirt track to the house. Raymond stiffens, and my heart sinks.

He opens the gate without a word and lets me walk through first.

We reach the house a little before the rider, and I go in to make sure there is something ready for him, while Raymond waits on the porch.

I hear the exchange of greetings, the creak of leather as the man dismounts.

"Well, come on in. There's food and you can get something to drink."

"That's all right—I'd like some, but I'd rather just get this over with."

My heart stills.

"The governor's sent me. He's asking for you to come back as soon as it's convenient. There's some trouble, a bad sign, out in the northwestern end of the territory. Cristobal Newton brought the word. They need some men deputized."

"That's a long way from here, that territory."

"And it's got a bad history."

Raymond sighs slowly. "Very well. You put that horse up and come get a bite to eat before you ride back. Tell him I'll start tomorrow."

"All right."

I step out onto the porch. Raymond's hand opens and closes slowly as he watches the young man lead the horse down to the barn.

"Tomorrow, Raymond? Shouldn't you—"

"Tomorrow." His hand finds mine and he kisses it. "You

may have married the marshal, but I'll be taking care of you first where I can. A few hours' wait won't hurt."

# 13

# CARNEGIE

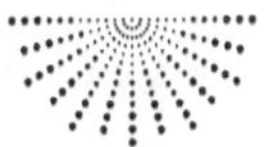

I MOUNT THE STEPS UP TO CARSON'S SALOON. THE SIGN'S had a new coat of paint, and he has new staff. The girl at the bar eyes me slowly.

"Got business here, ma'am?" Her hands never stop drying the glass. I feel like I'm looking into my reflection.

I hope she finds happiness.

"I do. I'm here to see Jack Selby." I reach up and tug my jacket where the star is pinned.

She looks slowly at the pistol on my hip.

"I'm a friend," I add.

"Room three," she says briefly and turns away. "He's in."

I cross the rough floorboards and mount the steps to the room. I know each of these rooms by heart, every knot and stain on the floors. There's a part of me that is almost sad, walking through my old haunts, belonging to them no more.

I knock.

No voice answers, but I wait quietly and he opens the door. He's not a man to announce his intentions.

"Kate—Miss Carnegie." His eyes light with concern. "Will you come in?"

"Thank you."

He ushers me in and pulls out the room's one chair for me, settling himself on the edge of the bed.

"I suppose you've heard it around town," I begin. "The news Cristobal Newton brought?"

"Yes."

"Governor Scott and Marshal Lacey are gathering riders to swear in and send out. I've come to ask you."

"If I'll ride?"

"Yes."

He's thinking. I have learned to tell when he is, though I doubt there is anyone living who can tell what. One hand goes to his smooth chin, stroking it.

"I don't need your answer right away. I don't even need it —you can keep this between you and them. But if I may be bold, I think by the end we'll need the very best, and you're one of them."

"They're saying it's dangerous...."

"Yes." This hasn't worried him before.

A little smile comes over his face and suddenly I feel cold. He wasn't asking because he was worried.

"Tell them to expect me. I assume they are meeting soon?"

"Day after next," I reply quietly. "Three o'clock at the Territorial Governor's office."

"I'll be there."

"I am glad to hear it." I force a smile onto my face and stand up, extending my hand. He just nods and takes my hand gently.

I'm seeing myself out when his voice stops me.

"Kate?"

I stop.

"Are you going?"

"Yes, I am." I pause a space. It sounds dire when spoken so simply. "I want to go."

"I—" He lets his breath out quietly. "I certainly will not stop you, or even try to dissuade you. There's no reason you should listen to me anyway."

I turn to look at him. He looks me in the eye and then drops his gaze.

"But I want to give you a word of warning. A word only. I don't know what lies at the end of this, but it's going to be hard, and I think good men are going to die bad. You're full of life and hope. It's men like me who are made for such jobs. We can't go back to what you have, Kate, but you can. When the time comes, just—remember that."

I just stand in the doorway, my fingers frozen on the handle, unsure what to say, chewing the inside of my lip.

"I'm sorry," he says. "I shouldn't have—"

"No. Thank you." I catch his gaze, smile at his solemn blue eyes, so worn and tired. "I mean it."

He nods, his shoulders and manner still apologetic.

"Let me give you a word in return, if you'll hear it?"

He nods.

"You sell yourself short, Jack Selby. You're a good man. When the time comes, I hope you remember that."

## 14

## GABLE

Edith is sitting in the corner sewing a patch on my jacket when I come in, take off my hat wearily, and hang it on the peg beside the door.

Her eyes meet mine and then return to the jacket.

"It's all over the papers," she begins. "This smoking mountain, all of them calling it doom, as if it isn't hundreds, probably thousands of miles away. Seems like a lot of nonsense, doesn't it?"

"What's that?"

She repeats herself, more or less.

"Ah—yes."

"Maria Pike used to talk a bit like that. She believed there was a curse on this land."

I lower myself wearily into the chair across from her.

"What is it, Lesley?" She sits up and leans forward to put her soft, cool fingers on my forehead. "Are you ill?"

"No." I smile to reassure her. "I—I must talk to you about something."

She threads the needle through the cloth of the jacket a couple times to save it and sets it aside, clasping her hands.

"Yes?"

"I suppose that you heard that the governor and the marshal are asking for volunteers to head west. I'm going."

A little scowl starts between her eyes. "What do you mean?"

"The smoking mountain. They have asked for men to ride out there. And I am going."

"To do what, exactly?"

"To try to stop it—end the curse."

"Are you crazy? Stop a mountain?" She nearly rises from her seat.

"Edith, someone's got to go."

"No, no—it's a fool's errand. I cannot believe that anyone is thinking of going."

"Doctor Sikes believes it is the only way. If we ignore it, we will die."

"What does he know about it?"

"He has lived in this territory a long time and he knows things no other man knows. If anyone knows anything, it's him."

"And his word is enough to throw your life away on?"

I don't answer. But I think she sees it in my face. This may be our goodbye.

"No, you can't. Don't do this to me, please."

"You were the one who said that you couldn't hold your head up around me." My voice breaks, though I fight to keep it steady. "Isn't it better for me to be gone and to have brought you honor?"

"You're bringing that up again? Didn't I say I was sorry?" Her voice is frustrated, sharp.

"Tell me it isn't true."

"Of course it's not true, Lesley." She reaches out and cups my face in her hands. "I'd rather have you here as yourself than dead and the best fighter there is."

I search her face for the truth, but I can no longer tell from her eyes when she means a thing. "It's too late."

"What do you mean? No, it isn't."

"The only way I can stand up as a man is to prove myself."

"Who else do you have to prove it to?"

"Myself and the woman I let down."

Her face falls. "And if you don't come back?"

"I'd rather die than come back shamed again."

She balls her small hands into fists. "Lesley, do you hear yourself?"

I draw a long, shaking breath. "I'll win you honor, Edith."

She stands in a rush. "You will not, Lesley Gable. This is a delusion—you're seeing what's simply not there!"

"Is that what it is?" I swallow hard and look up at her. "I'm incompetent? Why don't you come out and say it to my face, then?"

"That's not what I meant, Lesley. You know that."

"I don't know that."

She looks at me, her face working. "Don't go."

"It's too late."

I get to my feet and stalk back out onto the porch. I hear our bedroom door shut deep inside the house.

I had hoped to win her back tonight.

I sit out on the porch until the air grows chill around me and my fingers grow numb.

The door opens behind me.

"Lesley?"

I turn to look at her. She's holding a folded blanket, hugged against her chest.

"Come inside."

"I am not cold." I turn away.

"You are." She settles on the step beside me. "And you are stubborn and foolish, and I am angry with you—but we can talk about it tomorrow."

She touches my shoulder.

"Just come in."

Tears sting my eyes. I feel everything—I am angry, but I am angry because I desperately want to hear her say she loves me. I love her, which is why I cannot stand to be near her, not with her words still raw and painful in my ears.

I hate myself.

I am so, so tired. A tear slips down my nose and onto the ground beside my foot.

"Come in, Lesley."

Slowly, woodenly, I rise and follow her inside.

# 15

# THATCHER

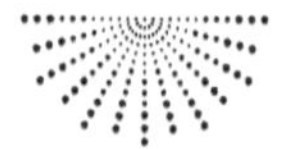

ARCHER IS NERVOUS. I SEE IT IN THE TENSE WAY HE SITS, in the way he keeps opening and closing his hands, as if trying to get a feel for a bronc before it lets loose on him.

I feel for him—he's like a man holding back a dam all by himself, and no one sees that it is about to burst and sweep him away in it. I think it's powerful brave of a man to get up in the morning and fight a fight no one sees, day after day.

And I'm mighty worried for him.

He notices me watching and he raises his eyebrows like a question. I shake my head and continue leaning on the edge of his desk.

The volunteers are here—some worthy, some less so— and I, fool that I am, am one of them. But Rosamund's baby is due soon, so neither Raymond nor I will leave until it is born and we know both mother and child are healthy.

Raymond is seated at one of the tables across from us, writing out commissions. The rest of the room is filled with the milling volunteers and a couple stray dignitaries—who knows where they came from.

I notice Jack Selby in particular. His face is set, and there's a light in his eyes I've never seen before. He usually looks like he's shrinking away inside, but today he looks bold, like he's seen a faraway glory.

When he speaks, his voice is still soft. I guess that hasn't changed.

Kate is a little behind him, dressed in her Sunday best, her usually wild hair neatly tied back. Now that's a girl who looks like she's seen glory. She's smiling and just flushed enough to have a little color in her cheeks.

Behind them stands a collection of individuals—Lesley Gable, solemn as a funeral; one of the older boys from Jensen's livery stable; a couple drifters I've never seen who look dangerously close to spitting on the floor; and Peter, standing against the wall, watching everything with his dark eyes.

I catch his eye and wink.

He winks back and gives me a nod.

I push myself off Archer's table and go over to him. "What are you doing here, kid?"

Peter shrugs.

"You're not aiming to ride with us?"

Peter shakes his head.

"You'd make a pretty good saddle partner, you know."

"Yeah."

"But you're not?"

"My place is here," says Peter. "It's not my time."

I laugh and raise my eyebrows.

"Did Sikes teach you to talk like that?"

"I talked like that before Sikes," he says. "Before he talked to me like that, anyhow."

"Then why are you here?" I press. It's easier sometimes to talk with Peter than any other man on this earth.

"I want to watch this. It is history, you know."

"I didn't."

Peter smiles at me, one of those rare, quiet smiles. "You'll be history too, Mr. Thatcher. You'll be one of the best of them all."

His comment hits me between the eyes. I'm not the sort you call best at anything. Not at shooting, not at riding, not even just being good. But I try. I reckon that's got to count for something.

"Just you wait," says Peter.

Raymond Lacey clears his throat and the whole room falls silent. "All right." He straightens the papers and looks up. "I'd like you volunteers to form an orderly line. I need your name, your firearm, and if you have a horse. If you agree to this statement, you'll sign your name and line up over there. I'll give you a commission and a badge and I'll swear you in. Is that clear?"

There's a murmur of assent.

Jack Selby is first. Name, Jack Selby, firearm, rifle, .45 revolver, has his own horse. He reads the statement silently and then nods.

Raymond gestures for him to go stand on the other side of the table.

Kate is next. Kate Carnegie, firearm, .45 revolver, army commissioned, has a horse.

And so on, for ten, twenty others. A couple read the statement and leave, a few more need it read aloud to them or explained.

At last I step up. Name, Jesse Thatcher. I describe my gun, supply my own horse, read the statement. I promise to uphold the laws of the territory, to conduct myself with honor so long as I wear the badge, agree to the penalties if I misuse the badge.

I am the last, so when I finish, Raymond stands up and faces us.

"It'll take time to gather the men we're asking as volunteers, so we will agree to meet and make camp at the Blue Lantern Rocks a month from today, which is the fifteenth. Be there by or before, or you're left behind. If any man decides between now and then that he no longer wishes to ride on Mount Spur, he may turn in his badge and go his way. Is that understood?"

There's a murmur of assent.

"Good. Now I'll ask for your patience—I've never sworn in a crew this size before."

One by one, we put our hands on the book and swear.

I solemnly pledge my life and courage to the cause. It's only afterward that I see Archer's face.

There are tears in his eyes.

16

ALAN

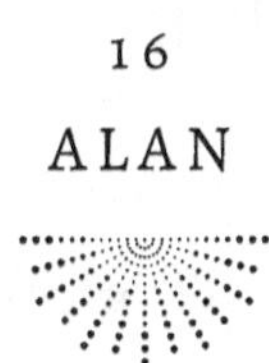

IT'S A COOL, SUNNY DAY, THE SORT WHERE THE SKY IS A
pale calico of white and gentle blue and the green and brown
of the trees stands solid against it.

We've only just arrived home, pulling off gloves, shedding heavy jackets, shaking our heads and remarking on the grazing for the season. It's been very dry and we're all afraid the grazing will be thin, let alone the hay crop. But the drive was good and the cattle have decent fat on them, so it's all talk for now.

But there's talk of a range war too, and that's like to turn into something more than talk.

Water sources are scarce and things are dry, and all it takes is one rancher strangled by the drought for there to be bullets and blood over water rights.

We Swifts are well situated up in the mountain country.

We have the mountain streams and hardy cattle used to tough conditions, but that's not everyone.

Some men would kill to get our mountain streams.

Our saddles are lined up on the rail outside the ranch house, the horses loose in the corral with the sweat drying off them, and the three of us head indoors at last to join our ranch boss and cook in a pot of coffee and some hot home-cooked food.

The fire crackles in the large hearth, so tall and wide that Jem could stand upright in it and his broad shoulders would fit. It's warm, it's good, and to a tired man's bones, it's heaven.

I'm the first to hear the rumble of approaching hooves.

They are faint at first, coming up the southern trail, which is hard-packed and sounds different from the others.

Max is still laughing over some joke and Jem's pouring himself coffee, agreeing with whatever had been said. Our ranch boss has his boots up on the coffee table and he's starting to doze.

Jem takes a sip and stops short.

"Is someone coming?" He sets down the cup with a clatter and goes to the door. Max trails behind, moving quicker.

It's the strangest feeling—it's like I know they're coming for us. And I want to savor this last taste of life as it is now, be together for the few minutes we have left.

I'm not ready.

"It's Carson!" Jem calls back into the house. "I don't think he's ever come up our way."

"Reckon it's a lot faster with half the route covered by train now," muses our overseer, pulling his boots off the table and sitting up.

Jem and Max stride out to meet him. I get up and pour myself another cup of coffee.

It's good, rich, strong.

"Alan, come on out!" calls Jem. "Carson's here to see all of us."

I set down the coffee and walk out.

Carson's horse is lathered and I can feel the heat radiating off it.

"No wonder you lads have such good wind," he's saying. "It's a long hike up here even in good weather."

He sees me and reaches into his saddlebags. "I'm bringing you boys word from Marshal Lacey. He's got a special request."

He pulls out a letter and hands it to Jem. Jem looks it over, Max and I reading over his shoulder.

My heart sinks.

"I have commissions and badges for all three of you." Carson reaches into his saddlebags.

Jem shakes his head. "We can promise two, but not three. As you know, there's a drought in these parts and we're about to have a fight on our hands."

"Sikes wanted all of you." Carson stubbornly hands down the items, three of each.

"I am the head of the Swift household and that's my decision. Come in and have something to eat."

"I can't stay."

Jem turns to Max. "Go get him something to eat and bring it out."

We wait as Max goes in. Carson clears his throat loudly.

"Jem, if I were you, whoever you send, you send them fast. The Blue Lantern Rocks are a ways away, and a lot can happen in between."

"Are you joining them?"

Carson shakes his head. "I'm getting too old for this."

"Well, a safe trail back, then. Give Archer our regards."

"I most certainly will."

Max comes out with what looks like a sandwich wrapped in a handkerchief.

"There's an apple in there too." He gives a quick grin.

"Thanks, son." Carson tucks the food into his saddlebags and gives us a nod farewell.

I watch him out of sight—around the side of the barn, down past the corrals, and below the crest of the hill.

"Jem, I think we should all go," I say quietly.

"Who will take care of the ranch?"

I don't have an answer.

"We'll draw straws," says Jem. "Fair enough?"


Our overseer holds the straws and we draw. Mine is long, and I'm not surprised. It's like I've known it all along.

Jem draws long as well, and Max gets the short one.

"I'll see you to the nearest junction, at least," he

mumbles. "What should I do if there's trouble? Or if you're not back?"

"You're a Swift," says Jem. "This is your ranch too. I have complete faith in your judgment. Do what you think is wise. We'll live with it."

"You have control of the bank funds," says Max. "I wish you were staying."

"I'll get you permission—we'll telegraph the bank when we reach the next town."

Max just nods.

IT DOESN'T TAKE us long to pack. We ride out of the yard on our roans, saddlebags packed, leaving the men with instructions to watch the ranch closely until Max returns. As we reach the last place on the path from which the ranch house can be seen, Jem reins in and looks back as if committing the place to memory.

But I remember this clearest of all: our saddles lined up on the rail just before we grabbed them and rode off, all of us together. As if we were coming back. But we're not.

We're never coming back.

17

## NEWTON

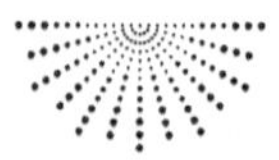

THE STAGE LEAVES GLORY MESA IN THE PALE HOURS OF early dawn when the steam stands off the big wheel horses's backs and the smell of the hostler's coffee is the only homey thing about the stark morning.

Glory Mesa has changed since the last time I was here. It's got the stand-up-straightness of a real town. It's no longer like an outpost or a scrap of civilization or even a boomtown.

It's here to stay, and it's going to do something great, I feel it.

But give me my hills and their steep valleys any day. That's the part of the Western Territory I want my brand on —not these perfect walls and shining windows.

"You ready, sir?" asks the driver, stomping up my way, checking the traces.

"Sure." I walk to the back and check my horse's tie once more, then climb in.

The driver shouts and cracks his whip and we roll out of Glory Mesa. I watch the town slip past and disappear into flat land and racing sagebrush.

A body can't really rest while traveling by stagecoach, nevertheless I lean back and watch the pristine landscape flow past, jerking and lurching at every rut.

The lash cracks overhead, one of the horses snorts long and hard.

I close my eyes and let the rhythm of the jangling harness lull me to an uneasy doze.

Not enough time has passed when I feel the stage stop below me and hear the brake grate into place.

"It's Travern Junction," says the shotgun, descending from the seat with a thud and a pale cloud of alkali dust. "We won't stop long, just picking up a passenger and watering. You can stretch your legs."

"Lovely."

I stretch and climb down stiffly. I know better than to turn down an opportunity to stretch my legs, especially with the trail to Keg Mountain up ahead.

The driver is checking traces and sweet talking the horses—most drivers are about the toughest, strongest hombres you can find and yet most of the sample I've known talks to their horses like they're children.

The shotgun brushes past with a trunk over one hand

and a carpet bag, delicate but worn, decorated with blue flowers.

He said *a* passenger. Just one.

"Looks like you're going to have some fine company," says the shotgun with a grin.

I'm not one jot superstitious, and I don't believe a word of the nonsense Doctor Sikes likes to pass my way, but I feel something powerful now, coming on the hot wind.

It feels a lot like destiny.

The door of the station opens and a young woman comes out, neatly dressed. I see a pale blue dress, honey-brown hair under a trim bonnet, pale fingers hands clutching a handbag.

It's dangerous enough for a man of my lifestyle and abilities, used to the land, to travel out this far, let alone a lady. She moves with a sort of tragic purity in this wild place, like a flower sprung up between mountain rocks where it shouldn't have survived at all.

"Are you ready?" calls the driver. "We're getting ready to leave."

"Yes, I am," she replies in a quiet firm voice that carries over the distance.

She passes me as if I am not there, and the desert wind brings me the scent of good perfume.

"Newton?" The driver looks to me next.

I don't need to answer. I sigh against the wind and trudge back to the stagecoach.

She's seated where I was before, so I quietly settle across from her, by the opposite window. Her eyes move to my face as a matter of course, take me in, and then go back to the window.

I smile, but she has already looked away.

She unfolds her hands, twists them, and refolds them. Nervous.

"Good morning," I greet, tipping my hat. "I'm Cristobal Newton."

"Pleasure. Are you traveling far, sir?"

"Yes. To the end of the line and then beyond. And you are?"

She folds her hands, eager but trying to be businesslike. "Hannah Milton."

"A pleasure, Miss Milton. Are you going far? It's unusual to find a young lady traveling alone in these parts."

"I'm traveling out here to meet the man I'm going to marry."

I've heard of this happening, but it's the first time I've seen it with my own eyes. She's even braver than I thought.

"Is that so?" I say after a moment. "There aren't many people out this way. What is his name?"

She pulls out a well-worn letter from an envelope and holds it out. "His name is Harrison Terhune, and he says that he owns a large spread of land. Is that true? Do you know him?"

I hold my hand out for the letter, and she gives it over.

Harrison Terhune, marrying a girl from out East he's never met? And there must be ten or fifteen years between them.

"It looks like his handwriting," I admit slowly, trying to buy myself time to think.

Her face brightens. "You know him?"

"Enough," I answer wryly, and fold the letter. "Here, you had better take it back."

"Is there something wrong?"

I don't know what to say. She's so bright and innocent, so ready to make a go of this territory and I have to be the one to smash it, take that away from her.

I wonder if I even should. But she's so excited, I think he couldn't possibly have mentioned the deal with the Governor's wife a year or two before. I like Harrison a good deal, but this girl has to know beforehand if she's going to have a lifetime of being looked at sideways or ostracized.

Or loving a man who is.

"Yeah, I know him."

"And? What's he like?"

"Well, he's rich, like he said." *Come on, Chris, think.* "He's a little—older. Not too old, you know, just—a man of the world, I suppose."

"He said he wasn't a *very* young man. Said he wanted to settle down."

"Yes, that sounds right." Settle down away from the eyes of the world that kicked him out.

"Is he kind?" A spark of worry starts in her eyes.

"Yes—he can be. He would be to you."

"I'm glad to hear that. Is he your friend?"

"Yes, he's a friend. A good one, even."

Her face relaxes. "Good. Then I shall see you sometime. Once we're married, I will have to have you and your—are you married?"

"No."

"Well, even so, we shall have to invite you over when I am settled."

"I should like that—though I'm one of his closest neighbors, and I'm still thirty miles away."

"Thirty miles?" she echoes softly.

"Give or take. And that's not much to speak of. These spreads are big."

"So you own a ranch too?"

"I do. I'm on some of the wilder country out westward."

"It sounds rugged. And beautiful."

"It is. Just that."

She leans back, a new shine in her eyes.

Something stirs in my heart. Here is another soul who feels it, the pull of the land.

I brace myself for what I have to say next. She's so hopeful that I hate to say it at all, but she has a right to know what she's getting into.

"Miss Milton...it may not be my business, but did Harrison mention any trouble in his past?"

She shakes her head.

"Ah."

"Is there something I should be worried about? Was he an outlaw once?"

"No. But he's not welcome in Glory Mesa and most of the surrounding towns."

"Why?"

"He tried to kill the governor's wife. It was a complicated situation, and he eventually went free, but—he's not exactly welcome in good society out here."

"Oh." Her eyes are horrified, and her hand goes to her mouth.

"He was under threat when it happened. He's proved his courage since, but he has to live with the consequences of that mistake—and as his wife, you would too. I wish he had told you."

"I wish that too," she whispers numbly.

"I'm sorry."

"It's all right." She gives a sigh and straightens her shoulders. "How far is Sherryville?"

"We're still a day or two away."

"I won't make a decision until then. There's no sense in going back before I've met him. Perhaps there is a good reason he couldn't tell me." She lifts her chin, calm and dignified. If she's merely putting a brave face on it, even I can't tell.

I only wish there was a good reason. But I smile.

"Perhaps."

18

SELBY

I never truly lived in Glory Mesa, so I am not sure why I feel the goodbye so strongly. But as I lead my dun out of the livery stable and throw my leg over his back, I feel a profound sense of loss.

I'm a man to whom the loss of anything should not be a shock, least of all a place and an experience that were not altogether pleasant. After all, Glory Mesa tried to lynch me once.

But I'm leaving now, and I suppose even years of hardening can't change the fact that I was once a sentimental man.

At least I'm heading the way I've always wanted to go— over those mountains to see what's beyond.

I watch the windows of the stores as I pass, see the windswept streets, see the marks of civilization on this place that was once wild.

A couple men touch the brims of their hats to me as I pass, and I return the gesture. The train is in the station, pumping steam, and people mill around it.

The whistle blasts. I should hurry, or I will be left behind.

I see Gable leaving the cattle loading area and heading up toward the passenger cars. He's wearing a long black coat, and he looks around, lonely-like, before climbing aboard.

I head toward the cattle cars.

Kate stands near the loading chute beside the train car, her pinto's lead in one hand and her saddle in the other, balanced on her hip.

It blazes up from somewhere I've tried to forget: the memory of sweat and blood and burned flesh, men packed together so tight that no one can lie down. Slipping in and out of fever, unable to sit up, your back seizing with chills, and all the while the chugging of the train pounding into your head the thought that it would be better to die than endure another minute of this.

I'll ride. I cannot get on a train.

"Are you ready?" Kate's looking fresh and happy and ready beyond a doubt.

"Yes—but I'm not getting on the train. I'm riding out."

She studies me for a long moment. If she was thinking of protesting, she decides against it.

"I'll go with you."

I take a deep breath. "That's not necessary."

"Why is it that you feel you must always take the hardest path forward?"

"Well—"

"And don't tell me because you were on the wrong side of the war, or because you were an outlaw and a killer or a convict. Have you seen Blue?"

Blue is different.

"I'm not forcing you to do anything, and I certainly wouldn't dream of trying to tell you what you should do. But it's like I said. You're a good man, Jack. There's no need to punish yourself for things no one else remembers."

"It is not that," I reply. "But I can't take a train."

"All right, then. I'll go with you. If we take our time, maybe Jesse and Raymond will catch up to us at the first junction."

She heaves the saddle over the pinto's back and turns her out of line.

"Do you need to lay in supplies?" she asks, bending down to fasten the cinch.

"No, I have enough."

"I should have enough to last me to Broken Tree if we stop there."

I nod as she straightens and dusts her hands on her vest.

"Well, let's be off. We can beat the train out of town, anyway." She swings up into her saddle and grins.

19

IRENE

I DON'T KNOW HOW RAYMOND COULD STAND IT IF HE ever became a father himself. Ever since the news came that Rosamund's baby is arriving, he's been pacing our small house in town like a caged tiger.

I settle myself in the front room with a cup of tea and open my book. I hear his slow, steady step in the other room.

"These things take time, dear," I say the next time he comes near. "It's better you find something to do."

He chuckles and comes to peer over my shoulder. "What is this?"

"Poetry."

"I should have guessed." He puts his hand on my shoulder and I reach up to hold it. He stands thus as I read serenely, enjoying simply being near him.

After a bit he presses my hand gently and leaves again.

A horse rides by swiftly. Raymond goes to the window and watches the strcet for a few minutes.

"Anything the matter?" I ask, looking up from my book.

"No." His face is stony as he turns from the window, but then he smiles at me.

"Just wait," I say. "The child will be beautiful."

His eyes light up gently. "I reckon so. You know, Rose was the most beautiful child I ever saw. I wept the first time I held her."

"Not long now, I suppose." I turn the page.

"I hope so."

A horse comes clattering up to the gate and a man dismounts, letting himself in and running up to the porch.

His hasty knock echoes through the room.

Raymond is at the door.

"Raymond Lacey?"

"That's me."

"I have a message for you."

Raymond steps out onto the porch and closes the door after himself.

They stand on the porch too long, their voices serious. But perhaps it is territory business. I must not worry until I know for sure.

The man turns away and heads back up the lane and Raymond steps in, his face pale. He closes the door very slowly, his fingers gripping the handle with white knuckles.

"Raymond?"

He snaps out of it, takes his coat down from the hook and thrusts his arms in.

"My love, what is it?"

"The baby—" His voice is steady and carefully controlled. "He was stillborn. I'm going to be with Rosamund."

"She might—"

"She'll want to see me." His face is grim and there are tears standing in his eyes. He comes over and kisses me gently. "Don't wait up for me. I don't know when I'll be back."

"I'm so sorry, love." I push his hair back from his forehead.

"Yeah." He sniffs and heads quickly out the door.

I'm left in the silent house with the measured, unhurried ticking of the clock on the mantel.


I HEAR him come in long after I first fell asleep. I don't want to guess the time. He sits down heavily on the edge of the bed, pulls his boots off.

I've never seen him move so slowly, so lifelessly.

I roll over and rub his shoulder. "Raymond?"

He presses my hand. "I'm just tired," he rumbles.

"How was she?"

He can't answer right away. I can feel him breathe slowly, searching for the words to say and the breath to say it with.

"She's inconsolable," he manages softly. "I've never seen her like this."

"It's grief," I whisper. "One of the deepest kinds."

"I was going to leave, but now—"

"Give her just a little longer. You have a job to do. I'm sure Jesse will be staying. Ride hard and you can make up the lost time."

He nods, wipes a tear out of his eye. "I reckon so."

He thrusts back the coverlet and climbs under, but he's not sleeping.

"Raymond." I move closer and he reaches back and takes my hand, but doesn't face me. "My darling, you should sleep."

"Tell me you'll be all right if I go on this venture," he murmurs. "If you say no, I'll stay here, with you. I'll find a way."

"No, Raymond," I whisper back. "Go. You've given me so much happiness that if I died tomorrow, I wouldn't have a single regret. I mean it."

He rolls over and kisses me tenderly on the forehead.

# 20

# THATCHER

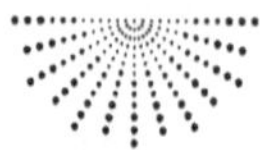

"You know I hate to leave you like this." I'm standing in the doorway of the parlor, my hat in my hands, facing Archer and Rosamund.

"That's all right. You gave your word. I'm—more grateful than I know how to say that you stayed. For all of it." Archer's voice is hollow.

Rosamund isn't even looking me in the eye. It's as if she's gone elsewhere and hasn't come back.

We had a small funeral with just the family, but the paper ran an obituary for William James Scott, born and died the same day.

There were flowers sent from the president of the railroad out East and a dozen other dignitaries. We drove out to the land Archer owns and buried him there amongst the wild purple sagebrush. Archer, Raymond, and I built a fence with our own hands—for a family plot.

They had a headstone made, beautiful and marble white.

Rosamund almost couldn't bring herself to return to Glory Mesa.

"Be careful, hm?" Archer reaches out to clasp my hand. I take it and then throw my arm around his shoulders, drawing him close.

"You watch your back, you hear?"

"I promise." He pulls back, looks me in the face with tears in his eyes. "I promise."

"Goodbye, Rosamund." I hold out my hand to her, and she takes mine. Her grasp is cold and spiritless.

"Goodbye, Jesse. Safe travels."

I wish I could say more. I wish I could take this away somehow or change the times so we could all stay and grieve together. Not take off as soon as he's in the ground, riding to the far ends of the Western Territory in the face of death.

This is the wrong sort of goodbye.

"Well—until we meet again." I put my hat on and head out.

"Jesse." Archer's voice stops me. He steps outside, closing the door. "I can't tell you how much, how badly I wish I could go with you."

I pause. That's not what I thought he was going to say.

"My hands want something to do. Some difference to make, right now. Something to throw myself into."

I shrug. "Come, then."

"You know I can't." His eyes are pained. "There are a

dozen things a day that need my signature. A thousand—Jesse, how I wish I had never said yes to this position."

"Perhaps it's time to pass the reins to someone else."

"To whom?"

I wish I had an answer. But I cannot think of anyone. Archer is standing guard for us all in a way most men wouldn't know how.

I slap his arm. "Stay strong. The cavalry will come. I don't know how or from where, but relief has got to come."

He smiles, but it takes an effort. "You come back, Jesse, you hear me? Don't you dare not come back."

"I'll come back."


It's windy and dry and mean as I saddle up my horse. I see Raymond's shoulders knotted through his coat as he pulls the cinch tight on his own horse. The wind makes the horses jumpy; mine blows long and hard at the wide nothing beyond town.

I throw my leg over his back, let him dance a little, get it out of his system.

"Do you think we're doing right, leaving?" I ask. The wind takes the words away as soon as they leave my mouth.

Raymond adjusts his hat, straightens the reins in his hands. He looks over at me with a grim set in his jaw. His eyes are like flint.

"We don't have a choice." He spurs his horse forward and we ride out of town into the fitful morning dust.

# 21

# NEWTON

THE STAGE PULLS INTO SHERRYVILLE A DAY LATER THAN predicted, thanks to a broken wheel. I've never been here before; the stage didn't run this far northwest until recently.

Thanks to the defeat of Mortimer, boomtowns are cropping up everywhere, which means more cheap hotels and cheap saloons for poor travelers like myself.

But Sherryville could be a lot worse.

I open the door from the inside and step out, giving Hannah a hand down. She thanks me with a smile and surveys the street with quiet determination, pushing a strand of hair back into her bonnet.

I reach up and take down her carpet bag, handing it over.

"I wish you all the best, and happiness, Miss Milton."

She accepts the bag, her knuckles whitening on the handle. "He said he'd meet me on the twenty-fourth. Would you be willing to stay in town that long? In case something goes wrong?"

"I'm not—" But my protest dies on my lips. She's alone. "Of course I will."

"Thank you."

"Do you have arrangements?"

"Yes, Mr. Terhune paid for a room for me in advance." She heads up the street just like that, again, quiet but confident. Unafraid.

I push my hat back on my head and walk the opposite direction in search of food and a bath.

THERE IS a whole day between our arrival and her meeting with Harrison Terhune, so I ask her to dinner in the hotel dining room the second evening, just in case any of the gentlemen around the common room or the hotel bar get ideas.

She's wearing a pale yellow dress this time, and she looks better for the rest.

"Good evening, Mr. Newton," she says as I pull out her chair and take a seat across from her.

"I hope you've been well? No encounters with unsavory characters?"

"No. But I have been keeping to the hotel," she admits. "I have no wish to attract the wrong kind of attention."

"Wise."

"I hope so."

Our food arrives—beef and potatoes and a few greens, nothing out of the ordinary for a cattle and mining town.

"Miss Milton, may I ask you a question?"

"Of course."

I toy with my fork, then set it down to rub my jaw.

"What induced you to accept an offer of marriage all the way out here?"

"There are many reasons...." She clears her throat, looks down at her plate. "I liked the sound of this territory, and I thought I could perhaps better myself in marriage out here, since women are scarce. But the chief reason is that I have no one else."

"No one?"

"My grandmother died last year. She was not well-to-do, and what she had went to creditors." She sets down her fork and rests her wrist on the table. "And that's why I am desperate. It's Harrison Terhune or I won't know what to do. But—your advice has given me pause. I am afraid of making a mistake."

I wipe my mouth on my napkin. "Do you think you will accept him?"

"I must see him first. Then I will decide."

Her voice is determined, her shoulders set. But fear and uncertainty linger in her eyes.

. . .

I DETERMINE to keep away from Hannah Milton the following day. I hope, for her sake, that she sees good in Harrison.

But I have a feeling deep in the pit of my stomach that it's not going to end well.

She is sweet and young and hopeful, and he's a man picking up the broken pieces of a life that will never quite be the same.

I see Harrison Terhune come past my hotel window around eleven in the morning. He cuts an imposing figure striding through the muddy streets with his high boots, broad shoulders, and stern blue eyes.

His chestnut trudges behind, mild and indifferent.

I watch as he approaches the hotel. I see him water his horse, comb his hair with his fingers, straighten his jacket, and go inside.

I wish them both luck.


I'M STEPPING out of the general mercantile with supplies for the trip to my place when Hannah approaches me, her face lighting up with relief.

"Oh, thank goodness! I've been looking for you."

"For me?"

"Yes. I have a question for you."

I shift the packages in my arms. "What did you think of him?"

"I'm afraid," she says softly. "I don't think I can go through with it."

"Then don't."

"It's not that he's bad, but you're right. He's hard. His eyes are closed off to the world. I don't know what else to do...I told him I'd think and give him an answer this evening."

"Decline him," I say. "I know you'll do it as gently as you're able."

"It's easy for you to say that," she says. "I have nothing to go back to."

"Then marry him. Like I said, he'd be kind to you."

"You are no help at all!" She clenches her fists. "You sit here with a ranch of your own, a horse, money, and the freedom with that gun to travel anywhere, and you tell me to make up my mind at once between two bad choices?"

I'm taken a little aback, but I see where she's coming from. "Easy now. I'd like to help if I can."

"Take me back with you to your ranch. Let me cook or clean. I won't require much more than food and board. I have no lofty aspirations...I just want to be somewhere where I can live my life happy and unafraid."

*Watch yourself, Chris. This is dangerous territory.*

I shake my head slowly. "Harrison Terhune is a good friend. To warn you against him and then take you home, paid position or not, looks an awful lot like betrayal."

Her face falls.

"Tell you what. I will pay your passage back and give

you enough to live on until you find a job. You can pay me back if it makes you feel better. Otherwise, consider it a gift from a friend. How does that sound?"

"I won't have my way paid like that," she says. "It's not how I was raised."

"Miss Milton." I pause, trying to think of a way to make myself understood. "In a place like this, time is of the essence. You stick around long enough and you'll end up in the dregs. And I have to get back to my ranch. The money is nothing to me. Please, just take it."

She wilts before my eyes and I suddenly feel as if I am the one stealing her hope and innocence, not Harrison.

"Look, make whatever decision you feel is right. And if you need me, come find me. I'm not leaving town yet."

She turns away and goes up the street.

Come evening, I go to the hotel and take a seat at the bar, just in sight of the restaurant. Perhaps it's not my business, but I want to see this interaction for myself. To know, if it is required of me, how to advise her.

Hannah comes down in her blue traveling dress and Harrison pulls out a chair for her.

I cannot discern the words, but she is brief, her voice soft and apologetic.

His shoulders sag.

"Very well." His deep voice carries to the bar. "I will compensate you for your fare here and give you enough for your fare back. How much was it?" He opens his wallet and licks his thumb to count out the bills.

"Oh, please don't," she protests, her voice clearer and bolder. "I feel terrible enough for the trouble."

"You went through far more trouble than I did," he says. "Let me pay it at least."

She reaches up and wipes a tear from her eyes.

"What are you crying for?" he asks, perhaps just a tad gruffly.

"I'm sorry that I can't do it. I wish—I wish I could, especially after everything you've been through, and—"

"What do you mean?" He goes very still.

"About your past?"

"Who told you that?"

She just shakes her head, gets up from the table and flees upstairs.

Harrison stands up, the chair scraping roughly. His hands are clenched. I see no more because he turns and comes toward the bar. I turn my gaze away and take a sip of my drink.

Last thing he needs is to know he's had a friend witness his disappointment.

"Whiskey," he says. "And no water."

He downs it and pushes the glass out for another. He knocks the second one back and takes a deep breath, bracing his hands against the bar.

"Are you all right, sir?" asks the barkeep.

"I will be," he answers briefly.

"A third one, on the house?" offers the barkeep.

"That's all right. I can afford it." He reaches into his pocket and a coin clatters onto the counter. He takes up the third glass, and that's when he sees me.

"Chris?"

I push my beer away and hold out a hand.

"What are you in town for?"

"Just passing through on my way home. Hear it's been dry."

"As a bone. Travel was good?"

"Yes. Quicker, thanks to the stage."

I start to catch myself and don't. But it's too late. Harrison's mind is working; he's staring at me slowly, as if the words on his lips no longer fit.

The stage comes through every other day. Cleaned up and well-rested as I am, it's not hard to discern that I didn't come in on today's.

"Did you meet anyone on the way? Traveling with you?"

"A woman."

"Did you talk?" His voice is hard, low. He's no longer looking me in the eye.

"Only a little. Mostly good, Harrison. But she deserved to know."

"I thought you were my friend," he says, tight and under his breath.

"I am," I reply, and reach for my drink.

His fist slams into my cheekbone, knocking me back against the bar. Someone's drink gives way behind my head and smashes. My own is pooling, pouring off the end of the bar.

I scramble up just as Harrison aims another punch at my face. He misses and hits low, on my shoulder. I hit the floor hard, but I'm scrambling up again in an instant.

Once you're on the ground, a big man like Harrison might never let you up.

I throw a punch back. He blocks and sends me spinning. I lunge for his stomach and he falls back with a grunt.

We're locked together, wrestling, as three men try to pull us apart.

I spring back, wiping the trickling blood from my face with my sleeve.

Hannah stands in the doorway.

"What's going on?" Her face is white, horrified. My face must be covered in blood, Harrison's fists smeared red.

He pulls out his wallet and throws a thick wad of cash down on the table in front of her. "Take it."

He strides to the door and turns back to me one last time. "And Cristobal Newton, if I see your face again, I'll kill you!"

He's gone. My heart is pounding and I have a dozen places that are throbbing, swelling up. I look at her, panting.

"You have the money. If I were you, I'd book a stage ticket out of here right now."

## 22

## PIKE

It is dark and cold, but I have been watching the lantern in the window of Stanton's hay barn, counting the men as they leave, one by one, until I am sure, very sure, that Holt is the only one left inside.

I leave my horse tied up around the back of the barn and slip in through the side door. I hear whistling in the loft and the sound of hay being tossed.

I wait. I have waited most of the day, and even in the cold of a desert winter, I can wait a few more minutes.

At last I hear the sound of his tools being put up and the heavy tread of his boots nearing the edge of the loft.

Holt comes down the ladder still whistling, shedding his work-worn gloves and stomping against the cold.

He stops short as he turns around and sees me. "You?"

"Yes, *me*. Stop staring like a bull calf. You knew I would be coming to see you sooner or later."

"I figured you'd send word," he says, scratching his nose with the back of a dirt-stained finger.

"As you see, I did not."

He grins, and I hate the wolfish look of it.

"How is Stanton's ranch?"

"We need water, but the cattle ain't dyin' yet."

"Tell him the Swift brothers are away from home. Two of them are gone on a long journey, and the other won't be back for a week or two at least. Move in and Stanton can seize the water on the southern border."

"Stanton ain't got enough men, but he might get Early on board with him. And Early ain't got much in the way of scruples."

"Then convince him."

"How come you care so much about Stanton's cattle all of a sudden?" He scratches the side of his head.

I wave him off. *Another idiotic question like that, Holt, and I'll cut you loose.* He really does try my patience. "It's not about his cattle. It's about the Swifts. I want you to take that youngest boy."

"I thought you said he was from home."

"Tell me, do you have anything more important to do in the next two weeks? Wait for him. Take him alive. Do what you like to him, but don't kill him. You can burn the ranch, take the stock, shoot the hands, I don't care. Stanton can do what he wants."

A smile is spreading slowly across his face. I know Holt has little love for the Swifts. Their enmity runs far back into the days of the reign of Mortimer.

"Sure thing." He spits with conviction. "I'll wipe them Swifts off the map, see if I don't."

HE'S TIRED. I WATCH HIM DIGGING HOLES FOR FENCE posts behind his house, covered in sweat and dirt. This boy I watched grow into a man, this man who is carrying the world. I wish I could reach out and take it off his shoulders, lay him down to sleep and wake him when the world is kinder.

But I have helped him come to this moment, and tired though he is, I know that he will not stop fighting.

He sees me and smiles in the sun, the wind playing with his dark hair, now shot through with gray in places. He leans his shovel up against a new post and comes over, pulling his gloves off.

"It's been a while, Doctor. How are you holding up?"

"I should ask you that."

"Well—you know how I've been. Rosamund's taking the loss of our son hard."

"And you?"

"I have a lot of work to do. I don't have the luxury of grieving how I want to."

"Your life has been nothing but that," I say quietly. He doesn't hear me, I think.

"Do you want to come in? I'm sure there's coffee on. Rosamund keeps the pot warm."

"No, thank you. I am perfectly happy here."

"Glory Mesa sure has changed, hasn't it? I hope the new doctor hasn't given you any trouble."

"Not at all. His work has made mine easier. The time is coming and is near at hand when my work here will be finished."

"Well, if anyone deserves a rest, it's you, Doctor. You've been practicing as long as I can remember."

"Since long before there was a town."

He whistles appreciatively. "You must find all this strange." He gestures to the bustling town.

I nod.

"Archer Scott, do you think that you can make this territory something?"

The question takes him by surprise. "I don't know. But I'm going to try. It's my job, isn't it?"

My heart swells with pride and something like pain, too. "I submit that you already have."

"Doctor, that's the finest thing anyone could say. I feel on the verge of giving up. Sometimes I wish I wouldn't wake up the next morning, just so it would be over."

"I imagine so," I say softly. "But you will not. You will live until you see the fruits of your labor, even if glimpsed from afar. I only pray that along with it you will get the rest you deserve."

"Well, I hope so. Legacy is a tricky thing. I just hope they're kind to me, you know? Or that something I did will stick." He rests one hand on the fence rail. "What do you think?"

"I think," I say quietly, "that your father would be proud of you."

"My father?" He stiffens.

"All of them, waiting, believing in the time to come, yet not being the one. But you are the one."

"You know who my father was?"

I smile. "It will do you no good now to know who your father was. But only a true son of the land can break the curse. And you have done it."

"Not yet."

I sigh and look up at the sky. "When I see clouds swollen with rain, thundering over the hills, I say rain is coming. I have not seen the water falling to the earth, but I do not need to see it to know that it is coming."

I put my hand on his shoulder, look him straight in his weary blue eyes. "And you have summoned this storm, my son. Not me."

He's looking at me, confused.

*Hang on just a little longer, my boy.*

Tears prick my eyes, but they do not spill over. I am going to miss this lad.

"May they be grateful," I whisper, and I drop my hand from his shoulder and close it to a fist.

It's the only blessing I know now to give.

# ALAN

We stop at Tapas Junction, a week into our journey, to say our farewells. Max, I think, has been dreading it. He desperately wants to come along, but he hasn't complained. He's man enough to take responsibility when it comes to him.

I water the horses and check the gear while Jem and Max go to get all the necessary business cleared up at the bank.

Our roans are hardy. They drink, I dry off the sweat under their saddles and down their chests, and they'll be good for another decent stretch before dark.

I pause to stroke my horse's head. He has more experience than the other two, and he's downright mannerly. I appreciate that in a horse, and I tell him so as often as I can.

My brothers come striding back up the street, looking as fine a pair as I have ever seen. Jem is well-built, tall and muscular like one of those racing horses breeders bring out here from the East. Max is taller than Jem now, nothing but lean height.

But they laugh suddenly—and it is the same laugh.

"Horses ready?" asks Jem, coming up.

"They'll be good a while longer."

"Good." Jem turns to Max and puts his hands on his shoulders. "Brother, what you do is of good value, same as us. You keep that ranch, you use that money well, and you treat man and beast just as square and right as you can."

"I will."

"Alan and I will be back before you know it. Don't you worry."

Max grins. "Sure."

He catches Max up in a big, hard hug and they stand thus for a few moments. Jem lets him go and Max comes over to me.

The late afternoon sun's in his eyes, and his forehead is creased with a slight scowl against it. "Well, Alan—" He's not sure where to start.

"Goodbye, Max. Stay out of trouble." I ruffle his hair and he grins.

"Same goes for you."

"You know me. I'm always good," I wink.

He throws his arms around me and hugs me hard. "I'm going to miss you."

"Me too." My voice almost fails me.

"You come back, hear?"

"And you stick around for me." I step back and smile.

"Always, Alan. I'll wait to the end of the world for you, you know that."

"I'll hold you to it." I punch his shoulder and he laughs, rubbing it sheepishly.

He unties his horse and swings up, backing it from the rail. His fingers sort out the reins, taking longer than he needs.

He's just watching us, swallowing hard.

"Well, you watch yourselves," he says.

"You watch yourself," replies Jem.

"See you two around. Don't stay away long." Then he gives his roan a kiss of the spurs.

I suddenly have a deep conviction that he didn't have to go, that the three of us didn't have to be split.

Not now, not at this time.

I watch as he lopes out of town, watch until he's out of sight. My heart hurts and my throat is thick. I love that kid.

"You ready?" asks Jem.

"Sure." I snap out of it and untie my horse.

Jem's already on his, backing it from the rail. "I've seen a few unsavory faces. Keep an eye on our backs."

"Sure thing." I take a glance, but see no one in particular.

Still, Jem's usually the first to spot trouble. And on this trail, it won't do to let our guard down.

# CARNEGIE

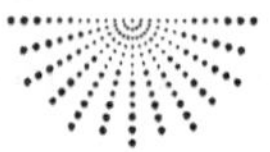

Two nights out of Glory Mesa, on the trail up to Black Flats, Jack Selby shoots us a pronghorn for dinner.

It's not the largest I've seen, but it's carrying good meat.

He smiles as he rides up to our campsite, the cleaned carcass slung over his horse's back. "Have you ever had pronghorn steak?"

"No, is it good?"

"Not fine meat, exactly, but I remember shooting one of these during a lean time. Best meal I ever had."

I smile and push my hair back. This wind is unforgiving to braids, especially when you spend all day on the back of a horse.

"Well, this fire will be going soon."

"Good." He heaves the animal down and leads his horse over to where mine is. "I'll have a couple good steaks cut for us in a minute. And I could do with a cup of coffee."

I get about brewing the coffee and pull a skillet out of my gear for the meat.

Jack comes over, bringing an impressively large knife.

"I've never seen that one before," I comment, looking up from my work.

"I don't usually carry it in plain sight." He knifes the air a couple times. "See, you can only display so many weapons before a town just decides to give you the boot."

I chuckle and he joins me.

He kneels down beside the pronghorn and gets to work. "How hungry are you?" He swivels around on one heel.

"Give me your best."

I am ravenous, but even in the middle of nowhere, it would be rather indelicate to say. I feel a strange need to maintain a level of good etiquette with Jack.

By my guess, he was a fine gentleman once.

We cook the steaks in the pan and use some salt and spices from Jack's dry goods to season it. I make a mess of beans on the side and we wash it all down with hot coffee to stave off the chill of the wind.

I'm pretty sure if I live to be a hundred I won't enjoy a meal more than this one.

"Kate." Jack leans back on one elbow, staring into the fire. "I have a question."

I'm beside the fire, enjoying the warmth, my face resting on my fists as I gaze into the wild flames. "Go on."

He rarely asks me questions unless it's a matter of business or preference. He's not one for conversation, though his conversation is very good.

"Why did you choose this?" He gestures to the wild country slowly settling into dusk, with the birds flying high overhead to some roosting place only they know of, the yip of a lone coyote hunting, the muffled blue falling over the brown hills.

"I can see you are quite well-educated, and I doubt your hands were used to work before you came here."

Oh, that man's sharp. In all my time out here, he's the first to notice.

"Well, the land speaks for itself," I say, looking around at the beauty falling so commonplace around our shoulders. "I'm sure I'm not the first to fall in love."

He laughs a little under his breath.

"And I came to a crossroads." I flick a stray sprig of brush into the fire. "For the first time in my life, I found myself with nothing to lose. I was young and strong, I had money in my pocket and an old life I wanted to move on from. It's not every day you also have a frontier a stage's fare away."

"I suppose not."

"And you were not disappointed when you came out here?"

"Disappointed? I never regretted anything less. This place is more alive than any newspaper or artist's sketch could ever capture."

"But working for Carson?"

"Well, I hated that sometimes. Sometimes I hated it with

every ounce of my being. I'm sure you know what a saloon can be like for a girl. But I never regretted it. Every morning I'd look out at the rocks and the wild land beyond the town and my heart just swelled. It didn't matter that I'd seen it every day before and I'd be seeing it every day again for the next year. It just moved me right to tears."

"I can see that."

He rolls over onto his back with his hand thrust under his head. A few silver stars have ventured out across the muted sky.

"What about you?"

He stays on his back, watching the stars for so long that I give up, assuming he is not going to give me an answer.

But then he says, softly, "I wanted to make something of myself. That's why I went to war."

I take the fresh coffee off the fire. There's not really a good reply to that comment, unless a person wanted to play dumb.

"I was so full of hope." He laughs to himself. "I really was."

"Sometimes hope just gets delayed a little," I reply.

"Not for me." He sits up fluidly, not even using his arms to raise himself, and reaches for the coffee pot.

I want to say more, but I shouldn't.

He offers to fill my cup and I hold it out without a word. We drink our coffee in silence and I cradle the hot tin against my chest.

It's going to be a cold night with this wind and no shelter.

"Are you going to take the first watch?" I ask, smothering a yawn.

"I may as well. Like I said, I don't really sleep." For the first time, he seems a little sad about it.

"Wake me up for my watch anyway." I toss out the rest of my coffee and get up.

# 26

## SIKES

When you've lived a dozen lifetimes, there are not many moments that stand out to you. But this is one of them.

Walking alone out of Glory Mesa, every dusty footfall a thunderclap. I knew this place when it was nothing more than a couple lean-tos for trading, a stopping place for men who could not stay. Now it boasts enough boarding houses and saloons to feed a small army.

And in only thirty years.

Thirty years, a mere stone in the riverbed of this territory's vast time. Yet it has been enough. Against all storms, evils, dangers, this place has stood, and—I believe—will stand.

The wind pulls at my coat. It's dry and barren out here. The drought has taken hold, and even I can hardly feel any dampness in the air.

But a good land survives even drought.

I turn my face to the hills. If he cannot do it now, alone, he cannot do it at all. The sounds of Glory Mesa are faint—the rumble of wagons, the sound of a horse or cow occasionally, the hum of hundreds of voices. Like pooled rainwater in the high desert rocks it sits, strong and good, full of living, thriving people.

I think this place is going to be all right.

There's a ribbon of dust, moved by the wind. It's growing, moving, beckoning.

I step into it, and I don't look back.

# PIKE

Just before dusk, I see the smoke signal, a column rising and halting and rising again. The wind is brisk—a perfect night.

*This is for every time you have thwarted me, Alan Swift.*

Everything is in place.

I watch the distant ridge closely, listen for any sounds. But it is a long time still before I hear the sharp crack of gunshots and see distant figures running.

A cow bellows, long and drawn out. Horses run down the hills like water from a broken dam.

Then I see it: the far-off flicker of dancing flames, licking the treetops.

The scent of smoke reaches my nostrils. I close my eyes and breathe it in. This is the beginning, the first step in setting things right.

Darkness falls fast. The burning ranch house and barn, surrounded by pines, light up the sky for miles around.

I can see my hands in front of me, far away as I am.

"Ma'am?" A voice comes at my elbow. "It's growing dark. Are you sure you want to be out here?"

"Yes, I am sure."

I stay where I am, and he leaves me be.

I watch the burning for a long time, see the flames pulsing and coursing over the land that was theirs.

It is a pity about those boys. You love them, somehow, even as you hate them. They are so inseparable from the land that you don't know what to do with them.

But they are in the way, so they have to go.


Sometime later in the night, when the fire has burned long, a man comes to report. One of Stanton's or Early's—sent by Holt, I imagine.

"A few of the hands were killed trying to stop us," says the man. "The rest fled, except for one we took alive."

"What about the Swift boy?"

"Holt's got him."

"Is it the youngest?"

"Yes."

"Very well. You can tell Holt to expect me tomorrow."

I look once more at the burning remnants of the ranch, the only bright thing in the cloud-covered night.

I smile. At last we're getting somewhere.

## 28

## ALAN

WE STOP FOR WATER NEAR A STAND OF TREES IN THE hill country where the grass is dry and brown from the heat. Jem is fixing a string that broke on his saddle and I'm checking my horse's legs when we hear hoofbeats.

It's hardly uncommon to see a rider in these parts, but I don't like the way he's riding, partly slumped over the horse, clinging to it as if trying not to fall off.

Looks like trouble's found us already.

The rider careens to a halt nearly on top of us. Jem looks up and runs to him.

"Paxton, what happened?" He's catching him even as he falls from the saddle. It's one of our steady, long-time hands. He's been beaten; his face is bruised and bloody, his shirt torn in a couple places. He has no jacket.

"They burned it," he gasps. "Right up to the sky. Drove off the stock. Some of them got away, I think, but—"

"The ranch?" It's not even a question. "Who?"

"Stanton's men, I think. But they were led by Holt. Never saw Stanton."

"The dog," Jem bites out. "He's after our water."

"And they've got Max," he breathes. "That's why I'm here. I didn't get away—they sent me with a note from Max. I'm sorry."

Jem whips his head up and we see it at the same time: there's another figure watching us from the crest of the hill.

Jem whips out his gun and fires. The man wheels his horse and disappears over the top of the hill.

"It's all right. You're with us now," says Jem. He goes over to his horse and takes down his canteen. "When did you drink last?"

Paxton doesn't answer, just reaches for the canteen. He drinks at first as if he cannot get enough, then forces himself to slow.

"Where's the note?" asks Jem.

Paxton rifles in his pocket with a scabbed-up hand and pulls out a crumpled note, stained with dirt and dried blood.

Jem takes a deep breath and opens it up.

"I don't think that's his handwriting," I say, craning my neck to see.

"No, it is." Jem smooths out the note against the saddle-horn. His voice is grim. "It's his."

"I saw him write it," says Paxton. "They made me watch it so's I could say."

*Brothers*, it reads, *there was nothing to be done. They had us from the very first. They want the water rights to the south quarter and the Hatchet Creek in exchange for me, in writing, due the tenth at Forger's Canyon, or Holt'll do me in. Please come. Max.*

Jem crumples the thing in his hand.

"The tenth doesn't give us a lot of time," I murmur. "And we'll certainly miss the rendezvous at the Blue Lantern Rocks."

"We'll split," he says, tucking the ransom note into his vest pocket. "You take Paxton, get him up the trail to the Horse Springs camp. At the very least, he'll be able to recover and get a firearm. You can go on from there and make it for all of us. I'll get Max."

The way he says it, I think he means he's going to get Holt.

I grab his arm, put my head near his. "This has the smell of a trap, Jem. Holt always hated you in particular."

He shakes his head. "Stanton never was particular about the sort of hands he hired. It'd be just like him to take on a man like Holt to look out for his interests."

"We could both go. Bring Paxton. He's tough. A day or two with us and he'll be right as rain."

"We gave our word we'd meet the company at the rocks. No need to sully our good name over a personal matter."

"I'd still feel better if you didn't go alone."

Jem nods, draws his gun, and starts reloading. He glances up at the crest of the hill, but there's no sign of the other man.

"I know. But it's the right thing to do. I'll ride fast and be there before the tenth to deal with Holt and shake some sense into Stanton and his boys."

Paxton, cattleman that he is, loosens the cinch on his horse and leads it to the water though he can barely stand.

I sigh. "All right."

I don't like any of this, but when trouble finds you, sometimes it's best to ride right into the teeth of it. "Go, then. Take anything of mine you think you'll need. I'd like to think part of me is riding after those dogs too."

"I'll take your knife," he says. "The little one. Spring's busted on mine."

I dig in my pocket and hand it over. It's warm from being close to me.

"Go get the brute," I say. "And tell him this is a present from me."

"Yessir." Jem puts it in his vest pocket beside the note and checks his cinch. "Paxton, I'm riding out to deal with this. Alan's going to stick with you until you get up to Horse Springs—I reckon you can do whatever you like then."

"What about the ranch?"

"I'll rebuild it. Takes more than a fire to stop us." There's a brief break in his voice. "That ranch house had all the worldly goods our parents left us. Stanton's not getting away with this, Holt or not."

"Then I reckon I'll foller on down when I'm set to ride," Paxton says. "Someone'll have to find the stock they scattered. You'll have a time rounding them up in those mountains."

"Thank you."

"Don't you worry none." Paxton steadies himself with a hand against his horse's flank. "Get Max, that's what's important."

"I'll do that." Jem heaves into the saddle and collects his reins. "You watch your backs."

"You too," I answer.

He pulls the brim of his hat, and he's off.

My heart sinks in my chest. We boys are meant to stick together, and I don't feel right about this one bit.

29

## GABLE

I stare at the food I have been trying to eat for the last twenty minutes, dead to the clamor of the boarding house around me. I may as well be eating sawdust.

Those of us who rode the train over have been moving through towns, getting out to eat now and again, letting the horses stretch their legs. Now we've reached the end of the spur and we're preparing to strike out on our own.

The men I'm traveling with, a few of them have been out to the Blue Lantern Rocks more than once. They say it's only five or six days' ride, if we make good time. We will be some of the first to arrive, and we plan to camp there until the rest of the company joins us. Our horses will have time to rest and graze, and we'll be the freshest of them all when we go to seek our territory's salvation.

And somehow, despite all that, I am listless. I watch the

people come and go, seeing but not comprehending. I couldn't tell you a single detail about a soul that's walked in or out.

But even in this state of dullness, a man like me always knows when his wife walks into the room.

"Edith!" I stand up so quickly I nearly topple my chair. "What are you doing here?"

She doesn't answer, just comes over, looking me up and down.

"Come home, Lesley."

"Don't be ridiculous."

"Come home."

"I swore an oath." I drop my voice. "What are you trying to do to me?"

"You're trying to get yourself killed," she whispers fiercely, "and I won't have it. If you insist on going on, I'm coming too."

Of all the—I take her arm gently and lean down to talk to her in a low voice.

"Edith, these are rough towns, and the country I'm going into is getting rougher. Go home. I'm worried for you."

"And I'm worried for you."

"I have to do this. At least let me discharge my duty, fulfill this oath. After that—" The words almost don't come. "After that I'll come home."

"Do you promise?"

I try. But I can't say the words.

"Didn't I tell you?" she whispers. "You're trying to kill yourself."

"No, no." I take her hands in mine, hurt. "Not trying. But I cannot in good conscience promise that. If my oath required it, and my oath might—"

"I asked you not to do it." Her voice cuts through mine like a knife. "And you went and did it anyway. Do you have any consideration for the fact that we have a duty to each other?"

*Then why did you say those words?*

She sees my thoughts in my eyes and something in my heart stirs. When we fell in love, that's what I loved about her. She could see right into me. She looked into my soul and saw what could break me, and somehow she still loved me.

But now, the knowledge just hurts. And I cannot stand to be here, with her seeing my thoughts, knowing how to hurt me.

She looks into my face and speaks slowly, earnestly. "Lesley, I don't know how else to apologize."

I give her hand a squeeze and drop it. "Let me go. Let me win back what you've taken from me."

And suddenly she understands. I see it in her eyes.

"I'm so scared," she whispers. "I'm angry with you because I'm scared for you."

Perhaps she should be. But it's too late for either of us to turn back now. We have to fight our way forward, not back, if we're to make it out the other side.

"I will try to come home," I say.

"Try." She shakes her head and turns her eyes away. "Try is the only word for you."

The noisy room feels empty to me after she walks out. I should go after her, walk her back to the train station—it's not the most civilized town, despite having a boarding house.

But I don't. I stay where I am and I eat my bitter supper.

# 30

# JEM

I RIDE THE STAGE ROAD. I HAVE TO KEEP A KEEN EYE OUT for coaches, but it's the fastest way back and the trail is smoother. I burn up the ground with my little roan, leaving dust like smoke in my wake.

I'm afraid for Max. Holt is one of the worst men I've encountered in my years of living. And on top of that, I'm angry. Angry that Stanton waited no more than a couple weeks after I left my home before raining fire on it. Angry because he's a neighbor and I never did him harm a day in my life. I had a thing, and he wanted it. Simple as that.

And he's put my kid brother in harm's way for it.

This is a vengeance road, and I'm coming for them.

It's late afternoon and the sun's starting to ride down toward the distant mountains when I see the trail's blocked. A stage is stopped in the middle of the trail, people wandering, gathering scattered luggage, loading it up.

"Anything the matter?" I ask, riding up.

A lady screams outright.

"Easy there, mister! Who are you?" The shotgun rider comes racing around the far side of the stage and shoves the barrel of his rifle into my face.

"Jem Swift." I jerk the bandanna down to my neck. "I'm just passing by."

"You'll forgive us," the shotgun says, withdrawing his weapon. "We were just held up, so we're a mite touchy."

"You folks all right?"

"No one's hurt, but they took the money and a passenger."

"A passenger?" That's not common.

"A girl. Pale blue dress. She sure didn't seem a ransom type."

"How long ago did they do it?"

"'Bout an hour ago."

"And no one went after her?"

"Look, mister," says the driver. "I'll risk what I can, but there were five of them. Going after them on one of these stage horses is like suicide. I have to look out for the rest of my passengers too, you know."

"Which way?" I'm already getting tired of this man's excuses.

"North, up into them hills. I'd be careful if I were you, mister."

"I'll worry about myself," I retort, and turn my horse northward.

It's not hard to see where they've gone. There are five or six of them, just as he said, and they left tracks everywhere. It's clear that they weren't worried about being followed.

But I have no time to lose and I've got to ride quick. Night is coming on and the last thing I need is to lose them and their trail in the dark.

I may never have lived with the Auki as Max has, but I've got their blood strong and hot in me all the same, and the dust and the rocks are my heritage.

I whistle up my horse and get moving.

Dusk is settling around me when I hear voices and the clang of a pan. They're setting up camp—loudly, the fools. Hope rises in my chest. I'll have this done in no time.

I dismount and leave my horse around the corner, tied to a piece of dead wood. He's pretty calm, but I'm taking no chances if shots start to fly. I check my pistol to make sure it's fully loaded and take my rifle out of its sheath.

I climb over the rocks, moving quick and quiet, easing myself over the ridge until I see the source of all the noise.

I smell food cooking. Three or four of the men are around the fire, another on lookout and another coming from the horses.

Their captive is sitting to one side, looking cold and tired but unhurt.

That's the trickiest part of cleaning out a nest like this. You've got to be mighty careful about bringing guns into the situation, lest the very person you're trying to save gets shot.

I count the men off carefully, account for their horses, then aim for lookout on the other side. If I take him out, the girl won't be in anyone's firing range except mine.

I draw a bead on him carefully and squeeze the trigger. The rifle goes off like a cannon in those cramped rocks, and every man jumps like he's been shot.

My man slowly loosens his grip on his rifle and slumps.

"Sorry, son," I whisper. "That why you don't take up outlawing."

They're all on high alert now, guns bristling, facing my direction. But they can't see me yet. The girl has started to her feet and looks ready to run.

I cup my hand around my mouth. "I don't want trouble with you folks! I just want that girl and the money you took from the stage."

"Come on and take 'em then!" shouts one fool, brandishing his gun aloft. If he wants to stay alive, he shouldn't be pointing it at the sky.

I shoot the ground by their feet, sending the rocks flying up at them.

This riles them. They start pumping lead in my direction, the bullets flying well over my carefully positioned head and striking against the rocks below me.

"Done yet?" I call down when they've quit. "That was a warning shot. Last chance before I start picking you off."

This starts a discussion. A couple for, a few against.

"I'm getting impatient," I call down. Truth is, I'm losing the light. "Make up your minds!"

A fight breaks out among them. A couple of the men run for their horses, and one of their companions guns one of them down. The other hightails it out of there, and the girl tries to slip away toward the horses.

"No, you don't!" shouts one outlaw, and she freezes. "Stay right where you are."

I fire down into them. They manage a couple frenzied shots in return, far wide.

And then it's over.

I stand up and descend the steep edge of the rocky hill, rifle held up in one hand so the girl can tell I'm coming in peace.

Even so, she reaches for the gun of the man shot going for his horse and holds it up.

"If you have any trouble in mind..." she warns.

"Nah, I passed the stage this afternoon and found out they'd let a girl like you just get carried off without resistance. I'm sorry, ma'am. They weren't much of men."

"That's all right. I'm much obliged," she answers breathlessly. "What's your name?"

"Jem Swift. I'm a rancher out a little south of here. And your name, ma'am?"

"Hannah Milton."

"You live in these parts?"

"No. I came out here to get married, but it didn't work

out."

"I see. Do you know anyone out here?"

"Just a man I met who helped me...his name's Cristobal Newton."

I raise my eyebrows. "Well, if you have to have one friend out here, make it Chris Newton. I'll get you to the nearest town and wire him to come get you. I'm on a bad trail and I can't bring a lady."

"But—"

"What's that?"

Her protest dies on her lips.

"Eat some of this, if you can bring yourself to. And get some sleep. We'll have to ride out of here before dawn."

She settles herself down beside the fire and finishes cooking the meat and beans the outlaws left.

Her calm, matter-of-fact ways impress me. We could do with a few more like her out here.

"Are you going to eat?" she asks.

Eating is the last thing on my mind. I feel the minutes and seconds counting down to the tenth; I'm going over the miles I have, the miles I've lost, and recalculating where I can make time back up.

Stanton wants me to get my brother back because he wants my water, but I'm not so sure about Holt. As for me, I'd be surprised if there wasn't some trap waiting for me there too.

But I nod to her and crouch down beside the fire.

She's scoured off the dirty plates with sand and she's

plating up the food. It smells decent for outlaw grub.

"Where's the nearest town?" she asks.

"A day in that direction." I nod back up the trail the way we came.

Her shoulders sag, but she says nothing.

I eat well even though my heart's not in it. I have to keep my wits about me, keep a clear eye. By the end of this, I'll need every ounce of strength I can get.

It was like this during the war. We didn't have good rations half the time, but I fought for good food, for myself and my men.

Whether you were clear and sharp or hungry and weak could make all the difference on the battlefield.

I LEAVE her in the small town of Sherryville, safely installed in a room, which she insisted she had the money for. I also left her with one of the outlaw's guns.

I head up to the telegraph office, write out a note for Chris. I keep it brief and don't mention the rescue directly.

"Look," I tell the telegraph operator, "you get an answer from that man, you take it to a Miss Hannah Milton, staying at the hotel."

It's not much of a hotel, but out here you can get away with calling a cow barn a palace if your sign's painted bright enough.

"Sure thing, sir. Will there be anything else?"

"Nope." I drop a coin on his table and light out of there.

3 1

# ROSAMUND

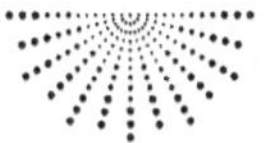

ARCHER'S GONE AGAIN. PERHAPS HE HAS ALWAYS BEEN gone this much, and I just didn't notice it. Solitude in happiness is so much shorter, brighter.

Whenever he leaves now, I feel each minute individually, every second drawn out.

When he's home, he is quiet. We used to talk in the evenings about our future, about what we would do when he's done being governor, about the life we're building together.

Now neither of us can bring ourselves to say even a single word. The best we can do is sit quietly together, his arms around me, and sometimes we cannot even do that.

Even that, the simple affection, breaks me apart.

I have cried more in the last three weeks than I have in my entire life before this, and I am so exhausted that I have become afraid to cry more.

I do not have the strength to cry anymore.

I sit down in the parlor chair beside the window and draw back the curtain just enough to see out into the street. There is no sun, but no rain either. Everything is numb and still.

A week ago, Doctor Sikes disappeared.

Someone said they saw him go, as he often did, towards the southern hills, but without his mule.

He never came back.

I want to feel something. He was a good man who was good to me. But beyond a little distant sorry feeling, I cannot feel anything about his departure.

They sent out men to look for him, and Trevain tracked him as far as the flats below the hills. Then all signs disappeared completely.

Trevain said it was no use looking. Doctor Sikes is gone.

Archer says I must do something to pull myself out of this cloud. He's afraid for me. But I am living in this cloud; I cannot see anything beyond it.

I just want my son back.

He was perfect. He had his father's nose. His fingers and toes were tiny, but long. A Lacey trait. The only thing the doctor could see wrong was that his heart wasn't beating. We'll never know why he didn't live.

Tears flood back into my already swollen eyes, my breath, already uneven, catches. I lean my arms on the back of the chair and rest my chin on them.

I just want him back. I want to hold him in my arms. I

want to sing him every song my mother sang to me, I want to see the way he'd reach for Archer's face. The way he and Archer would play when he was older.

I've never felt so alone.

I lean my head against the back of the chair and stare out the window, unseeing.

A knock at the door rouses me, I don't know how much later.

I straighten my appearance in the mirror and go to the door. The town has been more than generous in caring for us, but I cannot bear to talk or answer another woman asking how I am.

It's Irene, carrying a basket and a letter. "Afternoon."

I smile a little in acknowledgement.

"I brought some supper for you and Archer. Raymond told me what you liked before he left."

Of course he did. My brother is like that.

"Is there anything I can do?" she asks.

I shake my head. I wish I could feel something, anything. But there's nothing but a dull ache that lives in my chest, in my limbs.

I have lost myself.

She hands me the basket and I take it in cold fingers.

"We have been going through the things Doctor Sikes left behind," she continues. "Trasker and myself and Trevain. We found this with your name on it."

She holds out the sealed envelope.

"Do you think he's really gone?" I ask.

"I think so," she answers. "Trevain does, and I believe him. They're cut of the same cloth, those old men."

I take the letter. "Thank you."

Irene just nods.

She holds out her hand. "Please, Rosamund, if you think of anything, if you want—anything. I'm here."

I take her hand gratefully. I only wish I did want something. "Thank you."

She leaves and I shut the door, leaning against it as I open the letter.

It's a full sheet of paper, but there are only two words written on the entire thing.

I rub my thumb over the words scrawled in simple ink: *Take heart.*

32

# NEWTON

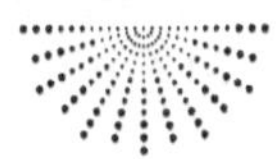

S‍HE'S WAITING FOR ME ON THE STAGE PLATFORM, HER carpet bag clutched in her small hands, her lips pressed tight.

I dismount, tying the horse I'm ponying up to the rail, and then tie my own. I mount the steps, stride across the bright, dusty platform to where she waits.

"I'm sorry for the trouble between you and your friend," she says softly. "I wish I could have answered him differently, I really do."

"You don't owe him anything." I take her bag from her small, tight fingers. She follows me down the platform to the waiting horses.

"The gray is yours." I point it out. "He's quiet."

She unwraps the reins and mounts up.

"Miss Milton...." I clear my throat, catch her reins a moment. "I'm sorry I sent you away as I did. I should have arranged someone to ride back with you. What happened should never have happened on my watch."

"You did warn me it was dangerous."

"Even so." I let go of her horse and swing up into my saddle. "You have my word it won't happen again. You're lucky a man like Jem Swift happened along. You couldn't have asked for a better friend out here."

"He said the same of you."

"He'll walk into the jaws of death for a stranger if it's the right thing to do." I turn my horse out of line and start up the street, and she follows.

"Where are we going?"

"Back to my ranch, until we can make other arrangements."

"How far away is it?

"Three days' ride, maybe four."

"I'll work hard," she says, urging her horse up beside mine. "I'm a fine cook, if I say so myself. And cleaning—I used to keep a large house, top to bottom. That's how I earned the fare to come out here."

"Well, I'm not putting you to work right away. I think you'd better rest awhile." I give her a half smile.

"I'm all right," she insists. "It takes a lot to wear me out."

"All the same, I'll be leaving just about as soon as I get there. I'm leading some men out northwest of my place, and I have to meet them a day's ride away. While I'm gone, how about you rest and let the place take care of you? We'll talk when I get back."

I urge my horse into a trot as we reach the edge of town and the road opens up before us.

"You don't have to do this." She has to speak loudly to be heard. "You barely know me."

"Strangers have to become friends pretty quick out here if they're going to survive. And—I reckon I wouldn't be much of a gentleman if I turned you away."

Her smile is shy, but it lights up her face.

# 33

## JEM

I'VE RIDDEN THE ROAN ALMOST TO DEATH, BUT I'M TOO late.

The night of the tenth falls over me and the dawn of the eleventh coats the canyons and arroyos pale gray as the roan collapses beneath me. I strip the saddle and bridle and let him lie.

Poor gallant boy. He deserved better than this.

I stroke his head and give him some water from my canteen before I leave him. If he has the will, perhaps he'll recover.

I continue on foot, running, running until my lungs burn and my breath comes in gasps. The landscape drags by, and the path to Forgers Canyon seems to go on and on.

The rim of the canyon is painted in golden fire. The rest of it is gray and still and empty.

"Max!" I cup my hands to my mouth. "Max!"

No answer. I see evidence of a fire the night before and a patch of churned-up earth where horses were ridden off some hours ago.

"Max!" I run through the canyon, searching, shouting. My voice is ragged, almost gone.

If there was a trap, it's too late. It's deathly still.

There's a prospector's cabin a couple miles from here. I can walk up there and borrow a horse, maybe. Pursue them. Maybe they took Max with them.

And then I see him.

Cast aside, broken, hardly the figure of a man anymore.

*No.*

I run to his side, cut his bonds, raise him in my arms. He moans softly as I move him, but there's no fight in him. His body's limp, sticky with blood, one leg is off at an angle it shouldn't be. His hands are criss-crossed with burns.

His face is like marble, cold and white and unresponsive under the half-dried blood.

"Max, no," I whisper. "Oh, Max."

He's covered in lashes and burns; his clothes are ripped to shreds. I retch.

And those devils left him alive.

"It's all right." I smooth back his hair, my eyes filling with tears so that the sight blurs mercifully. "It's all right, I have you now."

It's too late, but I take my shirt and rip it up to bind up the deepest of the wounds. I can hardly see as I work, tears streaming down my face, falling hot on the dust that clings to us both.

I shouldn't have left him.

"Fight, Max. Please."

But I'm only torturing myself. It's too late.

I raise him as gently as I can in my arms and sling him over my shoulders. The dawn is coming, spreading, the golden light mingled with gentle pink, bathing us in warmth against the cool of the morning.

Every step to the prospector's cabin seems like a mile, my arms holding my brother's limp body, going over every scenario, every minute, every hour.

I couldn't have done anything different. It wouldn't have been right to let that girl go. I couldn't have lived with myself if I had.

Perhaps they would have killed Max anyway. Perhaps they would have gotten us both and made us die together.

I have to stop thinking.

The prospector swears outright when he opens the door and sees me standing there.

"So that's what was going on down there," he says, shaking his head. "That was a bad lot, whoever they were. I stayed clear of them."

"Their leader was Mortimer's right hand," I reply, ducking in.

He gestures to a bed standing along one wall and hurries to lay down a fresh blanket.

I lay Max down gently and I can't see straight again. I

think I am going to wake from this nightmare. If it was a gunshot wound, I'd hold his hand and talk him through it. I'd get the bullet out and I'd patch him up. I'd give him eager root to slow his bleeding.

Cracked ribs I'd bind up, broken bones I'd set. Any ill, I'd get him through it. He lived with the Auki—he can bear pain.

But I don't even get to say goodbye. I don't get to tell him how sorry I am or why I was late.

"I'm sorry, son," says the prospector. "I don't think your friend's going to make it."

"Brother," I correct him.

I wipe my face and fight to regain my composure. "Look —I have to leave." I pull off my gloves. "Will you keep him as comfortable as you can?"

"Sure. Poor devil." He clucks sorrowfully. "I had a partner once on this mine, and it caved in. Took him three days to—well, I reckon you don't need to hear about that. I'll take care of him, son."

"Do you have a horse I could borrow?"

"Sure. Not the fastest born, but she'll move."

"Good. If you go down outside Forger's Canyon a mile or so, you'll find a roan. If he's not dead, he might be of use to you. Best horse I've ever had."

"I'll do that."

"Goodbye, Max." I bend down and move his golden hair back, kiss his forehead. "I'm so sorry."

The prospector sees me to the door.

"When it's time, send for Tagweiah of the Auki nation. Tell him I want my brother buried on our land." I pull my wallet out, count out a few bills. "This is for your trouble and whatever you need. Please, anything you can to make him comfortable."

He looks over his shoulder.

"Good news is, son, he's probably beyond feeling anything. There's nothing you could have done about it."

I thank him again, maybe a third time. I'm so numb I don't know what I'm saying anymore.

He shuts the door. I go over behind his shed and am sick until there's nothing left.

I stand in the strong, pulsing wind. I can hardly think straight. My hands want vengeance, blood to avenge my brother. My heart throbs hard in my chest, reproaching me for living while my brother dies.

I go and saddle the horse.

My brother's blood cries out for justice. I'll see it done if it's the last thing I do.

# 34

# THATCHER

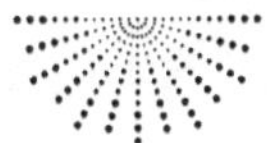

THE CAMP AT BLUE LANTERN ROCKS IS MUCH LARGER than I expected. Spread out in tent circles of two or three, there must be some seventy men. I've never been out this way before, and the land, I must say, is more than beautiful.

It stretches out wide and windswept, as far as the eye can see, broken only by the western mountains and some dark rocks of slate blue.

I still see no resemblance to a lantern.

"Ever been out here?" I ask Raymond, who's been even quieter than his normally taciturn self.

"Never have," he replies. "Lovely country."

We ride into the camp and a general cheer arises. It's for Raymond, of course. He doesn't acknowledge it much, but he gives a couple nods to familiar faces and strides on to the end of camp that's mostly Blue Harding's boys.

Blue is sitting on a stump by his tent, cleaning his gun.

His sleeves are rolled up and a cup of piping hot coffee sits on the ground beside him.

He looks up as we approach and gestures for us to join him. "Coffee's hot. Set yourselves down and share the pot."

Raymond and I dismount, tying our horses to a log that's been dragged out for a hitching rail.

"Blue, good to see you." Raymond holds out his hand and Blue sets his rag down to shake hands.

"Jesse Thatcher, right?" Blue asks, holding out his hand to me.

"That's right." I clasp hands with him. "How'd you know?"

"We boys make a point of knowing anyone worth over a thousand dollars in this territory. Or—we did." He chuckles. "Also, you being the governor's cousin made you a figure of interest."

He winks at me.

"Don't listen to Blue," says Raymond, reaching for a cup and pouring himself coffee. He takes a sip and leans back with a groan, moving his feet closer to the fire.

"Say, you didn't happen to bring that kid from back down in Glory Mesa, did you?"

"Peter?" Raymond raises his eyebrows. "No, I didn't."

"Pity." Blue dusts off his hands and takes a swallow of his coffee. "How was the journey?"

"Long, but uneventful." Raymond's looking around camp slowly. "Have the Swifts arrived? Or Jack Selby?"

"Haven't seen them." Blue returns to cleaning his rifle. "Kate Carnegie coming?"

"Far as I know. I swore her in. Is she not here either?"

"No, she ain't."

"That's a lot of good ones missing." Raymond scratches his head slowly. "Well, I reckon they have a couple days to show."

"I reckon. Most of these men made it here in the last day or two. I was one of the first."

"How's the weather been?"

"Fair to middlin'. I heard from a passing trapper that there's snow up in the mountains."

"And the smoke?"

"Smoke too." Blue takes a businesslike sip of his coffee. I reach for the nearest tin cup and pour myself some, then take a scalding swallow. It's not bad.

"He seemed to think it was awfully unusual," Blue goes on. "Smoked hard some days, hardly a trickle others. Said it was unnatural and he was leaving for better territory. Makes a man wonder."

"Sure does."

"I wouldn't be here if it weren't for your call, Marshal, I'll have you know."

Raymond chuckles.

"Give me an enemy I can see any day." Blue mimics aiming a pistol. "But I'm your man."

"It's appreciated, Blue." Raymond sets down his cup and stands up, stretching. "I better see to my horse now."

Blue sets his rifle aside with a sigh. "My boys shot some goats up in them hills today. You boys'll share supper with us, won't you?"

Raymond looks to me.

"Well," I grin, "if you insist."

"Reckon I do," says Blue.

# 35

# CARNEGIE

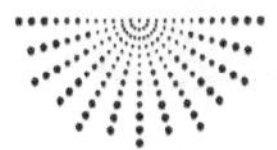

WE REACH A SMALL MINING TOWN JUST BEFORE DUSK on the thirteenth. There's no way to slice it, up or down, except that we are going to miss the rendezvous at Blue Lantern Rocks.

Jack's horse threw a shoe out in the middle of nowhere four days ago, and we've been moving at a walking pace since. Jack tried insisting I take off and leave him so only one of us would be late, but when I suggested he take my horse and leave me to walk his in, he said that was out of the question.

So we've stuck together.

This town is still on the upward climb, which means it's too early to know if it will live or die; but for now, it's on the way up. Saloons are as thick as flies on a steer's hide, hotels look seedy at best, and I'm eyeing the livery stable as our best option for a spot to sleep.

"Jack, do you think your horse could get fitted before dark?"

"Don't like the pickings?" he asks, with a quiet glance at my face.

"I'm thinking we might be happier camped out of town tonight."

"I'll tell them I'm pressed for time," he promises.

The blacksmith's shop looks like one of the more respectable establishments in town, thank goodness. Jack talks with the blacksmith outside the forge and I dismount to water my pinto.

She's grateful; she bends her neck down and it pulses as she drinks. I loosen the cinch and absently push her mane over her neck where it falls naturally.

A couple people pass by on the porch above me, a few more on the street. I can sense there's a few more around than is natural. Curiosity, most likely, but I glance around at the street just to be safe.

There are more coming.

"Jack?" I glance up to find him standing in the yard with his hands held up appeasingly. The blacksmith is taking his gun. There are three or four men standing around him now.

"I'm a deputy, I swear it," Jack says. "Let me show you."

I pull my pinto back from the trough and start over to him.

Jack slowly reaches under his jacket and into his vest pocket and produces the badge.

One of the men standing behind grabs him, another

knocks the badge from his hand. The men close in and I lose sight of him.

More come running from across the street, the porches nearby. There's a dozen around him now and more coming.

"Stop!" I shout, pushing through the mob, dragging my unwilling pinto with me. "I can speak for him, he's a deputy of the territory!"

I may as well be speaking to a herd of cows.

I unsheath my rifle and fire it into the air. There's a sudden, brief pause and Jack jerks his arms out of their grasp.

"I am a deputy marshal of the Western Territory," I announce. "And so is he. Let him go."

He wipes blood from his mouth. His vest's been half torn off.

The crowd takes a step back, but their eyes are on my rifle, and they're not dispersing like folks who respect the law usually do. I take a step toward Jack, and the leader, a rough-looking fellow with the chest of a bear, takes a step towards me.

"Jack."

Jack dives for my pistol, pulling it from my holster slicker than grease, and points it at the bigger man.

"What's that going to do, boy?" snarls the blacksmith. "You can't take us all. We're carrying iron too."

"I wouldn't try it." Jack Selby's voice is soft, almost gentle. "I could put two bullets in him and one in you by the time any one of you gets a shot off."

He motions quietly for me to move closer to him.

"What do we do now?" I mutter under my breath.

"Stick close and pick a man. No matter what happens, you keep your gun on him."

I raise the rifle and draw a bead on the brawny chest of the leader.

The air is so tight I can practically hear it hum. Jack's breathing is loud beside me, a little shallow from his dustup, but steady.

"Get a rope," says the leader, his eyes flicking briefly from me to Jack. "We're gonna hang us an Abernathy."

"I wouldn't do that if I were you." I steady the stock against my shoulder. I wish I had my pistol and Jack had the rifle.

"What, you'd shoot?" He grins. "I'd like to see you try."

I cock the rifle, a warning.

The sound of hooves comes over the noise of the mob. A horse is approaching town from the wilds, riding in, moving quick.

"What is going on here?" The rider reins in sharply, practically on top of the men who are running to bring the rope. He's on a sweat-stained roan, his golden hair equally dark with sweat, and he's covered in dust.

Alan Swift.

"We caught ourselves a would-be lawman and an Abernathy. We're going to hang them—or at least, him."

Jack's eyes flick to mine with grim amusement. "There's your advantage, deputy," he whispers.

This really isn't a good time to laugh.

"Well, I say you won't," says Alan, setting his hand on his gun. "Let them go, now."

"And who do you think you are?"

He draws his gun and cocks it. "I don't think that matters, does it?" He spurs his horse forward and they part, quickly.

Alan gives me one swift glance.

I swing onto my pinto and kick her into action. She doesn't need any more encouragement than that. She makes for the end of town like a hare with her ears flattened to her skull, her legs eating the ground.

I hear gunshots.

We don't stop, she and I, until we're more than a mile out of town, in a little hollow among the cedars where the light is already dusky.

She's blowing hard. Her blood is up, and when I rein in, she pulls back petulantly.

"Good girl," I murmur.

Hoofbeats pound over the sound of my heart and I see Alan only a little behind. He's got Jack behind the saddle.

"You showed up just in time," I say as he reins in.

He grins. "I'd say. Wonder if the drought has those folks a mite touchy."

Jack slides off the horse and drops to the ground.

"Selby, man, what happened to your horse?"

"He threw a shoe." Jack dusts off his hands. "I was trying to get a new one fitted when they noticed the brand on my arm. I showed them my tin and that just made it worse."

"That's a remarkable combination," says Alan, scratching his nose thoughtfully. "Opposed to outlaws and the law."

"Are you boys hungry?" I ask, pulling the saddle off my horse. "Because I'm famished."

"I could eat a bear," says Alan. "Got anything? I'm kind of lean on supplies."

"Dry goods. No meat except jerky."

"I'll take it." Alan shucks the saddle from his horse and leads it over to where I am hobbling mine.

Jack is already starting a fire, building it up with twigs and dead branches, since he doesn't have a horse to take care of.

I make a batch of fry bread and beans and we eat them with jerky and coffee.

As it grows dark, we recount our journeys over the fire. Until tonight, Jack and I haven't had much excitement.

Alan's story is much worse.

"You're worried for your brothers," I say, more of a remark than a question.

Jack's been listening silently to the talk, cleaning his gun.

"I've course I'm worried." Alan rubs his face wearily. "But there's nothing to be done about it but go on." He takes a bite and thinks as he chews. "Besides, I sort of think I've been meant to make this journey alone. Somehow I knew, deep down, it would happen this way."

The fire snaps.

"Do you think there's any hope of doing what we set out to do?"

"I hope so," says Alan quietly. "You know, legend used to say there was a great beast sleeping beneath those mountains. But Sikes never did. And he seemed to know—or talked like he knew—more than anyone else."

"What chance would we have against a beast?"

Alan just shrugs.

"Look," says Jack, glancing up. "There's no way either of you will make good time with me unhorsed. You ride out in the morning. I'll make it to the nearest town."

"We just rode out of the nearest town," says Alan. "You ride with me tomorrow and I'll drop you someplace more reputable. Kate doesn't have to be held up by us if she doesn't want to."

"I don't care," I reply. "I won't make it in time anyway."

Jack clears his throat.

Alan doesn't press, just snaps another large stick in pieces, slow and deliberate, and feeds it into the fire. The silence is stubborn.

"Well, all right." I shove my hat back on my head. "But it won't make one jot's difference."

I feel in my bones that Blue Lantern isn't where we're meant to end up now, and they know it too.

# GABLE

THE CAMP COMES ALIVE A LITTLE BEFORE DAWN. MEN saddling horses, campfires cooking the last breakfast before we move out. The smell of salt pork and flapjacks fills the cold morning air alongside the smells of horse and wood smoke.

I'm saddling up my horse, doing what I've done for days on end now. I'm getting used to life in the saddle, but I'm tired, body and soul.

Of nights, I dream of the days when Edith and I were in love. I'm afraid to die and win honor and leave her a widow. But something inside me keeps asking if perhaps she wouldn't like that better, in the end.

"Tired of jerky and fry bread yet?" Jesse Thatcher comes up beside me where his horse is tied and heaves the saddle over its back.

"Not yet, but I am missing home."

"I know the feeling. And I'm not even married," he grins, shoving his hat back on his head. "You'd think I'd know better by now than to answer every call for help that comes through."

I chuckle and he joins in.

"Between you and me, I wish my cousin could be here in my place. He wants to be here. And I—well, Sikes used the word 'worthy,' and I'm pretty sure that ain't me."

"Do you think it's based on worthiness?" I drape my arm over my horse's back and lean on him.

"Who knows. I reckon we won't ever really ever know. But I'm part of this territory, so I'll do what I can."

"I just want to do my part too."

Thatcher goes up to his horse's head and slips the reins over. "To be honest, Gable, I'm of a mind that in the end, just riding out here is worth something. Not everyone can be the man to slay the great evil or win the day. Wars are won by men who march, and that's what most of us will be doing, most likely."

I have never thought of it that way. Perhaps I have lived too long now among men I see as heroes. Jesse Thatcher is a man whom history will certainly remember, and he doesn't consider himself heroic in the least.

He finishes with his horse and backs it out. "Well, good luck. I'll see you on the ride." He smiles at me and pulls the brim of his hat.

.   .   .

THE AIR IS full of the sounds of preparation: horses stamping impatiently, the creak of leather, the jangle of bits and buckles. We mill, horses eager, as Raymond rides up, Cristobal Newton at his side.

Chris notices me and gives me a sharp nod, running the reins smoothly through his hands.

"All right, men!" Raymond raises his voice above the noise, his breath standing in the chilly air. "Cristobal Newton is here to guide us to the mountain. There will be no fighting among you and no straying or straggling until we know what we're up against. Is that clear?"

A rumble of assent from the men.

"All right, then. We're moving out!" Raymond spurs his horse forward and Chris takes off beside him like two men in a race.

We start after them in a trotting, loping band. We ride out from the shelter of the rocks, past the standing pines, and out into a space that opens beyond us for miles, deep and wide.

The mountain isn't just smoking; it's glowing, and the smoke trickles from it every which way like the smoke from an old man's pipe.

I don't think any of us knows what we're getting into.

# 37

# SELBY

I TRUDGE TOWARD THE LIGHTS OF A SMALL OUTPOST, MY saddlebags and rifle over my shoulder.

The black horse I bought in Perdition—a town aptly named—ended up losing his mind and his footing crossing a river. I barely rescued my rifle and saddlebags before he went under and the river carried him off. I am wet, chilled through, and fighting to stave off the numbness.

It's just my luck, losing two horses in five days.

A small group of wagons is clustered outside the trading post, and a fire burns beside them, but I make a beeline for the door. The smell of dry goods and spices greets me as I enter, and the bespectacled proprietor looks up. He takes off his glasses and gets to his feet.

"Evening. Looks like you ran into a spot of trouble."

"Lost my horse in the river crossing," I say, swaying a little. "I need a new one."

"I have a couple out back you can look at, but dry off first. If you stay the night, I have a spare shirt you can borrow."

"I'd be obliged." I sit down heavily beside the pipe stove. The water rises off me in steam. I put my head in my hands and close my eyes. Nothing is sweeter than a warm fire and four walls when a body is chilled to the bone.

The old man comes back out carrying a clean shirt. I shuck my wet coat and shirt and pull the dry one over my head.

Now I have a fighting chance.

Slowly I pull my boots off and wring my stockings out next to the fire. Unfortunately, my spare socks were lost in my bedroll with that horse.

"Go ahead and hang your gear up. Here's a blanket while you dry your jeans. I'm afraid I got nothin' that fits."

I thank him and gratefully slip out of the rest of my wet clothes, hanging them near the stove to dry. Once they're dry enough to suit, I'll ask if I can share the fire outside to cook something. Provided the folks outside take kindly to strangers.

"Who are the travelers?" I ask.

"Oh, a train from the south. They came north to Square's Run and all the way across, so I hear. But they're from that war-torn country, way back. Probably rich before it all burned."

"How many?"

"Forty?"

"None of them are going to come walking in here?"

The man just laughs.

I lean my chin on my hand and doze while my clothes dry.

SOMETIME LATER, with my clothes more or less dry, I dress again and pull on my host's borrowed jacket.

"You ready to see those horses?" he asks, bringing out a lantern.

"Sure." I take my rifle and sling it over my shoulder. It doesn't leave my side.

We head out into the cold night, the lantern showing the way, and he shows me what he has. A pair of scrubby, but sound mustangs.

I go in and check their legs and hooves for heat and unsoundness. I check their teeth and eyes.

"A finer couple you won't see," he says.

"Hm." I'm not given to praising a man's horses when he means to sell them. It rarely works out for a man's price or his pride.

I like the bay he's got a little better than the black, but I'm going to reserve judgment for the morning.

"Do you have a saddle I could buy as well?"

"If I did, I'd have to look around. I sold the last one I had in the trading post to one of those men over there, but you can see if he'd be willing to swap."

"Thanks."

I duck between the slats of the corral and head towards the travelers' fire.

A low nicker stops me, and a horse shifts in the dark. It's so familiar, I almost don't realize it right away.

The dun.

He's tied up outside one of the wagons, cropping absently at the grass around the wagon wheels. He picks up his head and nickers expectantly.

"Hey, boy." I come over and scratch his neck. His saddle is on the ground next to him—I was forced to abandon it when I had to get out of that mining town fast.

I pick up his feet and he's got a new shoe on. Whoever did it did a good job.

He whuffles in my pocket and then goes back to picking at the grass. I move my hands over his coat, he's been well groomed too.

"Jack?" A woman's voice speaks behind me, from between the wagons.

I freeze, my fingers stilling on the horse's shoulder.

"I'm sorry," the woman's voice goes on, suddenly apologetic. "It's just you reminded me of someone I—"

I turn slowly.

I can't look her in eyes. It's her. I'd know her anywhere, face, voice—that sweet, determined chin, that blond hair piled on her head, the matter-of-fact set of her downward turned lips.

"Wait, Jack...it is you!" She gives a laugh of disbelief. "Jack Selby!"

She starts forward to catch my hand and I pull back. "What's the matter?"

"Beatrice." I give her a nod, leave the space cold between us.

"Jack, I thought you must have died. You never came back."

"I know." I raise my eyes to hers. I can't stand it; they're confused, but they are sparkling, shining. She's happy to see me.

"Whose horse is this?" I ask, eager to change the subject.

"Mine. It reminded me of Polly and—and you, so I bought him off a blacksmith."

"He's Polly's son," I reply. "I had to leave him behind a few days ago."

She covers her mouth with her hand.

I reach out and touch his cheek and he lifts his head indulgently and blows on my arm.

"Well, you can have him back. And his saddle, of course."

I shake my head. "How much did you pay for him?"

"I said you can have him."

"How much?"

"Two hundred dollars." She flattens her mouth. "Jack Selby, I don't care if you're happily married or if you're an outlaw on the run, but I want to know why you never came back."

"It's a story I'd rather not tell," I say quietly.

She takes in a deep breath, soft. I remember what it was

like, when she would rest her head on my shoulder. Even the way she breathed was beautiful.

She reaches around her neck, draws up a chain. There's a ring on it. An emerald glitters in the firelight, accusing me. "I'm sorry, Jack. I think I should know."

I stare at the ring, hardly able to breathe. My chest is crushing in on itself.

"Jack?"

The firelight blurs. I can't look at her.

"Very well," I manage.

She reaches out and takes my hand. "Have you eaten, Jack?"

"No, I—" I gesture back to the trading post. "I just got in before dark."

"Eat first, then."


I MEET the rest of the wagon train—the stern master, the families, and Beatrice's father again. He's civil but a little distant. I wonder if he ever saw any of the papers about Square's Run.

She feeds me well, and I can tell it is her cooking. Bread with leavening, chicken with herbs, sorrel greens, and a cake studded with currants and baked over the fire.

If she's traveling with her father, I think she must not have married. Especially with my mother's ring around her neck.

I truly did cut every tie to home.

"Father," Beatrice says, putting her hands in her lap and lifting her chin. "Tell Jack to take his horse back. He only lost it a few days ago."

"Did he?"

I nod.

"Threw a shoe, did he?"

Again I nod.

"Well, Beatrice has my leave to do what she wishes. If she wants to give you the horse, I won't stop her."

"Father!"

He laughs, a little wearily. "Take the horse, Jack. Don't disappoint her again." He gets up and walks away from the fire.

Beatrice looks betrayed, as if someone has just smacked her. "Don't mind Father." Her words are small and proud. "He's just protective of me."

"As he should be."

The circle around the fire is empty except for the two of us, and my plate is empty. I sigh and set it aside. "I don't know how to go about telling you. It's hardly a good story."

"Jack, I'm not going to be angry." She stands up and comes over to sit beside me. "But if we must part ways, I deserve to know why."

"All right, then."

She holds out her hand. I start to reach for it and then withdraw.

"I spent the first few months of the war as a foot soldier," I plunge in, trying to think clearly. "My regiment was hit hard. My marksmanship was noticed, and with most of my comrades dead...well, I was a good shot and I was angry. So I accepted a position as a sniper with a reconnaissance unit. We traveled more than almost any other unit in the war. Went everywhere, including—once—back home. Right on the heels of Donovan's Creek."

"So you saw," she says softly. "I'm so sorry, Jack."

"With Mother buried and no home to go back to, I just didn't care about anything anymore. After that, I killed—I killed so many people, Beatrice. In battle and outside of battle. I just killed."

I fold my hands and stare into the flames.

"When the war was over, I was a wanted man. There was talk of trying members of our regiment for war crimes. So I didn't surrender. I didn't want to stand trial and I didn't want you to know. I came out West with Marion Abernathy, and I ran with him for almost a year. I did—terrible things, some-times. And I hated myself. I wanted out and I didn't know how. It's like—as long as you stick on a bucking horse, you're safe. You want off so it can be over, but you know if you try, it'll hurt."

Her laugh is sad, but it's a laugh.

"And then my band and another were caught in an ambush the army set. Probably a hundred of us caught that day. They gave us a quick trial and shipped us off to a work camp. If they hadn't been so rushed, I probably wouldn't have gotten off with only five years. But that's what I had."

"Oh, Jack." One hand is over her mouth.

"Three years in, a man named Archer Scott came into the prison, looking for a good tracker. I had a reputation, and he chose me. I did him a service that day and he didn't forget. He talked to the authorities and got me out before my time was up."

I sniff and rub my thumbs together.

"By then, I just—it didn't seem right, going back to you, or even writing. I took jobs tracking and being a rifleman for shepherds. They weren't particular."

"I wouldn't have minded. You know I wouldn't have."

"Perhaps that's why," I say quietly. "You could have done a lot better. And after everything I'd done, what kind of man would I be to come back to you, knowing you might just forgive me and take me back?"

Her voice is a little hollow when she speaks again. "What do you do now? Still guard sheep?"

"No, I've been deputized by the marshal of the territory. I'm headed north, to the mountain country."

"We're going beyond the mountains." Her voice is eager. "We're going where you are going."

I just nod.

"Jack, I still love you." She leans forward. "I do. And you can tell me no, you can tell me there's someone else, but if you still love me, I have to know."

"I've never loved anyone but you, Beatrice." The words are strangely hard to say. They come from a place I've kept buried far down, untouched for years. "But I haven't allowed myself to—to think about it. I knew you'd be much better off if you found someone else."

Her voice is quiet. "But I haven't."

She reaches out and takes my hand in hers. Her fingers are warm, and there's a gentleness to them that I don't think I've felt from anyone since the day I took her hand and kissed it goodbye, promising to come back when the short war was over.

"Come with us, Jack," she whispers. "We've left the old world behind. No one cares and you know it."

"They care. Some of them." I turn up my sleeve and show her the brand. It's better to get it all out now. "Especially if they see this."

"What did they do to you?" She reaches out, her fingers tracing it. Her eyes meet mine and I am shocked to see them blazing.

She rolls my sleeve down. "Dogs!"

"Shh, shh." I'm almost laughing. I'm relieved she's not afraid of it, and I reproach myself for doubting her. She hasn't changed a whit. "You'll wake the others."

She folds her arms.

"Why did they do that?"

"Faster than a tattoo. Like I said, they didn't have time."

She returns her hand to mine. "Well, I don't care. And I bet that they don't, over the mountains. Abernathy belonged to this side of the territory."

"You are right."

"Then come. Please." She takes my arm in her hands.

I hesitate, on the verge of shaking my head. Then Kate's voice echoes in my ears: *There's no need to punish yourself for things no one else remembers.*

"And don't say I couldn't love you, because I—" Her voice breaks. "Because I love you even more than I ever did. And your face, right here, is everything I want for happiness."

Tears well up in my eyes. One spills over and runs down my cheek.

She reaches up and wipes it away. "What do you say, Jack? Will you come with us?"


ALL NIGHT long I lie thinking. It can hardly be a coincidence that I have met Beatrice out here, of all places; that she should have bought my dun, thinking of me, after all these years; that she doesn't care what I was once; that she wants to marry me.

I never dreamed that a chance at happiness like this would come again.

But I took an oath.


I HAVE the dun saddled and my things packed by the time she wakes up, in the gray dawn. She looks at me, at my preparations, and I see the sudden sorrow in her eyes.

"You're leaving?" she asks, her voice carefully controlled.

I find I can't look her in the eyes again. I check my cinch again even though I checked it five minutes ago.

"Beatrice, I want with all my heart to go with you. But I swore an oath and I must at least try to fulfill my duty."

"I'll wait for you," she says quickly.

I brace myself to say it. "The task is one I may not come back from."

Her eyes widen. "Is it a sure thing?"

"No." My throat is thick, choked with tears that I didn't know I could still cry. "It's not for sure."

"Then I'll wait for you. Over the mountains." She takes both my hands in hers. "Only promise me, Jack. Promise me that if you live, you'll come find me. Even if—if it's to say goodbye."

I take her hand and kiss it tenderly, lingeringly. "If I come back, it'll be for good, Beatrice."

She swallows.

"Then goodbye." She musters up a smile. "Don't look back, remember. It's bad luck."

But I do. I can't help myself.

And I know I'll never forget the way she looks this morning, her hair swept back, a shawl wrapped tight around her shoulders, tears in her eyes and her lips parted in a whispered goodbye.

# 38

## JEM

THE HOT GOLDEN LIGHT OF LATE AFTERNOON BATHES Stanton's dusty yard as I ride in, my guns loaded, my knife strapped to my thigh.

The yard is empty except for Stanton's own horse. I'm almost disappointed. For once in my life, I wanted a fight.

I dismount and wrap my horse's reins over the hitching rail loosely. I want to be able to leave quickly.

"Joe Stanton!" I shout, giving the courtesy of one knock before I shoulder the door open. "Where are you?"

He's sitting at his desk in his study, the door open for air. I rush for him as he jumps up, running to slam the door.

I shove it open with my shoulder just as he reaches it and send him hurtling backward to the ground.

I haul him up by the dirty blue neckerchief around his throat.

"Jem—Jem, please, I can explain—"

"Explain fast," I whisper through my teeth.

"It's just water—I'll pay you back for it. No—no harm done."

"No harm done? Burning the ranch? And murder? How much are you going to pay for my brother's life?"

He goes white as chalk. "Murder? Now, Jem—I swear on my life, no one said anything about murder." He's squirming in my grasp now and I let him.

"Your note asked for water rights in exchange for him."

"Now—now Jem, you can't believe I'd do a thing like that."

"I didn't, until now."

"That must have been Holt's idea, or Early's."

"Holt?" I laugh, incredulous. "You hired Holt, knowing what kind of man he is?"

"He came cheap. And I've had trouble with fighting among my hands. He kept it down."

I wouldn't have hired Holt if he was the last man in the territory.

"I swear, Jem, I just wanted to use the water, seeing how you were gone."

"Max wasn't."

"Well, if Max got caught up in it—"

"They held him for ransom, Joe. They killed him slow. I'm holding you responsible."

"It must have been Early's idea," he whispers. "I'll pay you—" He reaches for his desk.

I draw my gun. His hand freezes on the butt of the six-shooter just inside the drawer.

"Reach, I dare you."

His fingers flex slowly and he moves his hand away from the gun.

"You really want me to ride you into Glory Mesa, don't you?"

"What would you do if you realized someone had killed and burned in your name?"

"I'd take responsibility."

"It's easy to say on that side of the gun."

If only he knew. If he only knew how much I've gone over every thought, every word. Why did we draw straws? I should have stayed, knowing the drought was a hard thing to leave to a boy like Max.

I should have put my foot down as the head of the household and made the decision.

"You listen to me, Joe Stanton. I am going to give you a chance. You tell me exactly what happened, and you give me Holt. There's a chance, if your story matches the others, you'll get off with stealing and nothing more."

"Holt's gone."

"Gone?" I pull him closer, my grip tightening. "Gone where?"

"I don't know. He doesn't work for me anymore. Soon as he came back from your place, he took off. Turned in his outfit horse and rode."

"Well, you'd better give me a better idea than that."

He looks up at me, the steel returning to his eyes. "I could call half a dozen men in here to kill you right now, Jem Swift."

I don't release my grip on his collar.

"You're the one who should be worried about dying," I whisper.

"Let go of my collar and there'll be no tricks. You'll strangle me before you ever get the story."

I drop him unceremoniously into his chair.

He coughs with a good deal more drama than necessary and pulls himself upright.

"Yes, I wanted your water. It's true. A man's got to live and I'm not above fighting a little dirty to keep my head above water. But if I'd known what they were going to do to your brother, believe me, I'd have never let them go."

"Talk is cheap, Joe."

"I'm a hard man but I'm not a murderer. This Holt, he comes to me and says your place was unguarded and you boys were riding with the marshal. They won't even know, he said."

"That's sure not what he was thinking when he burned the ranch."

Stanton makes a helpless gesture. "That's what he told me. Asked if he could take a few hands and go in with Early's outfit on it. Early just got in from selling three quarters of his herd up in Saguaro City. So I told him yes, and he went. I stayed where I was. With this weather and all, I'm not making myself a target for a rifle on a dark night." He laughs uncertainly.

"Go on."

"And they were back in a week's time, give or take. Early's men didn't come up to the ranch. I never saw them. Holt turned in his outfit horse and left the next morning."

"And that's it? They didn't talk to you about water, or how it went?"

"Some of my men said they'd got us access to the water now, that's it. They were a little—shamefaced. I figured they didn't like the scent of it. No one wants to run afoul of you boys."

"I reckon not." I holster my gun. "Look here, Stanton. I'm going to wire news of this and your story to the governor in Glory Mesa. You stay where you are, and maybe, if you're telling the truth, you won't swing."

"There ain't no place to go, Jem," he says.

"That hasn't stopped some men. I'm going to have warrants put out for Early and Holt. And I want payment for two weeks' use of my water."

He goes into his desk, a different drawer this time, and counts me out about fifty dollars.

I fold them up and thrust them into my vest pocket. "Goodbye, Stanton. Until next we meet."

He doesn't bother to reply.

I leave my gun out the whole way out to the yard and for the next five miles, but I don't see a soul.

. . .

THE DAYS after that are a blur. I ride to the nearest town with a telegraph and wire the news to Glory Mesa. I don't wait for a response.

I barely eat.

I return to the canyon and to the cabin, sick to my stomach. There are no bones where I left the roan. Perhaps he made it.

I ride into the trapper's settlement and I know immediately something is off. The corral is empty, the door to the shed hangs open.

"Anyone home?" I holler, watching for movement in the cabin.

Nothing.

I draw my gun and ease my way up to the house. For a long moment I stand perfectly still outside the house and listen.

Then I knock. No answer.

The door opens without resistance and I duck into the narrow cabin. It's empty, and the only things left behind are worthless items like a pick handle and a chipped mug. There's no evidence of my brother, no leftover clothes, no old bandages.

I don't know what I was expecting to find. Sometimes the desert tricks you, gets you kind of hoping for a miracle.

I wish I could have at least talked to the man.

·  ·  ·

So I go home. I kneel among the scattered ashes of the burned ranch. The beautiful trees that surrounded the house are just charred, limbless trunks standing against the pale blue sky. The house itself is a broken skeleton, blackened and twisted.

The only home I've ever known.

All the corrals are ash, the barn is half standing, the new loft of hay we'd put up is simply gone. I wonder what Max was thinking when they came.

He was still so young. He would have been hopeful, angry, charging out with all the confidence of a man who knows he is right.

And it made no difference. They took him and killed him anyway.

One of the only things untouched is the family plot. The grass around it was always spindly. The stones are there, a couple of them darkened with soot.

My mother, my father. A few of the steady hands, including Frank, the young cowpuncher killed when Mortimer attacked us.

Nothing for Max.

I walk down the hill among the thinning ashes and search for a good stone. My kin will do everything for Max that befits the memory of a brave man and a brave death.

But my hands and mine alone will carve his headstone.

· · ·

THE NIGHT IS WEARING THIN. My eyes are swollen from the stinging smoke of the fire I worked by, and I cannot keep back the tears.

My hands are scraped and cut, smeared with dirt and blood. My shirt is torn from hauling the rock up the hill, my arms are covered in rock fragments and dust.

But the stone is in place.

*Max Swift*, it reads. *Son of Ian and Tuala. Brother. Brave was his end.* And his dates. They are brief, mocking. So little time in between the first and the last.

I remember how, when I first brought him back from our kin in the Auki nation, he sang in the dawn for the next six months.

I knew the words—all of us did—but Alan and I didn't sing them here. It seemed almost a challenge against fate, calling attention to these hills where my mother bravely settled, the first of her kind to live where the land was cursed. It was a reckless thing my mother did.

But she loved my father and their love came first.

Dawn is red on the horizon, painting the tops of the trees a brassy gold. I smear my face with the marks of mourning, using ash from our home. I leave a smudge above Max's name.

Then I face the dawn and I sing. I sing with all the strength in my lungs, with every ounce of grief that weighs me down, with every streak of fire that courses in my veins.

The warm light of dawn embraces me like a welcome for

a son coming home. It floods Max's pale stone with golden fire. It seems as if dawn was created for this moment, and this one alone.

When day has broken, I saddle my horse and I ride away after Alan.

# 39

# THATCHER

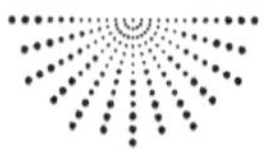

I DON'T KNOW WHAT I HAD IN MIND WHEN THEY TOLD stories of those colorful steaming pools, of the wide flats surrounded by wild hills and craggy mountains, but I can hardly believe my eyes when I ride over that first ridge and see them.

They're sprawled out below and around us, brighter than a party and shrouded in shifting smoke like a glorious threat. It's one of the most stunning sights I've ever beheld. Yet something else stirs in my chest, and the instinct that's kept this head on my shoulders for the past thirty years screams *run*.

I shiver, then shake it off. I sure as shootin' ain't turning coward now.

Raymond scratches his chin and regards the sight solemnly. If he's impressed, his steely eyes don't show it.

"That's something, ain't it?" I lean my arms on my pommel and take it all in again.

"Yeah, something," he echoes, as if he's reserving judgment.

"What do you reckon we should do?" I lower my voice just a shade. Raymond glances over his shoulder at the company following on our heels. Horses picking their way up over and around the rocks, men ready for a fight, ready to do something brave. Chris Newton, Blue and his men, the lean surveyor with his solemn face. None of them look as afraid as I feel.

If ever a river of gold and silver could bleed from a mountain, I reckon it's right here, but I'm feeling nothing but doubts right now. I don't care that it was Sikes himself who sent us.

There's no fight here we can win.

"Whatever lies ahead, we can't go back without trying," Raymond replies, matching my lowered voice. "I'll lead on."

I draw my gun and check the chamber, make sure I've got all my bullets, even though I checked it this morning. I cock it. "Whatever you say. If we're dying today, I'd just as soon meet it now as later."

I cluck to my horse and we start across the ridge, towards the trickling smoke.

Raymond signals the others to follow.

·  ·  ·

THE PATH down from the ridge is rough and twisted. You have to double back sometimes just to pick your way across. I look back once, see the men strung out like a mule train on the rocks. If we all make it back with our fool necks unbroken, I'll be plumb shocked.

My horse is lathered by the time we've made it a third of the way down the ridge. A glance back shows Raymond's horse is in the same state.

It's powerful hot down here among the steaming pools. It's like a desert in midday, but damp.

I reach up and pull my collar, but air doesn't help.

"Easy—" I hear Raymond behind me, and I see him, unfazed, straight in the saddle, easing his horse down a loose patch of rock.

The tumble of the dislodged rocks seems to go on forever before it reaches the ground. I hear a plop and realize we must be near one of those pools. I give my horse his head. He'll know better than I where to go in this shifting land.

My horse is weary by the time we reach the bottom. He's panting, sweaty. I dismount and lead him away from the slope, peering through the thickening air. My legs are tired too.

A hundred yards away, the air clears and I can see the colorful, scalding pools dotting the landscape like puddles after rain. I wait for the others to join, keeping a tight rein on my horse. He's watching and blowing and seems to like this just about as little as I do.

From the ridge I hear a noise like a groan. The ground

rumbles like thunder passing below my feet. My horse goes stiff and still, staring at the pool ahead of us.

For a moment I almost think I see something shift, deep in the hot spring. But I can't be sure it wasn't just smoke or steam blowing over the top.

Raymond materializes out of the trickling fog, leading his horse behind him. "See anything?" He makes his way toward me, waving to try to clear the air.

"Nothing but rocks and smoke," I reply. "I don't know what Sikes meant by his rivers of gold and silver."

"We'll keep looking," he answers, matter-of-fact.

I don't see how he isn't spooked by all this smoke and trembling ground. Maybe eeriness isn't the sort of thing that scares him.

Or maybe he already knows we're goners and just running out of time.

The others are coming down, appearing out of the smoke, keeping a tight hold on their horses. This whole thing feels bad, like I've seen it in a dream before and know already how it turns out.

Beneath my boots the ground rumbles and swells. Water, hissing, laps over the mouths of the pools.

Blue swears fervently somewhere back in the shifting smoke.

"Steady, boys." Raymond raises his voice just enough to be heard. "Keep ahold of your horses. We don't want them bolting into the springs."

He gives me a look meant only for me. *Keep moving.*

I chirp to my horse, pretending there's nothing to it, and keep walking, scanning the ground and the uneasy rocks for anything that looks like rivers of gold or silver.

"Fan out, men," orders Raymond. He's heading around the far end of one of the wider pools. The pale fog coats his boots, rises in clouds beneath every footstep.

My horse senses the danger before I do, snorting and starting back. I move with him, trying to hang on, settle him down. He drags me ten feet before I get him to stand.

The action saves my life. Where I was standing a moment ago, the earth is ripped open, as if a great claw has torn it from within.

The ground swells again.

"Get out of here!" bellows Raymond, fighting to keep his horse grounded. "Make for the hills!"

The men don't need any urging. Blue is calling his boys off, leading them away in a cloud of smoke toward the gentle, pine-covered hills on the far side of the pools.

A couple horses whip past me and I almost lose my grip on my own as he tries to follow them. Raymond meets my eyes directly across the steaming pool. "Jesse, get out of here!"

His words sound far away.

But he's not heading towards the hills. He's going further in.

"Raymond!" I cup my hand to my mouth and shout, but he doesn't turn back. I swing my leg over my horse's back and charge after him.

So this is how Jesse Thatcher goes—chasing after a hero like some blind fool.

"Jesse!" Raymond seems startled when I pull up beside him. "I thought I told you to get out of here."

"If you're not going, I'm not," I reply stubbornly. A poor speech, I'll admit it.

"Well, two'll get it done faster than one," he replies mildly, but I think deep down he's touched. "Let's spread out."

I turn my horse and head it back around the southern side of the pool.

It's a strange pool, I'll allow—all the colors of nature and awful-smelling. But still there's nothing that could be seen as rivers of gold and silver, even to a half-blind man.

I pick my way around the southern edge, gazing into the hot depths. My vision begins to tremble and blur. The whole world around me is blurring.

I look up to see Raymond moving along the steep rocks above for a better view. The ridge beyond him ripples suddenly.

"Raymond, get off the ridge!"

He whirls in the saddle, sees the ridge behind him shuddering the way a steer shakes his coat after standing up.

"Get back!" It's the last thing he says. The moving rocks rise up under them, catching Raymond as his horse rears. The ground explodes under my horse's hooves and we both slam to the ground.

Hooves and rocks churn around me. I'm scrambling over

dirt and rocks and leather to get out of my horse's way. The world and the earth swap places a couple times with me trapped in the middle.

My horse grunts and heaves to his feet as Raymond's mount streaks past. I catch mine before he follows, just barely.

"Easy, easy!" I turn him in the other direction. Raymond's horse is long gone.

I swing into the saddle and ride, hard, up the slope. He's half-buried in rocks and earth.

"Raymond!" I fall to my knees beside him, my hands digging at the hewn earth, tearing it off him until my fingers bleed.

He's just lying there, not moving. One arm bulges in his coat in a place it shouldn't. There's no telling where else he's hurt.

"Raymond!" I reach for his pulse. He's still with me. "Raymond, if you can hear me, say something."

Nothing.

The ground rumbles beneath me like a threat. It's now or never.

I lash him to the saddle, minding the broken arm, making the knots good and firm. The horse should be able to get him back, running to the men, away from the mountain. I just hope it's enough.

I take one more long look at his face, my last. He'd have finished it if he could. Maybe we're all doomed to fail today.

But this place won't take Raymond Lacey if I can do anything about it.

"Go on, get!" I give the horse a good slap on its rump and it heads off, nostrils wide, eyes white at the edges.

I shove my gun into my holster and start up the ascent.

I'll finish this if I can.

It's hot, powerful hot, even walking away from the steaming pools, and the smoke is thickening. I shield my eyes with my arm as best I can and trudge on, my eyes scanning every rock, every crag.

The ridge under me quivers like an edgy horse.

I had hoped that when I went, it wouldn't be like this—leaving my ranch behind, and with a lot of years left unlived.

But my choice is made, and if I had to make it again, I would.

Something catches my eye—a movement, perhaps a flash of color—below me. I scramble down towards the nearest pool. It's wide, wider than one of my sorting pens.

The ground rises and falls below me with a tremendous noise and I fall hard.

"Jesse!" My name is shouted by a faraway voice, faint against the roar of the mountain, against the tearing of the rocks.

For a moment I see it. It cannot be smoke or passing clouds—I glimpse a hint of something deep in the earth beneath us. Something living.

The water in the nearest pool disappears as if sucked

away, and I whip my rifle to my shoulder, emptying the chamber into its depths.

The world rocks and the water rushes back to its place as I fall to the ground.

*Jesse Thatcher, what have you done?*

The pool is filling with a new liquid, thick and hot, rising from the depths, flaming gold and molten silver.

This is it, and this is the end.

I whip out my pistol and empty the chamber into the cavernous pool. I load and empty and reload it again.

If I'm going down, I'll fight to the very last moment, the very last inch.

The ground shakes, heaving and swaying beneath me. I fall as rocks slam into my chest, twisting me backwards. Something in my leg snaps and grinds. I drag in one slow, painful breath, and the ground writhes viciously under me.

Dust and smoke fill the air, burning my lungs, blocking the sky. A desperate thought fills my mind as swimming blackness dulls the world: I just want to see the sun one more time.

A wrenching pain stabs me through the back and the world snuffs out.

# 40

# CARNEGIE

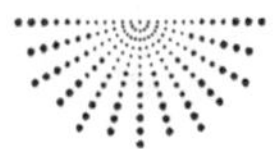

D ARK CLOUDS CLUSTER IN THE SKY, MATCHING THE smoke that's hung over the mountains above me for the last two days. I rein my pinto in, regarding the landscape ahead.

The peak has been fitful for days, glowing through the night long after the sun's light has left its jagged silhouette.

But the dark clouds bring a deeper kind of foreboding to my heart. My pulse quickens.

Whatever is happening up there, whatever is about to happen, is coming swiftly to a head.

If only I hadn't been delayed.

My pinto grinds the bit in her teeth, blows briefly through her nostrils. She can sense what is happening too, probably better than I can. And yet her ears are pricked and her body, though tense, is not tensed for flight.

She is cautious but curious.

"I wonder if they're up there," I muse aloud. She swivels her ears and turns her head back toward me a little.

"It's probably too late."

She just snorts.

I uncork my canteen and take a long swig. "Well, I reckon we won't know if we don't follow through."

I hang the canteen back on the saddle and pick up the reins. I whistle her up and we're off again.

The mountain is growing ever angrier. I hear thunder growling over its peaks, hear it echo down through the trees.

I lean over the neck of the pinto, urging her faster. I may have been too late for the rendezvous, but I can make up time on a large group of horsemen. I am light, and this pinto is half lightning.

If nothing else, I may see what comes of this terror, this curse, as it is broken or breaks over us. And if we die, at least I will have taken part in something great.

My pinto trembles suddenly, head to tail, and then again, so quick in succession that I rein in hard.

It's not the horse—it's the ground.

I pull my hat down harder on my head, tuck my hair that's flown free back behind my ears. "Last push, girl. Let's hit those hills."

We charge forward, up through the last of the long grasses, up toward the pine-covered hills that ease the hard mountain slopes into this fertile land.

The ground shakes and my pinto almost goes down. I give her enough rein to keep her head and whistle her up.

Again the ground shakes, this time harder.

I rein in. It's too dangerous. We'll go tumbling headlong and break both our necks.

Like thunder the rumble comes again, grows and rises in a crescendo. The whole ridge in the distance writhes like a snake.

A light, red and gold and blinding, flashes from the mountain.

I think I'm too late.

# 41

# NEWTON

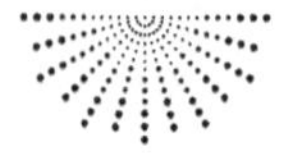

I ride down to the ragged party making their way slowly up the steep path toward the ranch house.

"They'll be ready for us," I say briefly.

Kate takes a deep breath and nods in thanks. She joined us late, the evening after it all happened.

"Any change?" I ask, turning in the saddle to look at the procession behind us.

"No. Probably a good thing though." Kate thins her lips.

The last two days have been long and harrowing. We recovered Raymond Lacey and Jesse Thatcher alive, but barely, and half a dozen others were injured by flying rocks and spewing steam. Raymond has shown some improvement today—he regained consciousness, at least—but I honestly expect to hear we've lost Jesse at any moment.

At least we're nearing my place now. There will be beds and clean bandages and hot water for washing wounds.

Blue rides up beside me and reins in. I know he's seen many bad things in his time, and probably done them, too; but there's a haunted light in his eyes today that unsettles me.

"How much further?" he asks.

"Not long. Half an hour."

"Would it be helpful if any of the boys rode ahead and got things ready?"

"I spoke to one of my hands already, but if your boys want to help, I suppose that's more useful than riding along here."

Blue looks relieved. "I'll gather a few of 'em and ride on ahead."

THE RANCH IS ALREADY in a flurry of activity when we arrive. Nathan meets us in the doorway—he has experience with horse doctoring, which is better than nothing. Raymond Lacey is well enough to walk inside on his own legs, supported by a couple men, but he's limping pretty badly. His arm is cradled in a crude sling and his face is white as a sheet, something I'm not used to at all. We have to carry Jesse Thatcher in on a stretcher. It's stained with blood.

The other injured men follow, limping or cradling bloody limbs.

Nathan directs the wounded to their rooms. Blue is bawling orders like it's the army.

I turn around and find Hannah Milton standing directly

behind me, her skirt held in one knotted fist.

"What happened?" she asks quietly, calmly.

Blue jumps to his manners, reaches for his hat that isn't there. "An accident, ma'am. An earthquake. The mountain—well, it was awful strange." He twists his hands around the brim of his hat. "I don't know if there's much hope, but we'll do what we can for 'em."

She raises her chin and her voice is very gentle, as if she is trying to spare Blue. "Well, we will give them hope where we can and comfort where we cannot." Her eyes meet mine briefly.

"Yes, ma'am. Thank you." Blue puts his hat back on and turns to the door. "I've got to see to my horse, Newton."

The door shuts. Hannah is already heading back towards the kitchen.

"Miss Milton," I call after her, quickening my step.

She pauses. There's something doe-like in the way she carries herself, dignified and collected, but on the edge of flight.

"Miss Milton." I lower my voice. "There's no need to—that is, there are more than enough of us to help. It might be ugly."

She nods, understanding in her face. There's a settled look in her expression, as if she has the upper hand on me. "Thank you," she replies. "But I want to."

She turns and goes into the kitchen without a backward glance. I hear the kettle clang onto the range, hear her stir the fire to life.

Kate Carnegie reemerges from Thatcher's room, her hair freshly tied back, a distinct smear of dirt dark against her pale face.

"Miss Carnegie." I wasn't expecting to see her in this mess.

"I've always wanted to see your ranch," she says softly, a little strained. "It's lovely."

"How is Jesse?"

Her shrug is so small I could almost have imagined it. "He's lived this long—that must count for something."

She breathes low and long, staring at the floor distantly. Sniffs, but her eyes are dry and clear.

"When was the last time you slept? Ate something?"

"I had a piece of jerky this morning."

"Come have a seat. Some water."

"Can't. There's no time." My suggestion snaps her out of her distant thoughts and she collects herself like a horse getting ready to head the other direction.

"You have a moment."

I lead her over to the sofa across from the hearth and pour her a glass of water. She accepts it with a soft word of thanks and takes first a tiny sip, then a long, deep drink.

"Word should be sent to the governor and his wife," she says, setting the glass down. "Where's the closest telegraph office?"

"Probably three or four day's ride from here."

She stands up abruptly and goes to the door, taking down her hat.

"Miss Carnegie, you're not going now?"

"Don't see much use in standing around."

"You and your horse are tired. I'll go get a volunteer right now. There's pen and paper in that desk over there." I gesture to the far wall. "You write them the message, huh?"

SHE HANDS me the note in cold fingers less than five minutes later. It's brief, respectful, and in a very good hand.

*Gov. Scott— Marshal and Jesse injured in earthquake— At Newton ranch— Will do everything we can— Mission partial success thanks to Jesse— You should be proud of him— Kate*

I take the note and scribble below it:

*Will wait for reply— CN*

"One of my best hands is going," I tell her. "He'll get it there as fast as any man can."

"Thank you." Her eyes are hollow and her shoulders braced. She's the picture of determination and dejection all at once. It's like I'm looking at two halves of a thing that do not fit together.

"Tell me," I ask, "if it isn't forward of me, is there an understanding between you and—anyone?"

An amused light enters her eyes for the first time since she's stepped into my house. "If you mean me and Jesse, no. There's nothing particular between us. But—" She swallows hard. "He's still my life. He and the marshal, and the rest of them. And I don't know what I'd do if I lost them."

"You should go rest," I tell her.

"After I check on them." She pushes her disheveled hair out of her face and strides out of the room.

I SEE my man off with instructions to wait for a reply and watch dusk fall like a curtain over the wild land.

The stars come out one by one, silent and distant, and slowly the house, with all its swift coming and goings, falls quiet.

I go in when it is too dark to see across the yard. The whole day feels like a strange nightmare.

I've never given Sikes and his prophecies much credence, but this one seems to be coming true, and now I cannot shake this foreboding. He always told me I was bound to die and that my death would be brought about by a woman.

Inside, I find Hannah Milton cutting bandages on the dining room table, her hands steady as clockwork.

"Aren't you tired?"

She pushes her long braid over her shoulder and it falls, rope-like, to swing against the dresser. "I'm all right."

"There are more hands to help. And Kate—that Kate Carnegie is as good as two. You can afford a break."

She looks up at me and gives a small smile, sad somehow. "You've done plenty for me, Mr. Newton. You needn't worry."

She gathers up the bandage neatly and moves past me, toward the bedrooms.

## 42

## SELBY

I spot the smoke of a campfire nestled in amongst the junipers down at the foot of a mesa, and somehow I know it's Alan.

He's still in his long duster, crouched industriously over the fire, a rabbit cooking over the flames. It smells so good it makes my head swim.

"Jack!" He smiles and waves me over. "You showed up just in time. There's more on this than I can eat."

"You sure?" The deference slips out naturally.

"Of course. Put your horse up over there. It'll only be another minute."

I lead my dun over to Alan's roan, shuck his tack, and hobble him to graze. Alan's roan is accustomed to us by now; he looks up with pricked ears and then returns to eating.

"I see you got your dun back," observes Alan as I come up to the fire, saddlebags and rifle in tow.

"Yep." I set them in the grass beside me and crouch down beside the fire.

"There's coffee. Help yourself."

I grab one of the tin cups off the end of the spit Alan's rigged and reach over the fire for the coffee pot. "I'll pour you a cup too," I offer.

"I'd take that kindly."

I take down a second and fill it, handing it over.

Alan takes a sip and lets his breath out in a long, appreciative sigh. "Trail coffee. Brings back memories. You ever drive cattle?"

"Not honestly."

He chuckles. "Well, I can't imagine honest or dishonest makes a difference to the cows. How far did you drive them?"

"A week. Drove them up to the plains."

"A week's long enough to make you a drover." He raises his cup to me. "To the droving men. May good grass and clean water always be ahead."

I nearly smile as I raise mine in return.

"Well, the food's ready." Alan sets his cup down. "Got your kit?"

We carve into that rabbit and for a time we don't speak. Just eat, refill our coffee, and watch the day fade.

"Which direction did you come from?"

"The low country. I—had some delays."

Alan nods slowly. He's got something on his mind and he's trying to find the right way to put it. I set aside my plate and fork and wipe off my fingers deliberately. If he wants time, he'll get it from me.

"I figure you know we missed the rendezvous," he says at last.

"Yeah." I stuff my handkerchief back in my pocket and reach for my rifle. We're overdue by a couple weeks, almost.

"I met one of Newton's men in the hills. He said things went badly."

"Badly?"

"Jesse Thatcher and the marshal are in a bad way. Sounded like the same thing that happened to the April brothers—did you hear about that?"

"I heard."

"Earthquakes, the mountain shifted—they're saying maybe Jesse won't recover."

I don't look up. I unsheath my rifle and shake out my cleaning cloth. Thatcher and I didn't talk much, but I counted him a friend of sorts. "So it isn't over?"

"No." Alan clears his throat. "He said the beast left those mountains. The few who aren't done in are trying to track it in the mountain ranges to the north and south, but they haven't had any luck."

I just keep cleaning the gun.

"Jack, you're in no way obliged to go along, but I'm going to stay on the trail, and I'd sure be glad if you shared it with me."

My hands pause on the barrel. For all the fanfare and to-do and gathering riders, it's come down to us at the end.

Somehow I knew it would.

"Why not? I have nothing to go back to." The words are out of my mouth before I remember Beatrice.

Regret stabs through my chest and I push it away, back to where I've pushed it for the last five, six years. I can't afford to let it out now.

Alan smiles. "Thank you, Jack." He pours us out some fresh coffee. "Here's to our venture and to the Western Territory. Maybe we'll be the ones to save her."

"To the Western Territory," I echo, and clink my cup to his. But for the first time, my resolve feels hollow. I was so ready to die, and now—

Thinking of Beatrice is about as pleasant as digging a bullet out of a wound. It's cruel, what I'm going to do to her.

I should have turned around and run the moment I saw her.

If she hadn't said it herself, I wouldn't have believed that she still cared for me. But she could never lie, even as a girl, and she said it not once but twice.

And now she's headed over the mountains where I've longed to go.

I can take comfort in one thing, at least. Even if I never see that far-off promised land, she'll be there; and if need be, I'll die with that thought held close.

"Are you going to tell me how you got your dun back?" Alan's voice brings a swift end to my thoughts. "Seems to me he must have passed you on the trail at some point."

I smile and scratch my ear ruefully. "I suppose he did."

"He looks in good condition."

"Some settlers bought him and we camped together one night. And so I got him back."

Alan laughs. "How much did he cost you?"

"They gave him to me." The words come out dry.

"Gave him to you?" To Alan's credit, I can see he doesn't suspect for one second I stole him back, but neither does he believe me. There's no getting around this one.

"I knew the folks from before the war. They wouldn't take money."

"They sound like good folk."

"Yes. The very best." I swallow hard.

"And they recognized you? After all these years?"

"They did." My hands quicken their work on the rifle, even though I'm really done cleaning it. Sweat breaks out along my forehead, prickles the back of my scalp.

"The war destroyed a lot of things," he says gently, and I realize he's guessed. He is too good-hearted to suggest the truth—that it wasn't the war, it was me.

"She still wants me," I say quietly, breathlessly, and I feel like I'm crossing some kind of line that cannot be uncrossed. "It isn't her. It's just that I made my oath to Archer Scott and I'm keeping it."

Alan is silent a moment before he speaks. "I thought you were a man when I first met you, Jack Selby. But now I think you're twice a man than most."

Tears prick my eyes.

It isn't the compliment, though that is one of the kindest

things a man has ever said to me. It's as if someone has taken a great hammer and started on the brick wall that's kept me safe. And now there is a great, gaping hole opened on everything I once was and had hoped to be.

The mere taste of hope hurts worse than bullets.

"Well...." I cast about for words. "That's good of you to say."

Now neither of us speaks. I sheath my rifle, tuck my cleaning cloth away in my saddlebags. Using my hands, working, doing what I am used to, brings me back to myself.

The only way forward is to put the dream down again.

I swallow. I am facing Beatrice again, but this time I'm braced and I know I can lick my heart, not just my will.

*Goodbye*, I say in my mind, and I shut the door deliberately.

Ahead of me lies some distant mountain. Like the one in the folk song, it stands high and proud and I must climb it. Not to get home, but to save home.

*Save it for her.*

"So." I buckle my saddlebags and swirl my coffee in my cup. "Where do we start?"

# 43

# THATCHER

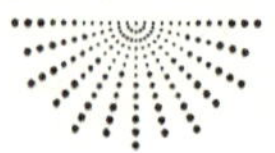

I WAKE TO A MUFFLED, DULL THROBBING MY EARS. I TRY to move my head and I can't. It's either held fast by something or I'm too weak.

I swallow, try to move my fingers. Those work. I move my shoulders next, and a racing pain shoots down my back into my legs. I go limp, gasping for air.

I guess I shouldn't move those yet.

"You are awake." A soft woman's voice speaks, and a face comes into my line of sight. A girl's face, almost, with a sweet smile.

Perhaps she is older than she looks. There is a measured maturity to her expression and her movements as she gently dabs the fresh sweat from my forehead.

"What happened?" I whisper. My voice doesn't work either.

"Just lie still," she urges. "You're safe here. You're at Newton's ranch."

Safe I could guess, with a woman like her taking care of me, but it's how I got here that I want to know.

"What happened?" I repeat. I accidentally shift and my breath is ripped out of my lungs again. I lie there as the world swims in and out.

When it clears, I don't see her anymore.

Blast, just as I was getting somewhere.

She comes back some time later. I've been in and out of a feverish dream and I have no idea what is reality and what my brain has invented.

"You need to take it easy," she urges. "Don't be so sudden or you'll hurt yourself again."

"How long have I been here?"

"A week, almost."

"A week," I echo. "How bad am I hurt?"

"Bad enough. You broke just about every rib in your chest and one of your legs, and your back is hurt. We don't have anything but a horse doctor here...otherwise we might know how bad it is."

*Not my back.*

But now I can remember. Being flung backwards, being buried by rocks and sliding dirt. The hiss of hot water spewing from the mountainside.

And then it comes to me in a flash.

"Where's Raymond?" I try to sit up, forgetting, and now she's the one who cries out. I don't fade out this time—I just lie there, unable to breathe again, feeling like my lungs have been ripped out of my chest.

It's a terrible feeling.

"Raymond's here," she says gently, trying in vain to make me more comfortable. "He's all right. Hurt, like you."

"Not so bad, I hope," I whisper, trying to smile as sweat breaks out over my body and with it, a little relief.

"No, not so bad. Here." She gives me a sip of something warm and I feel everything in my body relax.

"When can I see him?"

"When you aren't bedridden," she replies. "Or when he isn't."

"You'll tell him I'm all right, at least?"

She smiles. "I already have."

"Wait," I call out—or rather, whisper—as she goes to leave. "What's your name?"

"Hannah Milton. I'm just staying here for a bit. Now sleep."

When I wake up, I have to blink and look again. The figure sitting next to me is not Hannah, but Kate Carnegie. At least I think it is.

She shifts, pushing her hair out of her face, and I know it's Kate.

She gives me a half smile. "Jesse Thatcher, you sure gave us all a scare."

"Where did you come from?" I can't remember her being with us on the mountain.

"I came late, just in time to see the explosion on the mountain. It was awfully eerie. Just like the Black Shaft Pass."

I just groan. Even opening my eyes hurts today. "How long have you been here?"

"Ever since we brought you in." She puts her chin in her hand. "Hannah and I, we've been taking care of you and the marshal."

"Hanna said that he's not hurt as badly."

"No, but he's got a broken arm and it took him a day and half to open his eyes the first time. You were awake when they found you."

"I don't remember any of that."

She gives a short laugh. "Probably a good thing, too. It's better to forget the worst of things."

"I wish I could see Raymond," I murmur. My head's pounding, but I feel safe with Kate and I prefer asking her questions over the other girl.

"You'll see him as soon as he can move, I promise."

"When will that be?"

"You just be patient, Jesse, and leave that to us. We have it hard enough without a doctor here." She sighs and pushes her hair back, and I see how tired and worn she is.

"I'm sorry."

"Don't be," she answers, almost sharply. "I want you to rest, do you hear, and leave the worrying to us. When you're well enough, we'll talk more. And I promise I won't hold back. I'll tell you whatever I know."

"Thank you, Kate."

She pauses beside me, about to leave. "You gave us a scare, Jesse Thatcher." Her voice is hard and flat. "Next time, please don't be such a hero."

I hear her go out. I stare at the ceiling and wonder until I can no longer think straight—what was it that I did?

THE NEXT DAYS are a blur of pain and movement and trying to sort dream from reality. Food is hard to eat, even though it is mostly broth. Chris Newton comes to visit me and gives me his well wishes for recovery.

We are still weeks away from home. Since news travels so slowly, no word has come from Archer or Irene.

At some point, it seems, I turned some sort of corner for the better, so Kate feels confident enough to move my bed to the window and bring my horse around to see me. He's a little beat up and I can see someone has been treating gashes on his shoulder and flank, but he's in good spirits.

"Nathan has been doctoring the two of you," says Kate, reaching up to tousle the horse's mane. "He's coming along beautifully."

"Better than I am, for sure." I reach out to scratch his smooth cheek.

Kate gives a little smile, the first one I've seen out of her in a few days. "Don't sell yourself short, now. You're doing much better."

My horse lips at my blanket, looking confused. In fairness, I've never let him put his head through a window before. He blows and tosses his head impatiently.

"I think he's trying to get you out of there," says Kate, and she laughs. It feels strange to laugh, but I join her.

And even a faint, weak laugh feels downright good.

My horse loses patience with me and the window after a few minutes and Kate takes him away. The sun streams in where his head was a moment before, and the breeze is sweet and gentle.

I close my eyes and breathe. It's such a good thing to be alive.

Raymond comes to visit me the next day, and I'm shocked to see how thin he is—he was lean to begin with—and how carefully he moves. I wonder, then, how I look.

"How are you, Jesse?" he asks, his mustache lifting in a smile.

"I could be a whole lot worse. You're not exactly looking yourself either."

"Just a trifle," he rumbles. "Though they said I should thank you for my life. You gave me your horse."

"Well, I don't remember it, exactly. Just—vague pieces."

"I only know what they told me." He smiles wryly.

"What a pair we are." I finger the blanket where the end

has frayed. "I see you're walking, at least. Do you know what happens next?"

"Home, I think." he says. "I've been talking to Chris and Blue about the mountain. Seems whatever was ailing up there is gone from these hills."

"I think—I have a vague memory of those rivers Sikes spoke of. Silver and gold." I rub my head as if it will make the memory clearer.

"They said you shot down into one of those pools and it got to flowing. Perhaps you've done your bit."

"Some bit." I reach up and scratch my neck wryly. One arm doesn't hurt much to use, so I use it for everything.

"It was more than anyone else did." He sighs and leans back in his chair. "I think it's the end of the trail for you and me, Jesse. We had our shots and we're not much good to the cause now. At least if we're home, we can make some use of ourselves."

If I can walk. I wonder if he knows yet—if they've told him my back is hurt.

"Kate will be coming back with us on the journey, as well as Lesley Gable and Blue and his men."

"Is anyone staying here?"

"A few men may try," says Raymond. "But whatever it was that destroyed the mountain is gone. Those who weren't scared off by your brave stand will be hunting signs of it."

"Oh." I hadn't thought about that. Sikes hadn't mentioned anything like a roaming curse, out to destroy the land.

Somehow that gives me the creeps more than ever.

"I should let you be," says Raymond, getting up stiffly.

I want to protest, but I feel exhaustion stealing over me again. It's strange how I used to go days without sleep and now talking for a quarter of an hour wears me out.

"Thank you for coming to see me," I say instead.

He pauses in the doorway and looks back at me.

"You did good out there, Jesse. Real good. I think—I think it just wasn't meant to be. Not for us, anyway."

44

GABLE

M Y HORSE NICKERS IN GREETING AS I DUCK UNDER THE
bars; the others on the end of the corral pick up their heads
and come over to see me.

They've become used to me coming out to feed them in
the mornings. Since we came up to Cristobal Newton's
ranch, those of us who are uninjured have been attempting
to make ourselves useful, or at least to pull our own weight.

Even Blue Harding has been out back chopping wood
for the kitchen and running cattle down to the pastures.

The horses follow me down to the far end where the hay
wagon sits—it's been dry and I haven't seen it covered in
days.

I climb up over the rails onto the flat, hay-covered boards
and fork the stuff down. I've come to enjoy this work in the
mornings. From the top of the wagon you can see the land
spread out around the ranch house and the outbuildings—

and it's beautiful. Jagged forested mountains rise above the pines that surround the ranch house, and below I can see pastureland and timber abutting the wide lake that Chris says is mostly his.

"For an Eastern surveyor, you're looking pretty comfortable on a ranch."

I turn to see Cristobal Newton himself leaning against the rail, an ironic smile on his face.

"I'm just making do," I reply sheepishly. I fork one more pile down to the horses and lean the pitchfork against the buckboard.

"Well, I suppose out here it doesn't hurt someone, even a surveyor, to know more than one trade."

I laugh and climb down. "Surveying suits me better than ranch work."

"And pays better. Did you know Garth Levine?"

"I didn't have the pleasure."

He grunts.

"Was he the one who surveyed this?" I gesture to the vista I was just admiring. Chris's ranch is so vast I can't imagine one man being able to survey it in under a year.

"He was. It took a lot of work. He and I and three assistants were on it for I don't know how long. But we got it done. Now that man was a hero."

"Levine?"

"Yep."

"What did he do?"

"He probably set foot on more land than most of us will

ever cross in our lifetime. There were other surveyors out here who came and went, but Garth—he kept going, year in and year out. He blazed the trail for the rest of us."

"I never really thought of surveying—like that."

"Because it's your job. Garth never thought of it like that either. And he might not be remembered for it. But that doesn't take away the fact that we cattlemen, the railroad, the miners, the towns settled on the rivers—we all could do what we've done and have it stick because of him."

"I wish—" The words die on my lips.

I wish Edith saw me that way.

"Yep." Chris stretches and turns to view the land above the ranch house. "Surveying is a high calling out here."

I sigh. "My wife certainly doesn't see it that way."

"You know, Gable, unless you're born out here, you're bound to get one or two delusions about this land." He fixes me with a keen eye, as if he can see what I'm thinking. "I've been here longer than most, and I don't know half of what's out here, or what's to come."

I nod slowly. "I—when I came out here, I felt like I knew where I was headed. A year later, I feel lost. And I'm not sure I know where to go from here."

"Well, I'm not a married man." Chris pushes his hat back on his head. "But I'd say maybe you're chasing fool's gold, riding way out here."

"I don't follow."

"If a man's feeling lost, he should go back to what he

knows and start there. And whether she knows it or not, she needs you. This territory isn't easy for anyone."

"And the mountain?"

Chris smiles as if he knows something, but I can't guess what. "I don't think you'll have to worry about that. Everyone has a part to play, and I think your part's going to be back home."

One of the horses snaps at another over the hay and we watch the two of them sort out their disagreement for a few long moments.

"Look." Chris straightens with a sigh. "We're riding out to Plowshare Rock, which marks the border between me and Terhune. Another hand would be welcome."

"Today?"

"In a couple hours."

"Then I'll be ready. Thanks." I climb off the wagon and thrust out my hand on my way by. Chris grasps it.

THERE IS a small party waiting at Plowshare Rock, five men. The wind is whisking the tails of their horses, making them shift and sidestep. But the riders are like stone in the saddle.

I shade my eyes. "Is one of them Harrison Terhune?"

"The one on the right, with the blue shirt," says Kate.

I should have known. He carries himself like the boss of an outfit.

"Chris, may I?" Kate asks. She's wearing her tin star today.

"Of course." Chris Newton's face is quiet and a little grim. Whatever this meeting is, there's trouble in it.

Kate dismounts and leads her horse across the dusty ground, the rest of us following behind. The other party follows suit, Harrison leading the way.

He walks like a man with authority, every step of his tall boots leaving clouds of dust. His face is hard and distant.

"Afternoon," greets Kate, touching the brim of her hat.

"Afternoon," he replies, touching his own. "What can I do for you?"

"I heard there's been trouble between you and Chris Newton." Kate's hair had been tied back this morning, but now it's loose and blowing in the strong wind.

"And what business is that of yours?" His eyes flick to Newton.

"You heard of the trouble out in the mountains north of here?"

Terhune nods.

"We had good men hurt, and crossing your land is the fastest way to the railroad. We want our injured to be able to travel as little as possible. One of them needs to see a real doctor as soon as possible."

Harrison's hard eyes gentle a bit. "My trouble with Newton is between me and him." He steps forward, not looking at Chris. "There's no cause for there to be any ill will between us."

"So we may cross?"

"Send word when and I'll give you an escort all the way

to the train." His eyes flicker to Chris. "Just so long as that man doesn't set foot on my land."

"Thank you," says Kate. "We'll send word to you."

Harrison touches the brim of his hat. "My pleasure, Miss Carnegie."

45

# NEWTON

Hooves are pounding into the yard at a breakneck pace. Now that Marshal Lacey's men have been gone nearly a week, it's an unusual sound.

The cook, setting dinner in the next room, pauses to listen. I shut my ledger and return my pen to its inkstand.

"Trouble, sir?" he asks, seeing me head for the door.

"Let's hope not." I straighten my vest and go out.

The newcomer is one of mine. His horse is lathered and he's covered in dust. Nathan has already come out from the barn to meet him, standing in the yard with his strong arms folded, braced for bad news.

"Mr. Newton!" The young man meets me halfway across the yard.

"Tom! I thought you went with the herd going east."

"I did, sir. They sent me back. We've got trouble."

"Trouble?"

"We went to cross Mason's strip, as we always do, and he turned us back."

"Mason turned you back? Him or his boys?"

"Him. Said we couldn't cross. Said it with a rifle too. Seemed a little sorry about it, but he wouldn't budge."

"That's ridiculous. We have a land agreement."

"That's what the trail boss said. Trust me, he did everything he could."

"Well, it's not his fault. Where's the herd?"

"Back from Mason's boundary a few miles. Put them on good grass, a little water."

Water.

My heart sinks as I realize what's happened. Mason buys water rights from Harrison Terhune.

"Do you want to go talk to Mason yourself, sir?"

I shake my head. "It won't do any good. He gets his water rights from Terhune. I'm sure that's where our land agreement went."

Tom swears fervently at the expense of Mr. Mason's honor.

"Easy." I raise a hand to stop him. "Mason's a homesteader. He's not got a great deal of choice in the matter, not when his water's at risk."

"Well, what are we going to do?"

"Tell Evans to turn the herd and head it south."

"South, sir?"

"There's a junction down south, east of the mountains. You can skirt Terhune's land cleanly."

"That's a risky trail, sir."

"And I don't see another way. Go tell Evans what I told you, and tell him I'll meet you west of the Red Salt Flats. And leave Mason alone. His hands are tied."

"It's better than he deserves, sir. You've been nothing but good to him."

"He'll come around. All fights cool down someday."

"Yes, sir."

Nathan brings out a fresh cow pony and Tom mounts up. He's not happy with his orders, but he touches the brim of his hat respectfully and rides off.

I'm staring at the high crags beyond the ranch house when Nathan speaks.

"You're getting yourself in deep, Chris."

"I know." I rub my jaw slowly. "But there's nowhere else to go but forward."

"Just watch your back out there. This has the smell of a range war."

"Harrison is just angry and his pride's hurt. He knows he can't go too far."

"Don't underestimate a man whose pride is hurt."

"He's my friend, Nathan. I'm going to stay out of his way for a while. We'll come out the other side all right, you'll see."

"I just hope you're right." Nathan picks up his hammer from the hitching rail and walks back into the barn.

"Where are you going?"

"I'm going to give your sorrel's feet a check. You'll want him."

. . .

IT DOESN'T TAKE me long to pack. I'm taking a cowboy's kit, no more. Nathan brings my sorrel out and I tie my bedroll and duster up behind the saddle, fasten the saddlebags on.

I glance around the yard. It may be a long time before I am back, and I do not want to say goodbye.

"Don't forget this." Nathan comes out of the ranch house with my rifle.

"I was going to leave it."

"It doesn't do any good to pretend, Chris. You're heading towards trouble. May as well be ready for it."

"Thanks." I take it out of his hands.

"Mr. Newton, are you going somewhere?" It's Hannah, coming around the side of the house from the garden. She looks quietly at the rifle in my hands.

"I'm going down to see my herd south."

"Not north?" She looks to Nathan. "Nathan told me they were going north."

"We ran into trouble. We're heading back south to the mountains."

"It's my doing, isn't it?"

"Of course it isn't."

She presses her lips together and her bright eyes are solemn. "But it's because of Harrison Terhune. I should never have answered that letter."

"Look." I lean down, taking her gently by her shoulders. "Harrison is a fine man in many other respects. He's better than many you could have found out here. He should have told you the whole truth, and that is his responsibility and no one else's. You should not blame yourself for one moment."

"I don't blame myself for him, but for you. Taking me in has created more danger for you and your men. And you said yourself this land is already full of dangers."

I curve one corner of my mouth up at her. "So what's a little more?"

Her eyes warm, looking at me. "Be careful, I might—"

It looks as if she means to go on, but she swallows instead.

I smile and tip my hat to her as I swing into the saddle, my heart beating strangely fast.

It would be absurd to think she was about to confess love for me, but I saw the shine in her eyes and suddenly I'm not so sure.

## 46

## IRENE

It is gray, and the wind pulls insistently at the hanging laundry as if it has somewhere to be and is afraid to go alone. The clothes flapping and snapping would spook a more nervous team than mine.

The telegram had come while the town was still reeling with word of the burning of the Swift ranch and the brutal murder of Max.

It brought word of a tragic end among the steaming pools and steep ridges of the wild northern mountains, of the Swift brothers and Jack Selby missing, of Raymond injured.

The wind kicks up the dust in the road and brings the sound of a distant train whistle blowing. That would be the station stop, up in the hills. I chirp to the team in front of me and give their mild brown backs a light slap with the reins.

Not long now.

One of the station boys recognizes our team right away and ties them up for me.

"Afternoon, Mrs. Lacey." He pulls on his cap in greeting. "Want a hand down?"

He wipes his hand on his shirt and takes my hand as I step down on the wheel.

"It's too bad, isn't it?" he asks, sympathetically.

"I will just be glad to have them home," I reply, tucking a loose strand of hair back under my bonnet.

"Well, the train's due in fifteen minutes. You're welcome to sit inside, in the shade."

"That is very kind."

I mount the steps to the platform where many people are already waiting. Edith Gable, her face drawn and her lips pressed tight; Carson with a dark scowl; Archer Scott, his fingers tapping his leg nervously, his eyes worried.

I approach him quietly. "Archer."

The worry in his eyes snaps away as if locked out of sight and his face clears. "Irene. Good afternoon. How are you?"

"I will be all the better for seeing Raymond. Where is your wife?"

"She has a headache," he answers quickly. "The heat, I think."

"Well, once we're home she is welcome to come see him whenever she likes."

"Thank you. I'll let her know."

I try for a few minutes to sit inside the station, placed

near the door so I can see, but after a few minutes I find I am too impatient to sit.

My stomach is knotted, and the wind brings the rumble of the approaching train. The murmur on the train platform grows louder to match the sound of the train and the crowd begins to thicken.

So I stand in the doorway, waiting for him. The wind blows at my skirt, pushing it gently against the doorframe, like a flag caught on its own pole.

I can see the train now. I close my eyes, breath in the smell of the soot and smoke, mingling with the fresh, strong breeze.

He's home. Please, let him be all right.

The train grinds to a deafening halt and the crowd parts as the door opens. Kate Carnegie is first out, moving the crowds back with authority.

She looks older. Her face is quiet and dignified, and she carries herself like a soldier returning from battle.

Behind her come a couple men carrying Jesse Thatcher on a stretcher. Archer steps out to meet him and they clasps hands briefly.

Jesse looks so pale and languid, a shadow of his old self. But his eyes still sparkle, and when he smiles weakly at something Archer says, the old dimple appears in his cheek.

They pass me by, going to a wagon which will take Jesse to the doctor.

Lesley Gable comes out and his wife throws herself into

his arms. He holds her close, but there is something tired and very worn in his face.

She pulls his face down gently in her hands and kisses his cheek.

And then, suddenly, Raymond is coming down the steps and crossing the platform to me. His back is straight and his shoulders set, his stride steady.

There's nothing I can see wrong with him except that one arm is in a sling. His eyes are shining at me.

"Darling." I meet him halfway and stop. I'm afraid to touch him lest he disappear.

"Irene." He reaches for me with his good arm and I'm suddenly pressed against his shoulder, drinking in the feeling of his arm around me, the smell of fresh soap and sage, the steady beating of his heart.

We don't let go for the longest time, or perhaps it is only seconds—I'm laughing and crying at the same time.

"Look." I step back and let him see my figure. There's no hiding it.

"You've been gone a long time," I whisper. "We only have a few months to wait."

"Oh, darling." He catches me in another embrace, presses his lips to my head.

"They're already a quiet baby. I sing and they move, but they like peace and quiet."

He doesn't answer. I feel him take a long, shuddering breath and then he pulls back and kisses me slowly.

"I'm almost afraid to think how close I was to not coming back," he says. "How close I was to missing this."

"You're here now." I smile up into his face, soak in his glowing eyes. We're so happy in this moment that it hurts. "What happened to your arm?"

"I broke it." His voice is matter-of-fact, almost joking. "Don't worry, I'll be able to use it again when it heals."

"It might be a race between your arm and the baby," I laugh.

"It'll be ready to hold the baby when they come," he assures me, holding out his good arm. "Did you bring the team?"

"I did. Don't worry, I didn't hitch them myself."

He just chuckles.

Our team is waiting patiently, a matched pair of big brown geldings. Even with one arm, Raymond gives me a hand up into the wagon seat. Then he unties the team, climbing up beside me.

"Home?"

"Home."

He needs his one good arm to drive, but I lean my head against his shoulder, enjoying the familiar feeling of him beside me, of the rough jostle of the wagon's progress, of his calm, matter-of-fact handling of the team.

"Has it been quiet?" he asks.

"Mostly." I don't know if he knows about the burning of the Swift ranch. I don't want to ruin this moment, though. He's so happy.

"And Rose?"

"She's been keeping to herself more, but I think it's understandable."

"Certainly."

I reach out a hand, run it through his hair. It's graying. I hadn't noticed it before, how gray he is becoming.

"Please tell me that at least it was beautiful in those mountains."

He looks at me with a smile in his eyes. "Absolutely beautiful."

I look away, down the road in front of us, as my eyes fill with tears. It's almost too much, having him right here in front of me, whole and almost well. I want to capture this moment, hold it close to me forever.

Here and now in the dust-swept streets, with so much pain and uncertainty around us, my heart only sings.

I've seen diamonds and parties and rooms full of the best clothes money can buy. Felt the comforts of a good bed and warm room, food that you haven't worked for hours to prepare.

But one more day with Raymond, in this wild place, is worth more than all of that.

# 47

# ROSAMUND

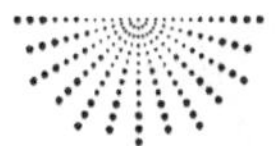

"Raymond." I open the door to the marshal's office and step inside. There's no one here except him, sitting behind his desk, bent over a map on his desk.

He looks up and his eyes light briefly with pleasure as he sets his pencil down.

"Afternoon, Rose. Have a seat."

"Should you really be here?"

He chuckles and adjusts the sling around his neck. "His injuries were found to be greatly exaggerated by the press," he quotes to me.

It was from a newspaper during the war, retracting the obituary of an officer who hadn't actually died. We had laughed about it, he and I, while he was home on leave.

It was one of the happiest weeks of our lives.

"You look well," I observe aloud.

"I'm fine, really." The corner of his mustache goes up in

a smile. He picks up his pencil and makes a final notation on the map.

"And back to work already."

"Yep." His face turns grim. "I didn't know how bad things were in my absence."

"The Swift ranch—there was no way of knowing until it was far too late." I swallow hard at the thought of Max.

"Was there a service?"

"At the church. Just a brief remembrance. I hear the Auki honored him in their way, out elsewhere. At least, they rode by through the southern hills not long after. Tagweiah came and told us everything he knew, which wasn't much."

"Max was a good young man. He had grit and he had heart."

"He was."

"I don't think I should have left, Rose." He reaches over and fingers a stack of papers on his desk. "I should have stayed right here."

"You did what you thought was right."

"Hmm." He fixes me with a deep look. "How's Archer?"

"All right, I suppose. His work keeps him out early and late most days. The more bureaucracy wants to help from the East, the more work he has, it seems."

"I imagine they're full of helpful ideas of how he should use his time."

"Yes. And he seems to be listening to them more than to me. He's never home now, it seems, and doesn't enjoy being home when he is."

"You've both had a mighty rough year." Raymond rubs his chin. "It'll pass, in time."

I hope so. I've never felt so alone.

"And how is Jesse?" Raymond asks. "You saw him yesterday?"

"He scared me when I first saw him. He's—well, I almost didn't recognize him."

"Jesse should have been dead weeks ago. The man's just ornery."

I laugh a little. I am glad I wasn't there. "The doctor was talking about sending him East for treatment, and Jesse said over his dead body."

Raymond chuckles low in his throat. "I know."

"So they're going to try some rest first. It is possible his spine needs only time to heal, not treatment."

"Let's hope so, for Jesse's sake. I've never seen a man so determined not to see civilization. Wore Kate and Chris Newton plumb out trying to convince him."

A shadow falls across the window and we both look up.

It's Blue, tying his horse up at the rail.

"Hm."

"Is something wrong?" I switch my gaze from Blue to Raymond.

"He's alone. I sent him out with a warrant to serve on Early's outfit, for Max's murder."

"Oh."

The door swings open and Blue saunters in with that

faint hitch to his step that men get when they've been in the saddle all day.

"Afternoon," he greets grimly.

"Did you find them?" Raymond stands up to greet him.

Blue nods to me and then to Raymond. His blue eyes are hard, his jaw thrust out a little.

"That's just it." Blue wipes the sweat under his nose with the wrist of his glove and shoves his hat back on his head. "Early's outfit's dead."

"Dead?" My brother's face doesn't change a shade, but his eyes get a hard glint. "All of them?"

"Yeah. Every last one of 'em, shot dead." Blue drags out a chair with the heel of his boot and slumps into it. "We talked to one poor devil on his last legs. Said he didn't recognize the man that did it."

"Just one man?"

"Sounds like it. He said he was one-armed. Shot them all down with his left. Mean piece of work. We tracked him a mile or two and then the trail gave out. He was headed south, but that don't mean much."

"Was it in the open or an ambush?"

"Our man didn't get that far. Most of the bullet holes seemed to be in the front, but we counted seven men. That's a lot for one man to take down less'n there's foul play involved."

Raymond is thinking hard.

"What did you do with the men?"

"Buried 'em. They were bad men, but they weren't even full outlaw."

"What about Holt?"

"Holt wasn't there. Man probably knows more holes to hide in than a rattler. He'll be lying low for a time, mark my words."

"Well." Raymond lets his breath out in a quiet sigh.

"Look, I'll go right back out there if you want, but I fancy a bath—I'm covered in three day's worth of dust. It's dry as a bone out there."

"Go, then. Come talk to me later."

"Sir." He brushes the brim on his hat with a couple fingers. "Ma'am."

The door slams and it is dead silent in the office. My brother's face is lean and grim.

"I'll leave you to work," I say softly.

"Thanks, darling. Take care of yourself."

"You too." I walk around behind the desk and plant a kiss on his cheek.

48

PIKE

I see Holt ride in and tie his horse up outside the shed. I can always hear when he comes up from the shed, grinding his boots on the steep, rock-strewn ground.

Uncouth brute. He's muttering oaths to himself.

He appears over the crest of the hill and trudges up to me, squinting at me in the mid-morning sun.

"Mrs. Pike," he pants. He takes his hat off, but only because he wants in. I stand my ground in the doorway, one hand resting gently on the doorframe.

"What are you doing here, Holt?"

"Is it a surprise to you?" he demands.

"Your coming is a surprise."

"Don't you play the innocent with me, Mrs. Pike. Early's whole outfit is dead. Every mother's son of 'em."

"Where were they? Did you see them, or just hear a rumor?"

"I saw it."

"And you think that I did it?" I widen my eyes and press my hand to my chest. "Really, Holt, you are becoming ridiculous."

"Then look me in the eye and tell me you didn't know."

"Of course I knew." I fix him with a haughty glare. "But that does not mean I did it, you fool."

"Then who did?"

"I didn't know you cared about them."

"I don't. I care about my hide. Anyone who's hunting them Early boys'll be a-hunting me."

"You know how to take care of yourself. You outlived Mortimer and Abernathy."

He grins, revealing a stained and jagged tooth. The man has the manner of a *darani*.

"That's right, I did. And I'll survive you too, if I have to." He says it like a threat.

I wave it off. "It's good you've come back, in any case. I have another job for you."

He sighs and thrusts his thumbs into his belt. "It'll cost you more."

I laugh smoothly. "Trust me, Holt, I have a price in mind and you will like it. When will you learn that you do not need to make demands so long as you are working for me?"

He mutters something about riding for the brand, with a little more color than is necessary. Riding for the brand indeed. That man is only loyal when it suits him or he knows he can't step out of line.

Today it is the latter. And gold will salve the wound well enough.

"So what's the job?"

"Are you familiar with Harrison Terhune's land?"

"As good as anyone's."

"The western side as well?"

"I been over there once or twice."

"Good. Stay here." I leave him standing on the doorstep and go back inside to fetch the survey map that is sitting under the window.

"What's it you keep in there so secret-like?" He licks his lips like a guilty child and peers past me.

"Nothing. You are not allowed in, is all."

"You've been keeping something in there this last month, mark my words." His eyes are shrewd, like he thinks he's caught me at something. As if he could match me at my own game for even a minute.

"Here is a survey map for his west side. I've marked what I want."

He takes the map and unrolls it, peering at it right here in front of me. The desert wind pulls fiercely at the corners, threatening to rip the parchment.

"This is Garth Levine's survey. Where'd you get your hands on this?"

"I had friends in Glory Mesa once. Unlike you, Holt."

He grunts and rolls it up. "How much?"

"Four hundred dollars at the beginning, six afterwards."

He whistles. "Let me see it."

I pull a small purse out of my pocket and give him a nugget of gold. "Go, get it done. If you need, send a telegram to the train stop at Pleasant Field. And do not do anything rash—if that is possible for you."

He is still eyeing that gold nugget. If he were more intelligent or less greedy, he might take the four hundred dollars and disappear, but I know he wants the six hundred.

He'll do it.

Holt pockets the nugget and tips the brim of his hat to me. "Ma'am." There's a hint of mockery in his tone.

I watch him down the hill until he's untied the horse and ridden away westward.

I'm glad he is gone.

There is another horse coming from the east, but still far off, the rider tall, his long coat sweeping back in the fierce, dry wind.

I go back inside the house.

49

ALAN

THE RIVER IS A SHINING BAND OF SILVER STRETCHED across the horizon like a mirage. The afternoon sun dances on its distant surface, promising cool, sweet relief.

I hope the drought isn't so severe back home, if home is still there. I cannot imagine trying to rebuild in this heat and dry.

At least Max lived for a few years in the south with the Auki. He's made for this weather, if any of us are.

Jack Selby reins in, his eyes quietly scanning the land around us.

"Is something wrong?" I stop beside him.

"Someone else is on this trail."

"Before or behind?"

"Before. It's a tinker, I think. I hear the sound of metal."

I listen intently. The gentle rush of the distant river has a harmony to it—a gentle, musical clinking.

248

That man's ears are worthy of a desert fox.

"Do you want to avoid him?" Traveling with Jack Selby has taught me he has strange instincts; sometimes, without a clear reason, he has a strong desire to avoid certain places or people.

"Not in particular. If he's headed in the direction of the river, he may have forded."

"Good enough for me." I ease up on the reins, following Jack westward. My horse can smell the water and he's impatient.

Jack leads the way for about a mile before we come upon a worn wagon with peeling green paint. Sure enough, it's a tinker's wagon, all the way out here.

The stranger spots us and waves to us to come on over. He's an old man, tall once, but bent now over the reins of a two-mule team. His pants are soaked to the thighs, half-dried in the sun.

"Howdy." He shoves his hat back and squints at us. "You fellers traveled far?"

"Far enough," I reply. "We're from down Glory Mesa way, or thereabouts."

He whistles. "Well, you boys are far from home. You looking for land?"

"No, not exactly. How about you?"

"Headin' the other direction. Just came over those mountains, through the eastern pass. There's a stampede of settlers coming through and over, headed for the valley beyond. I did a sight of patching for them."

Jack goes very still.

"They were well?" he asks.

"To be sure. They were keen on having houses built before the snow flies. And I reckon they will with that kind of determination. It's a good valley too."

Beside me, Jack lets his breath out softly.

"But I'd be careful if you're headed that way. There were some earthquakes in the mountains. Strangest thing."

"Which mountains?" asks Jack.

The old man turns in the seat and points with a lean finger due north. "See that river?"

"Yeah?" Jack's horse shifts under him. He seems tense.

"You go 'cross it, you keep on headin' north. You couldn't miss that range if'n you tried. It spreads north and west."

"Whereabouts were you when you felt the tremors?" Jack's eyes are on the river as if he can see the range already.

"Due north of here. But they were all over. Never thought I'd live to see a mountain shudder."

"Well, we're headed for those mountains," he says. "You may as well be specific."

"I was headed between the twin peaks." He reaches over and puts the brake on the wagon. "Let me show you."

He knots the reins over the brake and climbs down, finding a flat patch of dirt beside the wagon.

We dismount to get a better look.

"This here's the river." He makes a line in the dirt with a short stick. "Mountains are out here. You'll come up on the range, and out a little to the west is a pair of peaks that make the shape of a bird in flight between them. That's where I was. It was strong there, but maybe more on the next peak over to the west."

"Does that one have a name?" I ask.

"The White Horn. Some folks call it the Blessed Horn, say there was a miracle up there once. But I don't reckon it's all they say it is."

He straightens to wink at us both.

I feel it in my heart. These are the mountains that hold our fate. This was no chance meeting; I know now where we are to go.

Jack is mounting up, settling into the saddle and gathering his reins.

"Son?" The tinker jerks his head, inviting my confidence.

I duck close to hear him.

"Good luck and godspeed to you two and that other man. You are brave souls."

"Other man?"

"Met a strapping blond fellow riding a bay yesterday. He was asking the same questions as you. Seemed determined to go wherever the earthquake was strongest."

"Did he have a name?"

I'm breathless waiting as he mulls over the question.

"Quick?" he muses to himself.

"Swift? Was it Swift?"

"That's it. He said his name was Jem Swift."

# 50

# THATCHER

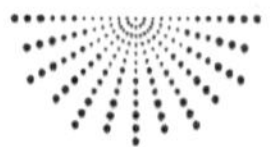

Dusk seems to fall faster here in Glory Mesa than out on the range. From my view on the doctor's porch, the buildings are everywhere now, blocking the sun to the west.

These days I'm what you'd call a real invalid. Sitting in a comfortable chair on the porch with a blanket over my knees and no vest. They tried to take my boots away and give me slippers, but I stopped them there.

A man needs some shred of dignity, I say.

I dig the tip of my penknife into the stick I'm carving and rub the shavings out with the end of my finger. Blow, when that doesn't work.

It's supposed to be a whistle, but I haven't made one since I was a boy and it's not what I'd be doing if I had a choice.

I want to feel a horse under me, feel the wind whipping

my face, be back driving cattle and riding range and end my day exhausted, sleeping under stars.

Instead I have cushions and blankets and salts and tinctures. Restless nights in soft beds.

And what's worse is I can feel it. My body couldn't take the range right now. I hate the comforts and the rest, but I need them.

"Jesse." My cousin is leaning against the rail of the porch. He's wearing a tie and coat, and while it suits him, the sight rather unnerves me. "What are you doing?"

"Whittling toys." I laugh humorlessly and toss the whistle aside. "I don't even want to."

"Would you rather have had Doctor Sikes?"

"Oh, heaven help me, no."

He chuckles and settles into the chair beside mine, putting a leg over his knee. "You're looking a little better," he says after a moment.

"Good. Perhaps Everett will think so too."

"He's been good to you, hasn't he?"

"Yes, as far as he's able." I shift the blanket on my knees and adjust my position subtly. It's starting to get uncomfortable. "The man's a bit newfangled."

"Probably not a bad thing for you."

"Doesn't make me like it any more."

Archer laughs. It's good to see him do that. He's carrying so many worries, and now he's got me on top of them.

His gaze wanders to the southern hills beyond town.

They are just vague shadows now that the sun's dropped over the mountains.

"What I wouldn't give to see a proper sunset again," murmurs Archer. "You can't see it for the buildings now."

I open my mouth to say he should ride out of town, as he used to, but something in his face stops me. He's got a powerful wistful look. Whatever is keeping him here, he'd have left it to see a sunset by now if he could.

"How's the governing?" I ask. It's not a subject I like, but by that face, I'm guessing no one else bothers to ask.

Archer reaches up and unties his tie, opening the front of his collar. "I'll be straight with you, Jesse, it's tough."

"I'm sorry to hear it."

My cousin acknowledges my sympathy and leans back in his chair.

"Would you consider passing it on? It's been a few years."

He laughs wearily. "Jesse, I would in a heartbeat if I thought I could. There's no one here who can, no one back East who should. I have to stand by my post a little longer. I promised Sikes."

"But if it's killing you, Archer...." I roll my head over to look at him.

"It's—not killing me. But I am lonely, Jesse. There are men out East who want this post and they want to find fault in order to take it. They lay what happened to the Swifts at my door. Knowing what happened, that Max died the way he did and that his brothers are nowhere to be found—to care that much and have to read it over and over on cold, unfeeling paper—I can't help thinking that maybe they've got a point. That a man who didn't love this territory could make his decisions without seeing his friends' faces when he does."

He sighs, rubs his face wearily with steepled hands.

"I can't stop it, but I have to try. And a man's got to wonder, how long does he stand between the bullets and the ones he's sworn to protect? Until he's wounded? Until his chest can't hold anymore bullets? Until he's dead?"

I stare at the fading line of light beyond the town, half obscured by a hotel that wasn't there a year ago.

I never guessed things were this bad.

"What does Rosamund think?"

It's quiet between us for too long.

"Rosamund doesn't talk to me much these days," he says softly.

"Oh."

"Since the baby died. I have so much work, and when I come home, she mostly keeps to herself. We talk, but—not about the territory, when we do."

"I think it'll pass," I suggest.

"I'd give it up for her if I could," he murmurs. "I want nothing but to go home, Jesse. I want to ride a horse, not a desk. I want to be out on the land I love, walking among the winter grass and driving cattle, not talking about it in figures with men who've never seen a herd of four thousand head."

"Does she say anything about the governorship, or—wanting to leave Glory Mesa?"

"Sometimes. Not often. I think she takes small solace whenever I do something particularly prestigious. She seems torn between her desires."

"I'm sure she's still heartbroken." It's not the kind of thing I'd normally say, but somehow I sense it's true.

"I wish I could reach her," he whispers, almost too low for me to hear. "It's like we're drowning, Jesse. Both of us."

The door opens behind us.

"Governor!" Doctor Everett's face registers genuine surprise. At least he wasn't listening to us. "I am sorry. I got working in the back and I forgot to come for you, Jesse."

I wave him off.

My cousin's face has changed to polite friendliness. His fears and worries are masked perfectly.

"It's all right. We were enjoying talking." Archer stands up. "Goodnight, Jesse."

I clasp his hand. It takes all my energy, and still my handshake hasn't any of the grip or strength a man's should.

He straightens his coat and heads down into the street. His shoulders are square when he walks, but I see it now—the visible burden.

My cousin is alone and I cannot protect him.

What am I to do?

5 1

NEWTON

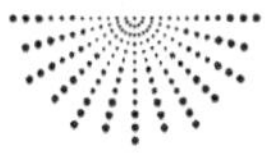

THE ROCKS OF THE PASS RISE ABOVE US LIKE A CLOSED gate, their jagged peaks brushing the sky and leaving pieces of cloud caught on their tips.

"Sir, this ain't going to be easy." My trail boss leans on his saddle horn and pulls at his gloves.

"No." I adjust my brim and squint to see the trail above us better against the painfully bright sky. "But we're doing it."

The calls of the hands below us and the heavy rumble of uneasy cattle drift up the steep rocks along with a cloud of fine dust.

It's going to be horribly dry up there. The ground will be solid, but the dust will be bad. And the trail's already thin as a knife's edge.

"Is Trace back yet?" I peer up the trail.

257

"No, sir. He was going to the fork and overlook to see which trail was sounder. He'll be back any time."

"Right. As soon as he's back, we're moving out. Don't want the weather to change on us. I don't fancy losing this herd and half of us to the snows."

My trail boss laughs. "No, sir!"

It's no laughing matter, but out here we laugh at danger and at death. It's how we get through it.

I turn my horse around and head it back down the trail toward the herd.

The cows are milling, stirring up dust. The men are trying their best to keep them settled, but the animals sense the difference in the air as we climb higher. At least these are mountain-bred cattle. A flatlands herd would be twice as dangerous to bring up this trail.

"Howdy, sir." A cowboy pulls his brim, another nods.

"Boys," I greet as I pass.

Everyone is tense. We're already covered in sweat and we haven't even begun the hardest part.

The sky above us is clear, the shelter of the surrounding mountains providing us some relief from the heat in the flat-lands below us.

Even with a tough job like this one ahead, a man's got to admit this is beautiful country.

A swift tattoo of hoofbeats approaches on the rocky trail above us and I see a lick of dust from the trail scout heading down our way.

"He's coming, boys! Let's hold 'em down a little longer," says the boss and word moves through the drovers.

Trace pulls up beside me and the boss. "The eastern fork looks good, and the Blue Bowl has water in it. We'll be able to split our run neatly with a stop there. At least they won't drop dead on us."

"Good." I slap his arm in thanks.

I nod to the trail boss and he hollers to the others. "Let's get moving, boys! This pass'll be powerful dry, but there's water in the Blue Bowl. Guard your canteens and keep the cattle moving slow. This is a narrow trail. Get a move on!"

He whistles and spurs his horse forward, up the trail. I pull my handkerchief up over my mouth and nose.

This is like to be one of the longest four days of my life.


Up in the pass, the air feels thinner. The dust is so thick that you're lucky if you can see the edges of the trail. The cattle seem to know the boundaries, but they still shove and jostle.

The edge isn't always a steep drop of a hundred feet, but five or ten will break the leg of man, horse, or steer just as easy.

The voices around me are carefully calm. Casual, even. Someone's singing down the line behind me, one of those hopeful songs travelers and gold-seekers sing.

I'm surprised how comforting it is in this thin blue air choking with dust.

The boss rides past, headed down the line, and I wave him over.

"Sir?"

"How's the point?"

"We're all right." His eyes, barely visible between his hat and his bandanna, crinkle at the corners. "We just have to keep them slow. The rear cattle want to get out of the dust and they're contemplating pushing the speed. I've got to talk to flank and drag."

"Don't let me keep you."

He moves on by and I turn my horse back in towards the herd.

CAMP TONIGHT IS A HILL—A gentle hill, for the mountains, but still not much of a place for sleeping. The campfire gets the only truly level spot, and our cook gets started on a pot of beans and salt pork with leftover bread from yesterday.

Rough as it is, I swear it tastes like heaven.

The stars are out above us, and on nights like these, I think of Buck April.

He was one of those men who would have thrived at university, if he'd ever thought twice about such a thing. Instead, his education was the mesas and trails of the Western Territory. His knowledge was in survival and in living.

Somehow I feel he'd have had his head on straighter than most in this world that's falling apart. I didn't know him long, but in this moment, I want to talk to him more than any soul alive.

"Coffee?" The cook drifts by in the dark and I can smell the pot he's carrying.

I hold out my cup without a word. He fills it and moves on.

Somewhere outside camp a steer bellows, and singing starts up among the night watch in response.

*Now comes the time for gathering, for reaping, for bringing*

*in,*

*the season of gold.*

*With my scythe and your twine we shall build a future*
*and know, come snow, we will be safe.*

*Let us go to the fields and be merry.*
*Do not cry, do not be afraid;*
*For we shall be glad in the abundance of the earth,*
*And we shall dance together in fields of plenty.*

I WONDER why folks picked a song like that for a place like this. You fight for your life against the land out here, and if you work hard enough and the weather and the stock cooper-ate, you might just have enough to eat come winter. In between, you might lose your whole lot to a swindler, a man with a gun, or just a wrong fall off a horse.

It's a place where men like Britt and Buck April, the toughest there were, can die at the snap of the fingers.

And here I am, one of the wealthiest ranchers in the territory, eating dust and a scanty meal on the trail. And for what?

A neighbor's slight? One man's fear of another? Pride?

I think only a fool dreams optimistically of places like these.

"You should sleep, sir," says the trail boss, coming by. It's dark, but I know his voice.

"I reckon."

"This next leg's going to be tough."

"Want to put me on night hawk? I'll pull my share like any of them."

"We're not that short-handed, sir."

I take a swallow of the coffee. "Glad to hear it." I swirl the dregs in my cup and finish them off. We can't waste anything up here.

THE TRAIL NARROWS on the third day. Dust fills the air, coats every inch of us, turns us all to pale dun. The cattle are thirsty, tired, and letting loose throaty complaints. My horse is streaked with sweat, the dust running down his sides like mud.

I want to stop, give him a drink, wipe the dust out of his nostrils, but we can't stop. There's no room.

"Sir!"

The ramrod reins in beside me. "Boss wants me to tell you we've had a couple cows drop. We're only a few miles from Blue Bowl, but the herd is wearing thin. They're choking on the dust and pushing the pace."

"Slow the front down, then!"

He shoots me a doubtful look and disappears into the cloud of dust.

The rear wants to hurry because they cannot breathe, and soon enough the front will smell water and want to run.

And the trail is simply too narrow here for that.

You can feel the urgency in the cows, the restlessness filling the air as thick as the dust. If we don't hold them now, we won't be able to hold them at all.

"Ho, cattle!" I call, moving my horse in towards the line. They're starting to break loose, heads tossing, backs lurching and heaving above the moving sea of bodies.

"Hold them back!" I hear voices but cannot see any of the men. "I said hold them back!"

The trail boss materializes out of the churning dust.

"Sir. These cattle want to break loose in the worst way, and if they do, we're liable to be swept over the edge."

"Is there anything more we can do?"

He shakes his head. "We're doing all we can. I just wanted to make sure you understood, sir."

"The only way is forward, like you said. We're all doing our job here."

He gives me a grateful nod. Then he disappears up the line, a creature of dust like the rest of us. I push the cattle back again and again. Shouts of "Ho, cattle!" and "Hold 'em!" sound up and down the line.

The dust doesn't let up. The cows are quickening their pace, shoving, jostling, horns rubbing. My horse snorts hard and long, shuddering the dust off his coat—a hopeless endeavor.

A whoop breaks out ahead.

"We've made it! We've made it!" The shouts are distant, up in the front, but they reach me clear enough.

The herd is moving down, running fast, eager at the scent of water.

"Slow them down!" bellows the ramrod. "Keep them steady!"

The dust is picking up, rising under the pounding hooves, filling the air.

I see the snow-fed lake materializing below us through the thick air, nestled between the peaks of the lower mountains. The sun reflects off it, raising a brilliant blue to match the sky.

I'm not sure I've ever been happier to see anything in my life.

The herd reaches the bottom, spilling out like water from a canteen, spreading onto the level earth and rushing for the water.

They wade in up to their bellies, sucking great gulps of cold water. The hands splash in around them, their horses knee deep in the cold water, chasing them off, keeping them moving, preventing them from drinking themselves sick.

The herd shifts constantly in a strange mix of relief and annoyance. I'll take it over thirst and panic any day.

I ride over to Trace, the trail scout.

"Good work."

He grins, shyly. "Thanks."

"I knew if anyone could get us through, it'd be you."

"One more day." He puts his hand on his thigh and regards the cattle.

"And one I'll be glad to get over with."

"Sure. But the eastern fork is looking good. If we've made it this far, I think we'll make it the rest of the way."

I let my breath out in a long sigh and watch the cattle and the men, relief in every line of their tired bodies.

It's a mighty beautiful sight.

# ROSAMUND

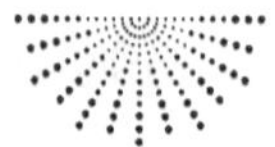

Dawn comes red with clouds hanging over the world. It looks like rain, but I know better than to hope. The air smells dry.

Archer and I used to get up together just before dawn. We would talk before he left about what we would do that day, dream of where we were going together, into the future. Every morning, even the simplest ones, were happy.

Now he's up at least an hour before the first cock in Glory Mesa crows, and I lie in bed staring at the wall until the sun falls in sheets over the wallpaper.

Dressing, pinning my hair, and going downstairs takes every ounce of my will some mornings.

Archer makes himself coffee and eats whatever is around. Sometimes he'll fry his own bacon and beans.

That is what he did today.

He always leaves the kitchen tidy, with a plate of food

for me. Out East that would never happen, but Archer has probably cooked more in his lifetime than I have.

I set the kettle on the stove and stoke the fire. I'll have a cup of tea with breakfast. I can no longer stomach coffee.

I take my plate to the table and sit down out of habit beside Archer's usual chair.

He's forgotten a letter on the table, crumpled. I pick it up and smooth it out. If it's business, I will not burn it until he's looked at it again.

*...we will be forced to take stronger measures if a resolution is not met swiftly.* The ominous words catch my eyes.

He does not usually bring his official correspondence home.

I look at the seal, the signature. It's from a senator out East.

They are threatening to take the governorship away. If they did, it would defeat the entire purpose of his taking this position. Wipe out all the sacrifices he's made.

I crumple it back up and set it aside.

He already knows its contents fully, I have no doubt.

The kettle begins to whistle and I pour out my tea, sipping it as I watch the day dawn, half in sun, half in shadow. And the thought comes over me: Today is not a day for fear.

I will go see Jesse and then visit Irene, who will have her baby within the month. Seeing her is painful, but I can be strong enough to be glad for my brother.

He knows it is hard for me, so he doesn't speak much to

me about it; but I don't think I've ever seen his eyes smile so much.

He is happy, and I have the strength to be happy for them today.

I clean up after breakfast and start a pie for Jesse. Doctor Everett says that rest is what he needs most of all right now and the best thing that can be done for him is cheering up and distraction, which are hard to come by.

Poor Jesse. All he wants is to go back to his ranch and be able to ride. Riding is one of the things Doctor Everett does not want him to talk about right now.

I slice apples and try to forget the letter. I'm humming a song—the first time I've done anything so ordinary in ages—when a rumble stops me.

I stand still and listen.

It sounds again outside, stronger this time.

My heart leaps. It is thunder.

But it doesn't stop. It grows and it grows. The frames on the wall shake, the glass panes rattle in the windows. The street outside is trembling.

One of the pictures on the wall falls to the floor and shatters.

# 53

# IRENE

THE SUNLIGHT STREAMS THROUGH THE WINDOW TO crown her perfect little head and turn her cornsilk hair to gold.

I have never known perfection until now. A place in my heart that I did not know existed is now full to bursting with her, and I can never go back to the way I was before.

She came early, in the quiet hours of the afternoon. Small, but with long fingers like her father and fair hair like me.

The moment they laid her in my arms, I felt her small heart beat, strong and fierce. And I loved her with all my heart.

Raymond cried the first time he held her. Cradled her in his newly-healed arm while wiping tears away with his thumb.

I want to go over and over that day, live it again, savor the joy of it.

I thought that I loved Raymond as much as I possibly could before, but now all I can see is the unspeakable gentleness of his face as he looked at his daughter, the way his eyes shone when he kissed me.

She moves and gives a squeak, looking up at me with her eyes dark in her fair face.

"Good morning," I whisper to her, and she kicks, waving her scrunched-up fists in response to my voice. "Good morning, beautiful."

I reach down and smooth her soft hair with one finger.

She kicks again, her eyes staring up at me wonderingly. I hold out my finger and she grips it in her tiny, cold fingers.

I tuck her small hands into her swaddling blanket and she does not stop staring, stretching her tiny neck out to keep my face in view.

"Ida," I whisper in a singsong voice. "Ida Lacey."

She answers me and kicks emphatically.

I lean down to kiss her tiny forehead. I haven't done anything but look at her for the better part of an hour and I could keep on doing it.

She's only been in my arms a matter of days, and already I'd do anything for her.

I lie down beside her in the sunshine so that our faces are level. All the pain and sorrow of my life thus far seem like nothing in the beauty of this moment.

It has all led me to this beautiful little girl, and I wouldn't trade her for the world.

It is just past dusk when Raymond comes home, entering the house softly, quietly removing his boots and hat and hanging up his gun.

I look up from my book and give a quiet laugh under my breath. "Evening, darling."

He presses his lips to the top of my head in a soft kiss. "Where is she?"

"In bed."

"Pity." He settles onto the couch beside me, his long arm around my shoulders.

I lean my head against his shoulder and close my eyes. I've missed him, and he's only been gone since this afternoon.

"How was your day?" I ask, still nestled against him.

I hear the slow smile in his voice. "I'd rather talk about yours."

"We spent most of the day just looking at each other. We're still well-supplied with food, so I've hardly had to prepare anything. She is perfect, Raymond."

"I know." A laugh catches in his throat. "I know."

He rubs his face wearily and I lean back, smoothing down his hair.

"You look tired," I murmur.

"Aww, it's nothing. Just the usual troubles." His hand meets mine at the side of his head and he grasps it. "One of these days, we're moving to the homestead to stay. But not while there's a range war simmering."

"You're still needed here." I squeeze his hand in mine.

"Mhm."

"But Raymond, I do want to take her out to the ranch. I want to spend what time we can out there, where her first sights are that wide open land, and the trees and brook and horses. Not a town...as beautiful as Glory Mesa is."

"You can say it. It's dusty," he says wryly, amusement in his eyes. "And you are right. I want my little girl raised on that beautiful piece of land, not in a town."

A knock sounds on the front door. At this time of night, it cannot be good.

"Stay here." He stands up and goes to the door. He takes his gun out of its holster where it hangs by the door and sets it on the front table close at hand.

He opens it. "Evening."

"Good evening, Marshal." It's a young man's voice, breathless.

"How can I help you?"

"There's been a shooting out at Miner's Creek, over the Mill and Creighton claim, I think."

"Anyone dead?"

"Yes, two men. And a man ran from the claim on a stolen horse."

Raymond doesn't move a muscle, but I can sense the change, the weariness that comes over him. "I'll be right there. "

He shuts the door and comes back over to me. There's disappointment in his eyes, hidden under a smile meant to cheer me.

"I reckon I'm needed again," he says. "I've got to go saddle my horse."

"I'll put you up some food. If you're riding on a fugitive's trail, it could be days."

"I love you." He kisses me.

He goes to the door and pulls on his boots, buckles his gun belt back on, and takes down his hat. I wish terribly that his job did not do this to him; he is so very tired.

But this is why I married him. Works all day and heads back out without complaint, minutes after he sat down to rest. I can't help it—my heart swells with pride.


A single lantern is lit in the barn. As I slip in quietly, I hear the usual sounds of preparation: the rustle of straw, the breathing of the horse, the scratch of the currycomb against the horse's sleek side.

He has his saddlebags near the door so they're easy for me to find. I pack the food in and buckle the straps, but I find I don't want to go back to the house, even in the evening's chill.

I step through the darkness of the barn toward the single lantern hanging outside the stall where Raymond is brushing his horse down.

The lantern light flickers gold against his long, hard

cheek, casting deep shadows along the rest of his face. His shoulder drops as he curries down along the horse's side, his arm moving in gentle, expert strokes.

I love even the tiniest, simplest things about him so much my heart wants to burst.

I just stand there and watch him, my man, standing in the golden light.

He sets the brush down and reaches for the horse's blanket, and that's when he sees me.

"How long have you been standing there?" His eyes get a twinkle.

"Not long." I unclasp my hands and come over, reaching out to scratch his horse's face. "I just want as long as I can have with you, is all."

"Can't say I blame you." Raymond heaves the saddle up over the horse's back with a creak of leather.

He reaches for the cinch and pulls it tight with a grunt. The straw rustles as he ties it soundly and walks around the horse, giving the saddle horn a pull to settle it.

"The nights are getting colder," I say. "Make sure you have your heavy coat."

"It's with the kit over there." He nods briefly to his saddlebags and bedroll.

He collects his things and secures them on the saddle. His movements are steady and experienced, but I sense he's reluctant as he checks and double checks and straps and buckles.

Finally he turns to me and holds out his hand.

We walk out into the yard in silence, me on one side, his horse led along behind us on the other.

"Irene, darling—you know I want nothing but to be with you."

"Of course. You don't have to apologize for doing your duty." I kiss his cheek gently. "I know you want to be with us."

"I'll be back as soon as I can."

He puts his arm around my shoulder and kisses me.

I watch him lead his horse out of the yard and mount up, the soft sound of his horse's hooves in the dust fading long after he's lost to my sight in the darkness.

# 54

# SELBY

THE MOUNTAINS TOWER OVER THE HORIZON, COLORED by the sun that rises behind us, though we are yet too low to catch its rays.

Jem is crouched over last night's revived fire, fixing the coffee.

We've fallen into a silent rhythm, the three of us. The two of them consult without me, talking in quiet tones. I remember they were laughing men, all three of them happy when we met in Glory Mesa and rode together against Mortimer.

They are no longer that. When Jem brought word of Max's death at the hands of Holt, they wept together freely and they talked of Max, of their times together and how much promise he had. And then the talk ceased altogether.

They speak to each other briefly, and when they are done, they ask me my opinion of the trail.

Beyond that, we've not spoken more than two or three sentences put together for days. I don't mind. I know what grief is.

It is a hard, hard thing to go on when loss hangs so heavy, even when one knows it is the right course. There is a measure of comfort in it, perhaps, but it is hard nonetheless.

I hear hooves approaching, a horse at a trot. Alan is back from scouting. He dismounts without a word and comes over, nodding first to me, then to his brother.

"Good trail," he says briefly, and pours himself coffee.

He pours me out a cup as well and hands it over. The mornings are cold here and they will grow colder still as we near and ascend into the mountains.

I wrap my cold fingers around the burning tin.

The mountains are aflame now with the light of the sun, beautiful and majestic and beckoning.

We're still a ways off, but I can sense that the end is coming, and coming soon. I wonder how a man should feel when he knows he has mere weeks left of his life. Does he think about the moment at the end, wonder if he will be afraid when it comes? Or does he press on and live and not think of the coming end?

It's a funny thing. I've faced death many times. I've stared it in the face and thought, with quiet resignation, that the sights before me would be my last glimpse of this earth.

And I've never been afraid.

When a man is so close to his own end, he begins to see

with great clarity the beauty of the things around him that used to be everyday.

But that feeling is stronger now than I have ever felt it. Everything is touched with gentle beauty, from the crackle of the flames and their glow against Alan's sharp nose to the way the horses come awake slowly, shifting and blowing quietly in the stillness of the sunrise. Even things like thick gloves or a familiar saddle or well-worn boots that have seen miles of dust and cattle seem strangely dear.

I wish, I wish that I had not seen Beatrice again.

No—I don't. It would have made what I must do easier, but her memory is sweeter now, not laced with guilt; and that alone is worth the sense of fresh loss and the pain of wondering what could have been.

The brothers are talking again.

Jem raises himself partway and gestures toward the twin peaks, now clearly visible in the range. The fiery light of the mountains is reflected in his cool blue eyes.

Alan turns to follow his brother's gaze.

They both regard it for a long while, their faces quiet and set. There is a nobility in the lines and bearing of their faces that lends a sort of hope to their grimness.

Then Alan stands up, dusting off his gloves. The sun falls over half his face, slanted through the trees.

"The sun has risen, brother. Come, let us go."

# 55

# NEWTON

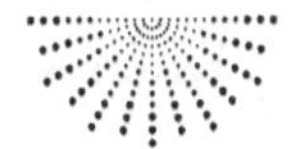

HOME HAS NEVER LOOKED SO BEAUTIFUL. THE RANCH house stands below the towering, jagged cliffs, crowned with frost-touched pines. It looks so solid and strong, a piece of goodness in the middle of the breathtaking, unforgiving land.

Most of my hands are still making their way back; a few stayed behind at the railroad to pick up more work at the ever-expanding cattle pens. Nowadays it seems like every man's got a herd he wants moved.

But I have my boss, ramrod, trail scout, and a few others besides, and a satchel full of the fine price these cattle fetched even after being driven over the southern Horn range.

Hannah is the first one out of the house when we arrive. She runs out, her skirt gathered in her hand, one arm flung up to greet us.

It's strange; I knew she was here, and yet somehow I am surprised to see her.

"It went well! I can see it in your faces." She comes right up to us, her face upturned and eager.

"Very well," I say, allowing myself to smile. "In fact, I think it warrants a celebration."

Behind me, the ramrod whoops.


THE COOK DID NOT DISAPPOINT. Today he and Hannah prepared a spread fit for one of those grand hotels out East, and the whole ranch celebrated.

We laughed, we were glad. For a time, all the dust and sweat and pain of the trail and broken friendships disappeared, and I want to savor it to the last.

On an evening like this, we are at peace with the world.

"Do you often sit outside at dusk?" Hannah appears from the doorway, a cup of tea held in her hands.

"When I can afford to," I reply, with a wry smile. "Come, have a seat if you like."

"Oh...." She pushes her thick braid off her shoulder. "I was just bringing this to you. Cook says you take a hot cup around now."

"Have a seat anyway, if you've a mind to. I don't want you to think I only want work out of you."

"Of course not." She settles in the rocking chair next to mine. "It is very peaceful here, this time of day."

"Yes."

I take a sip of the tea and give a long, contented sigh. Even the stars seem to hang low to enjoy the warmth of the falling darkness.

"Have you been East much, Mr. Newton?"

"I have. I have been East many times."

"I used to think I would stay out there forever. I loved the town I was in...I used to go out on the porch like this and memorize the stars and pretend they belonged to me. It made me feel as if I knew something worthwhile in this world."

"I think the stars are a worthy pursuit."

"They're so much wilder here." Her voice sounds so soft, so alone.

I had never thought of it that way. I simply thought that the stars in the East were like ones viewed through a cage, and they woke in me the desire to be free.

"When my grandmother died, I remember the only thing that comforted me was the stars. I hoped that even if I came out here to live, they would be the same."

"Do you think they are?"

"Not quite. But in time, I may learn to love them better."

Perhaps it is the way she said it, but my heart just lifts.

"Then you wish to stay here? In the territory, I mean."

She laughs, sweet and genuine. "Yes, in the territory."

The chair thumps against the floorboards of the porch as she stands up, folding her hands and straightening her shoulders. "Which brings me to a topic of conversation I wish I did not have to raise, but I must."

"Go on." My voice is calm, but my heart sinks down again, graver than before.

"I don't feel right about living on your kindness," she says, her chin raised. "It's been too long."

"I thought we agreed that you are not to feel beholden."

"I know. But I do think it is time to move on."

"I see." My heart sinks, but I set my cup aside and stand up, respectful. The last thing I want is for her to feel indebted to me or to believe she must do a thing simply because I wish it.

"Glory Mesa and Thrasher's Creek are both becoming civilized, I hear," she goes on. "I could take a teaching position, make my own way. I know that can be done."

She's so calm and collected, looking at me in the dim light. The lines of her shoulders are strong and set. There is nothing in her manner that speaks of disappointment or yearning or self-pity. Not even stubbornness.

But I remember how her eyes shone at me that day as I rode away, and I love her all the more for this quiet resolve.

"I am happy to accommodate that, if you wish." I clasp my hands behind my back, businesslike. "But I have a second proposition for you to consider."

She looks up at me, unsuspecting.

"How about marrying me?"

"What?" Her face has gone still, like she is afraid to hope.

"I have never met a girl like you, Hannah. You're

unspoiled and unpretentious. You're kind. And if you stayed, you would be doing me the greatest honor."

She looks at me slowly, her face melting from shock to wonder. "You mean it."

"I'd be a poor kind of man if I didn't."

She presses her lips tight, wipes her hand on her skirt. "Yes," she says, her eyes dancing. "Yes, I'll marry you."

"Well, then." I take her hand and kiss it slowly. "Welcome home."

"Sir." One of the hands comes in through the front door, whips off his hat. His face is grave. "It's Harrison Terhune."

"Here?" I set my pen down and stand up. I had heard a horse come into the yard a few minutes ago, but the hands were coming in from driving the trail horses to pasture, so I figured it was them.

"Yes, with seven of his men."

"Keep Hannah out of sight, if you can find her. I'll go speak to him."

"Do you want anyone to watch for you out the windows?" From his face, I have little hope that Harrison is coming to make peace.

"No guns, but keep an eye on us."

I leave my gun and my hat and step out onto the porch.

Harrison Terhune stands in the center of the yard, his arms folded, his face like stone. No, he isn't coming to make peace.

"Afternoon," I greet, walking straight up to him. "What brings you here?"

Harrison laughs bitterly. His soft blue eyes are hard as flint.

"Just talk straight with me," I say, buttoning up my sleeves. "You may as well do that, since you've come all this way."

"I thought you were an honest man," he says. "But you're just as dirty as the rest of us when the going gets hard."

"I don't follow."

"Two hundred and fifteen head." He shifts his feet and tilts his head back. "They all died in agony."

"If you think I did something—"

"You poisoned the water holes, didn't you? They weren't even steers. They were my breeding stock, Newton."

"Harrison, if you think I could—"

"It was only the holes that were close to your borders. Up near the mountain pastures." He spits. "I understand, I blocked your route. But if you have a problem with me, you come to me with your sidearm and face me like a man. Don't kill two hundred cows behind my back."

"I didn't."

"Oh, so you're going to lie about it now?" He laughs, disbelieving. "I didn't think you were a coward too."

"Says the man who threatened a weaker neighbor in order to hurt me. Harrison, I am more than willing to forget this disagreement and move forward. I don't know who did this to you, but I swear I had nothing to do with it."

"Who else could have done it? There's no one else within a hundred miles of that border."

"If any of my men did it, I will find out and I will turn them in to the law. I give you my word."

He looks me in the eye, nodding slightly, a grim, humorless smile on his face. "You want war. Well, I'll give it to you."

I return his gaze quietly. "So be it. But you'll not see retaliation from me. I wanted to remain your friend, Harrison."

He gives a soft laugh and jerks his head regretfully. "So did I, Chris."

# 56

# IRENE

I WRAP THE BLANKET TIGHTER AROUND IDA'S TINY BODY and hold her close as I step out onto the porch. I never tire of mornings at the homestead. From the doorway you see nothing but sweeping land, green from the river, open before you. It's such a change from the stark pathos of Glory Mesa, dusty and windblown.

This feels like a place to grow and live.

The sun is warm on our faces, the wind singing through the trees to us. Quietly, I hum her the song we sang the night before I met her father, the beautiful traveling song:

> *Home is fair and home is pleasant,*
> *Oft I dream, but ne'er I've seen*
> *This good place that I belong in,*
> *This good land of hope and peace.*

AND A GOOD LAND IT IS.

I see a single rider come over the far hills, cantering towards the house. It's not Raymond's horse, or his riding.

He's due any hour.

I watch, humming to the baby, watching the gentle morning as the man ties up outside the barn and heads up toward the picket fence around the house.

"Ma'am." He removes his hat as he comes through the gate. "I brought you something from your husband."

He's holding a note in his hand, white as a flower against the green earth.

"Is he all right?"

"Right as rain." He gives me a nod and one to the baby too, holding out the note.

"Thank you."

I open up the note and read over.

*My darling, I am sorry to say that I will be late by a day. There is no need to worry. Yours ever, Raymond.*

I fold the note and put it into my pocket.

"Any message to carry back?" he asks.

"No. Tell him I'm well."

"Ma'am." He pulls the brim of his hat and heads back to his horse.

I close my eyes and listen as he rides away. Next time I hear hoofbeats riding into our valley, it'll be Raymond, coming back to us.

.  .  .

Afternoon comes and with it the warm, still hours of the day. The baby is napping and I finally have a moment to sit and catch up on the mending.

Outside a bird calls. I take one of my dresses and lay it across my lap, examining a tear in the bodice. Perhaps I should cut this one up for rags. I set it aside and pick up one of Raymond's shirts. This one was new not two weeks ago, and it's ripped already.

I should start with this one.

The birds hush and I glance out the window.

Seven horsemen are riding down toward the house. I don't recognize their horses. I wonder where the hands have gotten to.

They don't tie up outside the barn; instead, they all ride up to the gate. One dismounts and comes up the path while another holds his horse.

He's a sun-browned man with sparkling dark eyes and a mustache.

"Afternoon," he grins, a bit boldly.

I stand my ground in the doorway. "What do you gentlemen need?"

"We need to speak to your husband, the marshal."

"I'm afraid he isn't here."

He continues to smile as if he hasn't heard me. I repeat myself and this time he reacts.

"Excuse me, ma'am." He goes back down to the others

and I watch them from the doorway. The wind picks up, carrying their voices and the grind of the horses champing their bits.

"...must be lying. He was supposed to be here."

"He's probably hiding."

The words strike me like a crack of thunder. These men are after Raymond.

"Well, she can't stop us. We'll drag him out if we have to."

Quietly, I shut the door and lay the bar across it. I take down the extra pistol from the hook where Raymond leaves it for me in case of an emergency, and I go to the hearth and take down his rifle.

Then I go to the bedroom and shutter the windows. Ida takes a loud breath through her nose but she does not stir.

"Sleep well, little one," I whisper, bending down to kiss her soft hair. "I love you."

I go back to the front room and load the rifle.

A moment later, there is hard pounding at the door. "Excuse me, ma'am! Unbar the door!"

"I'm sorry, but he is not here. You gentlemen must leave."

The pounding only comes harder and louder.

"Let us in or we'll kill him when we find him! Do you hear me?"

As if they were not planning to do that already.

A gunshot fires through the door. I am glad that I had the sense not to stand in front of it. I return fire from the window.

A volley comes through the windows. Two of them are smashed now—they'll be able to climb right in if I don't keep them away from it.

I run behind the sofa and prop the rifle over the top, aiming for the window that is missing the most glass.

Guns answer from the barn. The hands must have realized what is happening.

One of the men leans close to the open window to shout. "Give him up! We don't want to shoot you, but we will!"

I reply by setting the rifle off right through the window.

Another volley tears through the front room. The couch slams back into me, knocking the air out of my lungs for a moment.

I'm fighting to get my breath back.

"Woman, you tell us where he is and we'll let you go!"

*No chance, gentlemen.*

I fire again. The front room is filled with gunsmoke and splintered wood and glass, this place that mere minutes ago was beautiful and peaceful.

There's blood on the floor, soaking my skirt. I'm bleeding from my side.

One man shows himself in the window and I shoot. He falls with a cry. Two more bullets whistle through the room, burying themselves in the wall above my head.

In the ringing silence after, I hear the baby crying.

More shots ring out, but the world is strangely doubling, moving in and out like the pendulum of a clock. My pulse rushes and beats in my ears.

The silence drags out long. There's no sound but a thin whine; I cannot tell if it is my ears or a wounded man on the porch.

Either way, the firing has stopped. I pull myself to my feet slowly, shakily, leaving a smear of blood on the back of the sofa. I take a step and double over, almost crumpling to the ground. Ida is crying in her bed and I half crawl, half stumble to her.

She's unhurt.

"Mother's here," I whisper, and everything slides softly into darkness.

I WAKE IN A BED, my head swimming and dim, and Raymond is beside me. His strong hand holds mine. I try to squeeze it and cannot.

"Irene." His voice is so gentle and I have no strength. I cannot even turn my head.

"The baby." My voice is barely even a whisper.

"She's all right. Right as rain." Raymond's voice breaks. "My darling, you were—you were magnificent."

"What happened?"

"You were shot," he says, gently. "And—"

He's never been unable to say something before. It can only mean one thing. But at least he's here. At least his hand holds mine and his face is the face I see, and his voice is the one I hear.

He gives me the courage for anything.

"How did you get here?"

"One of the hands came for me, brought me to come see you." He tries to smile for me.

"The men—are they dead?"

"All of them. The hands found you and patched you up as well as they could. There's a doctor coming."

We both know there's no need for a doctor, but he must say it.

"Those men wanted me to tell them—where you were." I have no breath in my lungs.

"I know. I'd—I'd rather you had told them."

"Yes." I reach for his face and he brings my hand up to touch his cheek. I feel hot tears. "But Raymond, that's not love. That is not what I promised to give you."

A tear rolls down his cheek and lands on my hand.

"Where's the baby?" He looks up past the bed and nods. They bring the baby and Raymond holds her against me. She's quiet and content.

"Please—take care of her?"

"Of course, darling. She'll have everything. Don't you worry about a thing."

All I have the strength for is looking at her. Raymond runs my fingers over her soft face and hair and then someone takes her away.

He tightens his grip on my hand, fingers stroking my wrist.

"I love you, Irene," he whispers. "I love you more than anything."

I try to smile and the world dims.

I'm losing him.

"Raymond?"

"I'm here, darling. I'm here." I can feel his arms around me again; he's close, I'm resting against his chest, and his hand smooths back my hair from my face.

I want to tell him again how much I love him. I want to see my little girl's face again, feel her in my arms.

But I have nothing. I am slipping.

"It's all right." His voice is gentle. "You can go."

I try to speak, but all that comes is a sigh. His strong arms hold me close. His voice whispers gently in my ear: *I love you.*

57

# CARNEGIE

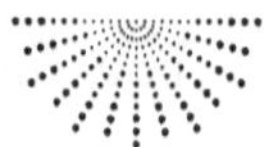

I'VE NEVER BEEN SO ANGRY IN MY ENTIRE LIFE. I'VE always been a level-headed girl. I know how to be patient, I know how to calm a situation before it turns to blows or bullets.

But right this moment, I know why men can kill in a fit of passion.

Blue Harding rides as the head of the posse. Takes an outlaw to root out an outlaw, he says. We're heading out to the spur of mountains that run nearest the Rio Jefe. Archer lamented Selby's absence more than once, but one of Blue's boys tracked the gang as best he could, and he figured the foothills were our best bet.

We are going to find whoever who sent those men and root them out.

I've not said it aloud, but my gut says Maria Pike.

294

Raymond rides with us, though he's not himself. He has always been silent, but he's strained now. There's a gauntness to his spirit that hurts me somewhere deep in my chest. His daughter is back in Glory Mesa with Rosamund.

I wonder, if not for her, if he would throw himself straight into a fight for the recklessness of it.

I'm not sure I've ever seen a pair so perfectly in love in my life, and I'm not convinced I'll see another like them.

Blue pulls the company to a halt with a swift gesture.

"We don't want to give them warning." He pulls a cigar out of his breast pocket and lights it deliberately. He takes a long slow draw and regards it thoughtfully.

"So?"

His piercing blue eyes meet mine. For such an easygoing man, his eyes are sharp.

"We'll split the company. You, Miss Kate, take twenty men and ride round the back. There's a pass you'll see, marked by a spindly tree growing every whichaway from the rocks. You watch that. They'll be spilling out through there if'n they get the chance."

"Try not to shoot unless you have to," adds Raymond. "We'd rather take them alive."

I pull my brim down in response.

Blue calls out twenty men—a mix of his own and townsmen riding posse—and we skirt north. We haven't even reached the pass when we hear the sharp staccato of gunfire.

My gaze meets the man's beside me. We spur on. If we

don't get there in time, we could be letting a whole stream of them escape.

Our horses race over the rocks, hooves clattering, the dust and small pebbles flying up into our faces and hitting our arms. The sun angles down, shining on the gathered hindquarters of the sturdy horses leaping and thundering toward the gorge.

My anger rises again. I feel the power of twenty men alongside me, the feeling of righteous vengeance, my heart rising to shout *no more*.

The trail is so narrow we nearly ride right past it, but just as we're approaching the spot, a horse run through it, wild and lathered.

One of our men draws his pistol and sends it back with a couple shots. It's tacked up but riderless.

We draw rein at the entrance and wait, our horses panting and blowing. I'm trying to hear if anyone is coming down the pass, but my pulse is pounding in my ears.

Again, gunshots.

Two outlaws venture down our way at a dead gallop, but when they see us, they turn back to try their chances elsewhere.

A bottleneck's a bad place to be in a gunfight.

We wait until the gunfire's been settled for nearly five minutes.

"Shall we head down?" I ask, glancing around at the men.

I leave ten behind and take ten others up the pass into the foothills. A distant settlement comes into view, soddies and shanties and some corrals. A few bodies are scattered around, and I give them a wide berth.

There they are. A crowd of men huddled together, covered by half a dozen deputies.

I catch up to Raymond as he's riding towards one of the soddies.

"Maria Pike was here," he says briefly. "But no one knows where she's gone."

"You think it was her doing?"

He doesn't answer and that is answer enough.

Most of the outlaws are herded together, but there's one man they're bringing from a distant shed, hauling him along by one arm.

"This one here says he's got nothing to do with the killing of the marshal's wife," growls Blue. "We'll see how long he keeps that story. The others say he's a leader."

The man they've arrested is tall, lean, and careful-moving, like a wild horse. He's wearing a long duster and dark hat and moves with a faint limp.

His right arm is strapped tightly to his chest, so one of the deputies holds him by his left.

There's something familiar about him—it's like I know him but I can't place this outfit, this manner. As for the man before me, his bearing is strikingly like the description of the lone gunman who killed Early's outfit.

His eyes meet mine. Blue, hazel-flecked.

"Hello, Kate."

My breath leaves my body. I wouldn't believe it, except that he said my name. I recognize those bright eyes, now haunted, that boy's face under a beard.

"Max Swift!"

5 8

PIKE

I can see the smoke from between the cracks in the rocks, hear the gunshots. They came upon us too fast and I had not the time to warn the men. It was them or me.

And without me, they'd be nothing.

The only one I mind is Max Swift. Time, careful planning, and patience has brought him into a tenuous partnership with me, and now, in the hands of his friends, there is no telling how he might be twisted.

But if they let him live, he may be won back, as he was won in the first place, with lies.

The wind brings me further sounds of destruction—orders shouted, horses driven off. I can see the men rounded up like sheep, hands in the air, moving at gunpoint.

But I do not see Max's long, uneven gait among them.

Perhaps he has escaped.

Max knows a great deal. He does not know it all—I have

made sure of that—but he knows much of my plans for the coming weeks, and he knows that Holt has gone to Terhune's land.

Terhune the coward. I laugh softly to myself. I hope he tears Cristobal Newton to pieces over it.

All this may be an obstacle in my path, but I will clear the trail. I will not be stopped by something so simple as thirty men in my pay being suddenly arrested.

Many a man is swayed by gold, and troubles abound in this unforgiving land. If these hang, I will simply buy more men. And if those hang, there will be still more.

I only hope that Max is spared. I have waited long for him, and my road to him has been long and arduous.

The sun is nearing the high rocks. In another hour, it will be past them and the foothills will begin to grow dark.

And then the wolves come out.

Holt is far away, a wolf himself, on Harrison Terhune's land. Max could have guarded me against them, but now he is gone as well.

I gather my skirts and turn eastward. On foot, I'll just make it to shelter before nightfall.

# 59

# CARNEGIE

It's two days' ride out to Raymond Lacey's homestead from Glory Mesa, so I was not expecting many people to be there.

The entire yard, halfway to the barn, is filled with people. It's a sea of black.

Death is common out here in the Western Territory, and none of us knows when our time will be up. But this death—a new bride, the mother of a new baby, standing against outlaws—that has moved our hardened people.

The papers have all painted her as a shining hero, printing stories with ink illustrations of Irene firing out a window and causing havoc among a crowd of men, captioned with sensational phrases like *The Marshal's Wife, Firing Upon the Wicked Outlaws.*

I do not see how Marshal Lacey can be so collected. He stands on his porch, perfect in his dark suit, his hands clasped in front of him, Governor Scott and Rosamund beside him. Rosamund holds the baby.

It's quiet except for the wind blowing through the valley.

Raymond nods to a couple men who stand at the foot of the porch, and they follow him and Archer into the house.

They emerge a minute later bearing the pinewood casket. I see someone has burned her name, her dates, and a beautiful flower into the lid.

They come down the path to the gate and pass right by me. The scent of soap and starch and cologne blows past on the wind, a sign of honor out here in its own right.

Rosamund follows with the baby. She looks beautiful and dignified, but so alone.

We follow them out to the plot beyond the house, where the grasses are soft and cool. A runoff creek from the river trickles near enough to hear it.

They've chosen a beautiful spot for her.

The men lay her down gently and Raymond takes the baby and brings her over as if for a goodbye. He lays an armful of wildflowers in and they cover it over.

So simple, so gentle—and far too close to their wedding day.

I look away to the beautiful land around us, wild and alive, the clouds passing over the sun and then beyond it, patching the sky in blue and white. The green hills rise against it, stark and beautiful.

I do not know why I love this territory so deeply. It takes and it takes, and often it takes the best of us.

Yet I still do.

THE SILENCE IS BROKEN over the meal. Folks seeing each other for the first time in a while. Homesteaders meeting townspeople.

I eat hearty, as I will have to change and get back to riding line this very afternoon, but I don't feel hungry.

Blue comes over, giving me a nod. His hair's been slicked down and the suit he has looks like he used a hidden outlaw stash to buy it.

"Lovely service," he says, as if he should know.

I nod. It wasn't much of a service—no singing and little speaking—but the pain is so very fresh, and we're in the middle of nowhere. The family had their own service yesterday, away from the eyes of the press and people who would sell it to the press.

"We'll have a trial coming before too long," Blue says with a sigh, making conversation.

"Really?" I've been out riding line. I only saw the first few hours of questioning, when the outlaws swung between sullenness, denial of guilt, and vile threats.

And that's the thing about Raymond Lacey. He had every reason to be angry and cruel. Every reason to take out his pain on the cowards who created it. Instead, he was the gentlest voice in the discussions. He showed nothing but patience with the stubbornness of these outlaws and was careful to listen to the men who insist they've done no wrong.

"Yeah. Max Swift's."

"Max's?" I feel as if someone's thrown cold water on me. "He didn't go after Raymond. He couldn't."

"No, you ain't wrong. But you see, there's a predicament there. Everyone's fired up about Irene Lacey's death, and they want payment. The papers, the troublemakers, the politicians out East. Sure, we can punish the outlaws. But they weren't the ones that did it. All the men who attacked the homestead were killed. The only way to see justice done is to find the one who gave them those orders."

"And that's Maria."

"So we suspect."

"Then what about Max?"

"It's looking more'n likely he killed Early's outfit. And he was working with Maria Pike."

"You think after what Early did to him they'd hang him?"

"Depends on the judge. One of ours, probably not. He's got scars, and Stanton knows names. But if they send a judge from out East, there's no telling. They're the ones that want blood for blood, and they ain't too particular how they get it, so long as someone swings."

A cold chill moves down my spine.

It sounds just like those folks out East to send a hanging judge.

# 60

# ROSAMUND

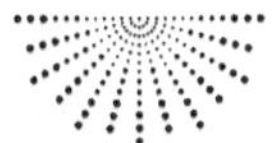

GLORY MESA FEELS LIKE A CROWD OF STRANGERS TODAY. Max Swift's trial begins this morning, and there are more people in town than normal, a great number of them crowded around the courthouse.

It is not right. Mere months ago they were mourning his tragic death, saying what a fine man he was, what a good lot those Swifts were, and how unjust it was that such things should happen to men like them.

And now they swarm in like a flock of vultures eager for blood.

Archer fought hard for a local judge, someone who understands the harsh realities of survival and the unspoken codes of honor by which we live in this territory, but to no avail. The Eastern judge came in on the train three days ago, and he is staying at the new hotel.

I feel sick to my stomach over it all.

I find my husband standing at the mirror, adjusting his tie, his jaw hard as flint.

He doesn't like this any more than I do. The more bountiful the yield from this territory, the further the reach of civilization, the harder they try to wrest the power from his good hands.

He turns to me with a shamefaced smile. "Do I look all right?"

"Like a governor."

He smiles at the compliment, but his eyes don't. He seems to like any association with the governorship less and less.

"I'll be back at the noon break," he says.

"Actually," I say, taking down my bonnet, "I want to come."

"Do you? You told me last night that you didn't."

"I can't bear to be alone in the house today." I tie my bonnet under my chin, keeping my fingers steady with an effort. "I would rather see the trial than stay and imagine the worst."

He pulls his jacket on and adjusts it over his shoulders. "Suit yourself."


THE CROWD PARTS for us as we approach the door of the courthouse, murmurs of recognition and respect arising around us. I just raise my chin and square my shoulders.

I am angry with all of them. None of them have a good reason to be here, and yet here they are.

They usher us in. It's nearly empty for now, but the judge is here, talking with Raymond. Raymond is polite, but his arms are folded across his chest and his manner is reserved.

He looks even more suspicious of this judge than Archer does. But when he glances over and sees me, his eyes soften.

The judge comes over, all smiles and reserved politeness. His dark robes give his shock of white hair a stern quality.

"Good morning, Governor, Mrs. Scott."

I muster up a smile for him that I do not feel at all.

"Good morning, Judge." Archer takes his offered hand and shakes it firmly.

"You and your wife have arrived just in time. As you can see, there is quite the crowd out there."

"You can hardly miss it." Archer's wry tone is lost on the man.

"Well, take your seats. The public will be allowed in soon and the prisoner will be brought in shortly." The judge looks to Raymond Lacey. "Will there be trouble with him?"

"None. I have a couple deputies bringing him over."

"A couple?"

"Trust me." Raymond's voice is calm, but I hear warning in it. "Two is more than sufficient."

I take my seat beside Archer and he reaches for my hand. He's looking gray up close, far more than he was even a year ago.

The public is let in with shifting and scuffling of boots and low, respectful voices. A louder murmur runs through them like wildfire, and I see Max Swift enter. He has a beard now, marred by a red scar that angles across one cheek. He's wearing a dark shirt and jeans—not unlike how I first met him—and manacles.

His eyes quietly take in the crowd as he walks up the center aisle and takes his place at the front of the room.

"All rise for the Honorable Judge Rattenford." The room rises with a great scraping of chairs and rustling of starched clothes.

Insufferable.

The red-faced judge comes out and sits, and we all follow suit.

"This court is now in session," he announces, and we begin.

THE PROSECUTION RATTLES off the charges: the murders of seven men.

Seven murderers is what they were, and there are no witnesses. This case should never have come to court.

The first witness called is Blue Harding, who comes up in remarkably good clothes, his stiff blond hair plastered down, his hat in his hands, his eyes brighter than the sky outside.

"Please state your name for the record."

"Blue Harding."

"Is that your given name?"

"I reckon."

"Very well, proceed."

"And what is your occupation?"

"I'm a deputy marshal of the Western Territory."

"That is your full occupation? My understanding is that you have been in this territory for some time."

"Well, yes I have."

"And you had a prior occupation?"

Blue squirms a little, loosens his collar.

"Well?"

"I was an outlaw."

A murmur runs through the room.

"And as such, you understand how outlaws think. Is that why you were sworn in by Marshal Lacey?"

"Well, not exactly. I know their dens and trails, not their thoughts."

"So you do not presume to know what other men are thinking?"

"If they ain't said it, why should I? In my opinion—"

"Mr. Harding, please answer the question directly."

Blue purses his lips a little in frustration. "No."

"Mr. Harding, were you the one who found Early and his men dead?"

"I was."

"And why were you looking for Early and his men?"

"To arrest them for murder. His murder." He nods to Max Swift.

"But he isn't dead."

"Well, now we know. But he sounded pretty dead then."

Another bout of whispering.

"Mr. Harding, how did you find the men of Early's outfit when you arrived?"

"Shot down. Most of 'em dead."

"Most of them?"

"One wasn't quite." Blue clears his throat.

"And did you speak to him?"

"Yes."

"Did they appear to be ambushed?"

"Most of them were shot in the front."

A silence follows.

"Please answer with a yes or no."

Blue looks at the prosecutor with a slow smirk. "That's a no. An ambush means you weren't expectin' it."

The whole courtroom breaks into laughter.

"Mr. Harding," the judge speaks, as the prosecutor begins to turn red, "you will please keep your remarks to yourself or you will find yourself held in contempt of court."

This threat rolls right off Blue's back. He looks rather like he'd enjoy trying to be in contempt.

The prosecutor is regaining his composure.

"Mr. Harding, when you spoke to the man, did he say who attacked them?"

"He described the man, but he didn't know him."

"So he said that it was just one man?"

"I think."

"You think?"

"The feller was dying. He said he didn't recognize the man. When you say the man—"

"Mr. Harding, please restrict your answer to the question."

Blue lets out his breath in a snort.

The prosecutor seems done as well. He's mopping his brow. "No further questions, your honor."

The defense stands up and presses Blue a little further on the matter of the bullet holes and the fact that the outlaw did not recognize his attacker, and then they are finished. The prosecution has a few objections, petty ones, which are all sustained by the judge.

Max remains silent through the whole thing. If he has thoughts, they do not show on his face.

They bring another witness, a drifter who had supposedly seen Early's outfit the same day, but his contribution seems superfluous.

The judge stands up. "After a break, we will cross-examine the defendant. This court is adjourned until noon."

Someone comes straight up the middle aisle and over to Raymond, putting his head close and speaking in a low voice.

Raymond nods and leaves with him immediately, walking swiftly.

. . .

ARCHER and I walk home for our midday meal. There's something about just walking, feeling the dust under your feet, that helps me clear my head. Everything has felt like one long dream for months, and not a good one.

And to walk down the street, my hand in his, the dusty wind blowing my dress eastward, feels like those early days when he and I were apart, when the world felt broken but we were free.

His hand tightens gently on mine as if he can read my thoughts.

"I have missed you, my love," he says.

"So have I." The wind almost carries my voice away, but he hears it.

I left our dinner already prepared, as the court will only be adjourned for an hour or so, but after this morning, I am not even hungry.

He opens the door for me and I untie my bonnet, hanging it up. Archer strides into the kitchen and pours out a cup of this morning's coffee, cold by now.

"You should warm it or make more," I say, but he downs the whole cup.

He's tired; every line of his frame is weary and his eyes are dull. But he smiles at me, his smile gentle and white. "You make a good cup, Rosamund Scott."

I laugh. It's been a while since he's made me do that.

A firm knock sounds at the door. I know immediately that it must be Raymond.

"What is it?" I ask when I see him. He's standing with his hat off, his stance apologetic.

"Rose, I need a favor from you."

"Of course."

"Irene's folks just came in on the eleven-fifteen train, her aunt and uncle. They—want to see the baby."

"How—?"

"Newspapers," he says, grimly.

Naturally.

"I have to be back to the courthouse in ten minutes, and they are certainly not seeing her without me. I don't trust them."

A small, cold misgiving settles in my stomach. These were the relatives Irene had practically fled from.

"If I had another way to do it, I would, but they need to be entertained, if only for an hour or so."

I raise my chin. "Invite them here, please. I'd be happy to have them for you."

"Rose, I don't know how to thank you."

"Don't." I reach up and kiss him. The poor man has been through so much this year. "Stall them a few minutes for me, will you?"

"My pleasure." He puts his hat back on and tips the brim to me.

I shut the door and go into the kitchen.

"Archer, dear, I'm afraid we are about to have company."

.  .  .

Archer, brave man, meets Irene's aunt and uncle at the door and ushers them in. The uncle is a tall, narrow man who looks like he wishes he had remained at home, and the aunt is a steam engine of a woman, older but with a forcefully youthful carriage and a face meant for ruling kingdoms.

"I was told the territorial governor owned this—house." She says it like it's a gracious term.

"I am the territorial governor," Archer supplies. "Archer Scott, at your service."

"Hmm." She looks him up and down with something like approval in her eyes. "War hero, weren't you? I think you came to a ball we had, once."

"I wouldn't be surprised," he says with a smile. "I went to many." He steps back and holds out his hand to me. "And may I introduce my wife, Rosamund."

I step forward and hold out my hand to both of them. The uncle's grip is like shaking hands with a cold fish.

"Please, if you will, there is some light refreshment in the parlor. You must be tired from such a long journey."

The aunt sails past me into the parlor.

Their names are Andrew and Agatha Davenport. I recognize the name. We were not in the same circles—not even in the same state—but money and power will make themselves known.

They refresh themselves on some cake and tea. It is not much compared to what we were used to out East, but this is the Western Territory. They will have to adjust their expectations.

"So you moved out here to be with your husband?" Agatha asks, once we are past the pleasantries.

"I did."

"And your brother, the marshal, he simply sold your family home and came as well?"

"Yes. He and I were the only ones left of our family. There was no reason for him to stay."

"Convenient for him that there was no law out here."

"Hardly." My blood is rising now. "We were both prisoners of Alexander Mortimer for two weeks. It was clear that a job had to be done."

"And that was how he met Irene." What is she trying to prove by asking questions she clearly knows the answers to?

"Yes. Your niece was a wonderful woman. They were very happy."

"Hmm." Agatha takes a delicate sip of her tea. "And yet it seems her headstrong luck ran out in the end."

I close my mouth on the sharp remark I could easily give. I wish I could simply fling the teapot at her self-righteous face and at her bored, inhuman husband.

"That would be a false assumption," I say, fighting for every gracious word. "My brother's position is a dangerous one and he has many enemies. She knew that when she married him, and she gave him the happiest months of his life. There was nothing unlucky about any of it."

"But her first husband—"

"Irene told me many lovely things about James. I promise you, she had no regrets worth mentioning. In the Western

Territory, we trade our comfortable lives for a place in history."

There—good gracious, I am beginning to wear thin.

This is going to be a long afternoon.

61

NEWTON

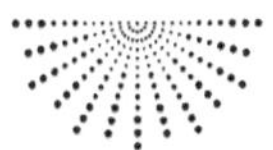

IT IS A CHILL MORNING, THE SKY A BRILLIANT FROSTY blue. I woke before dark to help feed the stock, as the hands will be our witnesses. They laughed and told me I had no right to be feeding my stock in the cold on my wedding day, but I just laughed along with them.

What else would I be doing?

I check my appearance in the mirror. It's been a while since I've needed to wear a good suit, but I could look a lot worse than I do. At least it still fits, and my hair has stayed where I combed it.

I missed a spot of cream from shaving. I reach up and rub it off.

Well—I suppose it is now or never.

I come downstairs and I see most of the hands gathered in the wide front room. They're grinning like fools in their cleanest shirts, elbowing each other and pointing at my suit.

Most of them have never seen me wear one.

The preacher is here too, the only other one in a suit. He's standing with hands folded, a pleasant smile on his face. He arrived last night with his wife and had supper with us.

He's one of those broad shouldered, boy-faced fellows and brand new to the frontier, but he strikes me as a good man.

Nathan comes over and shakes my hand. He's pleased as punch. "You look right smart, sir. Right smart."

I thank him and take my place beside the preacher.

The room takes on the sharp feeling of anticipation. The door opens and a hand comes in late, hair plastered to his head, his face sheepish.

All of them were excited to learn that Hannah Milton would be marrying me and staying on at the ranch. She's become a favorite, and while I was gone, they all looked out for her.

I suppose a big party full of food and cake with sugar frosting has its charms too.

I can even smell the food from the kitchen—roast beef and chicken, potatoes, fresh bread, pies, greens, preserves.

A door opens upstairs and I hear a collective indrawn breath from those around me. Hannah comes down the hall and appears at the top of the stairs.

Her dress is simple and trimmed with lace. She's carrying a bouquet of the mountain flowers that are in season, yellows, whites, and blues.

The pastor's wife trails her, a small smile on her face.

Time seems to slow and then still as she comes down the steps. I cross the room and offer her my arm.

"You look beautiful," I say softly. "Are you ready?"

"Yes." Her face is solemn. "I'm more than ready."

The pastor clears his throat. There is no one to give her away, so he just nods to her. She passes the bouquet off to the pastor's wife and puts her hands in mine.

He begins by asking the hands and the cook if there is any reason known that would prevent our marriage.

There is an almost offended silence, some of these men having never been to a proper wedding. Hannah laughs under her breath, a small, delighted sound that makes my heart beat faster.

The pastor reads the vows. We echo them, promising ourselves to each other in clear, steady voices.

We smile a little, almost shy with one another. I slip a ring on her small, delicate finger. She squeezes my rough hand in hers.

The pastor pronounces us man and wife.

I look at her face, and she's happy. Beaming like sunshine.

And I have no misgivings, no regrets.

I lean down and we kiss.

# 62

## CARNEGIE

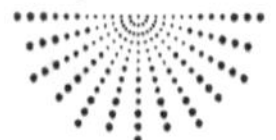

THE DULL LIGHT OF THE OIL LAMP IN THE MARSHAL'S office lights the small cell in the back of the building. Max sits on the edge of his cot, his hand folded. There's not much else he can do with it—he has stayed shackled since they brought him in, except for when Raymond Lacey is in the office.

Archer Scott sits across from him, just on the other side of the bars.

I lean against the wall, watching, my arms folded. I trust Archer Scott to be aboveboard in all respects, but rules are rules, and I have to remain within sight since I am the deputy on duty.

"Listen, Max. I am trying to help, I promise."

"Help, hmm?" Max studies his hands. "You think I need it?"

"I think the judge isn't necessarily on your side."

He laughs, bitterly. "You could say that."

"If you told me what happened, where you came from, I could probably speak for you. There are a lot of ways to show that you were provoked."

"I showed them my scars," answers Max, toying with one sleeve. "And they just said that it gave me motive."

"You could have told them more."

"Could I?"

"You haven't told us why you were in the outlaw camp after being presumed dead or why you were one of their leaders."

Max rubs his finger and thumb together slowly. "And why was your first thought not that I was a captive, but a leader?"

"We were told that by some of the men."

"And you believed the outlaws. About me." He chuckles under his breath and looks away.

"Is it true?"

Max doesn't answer.

"If you're not honest with me, Max, it makes it harder to help."

"I'll say what I want. I don't owe you anything, Archer Scott."

"I thought that perhaps, for old friendship's sake, you could trust me."

"I don't trust anyone." He raises his eyes to meet Archer's. "Not you, not them, certainly not that sorry excuse for a judge."

"What about your brothers?"

"You tell me where they are, Archer. You tell me who sent them away on a fool's errand. Tell me where my ranch is and the money my father sweat and bled for and then you tell me who I can trust."

It's Archer's turn to remain silent.

"It's ironic, isn't it?" presses Max. "They want to hang me for the deaths of men who tortured me?"

"Well, did you kill them in self-defense?"

Max shrugs.

"It's important, Max."

"Why?" Max smiles humorlessly. "They want my blood, they don't care how they get it."

"If you have the right of it, tell me, Max. I could still get you out of this."

"Let me tell you something, Archer." He raises his eyes and they are hard and haunted. "They deserved to die a lot slower than they did. Those men, dead and in the ground, got more mercy than they gave."

"They might beg to differ."

Max just gives a soft, mocking laugh and shakes his head. "Naw. A man's better off wanting to live and losing his life than living and wishing he hadn't." He stands up with a sharp clank and fixes me with a grim, dead look. "Kate, I don't want to talk to him anymore."

I look to Archer and he gets up, conceding defeat.

I wish Max would let him help, but there's a wall behind

his eyes now. If it wasn't Max's face staring back at me, I don't think I'd believe it was him.

I lock up and bring the light with me into the main office.

"Thank you, Kate." Archer shoves his hat on and heads for the door.

I follow him out onto the porch.

"Are you here for the night?" he asks.

"Just tonight. It isn't my usual place, but Raymond wanted deputies he knew well. Too much press, too many wagging tongues."

"Understandable."

He goes down and unties his horse. He is tired, every movement heavy as if it takes great effort.

"Archer?"

He stops.

"Do you think Max has a chance?"

"Any chance he has with the judge up there is in his own hands. But you can see he's not the same man. That boy in there—I don't know him."

I nod numbly. "He's endured unspeakable things. Doesn't that count for something?"

"It should." His shoulders sag. "But I don't know how much anymore. What would you do, Kate?"

I open my mouth, but anything I'd do would be without that old judge in the picture. He's like a bull planted in front of a gate.

A surge of anger washes over me. For the death of Irene,

for the boy Max used to be, for Archer standing before me, worn thin with grief and exhaustion.

And because Maria Pike and Holt both roam free while others shoulder the weight of their deeds under the eye of an exacting government.

"I wouldn't have held a trial so soon," I say, my voice hard. "I'd have looked for Holt first, and Maria. I would have addressed those crimes first, and when the truth was had, then I'd have dealt with this. That's what I would have done."

Archer nods quietly. "I like your thinking, Kate. If only you were a senator."

I nearly spit in disgust. "If I see another senator, I might collar him. I was tired of them before I came out here. If I had prior warning, I'd run to the hills just to avoid meeting one."

"You and me both," he says, and his face is haggard in the moonlight.

# 63

# ROSAMUND

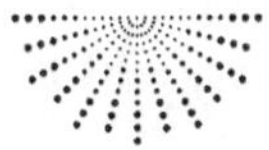

THE VERDICT IS EXPECTED TODAY. IF THE COURTHOUSE was packed before, it's even more so now. It is oppressively hot and the hungry expectation in the air is what you'd expect from a pack of wolves, not decent people.

The trial has dragged on for four days. Max got a chance to speak the first and second days, but he didn't say much. He answered questions about what Holt and Early did to the ranch, to the hands, to him. Supposedly he showed them scars on his arms. I wasn't there, so I only heard the gossip.

I do not see how showing the scars could hurt his case, but the judge seemed to see it that way.

He refused to answer when they asked him if he'd murdered the men in cold blood.

No one else was there as a witness, so the evidence is circumstantial and second-hand. Even so, I think this judge will deliver a guilty verdict because it is what's wanted. Back

East, they will call it progress. Out here it is more common for the lines between good and evil to roam beyond the normal bounds of law and society.

Raymond says he's recommended time rather than death, but haven't trusted this judge since the moment I met him, and not from prejudice alone.

He makes me feel the way Holt did when he walked into a room.

Both lawyers make closing statements. Why Max should hang, why Max should go free.

Archer's face is quiet and calm. I wish I could read him better, but he's wearing the face he wears as the governor—polite, nothing more or less.

And then the judge speaks. It is the verdict.

His voice echoes through the room that is so still and hot you can hear the workers in the railyard a mile down the street.

"Max Swift, you have been found guilty of the murders of Tom Early, Rob Hyde, Pete Washer, and Crooked Jim. You are therefore sentenced to hang by the neck until dead. Sentence to be carried out at dawn of Tuesday next." He bangs his gavel and adds gravely, "You have three days. If you have any kin to tell, we'll the carry the letters."

I clench my fist.

Max's eyes take in the faces before him. He looks calmer than I am, but he's angry, quietly angry. There's a spark of flame in his haunted blue eyes.

"No kin," he says softly.

The court is adjourned with the bang of the gavel and the noise and movement of the suddenly buzzing courthouse swarm up around me.

Max is led past by Raymond's deputy, a man I do not know well. Since the Davenports came into town, Raymond has been absent more.

Max looks over at me, but his eyes are hard and closed off from the world.

I start to rise beside Archer and the floor meets me instead.

I COME AWAKE WITH A START. I'm in bed and Archer is standing beside it, watching as Doctor Everett holds my wrist in his strong fingers.

"Just a little excitement," the doctor says calmly. "Nothing to worry about."

"What happened?" My voice is dry. I'm trying without any success to remember what happened before this.

"The courtroom was too hot. You fainted." Archer's voice is gentle.

It all floods back. The guilty verdict. The judge I do not trust. Max's face, closed off from the world.

I try to sit up in a rush.

"Easy, easy." The doctor pushes me back gently. "You need to rest."

He pulls a small bottle out of his bag and pours a little into a glass of water, stirring it.

"This will help you sleep, Mrs. Scott. Thankfully your husband caught you and you did not hit your head. You are just strained and exhausted."

He closes his bag and leaves the bottle on the bedside table.

"If you have any trouble sleeping at night, take a teaspoon of this in a glass of water. It should help."

He gives Archer a nod and leaves.

I finger the coverlet and stare at the ceiling. My head is pounding and my heart is racing.

"You should drink this," says Archer gently, picking up the glass and offering it to me.

"Not yet," I whisper, putting my hand over his, stopping the glass. "What about Max?"

His face darkens. "What about him?"

"You have to stop this. Write him a pardon."

"Rosamund..."

"Do not tell me you can't do it. I know you have the power."

"I can't just pardon him because he was my friend, Rose."

"I do not trust that judge. He's crooked."

"That still isn't grounds for—"

"Grounds for what? A crooked judge is grounds enough."

"It is more complicated than that. But I will look into it, I promise."

"You have to. There's no knowing how much of what he

did was in self-defense. And those men had tortured him. Surely that should have been considered."

"Darling, you need to rest. Please try to sleep."

"Archer, do you love me?"

His shoulders sag ever so slightly. "You know I do."

I press his fingers in mine, hard. "Don't let him hang."

"Just drink and rest. We'll talk later," he says gently.

I take the glass and drain it.


I FEEL MORE myself the next day, though I have a headache. Archer is here—he stayed home from the office this morning to be with me.

He's reading the newspaper, and the front page is declaring the results of the trial, complete with a picture. His eyes go to mine, looking at the paper, and he folds the paper in half to hide the front page.

"Archer, have you started on a pardon?"

"No."

"Why not?"

"I don't know if it is the right thing to do."

"That trial? It was a political move, Archer, that is all it was. And giving him three days? That isn't kindness, it's for spectacle."

"I know, Rosamund, but there is nothing that I can do about it."

"You can pardon him, right in front of their bloodthirsty noses!"

"And they would have me out on my ear in an instant. I have to think of the territory."

"So you'd let an innocent man die for the territory."

"He didn't deny killing Early's outfit. Rosamund, I know the Swifts and love them. I watched them grow up. But Max is a man, and he can face the consequences of his actions like one."

I slam the dish in my hand onto the counter. "You are not listening to me!"

He looks surprised, as if my anger has come out of nowhere.

"The evidence cannot be proven, they could be hanging the wrong man, and you're just going on and on about duty when the chance to save his life is right under your nose."

"But is he the wrong man, Rosamund?"

He looks at me, direct and hard.

Something deep in me knows he might not be. But stronger than that, sure as the earth, I feel that I cannot bear for him to die under these circumstances.

A confession, imprisonment, something—but not this.

"Rosamund, I said that I would try and I will. But I must do what I believe is right, and I cannot answer for the consciences of others. Will you trust me?"

I look him in the eye quietly, proudly. "No."

A hurt look flits through his eyes, but I am like ice.

"And if you fail to save Max by your means," I continue, "know that I will. By any means necessary."

"Rosamund, please. There are things in motion here that

you are not aware of. I must ask you not to intervene or even speak publicly about it."

"And why not?" I cross the distance between us, tear his hands off the paper. "Archer, I don't think you understand. I am so—so—sick of death. If he dies, I will break. I cannot take another loss, I cannot."

His face is held carefully still as he refolds the newspaper, inside out, and sets it aside. "Perhaps you should consider going East for a while."

The words hit me like a slap across the face. Who does he think I am? I've survived Mortimer, desperate rides for my life and his, and loss upon cruel loss—and his way out of listening to me is to send me away?

My breath shudders in my chest before I can get the words out. "Archer, if you force my hand, you will have no one to blame but yourself."

# 64

## THATCHER

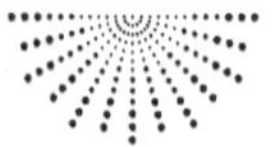

WHEN I HOPED THAT GLORY MESA WOULD GROW MORE civilized, I had hoped for two things: one, that I would not be around when it did (or at least not stuck in the middle of it), and two, that it would not become stuffy and nasty and fuller of gossip than Maria Pike.

I have been soundly disappointed on both counts.

The newspapers for the last three days have been full of the news of Max Swift's trial and upcoming hanging.

I wasn't anywhere near, or in any shape to know what the truth was, but in my opinion we're a mighty poor set of men if we are quickest to hang our old friends.

The worst of the newspapers have painted a lurid picture of Rosamund and Max Swift. She, the paper claimed, swooned upon seeing him led past, and—like a good newspaper—misremembers that it was Alan, not Max, who escaped with her across the desert. Put all of that together, and it comes just shy of saying that Rosamund and Max are in love, which is not a thing a paper should be printing about the governor's respectable wife.

"Don't tell me you are reading that," says Archer grimly, coming in the door, shutting it against the thick dusk.

"What else is there for me to do?" I throw the paper on the floor, on top of the others. "Really, Archer, have you spoken to the press? They shouldn't get away with that kind of nonsense."

"I spoke to them. But all they did was print a very unconvincing retraction. I will have to have a personal talk with the editor-in-chief, though I do not know how much good that will do, even as governor."

"Carson owns the building. You have a quicker way, I think."

"I stand corrected." He laughs wearily and settles on a chair opposite me. "How are you?"

"Better," I answer, and I mean it. "I can walk across the room now, if I have a cane. Still can't abandon the wheelchair for good, but progress is progress."

"Well, that is good news at least."

"You don't look well, Archer."

"I don't feel well. I'm sick over Max. Rosamund is taking it hard."

"So he's going to hang?"

"I think so." His voice is so soft I can hardly hear it, even in the still room. "I think he did it, and if I didn't know him, there wouldn't be any question in my mind."

"Is there a question in your mind? Are you unsure?"

"I think it is wrong that he should end this way. He was such a promising young man. But he's not himself, either."

"Haven't you told Rosamund that?"

"I tried. I can't find words to make her understand. She's beside herself."

"Have you considered resigning?" I can hardly believe the words as they come out of my mouth.

"And who would step in? Someone from the East, surely. We cannot risk that right now." His voice is determined, his shoulders squared, but he cannot hide his eyes from me. They look like a man in the desert who sees water.

"Archer, you know I can talk straight with you. I think—"

A sudden, urgent pounding starts at the door.

Archer stands up and runs to open it.

"Governor! Thank goodness you're here, sir. We have a problem." The man's face is pale in the robust light of the lantern outside. He glances at me, but Archer motions for him to go on.

"Max Swift is gone. He broke out and stole a horse."

"Whose horse? When was this discovered?"

"Just now, sir. We don't know whose horse, but we're looking. We just know he didn't have one of his own."

"Did he have an accomplice? Perhaps the horse was from them."

"Maybe so. The guards were drugged. We're not sure yet with what, but the marshal thinks it was a sleeping tincture. Doctor Everett keeps it."

"Is he the only one?"

"We're asking Trasker if he has any in stock, but we think Everett is the only one."

"Doctor!" Archer shouts. Everett appears in the front room just as another man comes running to the front door.

"Trasker doesn't carry the tincture, only—" He breaks off as he sees Doctor Everett.

"What is this?"

"Max Swift is gone and the guards were drugged."

"Drugged?" He's shrugging on his doctor's coat; I think the poor fellow was expecting an emergency.

"By a tincture only you carry. A medicine for sleeping?"

"Who have you prescribed it to?" asks Archer.

Doctor Everett's face darkens. "I'll tell you true, I have no interest in this—perhaps it was stolen."

"Just tell us who," urges Archer.

"Mrs. Long, as her rheumatism has grown bad."

"Is that it?"

"Only her and your wife, sir."

Archer's color and breath leaves him like he's been kicked in the chest.

"Excuse me, gentlemen," he whispers, and he runs out the door into the night.

# 65

# ROSAMUND

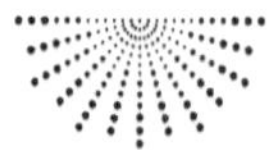

He told me, as he was holding his nervous horse firm, his eyes distant, that he'd killed the men.

He had gone after them, told them who he was and why he'd come, and then the bullets flew.

"I was used," he said. "And maybe—maybe I deserve to hang. But those men for sure deserved to die. And I owed someone a debt."

I asked him what debt, but he'd thrust his boot into the stirrup and ridden off hard into the night.

And now I'm alone in the house, in the dark, and my hands won't stop shaking.


Archer comes into the house not an hour later. I can tell from the rush he's in downstairs that he knows.

I knew he'd find out. If he hadn't, I'd probably have told him anyway. I told him if he wouldn't do anything, I would.

I hope he listens next time.

No lights have been lit—I've been standing in the dark this whole time. He's calling me, urgently. I hear him as he runs through the house, calling me.

His voice is full of fear and anger. I've never heard him crack like this, not ever.

A light grows in the open doorway and then his shadow falls over me.

"Rosamund—what are you doing in the dark?"

I turn to him, a bitter smile on my lips.

"What did you do?" His voice trembles.

"Only what you were too cowardly to do yourself."

"Rosamund, I'm going to ask you again—"

"I warned you." I'm so angry I laugh. "I told you I couldn't take it. You refused to listen. So I did what I said I would do."

"Rosamund, it wasn't that I refused to listen." His voice is soft, sad. "It is that I believed him guilty. And I cannot go against my conscience, and you betrayed me."

"You would believe a friend guilty? When you didn't know for sure?"

"I didn't want to! Rosamund, what kind of man—what kind of governor—would I be if I didn't hold to my principles?"

"And what about my conscience? What about protecting me?"

"You demanded an impossible thing from me."

"And I took care of that decision for you." I reach for his hand, trying to make him come back to me, to make things the way they were before.

He springs back as if burned. "Don't touch me!"

The air goes hot and still around me.

"Do not—touch me," he pants. "If you think you can do whatever you want, regardless of the consequences, you are very mistaken. What you did has implications you cannot possibly fathom."

This is a new Archer. I knew that he would be angry, but it is far different from the kind of anger I expected.

"Try me." I toss my head.

"I could be implicated. I probably will be. I will lose my position. We could both go to prison. It's the perfect excuse for one of those tall hats out East to take this territory, and this time it's ripe for the picking. You will certainly be arrested for aiding the escape of a convicted murderer. And the newspapers—they'll—"

"What about the newspapers?" There's something different in his face, something that makes my inside hollow and cold.

"They implied that you and Max could be" —he rolls the words around as if he cannot bear to speak them— "in love."

"They're fools!" Instead of crying, I laugh again. I cannot help it.

"I tried to protect you from it."

"Well, I guess it's too late."

"Yes." His voice is grim, resigned. "It is." He draws himself up, bracing as he says the words. "Come on, I'm turning you in to your brother."

Half of me wants to fight. I could turn this ugly, I could flee on a horse—I've done it before. I could probably make it by sheer stubbornness all the way to the Auki Nation. But the other half of me isn't sorry, not remotely, and I want, in a strange way, to lean into this trouble and see how deep I can go.

"Very well, then. I'll get my shawl."


THE LIGHTS ARE on at the marshal's office and jail; shadows move around and voices carry from inside.

But Archer will not be deterred. He marches onward toward the conflict, his hand gripping mine, and I keep step.

We're both half-mad, out of our heads with anger, and my heart is still singing at the thought of Max fleeing into the night.

Peter sits on the empty porch.

"You do not want to go in," he says. I have never heard him say it to Archer before.

"I don't?" Archer pauses.

"The marshal is locked in his back office and the men in there are all talking about hanging Max Swift if they find him." Peter unfolds his arms. "But they won't, though."

"You're right, I do not want to go in," says Archer wearily. "But I'm going in regardless."

He pushes into the office, dragging me with him into the smoky light.

"Where is Raymond Lacey?" he demands.

The talk stops abruptly. There are a dozen or more men standing around, red-faced. Some of them have been drinking and they're all wearing sidearms.

One thrusts his thumb towards the back room, just as Peter said.

Archer strides to the door and knocks. "Raymond Lacey!"

The men all stare at me, standing alone in the middle of the room, my face flushed and my eyes triumphant.

Let them know what I did, bloodthirsty dogs. I beat them at their own game.

Raymond comes out of the room, and I see his eyes are bloodshot. My brother almost never cries.

"Raymond, I am turning your sister over to you. She was Max's accomplice. You do your duty."

Raymond turns his eyes on me slowly. He looks haggard. "Did you do this?" He jerks his head towards the empty jail cell.

"My husband refused to pardon a man who was convicted on scant evidence. For show." I fling the words at the men watching. "So I took care of justice my way."

Raymond opens his mouth to speak and something broken crosses his face. Suddenly my triumph is gone. Something is wrong.

"Raymond, what is it? The baby?"

"The Davenports stole her." His voice is slow, measured. "Left on the afternoon train. I was going to go after her, until—"

Until I let Max Swift out.

"Oh, Raymond!" I cross the room to him, take his hand. "I'm so sorry."

He tries to smile to reassure me.

"Raymond—she released a convicted murderer, against my wishes."

I try to keep the cold anger out of my tone, but I can't help it. "His name is Max, and I think he helped save your life once. Raymond, tell him!"

"That doesn't matter, if he goes killing." Archer's voice is hard.

"After all this time, after everything, you dare say that to my face?"

I stalk over to him. How dare he, in front of all these men? He didn't even clear them out—probably so he could have witnesses.

"A man's life was at stake, Archer."

"He deserved to lose it."

I take in my breath sharply. How can he say that now, after he led me to believe he had regrets?

"Coward," I hiss before I can stop myself, and I raise my arm.

He catches it, instinctively, before it lands across his face. His fingers press into my arm.

Raymond takes a step closer.

"Archer." My brother's voice is slow and too gentle. "Take your hand off my sister."

Archer raises his head. Raymond has never issued him an order before.

"Go on, do it. Before I get—touchy."

Archer lets go of me and I have enough presence of mind not to hit him now that I'm free to do it.

"Now get, all of you." Raymond's gaze sweeps over the men, including Archer.

The loiterers don't stay. Even drunk, they know danger when they see it. They all head for the door as if there's a keg of powder ready to light.

I have never seen Raymond this angry either.

"Raymond, I brought my wife to you for justice. Just because—"

"Because of what?" Raymond snaps. "Are you deaf? I said get out!"

Archer draws himself up. "Raymond, we are all hurt and angry, but this territory—"

My brother strides to his desk. In seconds he has his shotgun down from the wall and cocked. "I said get out."

Archer looks wounded and suddenly I want to comfort him. "You would draw on me? After all we've been through?"

"Archer, there's only one person living anymore who could possibly induce me to draw on you. And she came to me for help."

Archer looks at me, suddenly pleading. "Rosamund—"

"Get out of here!" Raymond roars.

"Rose?" He makes one final plea.

The anger has faded from his face, and I can see he is beginning to feel regret. I start toward him, but Raymond's firm hand seizes my arm and holds me back.

"I'm giving you to the count of ten to be on your horse, or I'll shoot."

A spasm crosses Archer's face.

It's a nightmare, I am sure of it. I am going to wake from it. But Archer goes to his horse and mounts while Raymond holds the gun on him.

His horse's hooves clatter away.

Raymond shuts the door.

"Raymond," I whisper. The blood feels as if it's all drained out of me. "What have you done?"

He's calmly taking a rifle down from the wall, loading it. Now that Archer is gone, he seems as settled as stone. He takes down his saddlebags and starts to fill them with ammunition and provisions from a cupboard in the corner.

"He's lost his right to you, darling. No man touches you like that."

"What are we going to do now?"

"Let him clean up the mess he's made. I'm getting you out of here." He heads out the back door, where his horse is tied up to a post.

"And where are we going?"

"Home." He unties his horse and mounts up, holding out his hand to me.

I put my foot over his, and he hauls me up behind him.

"Your home?" I cannot think what else he means, but that's a two-day ride in good weather. But he's not listening.

One hand fumbles at his chest, and I see him toss his tin star onto the ground by the door.

We take off, trotting down the alley behind the building, out past the train station, out over the tracks themselves, stretching east and west in the darkness.

He stops on the train tracks, empty and cold.

"Forgive me, little one," he whispers to the east. "I'll find you, I swear."

And then he spurs his horse forward, so hard my head jerks. We're streaking across the wild night desert, heading away, away from Glory Mesa, away from Archer, away from my broken hopes and dreams.

The ground trembles beneath us, a veiled warning from the land itself.

6 6

ALAN

It has snowed overnight. The world is white and gray and soft pink. The rocks and trees and spindly sagebrush frosted with it like dusted sugar over a cake.

We have been ascending the western of the two peaks for nearly a week now, and I can feel it in the air—we are close to the end of our journey.

The sun is a great red-pink fire looming on the horizon. In all my years, it's the largest I have ever seen it. Everything around us feels beautiful and unreal. It does not fit with our aching bones and frozen fingertips and mud-caked boots. A landscape like this should be gentle, not brutal.

Jack is awake, as he always is come morning, saddling his horse. His hair and jacket are touched with frost, and he pulls off one glove with his teeth to adjust a buckle on his horse's bridle.

"Morning," I greet. We rarely talk now, except when we

camp. All of us can feel the weight of the journey growing as we ascend.

I think we all know that not all of us are coming back alive. It makes even a meal, a good morning, the soft push of a horse's nose special.

"Morning," Jack replies through shut teeth. He pulls the strap tight and reaches up to take the glove out of his mouth. "How'd you sleep?"

"For it being so cold, quite well." Our breath stands on the air between us. "And you?"

"I'm tired," he says, not quite answering the question. His eyes are weary. Like a man's when he knows he has little time left in his life and the charms of the world have dulled.

"Not me," I say, stretching my long arms. "In the mountain air, I feel a new man."

He nods and smiles, unsurprised, as if I deserve to feel that and he's happy for me.

We're camped beside a small mountain stream, cold as ice and clearer than the air in front of our faces. I kneel down beside it and wash my face. Jem's still sleeping; the man works hard and sleeps well, better than the rest of us.

Jack may sleep only a matter of a few hours in a night, and it's fitful. I wonder what it's like to be that way for years and years, as he has.

It seems wrong that a man should have to stay awake with his own thoughts so much of the time.

I know that we are headed in the right direction. I feel it. Not only that, but we've been feeling the rumblings at night, and we've heard from trappers and wandering clansmen that there's something strange about the mountain that had not been strange a mere five months ago.

In a few days, perhaps a week, all this may be over. And the words that Sikes always spoke, shaking his grim head as the clouds hung low on the horizon, will be fulfilled.

To think, we will have done it. One of us.

Jack mounts up and gathers his reins.

"Where are you going?"

"To scout," he says briefly. "The ground was uneasy last night."

"You can't go far on this mountain," I say with half a grin.

"No, I reckon not." He favors me with a small smile and chirps to his horse.

"I wouldn't complain if you found some game!" I call after him into the gray dawn.

He lifts his hand, holding the long end of his reins, in reply.

# NEWTON

I SEE THE SMOKE HANGING LOW OVER THE EASTERN hills and I know, beyond a doubt, that it's the hay fields burning.

They're only a day's ride from Terhune's land. By the time we get there, we'll barely have time to protect the timberland.

"What is it, love?" Hannah comes to the doorway, peering out at the eastern horizon.

"The fields are burning," I say, running past her back into the house. "I need every man we can spare, and quickly."

"What can I do?"

"We'll need water for ourselves. Have Cook hitch up a wagon and fill the canteens. We'll need shovels and feed sacks."

I snatch my gun down from the peg by the door and run to the barn.

A moment later, the cook is banging away on the supper bell, calling the men in.

"What is it?" Three of the hands come running from the barn. One catches a glimpse of the far horizon and stops with an oath.

"Come on, we've got to ride."

"I'll catch the horses, sir!"

It's mere minutes before they're ready, ten men and another seven coming from the near pastures soon. We're stocked with canteens, shovels, and feed sacks.

I stride back into the house to find Hannah. She's braiding her hair back and coiling it up behind her head.

"I'm leaving now."

She pins her hair quickly and calmly and comes over. "Be careful. I'll see you soon."

"It might be a few days."

"No, I'm coming down with the cook. He said I could." She kisses me. "It's my land too, now."

I don't have time to argue. I kiss her back, smile in case it's the last thing we see of each other, and pull my hat tight on my head.

Harrison Terhune doesn't have us yet.


THE FIRE HAS RAGED across the hay fields and is licking up the dry brushland between the fields and the timber.

The hay is gone. The brushland is roaring with fire.

I shed my jacket and hand my horse off to one of the men. He's collecting horses like we're dismounted cavalry, taking them back out of the range of the intense heat. It sure feels like we're at war.

"Start digging here! We'll dig a firebreak and extend it all the way down to the rocks."

They move into place quickly, digging into the earth deep and fast, dirt flying. The hot wind is beating on our backs, the sweat streaks down our faces and backs, and the dirt and smoke fill the air. Time flees in desperation. We work so quickly that we tear our nails, scratch our arms and faces, rip our clothes as we drag wood and brush out of the line.

If only the hay fields were not so broad.

THE SUN IS SETTING, shrouded in a haze of smoke, and that's when I see Hannah is here. Her hair is tied up under a kerchief to keep it away from the burning embers, her sweet face grim with concentration, her dress already stained with soot.

She's working too hard to see that I've noticed her. I return my concentration to my work.

We labor through the night with little rest. One of the men gets burned, and Hannah takes him over the far hill to bind it up.

We share a canteen once, a moment of tenderness

snatched between hours of fire and black, smoke-covered sky.

And then we part again.

Dawn arrives, weary, gray, and smoldering, revealing the devastated land. Hannah and I walk over what is left of the fields, spread out around us like a lake of destruction.

The ground is blackened, the hay burned to ash over dirt. The red morning sun spreads over the land in flat, blinding rays, turning Hannah's hair to fire.

"It's wrong," she says, bending down and touching the scorched earth as if it could feel her sorrow for it. "What does he think he is going to accomplish?"

"He's angry. Or his men are. Or perhaps the ones that poisoned his water holes did this. But you are right, it accomplishes nothing. It is wanton waste."

"It is not just waste. It is cruel." She straightens, pushing her long braid over her shoulder. "Cruel to the cattle, to this land, to you."

She reaches out and wipes a smear from my face. I cannot imagine that it will do much good; I'm covered in dirt and soot.

"It's our land, together," I remind her.

"Why must people be cruel?" She leans against me, her face in my shoulder.

"Because we are cursed," I say gently.

"I wish—I—" She cannot finish.

I hold her tight, sweat, ash, and all, as she weeps. The sun is turning everything to brilliant red-gold around us. It's beauty and destruction all at once, terrible and majestic.

I reach up to smooth her hair down. It smells like smoke.

This cannot go on. I must confront him.

6 8

ROSAMUND

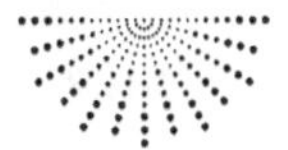

WE ARRIVE IN THE EVENING, TWO DAYS AFTER FLEEING Glory Mesa. Raymond helps me down and hands off his horse to a man who asks nothing.

Together we walk to the house in the gathering dusk. A year ago, there had been so much hope. Happy marriages, families to look forward to.

Now it is just us.

He lights a lamp in the doorway and hands it to me.

"The room upstairs is yours," he says as he bolts the door. "Anything you want, just ask."

"I'll take the guest room," I say quietly. "I won't have you put out."

He checks his rifle, cocks and uncocks it, and hangs it back up over the door. "Go ahead. I don't sleep there anymore."

I go upstairs and change out of my travel-worn dress. We

353

hardly rested at all on the ride, and the dust has wearied us both.

The hem is a little long, as are the sleeves. Irene was a taller, longer-limbed woman. Nevertheless, it feels good to be out of my dusty clothes. I'll wash my dress in the morning.

I walk downstairs to find a lamp lit in the kitchen. Raymond is there in fresh clothes, seated on a long bench beside the table. But he's sitting with his shoulders bent, his chin in his hand.

Like a sudden blow to the face, I see it. He looks old.

I want to comfort him. All he's ever done is be good to me, and this life's been cruel to him.

"Raymond—" I put my hands on his shoulders.

He reaches up and puts his hand over mine. "What is it, Rose?"

"I love you so much. The territory may have taken everything else from us, but it hasn't taken us from each other."

He chuckles, sadly, under his breath.

"I think there'll be better days coming, Rose." He says it so gently, but I can tell that he is weary.

"I hope so," I whisper, settling on the bench beside him. My voice abandons me.

"Come here, darlin'." His long arm is around my shoulders and suddenly it's me who is breaking, falling apart.

I turn my face into his shoulder and sob. Cry for my son, cry for his little girl, cry for the hopes and dreams and love we had and lost.

"It's all right, darlin', it's all right," he murmurs, stroking my hair, his own voice thick.

"How did it go so wrong?" I whisper. "How—how did it come to this?"

He doesn't answer. I want him to say something, something that will put sense into all this, fix the deep, gaping holes in me.

But that's a dream too. I will live with these holes the rest of my life.

"I—was ready to give up so much." I pull my face away from his sleeve, which is completely soaked through. He digs in his breast pocket and pulls out a handkerchief. I wipe my eyes, blow my nose. "But I didn't think it would take everything."

"I know."

I hold out his handkerchief and he pushes it back courteously.

"Rose, do you remember how excited you were? Back when you got that letter and we sold our house?"

I nod. I don't want to remember. It feels bitter and pointless now.

"I said I wanted to come with you, even though you were going to be married and have your own house."

"I remember."

"I didn't mind one bit that you'd have a place and I'd be on my own. I said I was glad to do anything, if it was for you."

"You did." I smile through my tears.

"And we knew it was going to be hard. It's been hard. It may get worse before it gets better. But you, Rose, know how to survive. And I'm right here with you, as I've always been."

I give a shaky sigh and reach for his large, rough hand.

"How can you be so strong?" I murmur. I faced outlaws and desperate rides, but I've never been so afraid of life as I am now at the idea of never having children or never getting Archer back.

"Irene and I...." He pauses and I let him think, collect his thoughts. "Neither of us had a fool's chance of finding happiness like that, and yet we did. The year we had each other, why, you couldn't beat it in a hundred years. I miss her. Some days I miss her so bad I can't breathe. But we made our choices. We knew that nothing's promised."

I tighten my hand on his. I wish I had even an ounce of that thinking. But my heart sinks heavy and everything feels meaningless the moment I think of life with no Archer, no children.

I want that so badly I'd give up anything for it.

"You're going to be all right, Rose," says Raymond, letting go of my hand to put his arm around me. "I know it."

I just lean against him and close my eyes against the welling tears.

THE FOLLOWING DAY, I am listless. I cry on and off through the morning. Raymond made coffee and was gone before I was even up. I woke to sunshine and the smell of it downstairs.

I do not see him until midday, when he comes back to eat and look in on me.

He is working in a far pasture, laying fence rail. I tell him to be back for supper. He promises he will.

I spend most of the afternoon on the porch, watching the wind sweep across the valley, running its fingers over the long grasses, drying the clothes and bedding on the line.

Raymond did pick some of the most beautiful land I've ever seen.

Supper is ready by six, and Raymond is back for it. He didn't have a great amount in the larder, but I was able to cook a chicken, bake some bread, and open a jar of preserved beans.

We do not talk as we eat. He's tired and neither of us is in the mood. Besides, what would we talk of? We have nothing to say.

The sound of a single horse riding hard reaches us through the open windows and I get up and hurry to the door.

"Careful," warns Raymond, but I open the door anyway.

It's Lesley Gable. He's just outside the gate, and he throws his leg over the back of his horse and drops down.

"Marshal! Marshal, sir!"

Raymond comes out, wiping his fingers on his napkin. "Lesley, I'm not the marshal anymore."

"Doesn't matter. Archer's coming with a posse for you—both of you, I think. I barely made it ahead of them."

"You rode all the way out here for that?"

"Well, I wasn't going to let them come out here and catch you unawares."

Raymond claps Gable briefly on the arm in gratitude. "Did you bring a gun? There might be shooting."

"I have my pistol."

"Good. You can put your horse up in that barn there and then come on inside. There's supper."

"I'm obliged, sir."

I'm at the table serving Lesley, who is tired and still damp from washing up, when I hear more horses—this time a score or more.

"Raymond?"

He's in the front room, stacking the ammunition he and Lesley have combined. He gives me a grim, steady look and goes to the window.

"It's Blue." He goes to the door.

I set down the bowl of beans and follow him out. I don't want to be far from him right now, and any man looking for trouble may think twice about something if there's a lady present.

Blue rides straight through the front gate at a lope, but his men stay outside the picket fence. There must be more than thirty of them.

He reins his horse in hard right in front of the porch and gives Raymond a sharp nod. "Well, Lacey, I reckon I've turned dishonest again. But I ain't letting them take you in. I gave that posse forty-three badges to litter their floor with."

Beside me, Raymond chuckles under his breath. "It's appreciated, Blue. You didn't have to do that."

"Well, I was getting stir crazy anyhow." He squints up at us with something like a grin.

"I hear the posse's close. Maybe get a couple of those men up to that high hill over there and give us some warning. I hope you boys are armed."

"To the teeth." Blue jerks off his gloves.

"Just remember, these are old friends. We don't shoot 'em like outlaws, hear?"

"Whatever you say." He salutes lazily and leads his horse off.

"That evens things a bit," says Raymond to himself.

"Raymond, do you regret this?" I ask. "People could die."

"While I have you to protect, no. I'm going to talk to them first, darling. Most of those coming are reasonable men, I figure. But we need to be ready to defend ourselves if we must."

The wind sighs through the grass. For the first time, I feel afraid.

THREE WARNING SHOTS break the silence. The men at the table look up, out the nearest window.

"That'll be my boys," says Blue slowly, reaching for

another piece of bread. "Better go see which direction it's coming from."

He goes out the front door.

Raymond stands up and dusts off his fingers. "Thank you for coming, Lesley."

"I wouldn't miss it," he says quietly. "It seems my lot to help you beat off gunmen on this land."

Raymond grunts deep in his throat and drains the rest of his cup of coffee. "Reckon it is. Rose?"

I look up.

"You can stay out of sight, if you like."

"I'd rather be there with you." I cannot say it, even to Raymond, but I want to see Archer again. If he remains stubborn, I will certainly not go back with him, but if he wants to mend things, I'm willing. I hate leaving things the way they were left between us.

Blue bursts back through the door, letting in the sound of pounding hooves. "They're a-comin'!"

"You ready, Rose?"

I give my brother a single nod and clench my fists so they cannot tremble. I hope Archer is coming to make peace, but I fear he is too principled. He will stick by his guns and men will die.

"We've got your back," says Blue. "Some of the men are down in the barn with a good view of the picket gate, if it comes to shooting."

"Thank you." Raymond buckles on his gun but leaves the strap over the pistol. "Let's go, gentlemen."

The posse is around twenty strong, with Archer at their head. Kate is there, her face hard against the light of the nearly setting sun, and behind her ride an assortment of people from Glory Mesa. I see a tall figure near the back that looks like Tagweiah.

"Raymond, I want to talk," Archer shouts.

"Come on up." Raymond hardly has to raise his voice to be heard. "Leave your gun."

Archer unbuckles his gun belt and leaves it over his saddle. He comes up the walk, easy and unafraid, but I see his eyes taking us all in.

He's not ready to yield.

Archer comes to the bottom of the stairs and stops, eyeing the guns on the men's hips. "Raymond, I've come alone and I left my gun."

"Looks like you brought quite a party over yonder. And they're wearing their iron."

"I just want to talk."

"I'm not drawing on you yet. Say your piece."

"I have to bring you in. You, Rosamund. The others now, probably."

"What are the charges?"

"Aiding the escape of a convicted man, three counts. Hindering an arrest, one. And for those men, aiding fugitives."

Blue guffaws loudly.

"I think I was still the marshal then," says Raymond. "It

was my decision not to arrest her, and you wouldn't take my answer."

"But it was the right thing to do."

Archer is stubborn. He believes it in his very heart, I can see it. He'd turn himself in if he believed it was right.

But I am not sorry for letting Max go.

"If I surrender myself, will you let Rosamund alone?" asks Raymond.

"I am not here to negotiate. I must take you both in."

"Then I'm staying right here. I have no trouble negotiating with a .45."

"Don't do this," warns Archer. "I want this settled peacefully." He looks at me pleadingly.

"We'll have peace when you finally stand up for this girl that you married. Until then, I'll keep on defending her."

Archer looks at me with a new expression. "Rosamund, is that how you feel?"

I give him a cool look. What I feel is far more complicated and cannot all be explained in this moment, in front of everyone.

I am certainly not going to have a personal fight with him right now.

"I'd speak for all of you," he says. "But the law cannot be cast aside based on personal feelings." He looks into my face and speaks quietly, just for me. "I am truly sorry for how angry I was, Rosamund. I can't—I can't tell you how betrayed I felt."

I swallow, fighting the urge to run down the steps and

put my arms around him, tell him it's all right, find a way to get over this together.

"She needs a better apology than that, Archer," says Raymond, his voice hard. "You'd best get out of here until you can give her one. And until you see reason."

The gentleness in Archer's eyes disappears.

"You are the one who needs to see reason." He strides back to his horse and mounts up.

Kate gives me a long look as she turns her horse after him. I cannot tell if she is angry or sorry for me.


FROM THE WINDOW THAT NIGHT, I watch their campfire up over the ridge, a flickering light against the night sky, so full of stars.

I wish Archer and I could sleep under the stars together again.

# 69

# THATCHER

I HEAR THE SOUND OF DOZENS OF HORSES RIDING IN, their rhythmic panting, the jangle and squeak of the tack, the occasional shout of a rider.

But Blue took his men and rode off in a great rebellious demonstration worthy of his Croix-Savannah days, and Archer rode out with a posse. If I know where they were headed—and I do—then neither of them should be back yet.

I know in my heart this means trouble.

My cane leans against the wall beside my wheelchair, and I take it up and haul myself slowly to my feet. If there's trouble, I am going to meet it on my feet.

At the door I stop and tie on my gun. There's no way I could outdraw a man the way I am right now, but I'm not going unarmed either.

I step out onto the porch and see a laughing, rowdy crew

of men congregating outside the saloon. Someone kicks the swinging doors.

Another handful gathers outside the governor's office. No one should be over there while Archer's gone.

I am watching the scene with growing unease when a horse lopes up to the porch, and I find myself looking into Max Swift's grim face.

"Jesse." He tips his brim to me.

"You'll forgive me, but I figured you'd be lit out in another direction right about now."

"About that." His gaze wanders slowly down the street then returns to me. "You won't like what I have to say, but I've always figured you for a friend. I hope it can stay that way."

My hand tightens on the handle of my cane. "Just say it."

"I am taking over the governor's position in Glory Mesa. The East is clamoring for a new face, and Archer's days are numbered. I can take it now and prove myself before one of their soft, arrogant politicians takes it from him."

"Max, you can't. Think about what you are saying. Who will support you? He'll come back, and the trouble you had before—it'll be twice that."

He takes a step toward me and sets his boot on the bottom step of the porch.

"Archer is days away, and I have enough men to keep him out. This wasn't a quick decision, Jesse."

"Do you know how it's going to look?"

Max shrugs. "I don't really care."

"I can't let you, Max."

He leans in, his voice gentle. "We are the heirs of this territory, Jesse. You, me, Archer. We were the first ones born here in ages upon ages of barrenness. Of anyone in this territory, I have the least desire for your blood, or for Archer's. Please do not fight me."

"I don't see that I have a choice." My hand goes to my gun.

"It's clear you are in no condition for it. Just listen to me for a moment." He starts up the stairs and puts his hand over mine.

"Max." I look him right in the eye. "I don't think there's anything you've got to say that I want to hear."

"I'll grant you safe passage home, if you want," he continues earnestly, ignoring the fact that I don't want to listen. "Or you can stay here, and these men will have orders to stay away from you and treat you with respect. I understand you don't like what I'm doing, but you deserve respect. If you want to go home, I'll make it happen."

I consider his words. Laughter and noise come from down the street, and he glances that way a moment. "Well?"

He's right. I cannot fight him right now. He has one of the fastest draws in the whole territory and steady nerves.

If I tried to draw on him now, I'd just be dying for principle, not for Archer or the territory.

"I would like to go home," I reply, my voice almost failing.

"I'll have an escort ready for you tomorrow." He turns his head and whistles to a couple men down the street.

"Boys, this here is Jesse Thatcher. He's heading home to his ranch tomorrow. I want a buggy and five men to see he makes it safely. If anyone, and I mean *anyone*, touches him— they're dead. Is that understood?"

"Of course, sir."

"Where is she?"

"Back at her house, I think. She was keen to go there."

"Good. You're not to tell her about Jesse. She doesn't need to know. And one more thing."

The men, about to turn their horses away, pause.

"Get a man to carry a message to Archer Scott and his posse. Tell them not to bother coming back unless they're ready to accept me as governor. And tell them there's going to be law and order here in this territory from this day forward."

70

GABLE

I NEVER THOUGHT THAT I WOULD BE THE SORT OF MAN to take a favor from an outlaw. Perhaps one act of defiance opens you up to more and more, and that's how a man ends up running afoul of the law.

In any case, I made my choice.

When the messenger came to Raymond's homestead with the news that Max Swift is the new self-appointed territorial governor, rendering both Raymond and Archer powerless, there was nearly a brawl.

But how can you fight a single messenger?

Right there, in that moment, with everything I've admired and worked for turned to ash, I only wanted one thing, and that was to be with Edith and keep her safe.

Hang aspirations. She is enough.

I asked, there in front of them all. I asked if I could go back to Glory Mesa with him, to be with my wife.

He said if I gave him my gun, he'd allow it. So I did.

As we near the town, I see a rider lingering near the end of Main Street, watching the road into town. He spurs his horse forward and meets us halfway, one hand hovering over his pistol.

"Afternoon," he greets. "Who is this?"

"Lesley Gable, the surveyor. He has agreed to cooperate."

The other man fixes me with a direct look. "Very well. But no starting trouble, you hear? We want our surveyors, but not bad enough to put up with antics. Things are just settling."

I nod. "May I ride on?"

My companion gives me a nod.

The outlaws begin to talk business—how the railroad magnates have already come to an agreement with Max, how there's been a strict penalty for stealing imposed and Max has already jailed three of his own men overnight.

And then I ride out of earshot. Before long, all the news will come to me whether I want it or not.

My house is just as I left it. I don't know what I expected —a fight, maybe, when they stormed in—but everything looks untouched.

I tie my horse up in the yard and run up the steps to the door.

I knock. "Edith?"

The door opens.

"Lesley, what are you doing here? I heard...."

Her eyes search my face. She's been afraid, and all I want to do is comfort her.

"I couldn't leave you alone. Not now, with this."

"That's why you're back? Just for me?"

"Just for you."

Something crosses her face, sweet and surprised, before she quells it. "I hope you haven't promised anything you can't keep."

"Just not to make trouble. And I won't, not with you here. Not unless it's worth dying for." I bend down and kiss her. "I should go put the horse up."

"Lesley...." She reaches out and takes my arm in her hand. "Would you go to the mercantile for flour and thread?"

"How much and what kind?"

"Twenty pounds, white and blue."

"I'll just put the horse up and I'll be on my way."

"I've have a meal started for you when you get back!" Her voice follows me out the door.


Trasker's General Mercantile seems relatively untouched. Other than a windowpane boarded up and fewer goods on the porch, it looks the same.

I duck into the dim, cool store. It smells of spices and dry goods—altogether pleasant compared to the livestock smell in the street.

"Lesley!" Trasker's eyes lifted the moment I stepped in,

and he shuts his account book. "It is good to see you. How did you get back into town?"

"I promised I'd make no trouble," I say briefly. "I'm here for twenty pounds of flour and white and blue thread, if you have them."

"I have them. But I'll have to bring the flour in from the storeroom."

"I'm not in a hurry," I assure him and drift towards the sewing goods.

Trasker disappears into the back as I pick out the threads and take them to the counter.

And then a heavy shadow falls across the doorway. The man's tall and broad-shouldered, with greasy hair down to his coat collar and a scruffy, gray-brown beard.

His eyes are like ice.

"Howdy," he greets with a wicked smile. "Reckon you're new in town."

"I think you are," I reply a tad stiffly.

"No, I don't think you understand. New, as in—since Mortimer's time." He smiles humorlessly. "Don't reckon you knew Mortimer?"

"No."

The man guffaws. "Nor been on trial for murder?"

"I would hope not."

This conversation seems to amuse the man. He picks up a stick of candy and snaps it in half, dropping it on the counter.

There's something about his behavior that makes me

dreadfully uncomfortable. I am glad that I came here instead of Edith.

He looks around the store and then reaches out casually and tips over an entire barrel of cornmeal. Right onto the floor.

Just then Trasker comes back into the room. "Holt, what are you doing in here?"

"Just lookin'," he sneers. "Got a problem?"

"Yes, I do. It's that barrel of cornmeal. Unless you are prepared to buy it, in that condition, you are not welcome here."

Holt saunters over to the counter and leans his hands on it. "And what will you do if I say I won't?"

Tracker plows a fist into the bigger man's face. Holt staggers back and then seizes Trasker by the collar, dragging him forcibly across the counter.

"This ain't a place you can get away with this anymore," says Holt nastily as Trasker twists in his grasp, trying to reach for anything to use as a weapon. "Not any more."

He throws Trasker back against the counter, hard.

I reach for the nearest tool—I am not a man to insert myself into a fight, but Trasker is outmatched in size and Holt's look is murderous.

"What is this?"

A gun clicks and I see Max Swift himself in the doorway, his gun drawn.

Holt and Trasker both go still.

"I thought I was clear on fighting." He looks at Trasker,

then at the mess on the floor, and finally at Holt. "You're under arrest, Holt."

Holt clears his throat. "I am under Maria's protection. I think you understand that."

"I don't." Max's voice is soft, unemotional. "I'm the governor, not her."

"And marshal too?" Holt sneers.

"Did you think you would be safe in my town after what you did to me?" Max chuckles in disbelief. "Even so, I will be the man you never were, and when you go on trial for your life, I'm not bringing those charges. You'll die for the rest of it. That's my gift to you."

He jerks his head to a couple men standing behind him in the doorway.

"Take him."

Holt is cuffed and led away, snarling and twisting. He spits at Max, but Max doesn't move a muscle.

Not until Holt is out in the street does Max move. He digs out a coin and tosses it at Trasker, who is flexing his hand gingerly.

"That man ain't bothering you again," he says. "He's got no chance against a judge or a jury."

He strides out into the sun.

# 71

# ROSAMUND

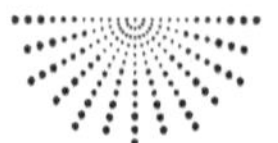

I leave a note for Raymond and ride away before the sun is fully risen. When the messenger returned, I gave him a note to give Max. He said he'd deliver it.

I hope he meant it, otherwise I am on a fool's errand.

The land surrounding Raymond's homestead is unfamiliar, but I know how to ride from one place to another, and I know there are secluded hills down between here and Glory Mesa.

The horse picks its way over thin, trickling streams, probably healthy brooks when there is no drought. This place, with its natural springs, has not been hit as hard as Glory Mesa to the south or the ranches to the west.

I arrive in the hills by noon, too determined to be tired or sore. A cluster of trees stands at the foot of one hill, and there I see a lone rider.

He is here.

I head down between the hills to the trees and rein in just under their shade. Max takes off his hat.

"Rosamund."

"Thank you for meeting me."

He dismounts and leads his horse over to the nearest tree, tying it to a low branch. "Well, I'd be ungrateful if I didn't."

"And yet you kick my husband out of office?"

"As I recall, you were having a fight. One big enough to make him abandon his post."

"A governor can leave town. I see you have no problem with that."

He stops short and then laughs. "I can see why you might get into a fight with Archer."

"That is none of your business, Max."

He shrugs. "You're probably right." He turns around and loosens the cinch on his horse. "What do you want to talk to me about?"

"I want you to reconsider, Max."

He glances at me and pushes his hat back. "I can save you time and give you my answer. I'm not changing my mind."

"I want you to hear me out first."

He folds his arms and leans against the tree in something like acquiescence.

"Archer has fought for this territory. He's given so much of his life for it. So has my brother. The two of them together have made it what it is. If you take it from them like this, you destroy a whole legacy of good. Why not partner with them?"

"Do you really think your husband would agree to that?" Max chuckles. "No, and he has no power anymore. Whatever happens, it must be without him, from this time forward."

"Please, Max. You wouldn't even have been able to do this if I had not freed you."

"And I am grateful, but I won't change my mind."

"You cannot take the whole territory."

His eyes soften, just a little. "Rosamund, if you want to come back to Glory Mesa, no one will bother you. You can have your house, you can live in peace. Any troubles the law would have had for you—they'll be struck from the record."

"And Archer? Raymond?"

"Sorry. Not them. I think you can understand why."

"Then no." I draw myself up. "I'm sorry, I am not interested."

"Then our time was wasted. If you ever reconsider—"

"I won't. Not without them."

I study his face. It's the same man, but there's a deep iron in every line of him that wasn't there before.

"But, Max..."

He's collecting his limbs, adjusting his hat on his head. He pauses.

"I'm not sorry I saved your life. Know that."

A tiny smile crosses his face. "I'm glad to hear that."

He tightens the cinch on his horse with a grunt. Without

turning around, he says over his shoulder, "I'll board up your house in case you want it back."

I don't answer. I shove my foot into the stirrup and mount up, spurring my horse away.

I RIDE hard over the hills, anger and sorrow and deep, deep weariness welling up in my chest. Archer and Raymond at each other's throats, Max pulling a coup on Glory Mesa, Maria Pike probably pulling his strings, and me—caught in the middle of it all.

All I ever did was walk straight in the direction I meant to go, and I find I have walked into a web so tangled someone is bound to die before it's all over.

Did I do this? Was it Archer? Did it happen with Max's capture by Holt?

Where did we go wrong?

The late afternoon sun slants over the hills as I ride nearer to Raymond's homestead. Another couple hours, perhaps.

At the crest of one hill, my horse snorts and his ears prick forward.

A figure stands in the river below us, up to his knees, casting a rod.

I rein in, watching him. There is a serenity to his movements. The world may be falling apart, but this man is content.

I urge the horse forward, down the hill toward him. He

looks up as we are halfway down and lifts an arm in greeting. There is something familiar about him.

It is Mortimer's father.

He looks no different than when I saw him last, the day I shot Holt and fled for my life over the flats north of the camp.

How much has changed since them.

"Do I know you, miss?" He squints at me over the shining water.

"My name is Rosamund. I...stayed in your house for a couple weeks once."

He continues to squint, and then gives a stout nod. "Yes, I remember. My son was fond of you."

I don't know how to answer that.

"What are you doing in these parts?" He collects his line and casts it again, further into the river.

"I was riding past on my way to my brother's home. Marshal—Raymond, I mean—Lacey."

"Oh, him. Good man. Is he up at his place? Last I heard, his wife was killed by outlaws."

"Yes." I let the answer stand for both.

"And you're visiting? I figured you married that Archer Scott."

"I did." My voice sounds hollow.

He turns and fixes me with a keen expression. "There's trouble, ain't there? I've lived long enough, I can feel in my bones when there is."

I just nod.

He shakes his head wisely. "You know, you can't make a

person do what's right. You can try, of course, but in the end, if their hearts are set on a thing, that's where they'll go."

"I think that I am partly to blame," I say. I do not know how, even, but I know that somewhere I went wrong.

"Every man's got his part to play, good and bad. Many's the day I gave myself grief over my son's wild ways. But he had the stars in head and I couldn't get them out."

"What did you do?"

"I reckon I gave up. Sometimes you've got to just let the wild horse break its neck, if you forgive the term."

He squints at the river and lets out a long sigh.

"He wanted bad things, and he dug his own grave, God rest his soul. But he had it hard, my son. He grew up in a cruel world that I couldn't protect him from and it turned him cruel."

"I suppose it happens." I think immediately of Max, hard and detached when he used to be bright and laughing.

I draw in a deep breath. "You didn't ever believe in the cursed land or in that great destiny your son spoke of, did you?"

"No...I reckon I didn't." He scratches the side of his nose. "I never did put much stock in it."

"Mortimer believed that Archer was cursed."

"And do you?"

I don't answer. I remember the moment when Mortimer touched my forehead beside the smoking train and told me I'd saddled myself with a cursed man, and that the curse was on me. He said one day I'd wish I had accepted his offer. He said I'd remember that moment.

And I do.

"Are you all right?" His voice breaks into my thoughts.

"Yes." I catch my breath.

"Just you sit down a spell," he directs, pointing to the long, half-dried grass. "Fishing is good for the heart, you know."

"I didn't know."

He chuckles and winks. "Ever eaten brook trout?"

"No, I haven't."

"Best food you'll ever taste. It's fresh and pure as this land."

I let the horse graze and I watch him fish. It takes him a little while to catch one, but then he catches another and another.

By the time he's done and wading like a heavy horse out of the water, I realize that I've lost an hour or more.

"I should go," I say, standing up, brushing my skirt off. "At this rate, I will not be back before dark.

"Not to worry," he says, peering at the sky. "You needed the sun and the water, mark my words. My place is over yonder a mile or so. Walk your pony over and I'll stake him out on some good grass. It's quiet there, and we'll have fresh caught fish for supper and I'll make you the best straw bed you've ever slept on."

"My brother might worry."

"Nonsense. He wouldn't want you traveling in the dark.

I roam these parts high and low—if he's worried, I'll be the first stop he makes."

"Are you sure?"

"Sure as sunshine. Come on, the fish in these rivers are the best you will ever taste. I'll prove it to you."

# THATCHER

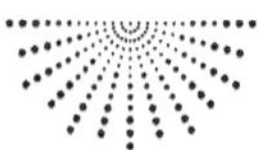

I CLOSE MY EYES AND BREATHE IN. THE WIND IS sweeping down from the hills, strong but not harsh. The distant sounds of cattle and horses are like a balm to my soul.

There is nothing quite like home. I never dreamed I'd be away for so long. I have missed nearly a year's worth of doings—sure, my foreman and I have talked and all—but it's not the same as being home, seeing the cattle, smelling the hay and dirt and clean air.

I feel stronger already.

Archer comes out of the ranch house, finally wearing jean cloth and cotton.

"You're a sight for sore eyes," I say.

He gives me a half-hearted smile and hands me a tin cup of coffee.

"I spent the last year pining for this." He settles in a chair beside mine. "But this is not how I wanted to get it."

I shift in my chair; it's been hard to stay comfortable. But I've been walking more. And out from under Doctor Everett's sharp eye, I've gotten into the saddle once or twice with a little help.

"None of us wanted this, Archer."

"But I should have been watching."

"I don't know about you, but Max Swift becoming governor behind your back wasn't exactly something I predicted. I doubt he even predicted it before he up and did it."

He smiles, humoring me, but it doesn't reach his eyes. "I just wish I knew what kind of hold Maria has over him. I never thought one of the Swifts—"

"It's unnatural, I know. But I believe, Archer, we'll win it back in the end."

He takes in a long breath. "This land is going to require my life of me," he says. "I feel it. These moments here, Jesse, are the closest thing I will ever get to peace."

"A man can't know his end. Not for sure."

"This is different, Jesse. My purpose has been to defend this land, to make it a good place, and all I've done is ruin my own life."

"I dunno." I reach up and scratch the back of my head thoughtfully. "I reckon you've done a sight of good here."

"At what cost? My wife? The territory and my reputation?"

"Have you talked to her?"

"I can't get past Raymond."

I sigh. I'd like to see the person who could get past Raymond once his mind was made up.

"Have you apologized?"

"Yes. But she didn't respond."

"She's hurting, Archer. I could see it in her eyes even before, when she came and was asking after me and my recovery. She was hurtin' awful bad."

"About the baby, do you think?"

"I reckon. Wasn't my place to ask."

Archer sighs and looks away over the fierce landscape beyond the ranch. "My house is still over there," he says. "Unfinished. Oh, the dreams I had, Jesse."

"Yeah, I reckon we all did."

"I could see it in my head. I would make this territory a beautiful place for people, and then I'd come back here, where my heart is. And it would be Rosamund and I, and a family. And we'd sit in the purple evenings and talk as the children played, and every morning would be more beautiful than the next, simply because we were together."

He chuckles sadly and raises his eyebrows.

"And now I don't even know if I'll be seeing her again."

"It's the curse." The words come out stronger, more sure than I mean them to be. "Those of us who are closest to the land—I'm crippled, you're without home and occupation, Max has been corrupted. The other Swifts, we don't even know if they are alive. We've opened this land, broken its dirt, brought it to heel, but maybe that's the cost. We'll be broken and everyone else will get the fruits of our labor."

"Perhaps." He rubs his face wearily. "Perhaps you are right."

I do not want to be right. I want to run and ride and work, not be a young man who needs a cane to walk painfully across a distance I used to cross in moments.

But I can't complain either. I should be dead.

"I would be happy," Archer says, his eyes going to the quiet land in front of us, "if I could be together with Rosamund just one more time, and we could be at peace with each other. That is all. Then I could die content."

73

PIKE

The office looks almost as it did when Archer was the newly-appointed governor, but this time I come in as a conqueror, not bearing congratulations.

Max looks up as I come in. He looks smart behind that desk.

"You should buy a suit, Max," I remark, setting my basket on the cold stove. Archer Scott rarely used that stove, except on cold winter nights.

Desert nights can be cruel.

"When I need one, I will get it," he replies briefly, uninterested.

"Any trouble with the locals? I heard Carson had words with you."

"Carson always has words. He's not a threat so long as I leave him alone."

"Max, you do not take charge by leaving people alone."

He looks up at me, a faint scowl on his face. "Are you the governor?" he asks, almost sharply.

"Why, no—of course not, but—" I lean close, so that my lips nearly brush his ear. "Max, let me tell you a secret. I will make you unstoppable."

He turns and looks at me. The scar on his face, cutting through his beard, stands out red as blood against his pale face.

"I don't need you. I am already unstoppable."

I draw back. This is new behavior from him. I have allowed him to act independently, of course, as he must feel himself in charge, but he has always understood that he owes me his life. After all, I was the one who came upon him half-dead in the canyon and nursed him back to health out of the goodness of my heart.

Or so I've led him to think.

He straightens the papers on his desk and stands up. "I talked to Holt right before he hung." He's rearranging the stacks, not looking at me as he talks. "I wanted to ask him why he attacked our ranch, why he tortured me within an inch of my life and left me for dead. Why even a man as evil as him would do such a thing. Do you want to know what he said?"

He's looking straight into my soul and a stab of fear races through me. He knows.

"I saved you," I counter, taking a step back. My heart is in my throat as his eyes burn into me, unwavering.

"He said it was you."

"Holt was about to hang! He'd say anything."

"He also had no reason to lie anymore."

"Max, after what I did for you—"

"What did you do for me?"

"I healed you. I put you back together and I made you something."

He takes a step towards me. Slow—lazy, almost—but I know better.

"I want to hear it from your mouth, Maria Pike. No lies. What did you do to me?"

I take a step back and the wall meets me. Max takes another step, his fingers toying with the handle of the switchblade in his belt. "Say it."

"I told Holt to burn your ranch."

"And?"

His eyes bore into mine. "Say it. I'll know if you're lying."

"I told him to take you alive!" I take a shuddering breath and cover my eyes. "Not to kill you. I told him not to kill you."

"And what a good man," says Max, rolling up his sleeves, holding out his palms, turning his neck so I can see the scars. "I'm not dead."

I close my eyes against the sight of his scars. I've seen them all, but held out before me like this, I can't bear it. Each one stands dark against his pale skin like an accusation.

Curse Holt. What I'd do to him if he wasn't dead already—

"But do you know what the worst of it is? You manipulated me. You cursed the men who did it as you treated my wounds, and all the while you knew they had been at my ranch on your orders. Why did you rescue me, Maria? Was it guilt?"

I feel my eyes waver under the white heat of his anger.

"Don't be afraid," he smiles bitterly, rolling down his sleeves. "I won't hurt you and I won't hang you. I still owe you my life."

I try to smile my old, charming smile, all sweetness and innocence.

He has nothing. Of course. And Holt is dead.

His eyes remain hard and there's a glint in them. "But your time is coming. I may owe you a debt, but you cannot outrun your fate, Maria Pike. Remember that."

"Governor, sir?" A man comes into the doorway, stops respectfully. It's one of the boys from the telegraph office. Not one of ours, but not looking for trouble.

"Excuse me. I have important business." Max turns his back on me.

"Ths came for Archer Scott." The boy holds out a telegram.

Max reads it and then crumples it up and drops it on the dust-covered floor.

"You wire back and tell them Archer Scott is no longer here. Tell those men back East, sitting in their fine offices and comfortable chairs, that there's a new governor—and he's bringing order to this territory. Tell them I started with Holt."

But I am the one he looks at, and there is a deadly warning in his eyes.

# 74

# NEWTON

I REIN IN BEFORE HARRISON TERHUNE'S SPRAWLING ranch house and dismount, ignoring the hands that stare at me as if they cannot believe their eyes.

But I am not afraid. Harrison Terhune might be playing dirty, but he cannot afford for even the suspicion of a killing to fall on him. He's felt the shadow of the noose, and that changes a man.

"Is your boss home?"

The man just nods, but his hand won't stop hanging over his gun. These hands of Harrison's are a suspicious set, carrying iron around the yard.

I unbuckle my gunbelt and carry it folded up in one hand. This way there can't be any confusion about my intentions.

I knock, out of habit only, and push through the door.

"Harrison Terhune?"

I catch him standing over the hearth, a stack of letters in his hands. His face shifts immediately from curiosity to hostility.

"What do you think you're doing here, Newton?"

"I am here to talk."

Harrison gives a bitter smile. "Did you like my wedding present, then?"

"You have a twisted heart if that's what you consider a response to a neighbor's happiness. I never thought in all my life you'd be the first neighbor to betray me."

"You married the girl who came out here to marry me. How is that not a betrayal?"

"You know it wasn't like that. She tried to go back and was forced to return. What should I have done, left her alone in a frontier town?"

"She is the one that chose that."

"And would you have her marry you by force?"

"Of course not! But you poisoned her against me."

"I did no such thing, and you know it."

"The same way you did not poison those water holes?"

"I'm not the one who moved against you, Harrison, I swear. I've done nothing to harm you save telling a young woman a few things about your past—things you didn't see fit to tell her, even though she used the last money she had in the world to come out here for you!"

"It wasn't your business."

"I did what I thought was right. I said only the truth about you."

"Only the truth? Did you ever think that if a man has put a thing behind him, it is behind him? Even outlaws can be pardoned. I was used and I made a mistake, and I owned it."

"It was a pretty big mistake."

"Big enough that I should never deserve happiness again?"

"Big enough that she needed to know before you married her. Marriages, like any other partnership, are built on trust. And you are obviously incapable of that."

A spasm crosses Terhune's face as if I've hit him. "Leave. There's nothing more for us to talk about."

"I will," I answer calmly, "if you leave my land alone."

"And you?"

"I never touched your land. If I wanted to hurt you, wouldn't I enjoy telling you, not deny it up and down? Use your good sense, man."

Harrison storms past me out onto his porch and I am left in the silent house.

The ghosts of yesterday seem to hang about this place. It was hardly any time ago that I was here vowing friendship with the April brothers, all of us eating at that table.

And now they're gone. It's all gone.

Harrison comes back with two men.

"I want you to see Mr. Newton off of my land. And you let the boys know—if he sets foot on my land again once he's crossed the boundary, shoot him."

# 75

# SELBY

THE MOUNTAIN TREMBLES BELOW US IN LONG, rhythmic quakes. We've been forced to stop for the night while dark is still hours away; the summit looms above us, and the horses cannot go any further. We will camp tonight and press on by foot tomorrow.

There isn't much by way of fuel for the fire, but Jem packed along a little dry wood from further down the mountain, and I am able to find a little bit of dry grass here and there to twist together for a fire starter.

The odd thing about this mountain is that while the hills and crags below were snow-covered, the summit is not.

Everything is melted and even dry. I have never felt it both warm and dry so near a summit. It isn't natural, and we all know it.

Tonight is probably our last night together.

I continue up the uneven rocks, searching for a few more

stubborn stands of mountain grass. The air around me is so thin, the sky so near.

And then I see it: past the rocks, through a crack between the mountains, I can see down beyond the northern edge of the range, and below me is the valley, fair and sun-soaked, green with growing things. Perhaps it is my imagination, but I fancy I see a wisp of smoke from a settler's fire.

It's beautiful.

I stand and stare, thirsty for it like a man offered a swallow of water on a hot day.

It's a gift, a glimpse of my faraway home. I may not live to see it but from afar, but seen it I have.

I stare at it until my heart is full. A tear runs out of one eye and I let it be. Let me cry for beauty and a home just once.

Once, before I steel myself for death.

I bend down and pull up another twist's worth of grass and then I head back to camp.


JEM IS STARTING SUPPER. We're down to beans and bacon grease and the last fistfuls of flour.

"I hope you found something," he says with a smile. "I'm already committed."

"I found some." I kneel down on the rocky ground beside the fire Jem's begun to build, and I feed the twists of grass into the sparks.

"Where's Alan?" I ask.

"Scouting out a spot for the horses for tomorrow. If we can't take them, at least we can find them a safer spot than this."

I look around at the barren ground. He's right; it's bad ground, completely devoid of forage. I hope, whatever happens, that my dun will be all right.

I reach into my shirt and pull out a match.

"Well, here's to the last supper," I say, a sorry stab at cheer. I strike the match and coax the fire to life.

By the time Alan comes back, the comforting smell of food has invaded these barren parts and the first cup of coffee is cradled in my calloused hands.

"Find anything?" asks Jem, glancing up.

"Sure. There's a plateau just a little southeast of here, they'll do well enough there for a week if needed. They sure won't find anything better that I know of."

He crouches down beside the fire and pushes his hat back.

"Is there snow down there?" asks Jem.

"A little, but it was melting. Wind was bad on the way, though."

"How far is it?"

"Oh, a few miles. One of us can drive them down while the others start in the morning, I imagine."

"Strange to think we're almost finished," muses Jem. "If such a thing can be done."

"I have hope it will." Alan speaks with a strange surety. "Our paths have all led us here, and to—this mountain."

"Did you see something?" Jem looks over at his brother sharply.

"Do you remember how Sikes spoke of rivers of gold and silver? And how Jesse Thatcher said it looked that way too? Right before the mountain collapsed?"

"Yeah?"

"Well, I've seen rock, dried rock that looked melted. It was gold, Jem."

"Where?"

"Scattered here and there. I saw it while I was scouting."

"Well, I'll be." Jem laughs and shakes his head. "Perhaps that old fellow was right."

I take a deep breath of the stiff mountain air and close my eyes. I hadn't much doubt at this point, but this drives it home.

Signs upon signs.

"What do you reckon?" asks Alan, drawing up his knees and wrapping his arms around them. "All those years back, I'd never have believed I'd actually go, at Sikes's behest, to a far mountain of legend. But now that I think on it, he always seemed to talk to me that way. As if he knew."

"He never spoke that way to me." Jem ladles out a generous portion to each of us. "But, of course, Alan was always the quietest. Maybe Sikes figured he'd take in more than Max and I."

Alan just chuckles.

The sun is beginning to set to the west, the palest stars coming out over the fading canopy of eastern sky.

It's a muted, gentle dusk.

"I always wanted to see the ocean," says Alan quietly. "Not the one back East, but the one they say is out beyond these territory lines, bright as the sky. I always figured it would be quite a sight."

"I reckon it would."

"Max and I always said we'd go find it after you came home from the war, Jem. It's how I consoled him when he had to go to the Auki. But once you got back, I reckon we just got too busy."

"Poor Max," murmurs Jem. "I hate the idea of our ranch going to the land. I was so proud of that house father built, of the cattle line we had, and the way the sun slanted through the trees. It was the most beautiful sight I think I have ever seen."

"Do you know...I would have gotten married if I hadn't come here?" I say quietly. Even if we all die, I want someone in my life to have known, even for a short time, how much I loved her.

This is a surprise to Jém, he nearly drops his plate. "You, married? Who's the girl?"

"I proposed to her before I marched off to the war." I stare into the flames, not trusting myself to look up. "Her name is Beatrice. And then I ran from the surrender, I joined Abernathy, I did things I am ashamed of. After I spent those years in a prison camp, it didn't seem like the right thing to go back. But I met her again. I spoke to her and she didn't care.

She wanted me to come back and settle with her beyond these mountains."

"But you told her no?" Jem's voice is still.

I shrug. "I swore an oath." If it was not my oath-bound duty to be here, I would go tonight, in the dark, without sleep.

"I think," I add quietly, "if I had not done those things, I would not go so willingly to death. But for me, to be on this mountain at all is an honor. Every man has regrets, but you two, I imagine, have far fewer than I do."

"I reckon it never does to compare your past with another man's." Jem pushes his hat back and reaches for the coffee. "A man can excuse an awful lot that way."

"And the other way around," adds Alan.

We scour our plates with the gravel from the ground and stow our packs, ready to go for tomorrow, even if we won't be bringing them.

Old habit, I suppose.

Jem banks the fire for the night and Alan pulls out his bedroll.

"I'll take the first watch," I volunteer, as I do nearly every night.

Alan stretches, looking up at the night sky. "There's no need, Jack. Out here, I don't think we need to set a watch."

I lay back on my bedroll and thrust one arm under my head.

The stars above me lace the night sky with a thousand spidery lines. Pictures and stories, the heroes I thought I'd be someday when I was a boy, dreaming glory. How dusty those dreams became.

And here I am, a broken man, perhaps, but one who has found his place in them. It was a bad road getting here, but it has brought me to a place that I could nearly call fulfillment.

I am content.

I WAKE with no memory of the darkness. The pale light of dawn stretches its rays over the rocky ground.

I slept through the whole night.

# 76

# ALAN

Our goodbyes are simple. What do you say after months of travel together, years of knowing each other? What do you say to a brother you've grown up admiring, knowing you're probably seeing him for the last time?

Jem will take the horses down to the plateau. We drew straws, and his was the short one. Jack and I will head up the mountain, and my brother will follow as he can.

"I'll see you after," he says, holding out his hand to me.

"There may not be an after," I say, taking his.

"I'm saying it anyway. Look, if you make it out of here and I don't, you live for me, you hear?"

"If you'll do the same."

"Of course."

He throws his arm around my neck and hugs me close. He's all hard muscle and cold mountain air and dry, clean horse smell. It's gray today; otherwise his hair would be the color of the sun.

No, there's nothing to say that hasn't been said. Nothing we don't know of each other's hearts. To say much more would only be repeating what neither of us needs to say.

He tousles my hair and I laugh, deep in my chest, with all the air in my lungs.

"Be careful, brother," he says. "I love you."

"I love you too. Tread careful on those paths."

"I will." He gathers the reins of our horses.

Jack Selby is saying goodbye to his dun; he presses his forehead to the dun's and whispers a brief word. Then he hands him off to Jem with a quiet smile.

"Watch that rear hoof," I call after my brother, nodding to my roan. "It's dry and cracking a little."

"I will!" he shouts back.

Then he's gone, around the side of the sloping mountain.

THE ASCENT GROWS ONLY STEEPER AS Jack and I tread the twisting deer paths upwards. We don't speak, save for a "watch your footing" or "easy there" as we fight our way upward. Jack's face is straight and cool as marble. He's traveling light, just a knife and a canteen. He clearly doesn't expect to live much past today.

We reach a tricky spot—a sheer climb up about six feet by your fingers and the toes of your boots. I shed my light pack and jump to get a hold. Jack shoves me up and I gain footing above.

"Would you like a hand?"

He smiles and reaches for mine. I haul him up and we survey the ground around us. There are two paths, splitting off. The tremors in the ground are actually lessening up here, near the top, but the air is thinning.

But below us—below us nearly takes my breath away.

It's the Western Territory we've just crossed, spread out to the south, stretching east and west as far as the eye can see. Rivers in shining bands, distant flecks of color that are fields—wild, plowed, burned even, and trees and dust-swept flats.

It's as if the whole territory has been represented below us and we get a glimpse, just a small one, of the world we've come to free.

"It's like poetry," whispers Jack. The wind whistles past our ears, blows through our hair, thin and cold.

I look at him and smile. "It almost makes me feel all the terrible things I've seen might just have been worth it, for this."

He looks out over the expanse with a faraway look in his eye, as he does in the evenings when he quotes poetry.

"It may be that we will not live to see the glad ending," he recites. "But when we are gone, these darkened fields that have held so much sorrow—they will be called glorious."

"Glorious," I echo softly. "I think you might be right."

·  ·  ·

WE SPLIT ON THE PATH. He takes the eastern fork and I the western, and he's lost to my sight. The path before me winds out and then steeply upwards again.

It ends in a crevice—the mouth of a cave. Above it, ancient, is painted a white stag.

Drawing my gun and leaving my pack on the ground outside, I step into the cave, and I do not look back.

Inside, it is not dark; there is a golden light radiating from within. A steep path winds downward and I follow it, deep into the mountain.

For an hour or more I follow it as the air around me grows still and hot and the light grows brighter yet, until it is nearly as bright as day.

And then the path ends abruptly.

I do not know if what is before me could rightly be called a cavern. It's as if the very heart of the mountain has been carved out from below and a towering heap of scaly ridges, tall as the pines, has taken its place. From one such ridge, a river of gold and silver pulses out as a stream, some pooling on the wide ground before my feet, some trickling below to unseen places.

A rush of steam and hot air shoots forth as the ridge shifts and a great groan breaks through the entire cavern.

Above, the ceiling begins to crumble, rocks and dirt falling, and a needle of sunlight breaks through.

This is the Guardian, and he has tunneled upwards from the heart of the earth, now just inches from breaking through the mountain, bringing fire and ash upon our world.

It has been a question in my heart for a year, perhaps two, and now I see it with perfect clarity.

He is the serpent and I am the white stag.

Thrust into the ground between me and the beast is an ancient spear, sun-bleached, its head thrust into the ground.

I pull it out. It is not rusted, not worn.

How such a thing came to be within the mountain, I do not know, but I see my course before me as if I have known it all along.

I have one chance, an impossible shot. Yet I am not afraid. My palms barely sweat.

I grip the sun-bleached shaft of the spear and I start up the scaly hills that rise and fall below me with every hot breath.

Halfway up, I must sit and catch my breath. The heat is almost unbearable; my head is swimming and light.

I take my canteen off my shoulder and swallow down the last of the water. I need not worry about coming back—I must use everything to reach that wound from which the gold and silver flows.

Still, by the time I reach the source of the flowing river, I have sweated away nearly everything, and heat exhaustion is setting in.

*Steady, lad. Not much longer, either way.*

I plunge the spear home.

Immediately the ground beneath me thrashes, twisting, turning, knocking me onto my back. The gold rushes upwards like a spring, strong and hot, and steam fills the air.

A sound like thunder in the mountains rises, crescendos upward so loud I think I will die of the sound alone.

And then a crash like dynamite splits the air and rushes from this place, through the earth and away.

It is still and quiet. My ears ring with it.

I can hardly breathe. Spots of black swim before my vision. But I know, like a needle pulled north in a compass, that I must see the sky again.

I drag myself painfully down, stumbling across the open ground. I black out many times on my way up the path. Sometimes I walk, sometimes I crawl.

How I manage it I do not know, but at last fresh air breaks over my face as I drag myself out onto the cool ground.

It is the golden time of day, when the sun is magnificent before setting.

The world swims around me, but I can see the colors of the land below me. I drag myself up against the rocks, prop myself up to face the valley.

A ray of sunlight breaks through the clouds and a patch of gentle blue appears. Already I know it—this land, these people, they will be all right.

I close my eyes, draw in another slow, heavy breath. The sun warms my face as I fall asleep, and I know that if I never wake, even so, it will be well.

# 77

# SELBY

THE LAST THING I REMEMBER WAS THE MOUNTAIN shuddering, beneath me and then beyond me all the way down, the way a shiver runs across a mustang's back.

Now here I am, covered in dust, staring at the empty sky, the breath gone from my lungs. Have I been laying here minutes? Hours?

I dig one elbow into the ground and haul myself up.

A stab of pain shoots through my shoulder and arm. My chest hurts, but I force air into my lungs again and again until I can breathe well enough.

I check my arm—I think it's just bruised and strained.

My face is bleeding all down my neck and into my collar. I find a patch of melted snow in a hollow and wash the sticky, half-dried blood off. It's a decent gash that will need stitching, and I don't have needle and thread with me.

I untie my handkerchief from around my throat and press it against the cut.

The world is so still.

The mountain has fallen into shadow as the sun has dropped behind the western side, dusk falling over everything; but this is a different sort of stillness.

The air is still. The mountain is still. The only thing I can hear is the high pitched whine in my ears, left from the last earthquake.

It's no longer restless. Somewhere, a bird begins to sing, light and hesitant, the way they do in early spring.

I crane my neck upwards—the path is gone, covered in rock. I could go back and try to find Alan or Jem, but I have a feeling that whatever we came for just happened. And the light is fading quickly up here. It will be even darker further down.

I start back down the path, stopping now and again to call Jem and Alan.

"Halloo, Jack!" It's Jem.

I limp down to him.

"Have you seen Alan?" His face is grim.

"No. We split on the trail up that way. I haven't seen him since."

"Well, you're bleeding something awful."

"Rockslide," I reply.

"Yeah, it hit me too. I've got a bad cut on my leg."

"Need stitching?"

"I took care of it already. I'll do yours if you'd like."

"It's all right."

"Nonsense, man—I'll do it." He slings his pack down.

So right there on the trail, kneeling in the dirt and wet rock, he cleans it off and puts in a few stitches.

"That'll do you for now," he says, eyeing his work with approval. "Didn't hurt too much?"

I shake my head. I don't feel much of anything right now.

"Show me where you and Alan split."

He follows me as I head down to the fork and up the other side. It leads out to a flat place, then steeply upwards.

My sore body protests the climb, but Jem pushes ever faster.

At the top, lying peacefully against a wall of rock, is Alan, lying as if asleep.

His face is white and still as a marble statue, and his clothes are torn and burned in places.

"Alan." Jem kneels down beside him, takes him in his arms. There's something so tender in the way his strong hands hold his brother, I daren't touch him even to feel for a pulse.

But I know the answer.

"He's gone," whispers Jem. He presses his face to his brother's hair and kisses him. "Brave lad."

Gently, he crosses Alan's hands on his chest and lays him back onto the ground.

I wonder what he could have met that left him thus, burned in a few places, but not many—dead, as it were, of exhaustion.

Jem stands up, dusting off his hands quietly.

"It's too dark to head down now, too dark to bury him without light." His voice cracks. "He was the best of us. He truly was."

"He looks peaceful," I say, knowing it is little comfort.

But Jem puts an arm around my shoulders anyway.

"Noble heart, I wonder what sights you saw," he whispers.

Above us, the stars are coming out, scattered across the night sky. I count two, three, four comets streaking through the sky.

Jem looks up.

"Jack, the stars have changed!" His voice is reverent. "The stag has fallen on the mountain. But the serpent—the serpent is gone!"

I look up where he points, and I see it is true. The serpent is gone.

He lets his breath out in a choking laugh.

"He did it. Beautiful boy, you did it."

# 78

# THATCHER

THERE HAVE BEEN TREMORS ON AND OFF, GROWING LIKE a muttered threat, tying my stomach in knots with memories that I only half remember but haunt me anyway.

But this one, the one that just ripped through the ground below us, was different. It was as if a blast of wind from an explosion had gone over us.

It frightened the horses. They plunged and ran themselves hot and slick in their pens. The hands are out there now trying to make sure the yearling colts don't jump the fence.

But Archer, when it happened, stood up as if he'd heard a distant call. And he stood facing the west as if trying to hear it again.

Then, over the hills, I heard the rumble of thunder, and the wind picked up, sweet and cool, smelling of rain.

It is too much to hope, perhaps, that something good will

come after bad upon bad, but I have always been too much of an old fool.

I am hoping from the very bottom of my soul.

Kate comes out from the ranch house, her hair in a braid.

"It almost looks like rain," she says. Her eyes go to me, just me, standing against the post of the porch, trying not to lean on my cane.

But she says nothing.

"How do you like being an outlaw?" I ask her.

She laughs and tosses her braid over her shoulder. "I am not an outlaw. I am an outcast. I wouldn't go back to that old town anyway."

I snort. "I have heard there might be rewards out for us soon. We're dangerous to them."

"We haven't done anything."

"I don't think Maria needs a reason. She'll find something."

"And Max?" She looks at me.

"Max has lost his way, but he isn't cruel. He's a Swift deep down."

Kate just shrugs.

"Are you hungry?" she asks.

"Sure." I am not very hungry, but a man should eat. These are strange and uncertain times.

She just nods and goes back inside.

The clouds are hanging dark and ominous over the nearer hills now. Archer comes around the side of the house and climbs slowly up the porch steps.

"Tagweiah says that the white stag has been slain." His voice is tight, and there's a note in it I cannot detect.

His face is still and his jaw clenched, his eyes gazing out on the land beyond the corrals.

"What does that mean?"

Archer doesn't answer.

From somewhere beyond the corrals, I hear a lone voice singing, clear and strong and mournful. It's the Auki song for the fallen warrior.

A drop hits the hard dry dust, and then another. The air over the distant hills turn blurred and gray and somewhere down at the pens, one of the hands lets out a whoop.

Sheets of rain sweep down over us, powerful as a herd of running cattle, pounding over the roof of the porch and the ranch house.

Kate runs out onto the porch, her skirt held up in one hand.

"It's raining!" she gasps. "It's raining!"

She runs out into it, her arms outstretched, her face lifted to the gray sky, laughing. Her laughter and Tagweiah's lament mingle together in harmony with the driving rain.

"It means—" Archer turns to me and I see tears streaming down his face. "It means the curse has been broken."

"Broken?"

"Broken." A smile spreads slowly across his face, and he lets out a sobbing laugh. "We're almost there, Jesse." He throws his arms around me in a crushing hug. "There's hope for us yet."

He runs past Kate and out to the barn.

More men are coming onto the porch, some out of the house to see, some out of the rain for refuge, their voices excited.

This means the drought will end, the rivers will flow, the cattle trails can be used, and the stock will arrive in good condition.

Kate is next to me now, drenched and panting. I swear, that girl finds everything beautiful.

Archer leads his horse out of the barn, a mere blur in the heavy rain, but I'm well acquainted with how he moves and walks. It's him.

He mounts up and rides out, trotting past the house, headed for the far gate.

I limp out into the rain, sheltering my eyes from the pelting water. "Where are you going?"

He reins in, his horse dancing under him, eager and nervous with the rain and wind.

"I'm going to take the territory back," he says, looking into the rain with a determined grin. "But first, I'm going to see my wife." He lets the horse go and passes in a splatter of rain and mud.

Hang this bad back and hang the doctor's orders. I hobble as fast as I can back to the porch and motion for one of my hands to come quickly.

If Archer's taking the territory back, I am going with him.

# 79

# ROSAMUND

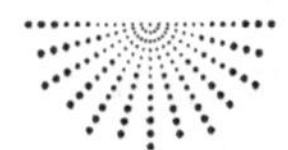

A LONE RIDER COMES OVER THE HILL AND DOWN INTO the valley towards the house. For a moment, I do not believe it. I recognize the horse and the way the rider sits in the saddle.

It's Archer.

I glance around the room and then run out onto the porch to check the yard. I do not see Raymond or Blue. All the better. I gather the skirt of my dress in my hands and I run, I run as fast as I can to meet him.

We meet halfway and he dismounts. No words pass between us—we just throw ourselves into each other's arms.

I can't get close enough to him. My face is pressed into his shoulder, and I drink in the fresh-air smell of him. His coat is damp from riding in the rain.

He is crying, his tears falling hot into my hair.

I missed him so badly.

"Rosamund." He pulls back to look at me, reaching out to cradle my face in his hands. "You ran to see me. Why?"

"I just saw you and that's all that I thought of."

"Thank you." He wraps me in his arms. "Thank you."

I reach up and rub his shoulder.

"I am sorry," he says. "I'm sorry I did not care for you better and I did not protect you when you needed me. I lost sight of you."

"I'm sorry too," I whisper.

"I've been a fool, but if you'll have me back, I swear I will do better. Let's put the past behind us."

"We've both been fools." I reach up and kiss him. "But what brought you back?"

"The curse is broken," he says gently. "Someone out there made it. And now I have to finish it."

"Finish it?"

"I am going to take the territory back. While it's still fresh in Maria's hands, I must try to get it away from her."

My heart sinks, but I love him all the more for his courage.

"I would like to talk to Raymond, if he'll talk to me."

"I don't know where he is, but I don't think he's far." I turn around and see him standing in the gate, his arms folded.

I wonder how long he's been watching us.

"Raymond." Archer takes a step toward him, another when Raymond doesn't move. "I want to talk with you."

"Go on," my brother urges quietly, his arms still folded.

"I want to tell you that for my part, I am sorry. I was not thinking of you nor of her that night, or in the days after."

"You tell her that?" His eyes flick sternly between us.

Archer just nods.

I nod too; I want Raymond to make peace.

"I'm going to take the territory back. I'll go alone, if that's what it takes, but I wanted to ask if you'll ride with me again."

Raymond casts his eye over the land as if he's seeing the whole territory, Glory Mesa, outlaws, and all.

"Well, I'm not bringing my daughter home to this," he says and heads back towards the house.

I grip Archer's hand in mine. That's good enough for me.

THE LIGHT on the table flickers over the map laid flat on the table as Archer, Raymond, and Blue lean over it, hands splayed on the table edges.

"I wish Lesley Gable were here," says Archer, rubbing his chin with one hand. "He was laying plots for some new buildings out to the south. I don't know how far they've come."

"I could ride down and scout," says Blue. "Or send a couple men."

"It's dangerous," says Raymond. "There's a lot of open territory there between the hills and the town. I wouldn't, not yet."

"Shouldn't we strike fast?" asks Blue. "The longer we

wait, the more's the chance he'll find out what we mean to do."

"Is he sending out scouts?" asks Archer.

"He's breaking folks in fast," says Blue. "He had Holt tried and hung like that." He snaps his fingers. "We shouldn't underestimate him."

"Well, Holt's been asking for that a long time," says Raymond slowly. "There was no love lost between him and those Swift boys, I can tell you. But I agree Max is dangerous, and because of that, I don't want to rush in."

"I never thought I would be planning an attack on Glory Mesa," Archer sighs, just to himself. I reach out and rub his shoulder gently.

"We could come in on the train," says Blue. "My boys know how to hijack a train."

Archer looks at him slowly, eyebrows raised.

"During the war," adds Blue, just in case.

"We could use that as a diversion," says Archer. "Start something down near the depot and then smuggle our other men in from the south. If we come from any other direction now, we'll be spotted too soon. We need to be able to get into town and clamp down on the main places—Maria, the governor's office, the boardinghouses and saloons where their men will likely be."

A knock sounds on the door, startling me. Raymond and Archer both look at it as if expecting bullets to follow.

The knock comes again.

"It's me, Jesse! And it's darker out here than a black steer in a tar pit."

I rush to the door and open it. It is Jesse, as he said, barely visible in the dark, shoulders hunched sheepishly.

"Jesse! What on earth are you doing here? Come in, out of the dark."

He gives me a wry smile as he limps past me, into the house. He is looking better. He's walking, at least.

I take a match and light a lantern outside the door.

"You may as well leave the door open," comes a voice down by the gate, in Kate's dry tones. "I'm coming up too, and Tagweiah was behind us."

I leave the door and run to get Jesse a comfortable chair. He may be stoic, but a ride all the way from his place must leave him in considerable pain.

I find a chair with arms, drag it over to the table as he's greeting the men, and put a pillow against the back.

"Rosamund, you sure know how to make a man feel his best," he sighs gratefully.

Kate comes in and sets down her saddlebags, looking at the table with silent interest.

"Jesse, Kate, tea? Coffee?"

It's tea for Kate and coffee for Jesse, and as I pass by with the pot, Blue holds out his cup for more.

"We were talking about getting into Glory Mesa," says Archer. "I mean to take it back."

"Jesse told me on the way," says Kate. "There's no

chance of you coming from the northeast as Mortimer did. The trail's too busy now."

"We were thinking the southern hills," says Archer. "It's the only place we can go where we won't be seen beforehand."

Tagweiah comes in quietly, giving me a respectful nod and declining a drink.

"It's a mighty long stretch of flat though," says Jesse. "They'll mow us down."

"Not if they're not looking. Blue thought we could hijack the train coming into town and then we'd have a diversion."

"It would be ideal if we had a couple men on the inside," says Raymond. "Maybe we could talk to Sam. He runs the line between Saycook and Santos Flores now, but he could arrange to get the stage into Glory Mesa."

"If he can find Peter, Peter could do the rest." Kate looks at the faces around the table, businesslike. "I know he can."

"I'd want Carson, Gable, Trasker, and Doctor Everett," says Raymond. "They wouldn't need to do much. Just a signal in the window, maybe lock a few doors."

He looks around at the table, his hand pressed on the map. "We can call in favors with a couple of the outlying ranches too, if they'll come. Particularly Cristobal Newton. Maybe Terhune. He's a good shot, and he owes us, I reckon. Could a few of your men go round 'em up, quiet-like?" He looks to Blue.

A slow smile crosses Blue's face. "My boys don't sleep a wink anyway when they smell a fight."

He heads out into the night, touching his brim to Tagweiah, who has been listening in silence.

"Do we need the ranches?" asks Kate, sounding doubtful.

"This ain't poker we're playing," says Raymond. "I don't aim to take chances."

Tagweiah stirs.

"I will ride to the Auki nation and bring back warriors." He looks at Archer alone. "For my friendship and yours, they will come."

"Even to ride against your cousin?" asks Archer.

"He is more than a cousin. He is a brother." Sorrow crosses Tagweiah's face. "But that is why we will ride against him. It may be that what is wrong in his heart can yet be healed."

Archer rubs the bridge of his nose wearily. "Then ride swiftly, my brother. I will take whatever help you can bring."

Tagweiah flashes a rare smile, and he too leaves.

We buried him there on the mountain. Raised his grave high with the scattered rocks. We had no wood for a cross marker, so Jem found pale rocks and laid them on his grave in the shape of a cross. He said a few words with only me and the mountain birds for witness.

We are hungry and cold and hurt and we must go back down the mountain if we are to live, but even so, Jem lingers as long as he can.

"I'll come back and visit," he says, kneeling beside his brother's grave. "I promise."

He puts his hand on the rocks as if they're Alan's shoulder and then stands up, wiping tears from his eyes.

Still he stands there, unmoving, as if trying to form words.

I turn away. It's a time for the brothers to be alone together.

. . .

WE SLEEP below the summit at our former camp, using the charred leftovers to rebuild the fire, and we clean each other's wounds in its dim light. The next morning, we catch our horses from the mountain pasture where we left them. Jem's horse is so content it doesn't want to be caught, but Alan's roan comes over inquisitively as if to see where we might have hidden him.

As for my dun, he is resigned and not unhappy. I whistle to him and he comes.

He stands quietly, indifferent as I buckle the straps on his bridle and lift the saddle to his back—things that are so normal I don't even think about them, yet I never thought I would do them again.

Jem is ahead of me, working quickly. He has his horse readied and he's tying his pack over Alan's saddle.

"Where will you go?" I ask.

Jem gives his pack a pull to straighten it.

"I am heading home to rebuild the ranch. Alan should have a headstone on the family plot. Tagweiah and our Auki cousins will come and we will mourn him as a hero."

"He deserves it."

"And you? After this, no one will have any cause to say you shouldn't settle wherever you want."

"No. I'm going on, north over these mountains." The words are sweet in my mouth.

Jem smiles.

"Good luck then, and godspeed."


So we part ways, probably for the rest of our lives, as if we haven't just lived through a miracle and a hundred near-deaths.

Jem ponies Alan's roan behind him, trotting off in the direction of the rising sun. Back toward the hills and flats and cliffs that held me prisoner, yet also offered me my redemption.

I mount up, settle into my worn saddle as I have a thousand times.

During all my years as a wanderer and an outcast, I had given up hope. To feel it again is strange, ill-fitting. But I could get used to it.

I turn my face to the north and I do not look back again.

# NEWTON

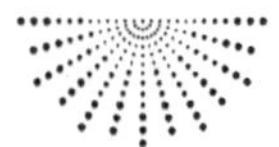

THE MOMENT I HEAR HOOVES, I KNOW SOMETHING IS wrong. It is too early for even the cowhands to be up, and if they were, they'd not be riding like that, or in such large numbers.

I move the quilt over carefully so as not to disturb Hannah and roll out of bed. If it's Harrison Terhune or his men, I'd rather she stayed upstairs, safe.

I hear boots approaching the door even as I am reaching for my coat and gun. I open it sharply on a man with his hand raised to knock.

"Odd time to be coming to a man's house," I say. My gun is in my hand, held out of sight behind the door.

"It couldn't wait," he says. "I'm awful sorry about waking you."

"Who sent you?" I look past him at a cluster of riders, worn-faced, grim, a few of them carrying lanterns.

Harrison's face is illuminated in the harsh light of one.

"What's this?" I demand.

"Terhune hasn't anything to do with it. He warned me he might not be welcome."

"He isn't."

"Hear me out." The man steps closer to the door. "I've come from Raymond Lacey. He asked for you by name."

"Lacey? What happened to him?"

"Glory Mesa's been overrun by outlaws. Max Swift is their leader, and he's declared himself governor. Marshal Lacey and Governor Scott need help taking the territory back."

"And he wants me." I rub my chin slowly. "I know Max. This doesn't sound like him."

"It's him, all the same. Terhune's agreed to ride with us, him and a dozen of his men. But like I said, the marshal asked for you particular."

I sigh. "I will come. Let me pack my things. Feel free to go over to the bunkhouse, see if there are any volunteers."

"Thank you, sir."

I close the door.

Hannah is standing behind me, her shawl wrapped tightly around her. "What is it?"

"I have to go." I reach out and rub her shoulders. "Glory Mesa's in need of some help."

"Is it dangerous?"

"Yes. But don't worry, I'll be careful."

She looks at me slowly, lovingly, and for a moment she

looks inclined to speak. But she just reaches up and kisses me softly on the cheek instead.

"I will get you something for the trail."

PACKING DOESN'T TAKE LONG. Years of living on the trail and traveling have made that easy. An extra shirt, a couple clean handkerchiefs, ammunition, spurs.

Hannah meets me at the door. If she's afraid, it doesn't show on her face. "There's good journey bread and jerky in here."

"Thank you. I will think of you all the way down the trail."

"Be careful," she says.

"I will." I lean down and kiss her tenderly.

She presses my hand in hers.

"When you get back—"

"What?"

"We'll celebrate. Steak and pie."

"Now I'll think about that too, all the way down the trail," I tease her, grinning.

"I love you."

"I love you too." We embrace one last time and I take my hat off the peg, pressing it solidly onto my head.

"Don't forget about that steak and pie."

"You're the one who would forget," she replies, folding her hands in front of her. "Now get going."

"Not that, I won't."

I give her one last grin and head out the door, shutting it firmly after me.

# CARNEGIE

THE SUNRISE IS A LINE OF LIGHT ON THE FAR EASTERN ridge beyond town, thin as a horsehair. Above it, the sky turns pale gold.

Down here in the southern hills we are without fires, and the air around us is a thin gray. We're chilled and stiff from nights on the cold ground, and the food is dry.

I roll up my bedroll and scan the shifting dark shadows for the slim shape of Peter. He's supposed to be back any time, if not already.

I slip away from the men who are waking up and breaking camp and trudge up the hill just beyond.

Everything is especially beautiful this morning. It reminds me of the morning I walked down Main Street with Trasker, preparing to defend Glory Mesa when we were badly outmatched. Only we're on the other side now, hiding in the same hills where the outlaws were.

"Morning, Kate." Peter materializes from the rocks north of me, his hands in his pockets. His voice is getting deeper every time I hear it.

"Where did you come from?"

He shrugs and gives no answer.

"I was watching the hills coming in from town...why didn't I see you?"

He grins. "I guess I'm just getting better. Or else you're getting worse."

"You're getting better," I answer wryly and start back towards camp.

We find Raymond Lacey talking with Sam. Sam is standing hands on his hips, still in his driver's clothes with his long coat and heavy gloves, the coat drawn back to reveal a pistol in his belt.

"Peter, Kate," greets Sam, touching his brim. "Pleasure."

"What do you have for me, Peter?" Raymond asks, a faint smile in his eyes. I can tell he likes that boy.

"I have the train schedule," he says. "Memorized. And Carson says he'll lock his back doors and shutter the windows and slow patrons down, if it's the right hour, but he won't do anything else."

Raymond just chuckles under his breath.

"Gone soft," whistles Sam.

"Well, if you'd gotten prosperous, you might feel the same," Raymond says dryly.

"What about Lesley Gable?"

"He will do it."

"Is he signaling from his house or from the survey office?"

"Survey office."

"Good, then. Thanks, boy." He holds out his hand and Peter takes it solemnly.

Raymond turns to me. "You better get a move on, Kate. Blue's dozen and Chris are about ready." I glance over to where they're saddling their horses, checking cinches and bridle buckles solemnly.

Chris Newton raises his hand in greeting. I haven't seen him more than a time or two in the last few years, but it seems he still remembers me.

I saddle my pinto, talking to her all the while. This feels like it could be goodbye, and I want to tell her how good a horse she's been.

She stands half-asleep as I ready her, but as I buckle on her bridle, she looks at me and nudges my arm.

I think she understands. She'll take care of me.

Blue's dozen are getting into their saddles, laughing and joking about death. Chris flattens his mouth wryly and gives me an apologetic look.

It's all right. If I put stock in everything said by a man facing his mortality, I'd have been long gone by now.

"You got enough ammunition?" asks Raymond, coming over.

Chris nods. We all have two pistols, some men three. It's going to be hard enough to jump on a train without extra weight. Once aboard, we'll have to make do with what we can find.

Raymond looks us over, one side of his mustache lifting in a smile. "Godspeed."

THE TRAIN CHUGS swift and steady up into the Black Shaft Pass. I find it ironic that this, Mortimer's favorite haunt for sweeping down on stagecoaches, is now ours. Because the pass is so narrow, they won't be able to see us until it's too late.

Two of our men will be jumping down onto the roofs of the train cars—they'll be the ones to go forward and mind that the engineers are safe and out of the way.

My pinto swivels her ears forward and back and snorts.

Sure, she has been around trains, but she can feel the difference in the air this time. She's like me, a little cautious and mostly excited.

"Steady," says Chris as the train approaches. "Easy does it."

My pinto stomps, impatient.

And then he's off, racing with his hand well over his horse's neck, giving him his head as he streaks like lightning after the train.

We're only seconds after him. My pinto needs no urging. She's eating up the hard ground beneath her, running like a true cow pony. I ease her up against the side of the train car, stand up in the stirrups.

Chris reaches out, takes hold of one of the handles on the side of the train car, and kicks off. His horse knifes away and he's climbing over the railing between the cars.

Now or never.

I reach out and grip hard, kick free of the pinto.

She's smart. She peels off from the direction of the train and slows. I left her reins tied loose so she wouldn't catch on anything. We brought an extra man to collect the mounts—a thankless but necessary job. She'll be all right.

"Nice work," says Chris with an approving smile. He looks over my head to check the others. We all made it.

"Let's move." He opens the door through the mail car and we move up into the passenger section.

The first ones to see us start to their feet, Chris holds up his hand in a steady, placating gesture.

"Good afternoon, folks," says one of Blue's men in his gentle drawl. "This ain't really a hold up, but if you'll kindly move yourselves to a car without windows or get down on the floor, we'd be obliged. There may be shootin' in a bit."

There are not many passengers in this car, and most of them are more than happy to give us no trouble. A few head toward the back, the rest hunker down among the seats.

I have no idea what the newspapers have been saying, so I don't know if we'll be hailed as heroes or outlaws.

But I do know this—we are on the right side.

"Guard this car, will you?" Chris thrusts his head beside mine and speaks quietly. "I don't think there will be trouble, but we can't have any before we arrive or the train may not stop at all."

"You've got it."

He gives a nod and jerks his head to the others.

I lean against the wall beside the door, my arms crossed, my pistol in one hand.

The passengers watch me with quiet trepidation. I smile at them, but I am not sure that helps.

My, but the land is pretty from the racing window of a train car.

83

PIKE

I stride out into the hot street and listen to the sounds of violence. The resistance I thought they would be too wise to mount.

Of course, I should have expected this kind of stubborn stupidity from the likes of Archer; but with him being at odds with Raymond Lacey and, consequently, half the lawmen in the territory, I had counted on him being unable to do it.

Never mind. It will not stop me.

"Mrs. Pike, you should be out of the street." It's one of the outlaws I brought in, tall and deep-voiced with a dark beard.

"What is going on?" I demand.

"There's a fight down at the depot. Looks like some outlaws hijacked the train and got in through the station."

"I see. How many?"

"Hard to say. They're still in the cars, mostly. The civilians are sheltering in the depot."

"It would be a pity if one of those outlaws set a fire. They'd hang for sure when we caught them."

A glint comes into his eyes. "But the governor won't like it."

"The governor won't know you've done it. He will blame them."

He hesitates. "What's it worth?"

"Your life and four hundred dollars."

"I'll collect tonight." He touches the brim of his hat and heads away up the street.

I watch from the porch, waiting to see the rush of flame that rises above the depot.

At last it is burning, and with it, I hope, the ashes of Archers Scott's cause.

A handful of men run past from the direction of the station.

"What is it?" I call. "What is burning?"

The bearded one gives me a knowing look. "The depot. Must be one of the outlaws set it—one of Blue Harding's men, maybe Archer Scott himself."

"How horrible. Where are you headed now?"

"There's word of another attack at the south end of town. We're going to repel it."

"What are you doing?" Max storms up to me, his face like iron. He's covered in dust and blood and his hands are stained black.

"I was helping direct the men," I reply with innocence and a touch of hurt in my tone.

It's lost on him. He takes a step towards me.

"And I told you to stay out of this. I am the governor, Maria Pike, not you. Get back in your house and stay there before I find a reason to throw you in jail. I swear, it wouldn't be hard."

Max looks at one of the men and jerks his head. Then he walks on. He doesn't even acknowledge me.

The man obeys him, not me.

He leaves me at my doorstep with an apologetic tip of his hat. "He's governor," he says by way of explanation, as if that were not clear, and leaves.

Max Swift has outgrown his usefulness. I had hoped that the days of keeping him under my thumb were to be longer, but Holt ruined that.

I take a smart green jacket and a holster down from the rack beside the door. With all the bullets flying around, it will be easy enough to do what I must now do.

No one can say I wasn't defending the town, as is good and right. But in case the pistol fails, I take a knife down from a box on the mantel and slide it into my boot.

As sorry as I am that I must be rid of him, he'll be sorrier.

# THATCHER

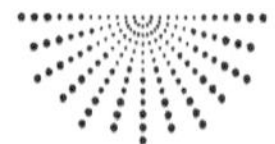

The signal comes, a quick, blinding flash from the rear window of the surveyor's office. The train is in, shots fired at the depot. I hear them distantly, and nearer a bell ringing, calling men to defend the train and the station.

I've wrapped my back up as tight as I can stand it—at the least it will stave off the weakness for a while. It makes me stiff in the saddle, but it's better than not being here at all.

Archer and Raymond ride together in the front, Archer light in the saddle as if he has no need for one, Raymond steady and quiet, ready to ride into any danger.

"When we go, we go hard," says Raymond, turning in the saddle to look at us. "The longer it takes to get across, the more of us are dead."

There are nods, ripples of agreement through the men.

Archer swings his glance back at the men and then to me and Raymond.

"Let's give it to them, gentlemen," he says. Raymond gives him a nod.

He spurs his horse forward and we're off after him, riding as hard and close as we dare, the wind whipping sharp mane into our faces, feeling the pounding of the horses' hooves through our saddles, in our boots, knowing this might be our last ride, the last time the wind blows in our faces, the last time the hot sun beats down on our backs. And for a moment, I don't think we care.

We men are the very spirit of the Western Territory, and it doesn't matter if we're on the winning or losing side of a fight, as long as Archer Scott and Raymond Lacey lead us into it.

We shoot into town like a herd of stampeded cattle, guns blazing, driving hard for the governor's office.

From above us, one of the boarding house windows comes alive with gunfire. Someone is watching their back. Then I see the depot. It's on fire, billowing black smoke rising above it, screams coming from around it. Our men wouldn't have done that. It must have caught somehow— maybe a careless flame knocked over when the shooting started.

"Get around that boardinghouse, check the back alley!" orders Raymond, his voice carrying over the noise. That man has a voice made for war.

Archer turns his horse around and heads for the governor's office. That one is on the other end of town, the furthest objective besides for Carson's saloon.

Raymond motions for half a dozen men to follow and rides after him.

A few moments later, the sharp staccato of rifles, like a firing squad, cuts the air in half. Up the street, I see the smoke hanging on the air, see the horses—Archer's horse—rear up and nearly fall.

A couple of the men are returning fire, but it's not clear where the shots came from. The men are dismounting, ducking into the shelter of the houses and shops beside them.

Another volley of fire comes and the horses run, one of them bleeding profusely. Archer's on the ground, down on one knee. Raymond seizes him and carries him out of the way as more shots come.

"Archer!" The words tear from my lungs like a kick to the chest. "Archer!" I run to him, caught like I'm wading in deep water, my voice muffled, my limbs slow. I duck around the corner as more shots come, and this time we answer with twice the number.

My ears are ringing.

Archer's not on the ground with a bullet in his gut—he's standing there, white and shocked and still.

In front of him, quietly, calmly, Raymond unbuttons his vest and he's blood from rib to hip.

"Raymond," I choke.

Archer and I rush to him at the same moment, as he takes a step and his leg buckles.

"Easy now," Archer's saying, his voice calm and clear. "Don't try to move. We'll get help."

More people rush around us, men sheltering us with their fire, with their bodies. There's a horse, nervous and pulling on its reins.

"Quick, we need a doctor!" It's Sam's voice, shouting. "Get Doctor Everett, someone!"

As if in a dream, I see men rushing forward to hold this ground, block the road, pound on the door of the nearest house, asking to be let in.

Raymond looks at me, direct and sure. "Don't you worry, Jesse," he says. He's calm, but he's out of breath.

And then he's gone, carried off by half a dozen hands eager to get him inside.

The gunfire is dying down. I think we've managed to take this much of the town, at least. I've been in fights, but I forget how fast things can happen and be over.

My back feels hogtied by a hundred ribbons of fire. My right shoulder aches and my fingers are numb and disobedient to my will.

I've had it.

I stumble over to someone's broken and crushed ornamental bush and I'm sick in the dust behind it. Sick until I've got nothing in me.

My knees give out and I let myself crumple to the dust.

I reckon I look like a dying steer, lying here in the sun, but I haven't the heart to care.

# GABLE

THE STREETS HAVE FINALLY QUIETED, SAVE FOR A FEW shots here and there, but I don't think either side has the town.

I don't dare go home yet. A stray bullet could take out anyone moving on the street. I warned Edith there could be trouble—didn't say what—and warned her she should go to the cellar if she heard any shooting. I just hope she's listened.

"Lesley Gable!" I thought I heard my name, but perhaps I'm just a little nervous.

I look up and there's men, a dozen of them, coming towards my office. They're carrying guns and rope.

They know what I did, little though it was.

The door of the office splinters open and they pour in. It wasn't even locked. Hands seize my arms. If I had words to protest with, I wouldn't have the time to get them out.

But I don't. I'm shockingly calm, resigned. I do not regret my actions, and however they found out, I don't care.

I'd do it all again.

They drag me out into the street, shoving me between the shoulders. I can hear the sound of crashing furniture in my office.

"Easy, easy!" shouts one of the men in charge. "Not the surveys, you hear? Not the maps! We need those."

The crashing lessens, but I hardly notice. I'm watching everything unfold as if I'm a spectator, barely caring what happens.

They tie my wrists behind my back and one of the men leans up into my face. "Did you know they were coming?"

I keep silent.

"Did you signal them?" he shouts. He hits me across the face.

To remain silent is as good as saying yes. Saying yes would only serve to further rile them, and I refuse to lie about this.

"Hang him here, from his own office, the traitor!" shouts one.

"Quiet!" The one who seems to be the leader shouts and turns on his men. "Take him to the jail, those were the orders. We'll have no hangings here. We shouldn't be out on the streets."

He jerks his head. "Get moving!"

•   •   •

I'M NOT ALONE in the jail. There are a few vagrants who were only dragged in for questioning, so I overhear, and Carson, who has not been arrested but is having a most heated argument as to his innocence.

One of the men comes to my cell, crouches down on the other side of the bars.

"They're not going to last out there, you know," he taunts. "There's only a handful of them. Holed up in lofts and sheds and houses. They're separated. We'll weed them out in the next couple days, and you'll get a good view of what a hanging looks like."

He smiles.

"You do know what a hanging looks like?"

I don't answer. He wants trouble, and I'm not giving it to him.

"And after you've gotten a good look, it'll be your turn. Or you can tell us who your accomplices were."

I look away. That's enough for him.

"All right." He stands up and dusts off his hands. "We'll find another way."

He leaves the room.

I don't like the way he said that, but I figure many a man's cracked himself just by anticipating bad things to come.

I fold my arms on my knees and rest my head against them. I can't sleep, but I'll rest while I can.

Some time later, the door opens, and one of the outlaws enters, stepping aside to let another in.

"Edith!" I start up, despite myself. She's looking at me, her eyes wide, her lips parted in soft horror.

I want to comfort her, tell her it's all right, but I'm on the wrong side of the bars. I can't do anything about it.

"Get him out of there," orders one. "We're doing it out there."

They unlock the doors and lead me out. Edith is watching me, her eyes afraid. I could have been afraid five minutes ago, but I find I fear nothing now, as I try to reassure her.

I give her a small smile. She just presses her lips together.

We enter the large front room of the marshal's office where several men are waiting. Carson is nowhere to be seen —he must have talked himself out of it.

"Your husband signaled to the southwest this morning, after which there was an attack on Glory Mesa." He turns and looks at me. "Who did you talk to?"

His fist smashes into my face.

"Stop!" Edith cries out. "You didn't even give him time to speak."

"He's had his chance and he doesn't want to," says the outlaw. He's smoking a cigar right in front of her, and the smoke is everywhere.

"You just tell us who your husband talked to, who he planned this with, and we'll stop."

He lands a punch to my stomach and another to my ribs. He's got a fist like stone; my knees buckle.

"Please, no...." Her voice is soft and gentle. The way she

used to speak when we first met, when we were falling in love and she was shy.

"Then tell us," the man demands, and turns on me again.

I cannot tell if she has gone silent or if I am beginning to fade out. I can't hear anything besides the pounding of my own heart, the way the blood rushes in my ears every time he hits me.

He stops. "Well?"

Everything settles for a moment. I feel the throbbing in my ribs now. She's looking at me with the expression she wears when she is angry, yet the light in her eyes is new.

I didn't tell her, but she knows I did it. She knows me.

And she isn't a fool. If they're trying to force her to tell, they must need something they think they can't get another way.

And this I know: my wife can be as stubborn as she pleases.

"Stupid woman, just speak!" He slaps her.

The world rushes up around me in a surge so dark and red that I am at his throat before I even know I've moved. I smash him against the ground and he doesn't stir.

"Lesley!"

I turn as another man rushes me—two of them—and I catch one in the eye socket with my elbow and smash the other one under the jaw with my bound hands.

The rifle he had in his hands clatters to the floor.

I snatch it up and manage to get my finger around the

trigger. They did not tie my wrists as tightly as they should have. "All right, drop them now!"

The remaining two men freeze.

"I said drop them! I can cut you in two with this before you have time to blink."

I'm shocked at the voice coming out of my own head. Somehow I know beyond a doubt that I can make good on my threat.

They drop their guns at once.

"Now get in those cells. Take them with you." I gesture to the men on the ground. Slowly, they take the men—the third is getting up on his own—and head towards the cells.

"Edith, fetch those keys, please." I don't take my eyes off the men. She goes and comes back, her hands pressing mine.

I hold the gun on them while she locks the cells.

"Now shut the door behind us," I instruct softly. We walk back to the main room of the marshal's office together. Edith shuts the door.

It is oddly quiet and there are blood smears on the floorboards. The outlaw's cigar smolders where he dropped it, and I step on it to smother it.

Edith is rifling in the marshal's desk. She emerges with a penknife. "This will have to do." She tilts her head to examine my bonds.

I sit on the marshal's desk, leaving the rifle within quick reach, and I stretch the rope over the corner of the desk so she's got something to saw against.

It takes her a few minutes of hard work, her brows knit

and her lips pressed into a hard flat line, but she soon has them thin enough that I can jerk them apart.

Immediately she moves on to the next task, not even impressed with her own work. "Lesley, you're bleeding." Her delicate hands reach up to dab at my lip.

"I don't feel anything."

"You will as soon as your heart stops pounding so much. Now, are we staying or are we going?"

"Staying." The answer comes to my lips immediately. "We can't risk the streets right now."

"Very well." She gathers her skirt and heads into the marshal's cupboard.

It is so strange to have him gone, to have these rough fellows desecrating the place he made good and safe.

I settle on a chair beside the window where I can watch and make sure no one is coming. She comes around with a cloth and a bottle of witch hazel and drags over a chair.

"Hold still. I will be gentle," she says, tipping the bottle against the cloth.

The feeling of uncertainty that lay between us for so long is gone. She defended me, I defended her. We are not afraid anymore.

I look at her and smile, though I must look rather hideous.

She doesn't seem to see it. Quietly she stands up and kisses me above the temple, where there is no blood or bruising.

"I love you," she says softly.

I reach for her hand and press it gently in mine.

After a minute she goes back to work on me, unbuttoning my shirt and checking my stomach and ribs, though there's not much she can do for them at the moment.

She dabs witch hazel on a spot that's starting to swell and then she sets it all aside.

"What are you going to do next?"

"Watch for a while," I say, wincing as I button my shirt again. "If it gets safer out there, I can take you home and go find wherever Governor Scott and Marshal Lacey are. You should rest."

"I'm not leaving you tonight." She slips her hand into mine and leans her head against my arm. My heart swells with contentment.

I turn my head and lean down to kiss her thick, soft hair.

She laughs under her breath.

A man told me once that this land will make you or break you, but it won't leave you the way you were. I didn't know what to think then. But now I understand. Edith and I, it nearly broke us—I'll admit that to anyone now.

But I think we've made it. And if we keep fighting, side by side, maybe one day folks won't have to.

# CARNEGIE

THE ROOM HE'S IN IS DARK AND THE MEN CLUSTERED outside smell of sweat and horse and acrid smoke, but their voices are soft and reverent. For a day and a half we've held half the town, the men taking shifts on guard.

Little has happened since. Lesley and Edith Gable came to us after the first day, having made a rather brilliant escape from the jail, so I heard. A couple men have been shot since —one killed, one wounded—but Marshal Lacey's shooting is a dark cloud hanging over us all.

Doctor Everett has been caring for him and the others since it started. He hasn't said much, but I don't think it's looking good.

The doctor comes out, drying his hands on a clean towel, and goes to his physician's bag on the table along one wall.

"How is he?" asks Jesse hesitantly.

"Where's his sister?" Doctor Everett looks up grimly. "Can she come?"

"She was sent for as soon as it happened," he replies. "One of Newton's boys is getting her."

"Good. I don't think he's got long."

The world jolts to a halt like I've just been thrown from the saddle. This happens to other people, not to Raymond.

These words don't fit him.

Jesse is calm. He just licks his lips and nods, but he's got his eyes on the ground when he asks softly, "Can I see him?"

"Go ahead."

Jesse goes in and shuts the door.

Word passes through the men in the room. It doesn't take it long, I think, for it to spread even further, for soon there are men crowding the front room, packed so tight one can hardly move.

Even if he'll never see them all, being there is enough for them.

Harrison Terhune comes in from the kitchen, his hat in one hand and his other sleeve rolled up to show a bandage stained with dried blood.

"You wanted to see me?" he asks the doctor.

"Yes, just wanted to look at the arm. Have a seat. How is it feeling?"

"Hardly feel it," he replies gruffly, lifting a chair with his hurt arm and placing it against the wall.

"How are the streets?" asks one of the men. It's still quiet in here, respectful.

"Nothing happening out there." Harrison holds out his arm as the doctor unwraps the bandage. "Chris has it handled. I'm hardly needed. The marshal any better?"

Silence follows the question. No one wants to be the one to say it out loud.

"It's not looking good," I say. Somehow saying it makes it better and worse.

Harrison's face darkens. He looks from me to the doctor. "No?"

"Keep it clean," says the doctor. "Burns get infected too."

The door opens and Archer steps in, parting the way.

Doctor Everett glances up, his hands rolling up the spare bandage and putting it away.

"Doctor."

"Governor."

"How is he?"

The doctor hesitates, and Archer looks at me. I can only stare back, feeling the same weight I felt a few minutes ago at the doctor's words.

"I'm sorry, Archer," he says, slow and measured. "I've done everything I can, and he's the toughest man I've ever treated. But he's not going to make it."

Archer doesn't answer right away. His face is blank.

"How—how long?"

"Hours, probably. A day or two, perhaps, if he hangs on. He's been asking for his sister."

It's painfully silent for the space of a heartbeat. A muscle twitches in Archer's cheek. "Can you tell him something, from me?"

"Of course."

"Telling him I'm going to end it. Tell him not to worry, for the territory or for Rosamund."

He checks his gun, feeding another bullet into the empty chamber and giving it a spin. "Thanks."

He strides out into the hot street.

# 87

# ARCHER

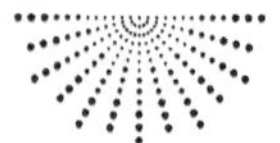

THE STREETS ARE EMPTY. WE DID THAT. CLEARED THEM of life, made them dangerous to walk in once more.

The sun beats down upon the dust, packed and rutted from use and from the rain that passed through a few weeks ago. There are bullet holes in the buildings I pass—bullet holes that we made, firing on our own town. The sky is clear.

I wonder what would have happened if Sikes had been here when they came. What would have happened if I had stayed here, as I should, instead of leaving my post, chasing after Rosamund.

Perhaps he wouldn't be dying right now.

"Max Swift!" I shout, my voice ringing against the closed doors and shutters of the fearful town. "Max Swift! Come out, I want to talk to you!"

A bullet whines past my ear and another buries itself in the dust by my feet.

I keep walking. Nothing's going to stop me now, not until I get to Max.

I shout his name again.

"Archer." He's standing on the porch of the governor's office, under the territorial flag, waving proudly in the wind.

"I have business with you, Max Swift."

"That so?" He comes down and crosses the space between us until he's standing only ten yards away. His hand rests lazily on the butt of his pistol.

"I'm calling you out."

Max grins, chuckles to himself.

"You want to do that?"

"I think you heard me."

"You seemed happy enough to hide behind men and walls before this." His lip is raised in a sneer.

"Raymond Lacey is dying, and I hold you responsible for his death."

"I didn't pull the trigger. You come after me, you take what you get."

"I wasn't the one who snuck in the back door and stole what wasn't mine. Get ready to draw."

Max takes a step back.

There's no one to call between us. I don't dare look over my shoulder, and as far as I can see, Max has no one behind him.

His eyes stare into mine, squinting a little against the bright sun. His hand hovers over his gun. My heart pounds steadily in my ears. It may have been years since I've stood facing a man down like this, but my eyes and my hand know this like they know the feel of the earth or the lines of the southern hills.

Hoofbeats come on the wind, a swift tattoo, distant and growing stronger.

Max goes still, his eyes on the horizon behind me. I turn, slow and easy, and glance back. There's a lone rider approaching, loping over the dusty flats, riding down into town.

It's a roan.

Max doesn't move a muscle. Every line in his body is taut. It's as if he's forgotten that I exist, forgotten that we're gunning for each other.

The horse pauses, dancing, as the rider speaks to a figure up the street—Kate, I think, by the movement. And then he lets the horse go, riding hard up the street toward us.

"What's going on?" the rider demands. I recognize the voice. It's Jem.

He reins in beside me and dismounts, running between us, throwing his arms around Max, who stands white and still.

"Max! I'm sorry—I came too late. I rode my horse nigh to death trying to reach you in time. I thought you were dead."

Jem's hands are roving over Max's head, over his shoulders, as if he cannot believe he's whole.

"I figured you for dead too, Jem," he says slowly. "You didn't come, so I figured you for dead."

"But I did come. I took you back to that cabin—Max, if

I'd thought there was even the smallest chance of you pulling through, I would never have left your side."

Max looks at his brother, confusion giving way to white, sick realization. "It was you." His eyes wander to my face. "Archer—"

Jem turns to look at me, sharply. "What is going on?"

"This is for the territory, Jem," I reply. "It's between us."

"Between you? Max, what have you done?"

Max is staring at the gun in his hand. He looks up at us, the wind blowing his fair hair, his brows drawn in a slow scowl.

"No it ain't, Archer," he says, as if half in a dream. His gaze trails slowly to the porch of the territorial governor's office.

Maria is standing on the edge, one hand grasping the post beside the steps, the other her skirt.

Her lips are curved in a slight smile.

88

PIKE

THEY LOOK SO SURPRISED. AS IF I SHOULDN'T BE watching them. As if I wouldn't know or care about the outcome of this territory's fate.

"Gentlemen!" I step down from the porch into the hot, windblown street. "What's this, a duel?"

It's too bad, really, that it has come to this. I had been hoping to watch them gun each other down. They are both quick, clean shooters.

Both of my problems would have been eliminated without an ounce of blood left on my hands.

But I have never been one to waste time mourning what isn't to be. I do not change my destiny simply because a plan fails.

And Max, I can see, is failing me.

"Maria Pike." Jem meets me in a rush, towering between me and the sun. "I want the truth."

"The truth?" I stop, smiling at him. "About your brother? Which part, the murder of Early's outfit or wresting the governorship from Archer Scott?"

"The part where you—"

I don't wait for him to finish. I seize his shirt and plunge my knife into his side, above the hip.

"There's my answer," I whisper, snatching his gun from his belt. The air rushes from his lungs and he falls to one knee.

I pull the knife from Jem's body and hold the gun to his head. Archer and Max are staring at me, horrified.

"Drop your guns, both of you."

Slowly they obey.

They are so painfully predictable. You threaten a life, and they'll do whatever you say.

"Throw them over there." I jerk my head to the dust, beyond us. This, too, they obey.

And then I bring the pistol up from Jem's head, brush right past him, and aim for Archer Scott.

I am sick of the facade. First it was Sikes, now it is Archer. They've done nothing but stand in my way, taking the glory for themselves without a thought for those who deserved it more.

Archer will pay a dear price for that.

"Maria, no!" The boy steps between us.

"Step out of the way, Max."

"No." His eyes bore into mine. "I don't owe you a thing,

and I never did. If you want him, you'll have to go through me."

"I'll shoot you," I threaten sweetly. "You want your life to end like that?"

"At least I'll have stood for something," he says.

I cock the gun.

"Max." At the sound of Archer's voice, a thrill of victory runs through me. "Step aside."

"I'm sorry, Archer. I won't do it."

"You'd better listen to him," I say softly.

Max doesn't move. But Archer does.

Gently, slowly, he steps out from behind the boy, his hands raised slightly. "Maria, may I speak?"

"Make it quick. And good, because they'll be your last words."

He swallows. "Maria, if you want my life, you can take it. But it won't give you the territory. It no longer matters if I die today or not. This land will endure, and it will do so without you or me."

"Stop it," I snap. He's not even dead, and he's already trying to be a martyr. "Get on your knees. You too, Max."

Max remains on his feet, daring me to fire.

"Max, please," urges Archer, obeying. He thinks his compliance might induce me to spare Max. Again, so easy to control when there's someone he thinks he needs to protect.

Max's face burns with anger, but he obeys Archer as he would not obey me.

I smile. All their struggles, good and bad, have led the two of them to the same place: on their knees before me.

I level my gun. Archer will go first.

A crack splits the air. Smoke clouds my vision as the reality dawns like a lightning flash. I'm hit.

Through the parting smoke, I see a pair of cornflower-blue eyes, grim and hard as stone.

"You—?"

# 89

# ARCHER

Harrison Terhune lowers his gun, smoke trickling from the barrel.

"You are not ruining another life, Maria Pike," he says, his voice low. "Not a single one."

The gun falls from his numb grasp into the dust of the street.

"Jem!" Max scrambles up and runs to his brother who's bent in the dust, clutching his side as blood drips onto the ground.

I'm torn between the two scenes—Max kneeling beside Jem, pulling out a handkerchief; Harrison staring at Maria's body, his eyes dull. My ears still ring from the gun's report.

I get to my feet. "Harrison."

He gives me a quiet nod.

"I couldn't let her do it." He stares at his hand, flexing his fingers slowly. "I'll stand up to the consequences, whatever they are."

"You saved my life and Max's. As far as I am concerned, it was the only thing to do."

"Thanks." His gaze drags from Maria's still form to the Swift brothers. "Does he need a doctor?"

"Please," Max says, unbuttoning his shirt. Harrison turns and runs up the street.

I go over and crouch down beside them. Max crumples his expensive white shirt into a ball and presses it against his brother's side.

"Jem?"

He gives me a half smile through his gritted teeth. "I'm all right, Archer."

"You're white as a sheet," I reply. "Where'd she get you?"

"Above the hip." He gasps.

"Easy, breathe slow," urges Max. He glances up the street. "The doctor's coming."

Doctor Everett appears, trailed by several armed men, among them Tagweiah, Harrison, and Jesse.

The doctor takes one brief look at Maria's lifeless body and turns his attention to Jem.

"Are you all right?" Jesse demands of me. My mild cousin is almost angry. "What were you thinking?"

My gun is still on the ground. I walk over and pick it up, buckling it back on.

"I was thinking of the territory."

"The territory." He shakes his head in exasperation, his

gaze straying to Maria. Tagweiah has brought a blanket and he is covering her.

The doctor and a couple others are moving Jem; the rest stand around talking. I walk up the street, away from the noise.

The world slows around me. I can feel the power of this moment, the significance of it all. The curse is broken, the territory is safe. And I am alive.

The wind picks up, sweeping past me, carrying the low rumble of thunder from the hills.

I STEP out the back door of the doctor's office into the cool night air. The light from the door casts a golden square onto the ground around me and touches the brim of Max's hat. He pulls his eyes from the stars.

"Jem told me Alan did it." His voice is soft. He tilts his head back, looking at the stars. "He changed the constellations, my brother. Who would have thought."

He smiles, but his eyes are still haunted. I wonder if they'll ever be the way they were before.

"The doctor says Jem has a good chance."

Max nods. "He was gored once. Maria's knife was probably a sight cleaner than that steer's horns."

"You cattlemen."

"You were a cattleman once," he cuts in wryly. "Don't forget that."

"I pray I will be again."

"Look, Archer—it's been a bad road, however you look at it." Max pulls out his switchblade and springs it open and shut. "And I did you dirty a couple times. If you want to charge me over it, I won't go anywhere."

I lean against the wall and look down at my hands, worn and calloused. "You know, Max, things aren't always straightforward in life. Just how it is. But what you did today was a good thing, and I think if you took to the trail, you wouldn't find any charges waiting for you when you got back."

He looks at me. "I'll ride out, then. Can I stay until Jem's a little better?"

"I don't see why not."

Again, he looks up, as if reading the stars. "You won't regret it, Archer. I will earn my redemption. This territory wants settling far out, and I can help. I want to see the far west, perhaps the sea. Visit Alan and tell him about it." He laughs, and his voice cracks. "And then I'll come back to the ranch. It's where Pa wanted us boys."

I hold out my hand to him. "Then godspeed, my friend, and a straight path to travel."

90

# NEWTON

THE STREAMS ARE FLOWING AGAIN. WE STOP OUR horses knee deep in the swift, clear water and let them drink their fill.

I lean down in the saddle over my horse's shoulder and fill up my canteen. I drink deep, savoring the cold rush down my dry throat. My horse lifts his dripping muzzle and snorts, pleased.

"I can't say how relieved I am to have these streams running again." Harrison squints up the stream to the bend. "Sure's going to make the drives this year better."

"Better than last year, anyway," I say, shaking my head.

Harrison chuckles low in his throat. He's been quiet, almost resigned, since we rode out of Glory Mesa, but I sense for the first time in a long time that he's at peace.

"Look, Chris," he says after a minute. "If you want to say you haven't forgiven me for that—"

466

"I've forgiven you. As long as I don't have to ride over a mountain's backbone again just to suit your mood."

He laughs. "That's over. I have a temper, I know it."

"I knew it was over the moment you rushed the depot to get us out of there."

"I don't think I could have stopped Blue's men anyway. They were set on it even if it took 'em straight to perdition."

I laugh. "Now if only we all had men that good."

There's a general laugh from the hands at the oblique ribbing.

"Look here." Harrison leans on his saddle horn. "I know you'd like to get home, but I'd be honored if you stuck around tonight. Have a good meal, sleep in a bed. What do you say?"

A murmur of excitement runs through his men.

I want to get home, but this is a fresh start with an old friend, and that's worth a night's delay. "Sure."

Harrison sits up straight. "One of you boys ride on ahead. Tell the cook to start a big meal and spare no expense. The rest of you, let's get a move on," he grins. "I'm hungry."


WE RIDE out of the bottomland toward the clustered rocks that are strewn around the brushland like a child's jacks. As we approach the first formation, I get a sudden feeling of disquiet. Perhaps a dislodged rock or a shadow, but it's brief and strong.

Something slams me back in the saddle. I hear a gunshot.

The world has slowed and focused, and I can feel hot blood soaking my shirt.

The others are shouting, pointing to the rocks just north of us, men scrambling for cover, and Harrison is beside me, helping off my horse, dragging me to shelter behind the rocks.

His men are shooting up at the gunman, preparing for a shootout, but it doesn't come.

"Halloo! Terhune!" the gunman is shouting down. His voice is surprised, panicked.

"No, no, no—" Harrison lets out a short string of oaths.

The gunman comes down, hands in the air, his pistol dangling from two fingers. "What were you doing together?"

He's looking at the two of us, at our hands who have backed away, guns drawn.

No one is sure what to do except for Harrison, who strides right up to the gunman. "What were you thinking? Where have you been? Don't you know this is over?"

The man is inspecting me with hard eyes. He is the sort of man who'd shoot for money, I am sure of it. The sort to get in on a feud if there's one to be had.

"Four hundred dollars, is that what you want?" Harrison shouts, ripping his wallet out of his shirt and throwing it to the ground. "Take it, and if I see your face again—"

He stops himself.

"Go." He pulls his hand off his gun and thrusts a finger out towards the horizon. "Before I do something I regret."

Harrison comes back and kneels down.

"Chris." He reaches for my hand. "Hang on, my boys are going for help."

I meet his eyes. "I have a letter to my wife in my saddlebags. Make sure she gets it."

"I promise."

"It's—it's a hard life for a woman alone."

A wave of pain sweeps over me. I grit my teeth against it. I want to see her one more time.

"I won't let your ranch go down," he says steadily. "I promise. I'll keep an eye out. Don't worry for one moment about that."

"Thank you." It has suddenly become hard to move; a great effort moves my hand only a little.

His voice is thick. "Chris, I wish it could have been me. I mean that."

"I know." I try to laugh but can't. "Wasn't meant to be."

"Forgive me, please."

"It's forgiven. Don't—"

I don't have the strength to pick up where the words left off. It takes too much breath.

Harrison raises me in his arms and I can breathe easier.

"Remember the cliff above the hay fields? The one you can see from your place too?" Every word feels like fifty pounds on my chest.

"Yes." He's leaning close, trying hard to catch every word.

"Tell her to lay me down up there."

"It'll be done."

The sky swims above me, so bright and fighting alive. A good sky to go out under, to join the brave ones who died for this territory. A good land to shed your blood into....

# CARNEGIE

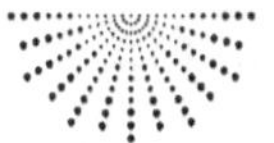

Rosamund comes the following morning, on the train. Once Glory Mesa settled down, we were able to telegraph her that it was safe to come to town.

Archer's gone to meet her at the station. The rest of us have been around the house since the night before, waiting for news of any change. Sometimes a few will go into Raymond's room to see him, but he's been sleeping mostly.

"Here comes the governor," comes the murmur. The men gathered on the porch part as Archer comes through, Rosamund on his arm.

There are no tears on her face, but her eyes are wide, her lips pressed together in worry.

"Doctor Everett." She reaches out to take his hand in greeting. "How is he?"

"He wants to see you," begins the doctor, fishing for words.

"There's no chance then?"

His face falls.

"No. Any other man would have been gone by now. He's been waiting for you, I think." He presses her hand in his. "I'm sorry."

Rosamund just nods faintly. She goes in, followed by Archer first, then myself and Blue.

Marshal Lacey is lying in a four-poster, propped up on a couple pillows. All the color is gone from his sun-tanned face, but his eyes light up at the sight of his sister. Jesse's sitting beside the bed, and as he sees us, he stands up to give Rosamund his chair.

"Rose," Raymond says fondly, moving his hand on the blanket toward her. She takes it in hers and leans over to kiss his forehead.

"How are you feeling?" she asks gently, but he waves her off with an "aww" and a faint shake of his head.

"I don't have much time, darling."

"The doctor told me."

"Listen, Rose, I don't want you to be sad. You're young and you have a good man who loves you. You go live and be happy for me."

"I will," she says, her voice thick but steady.

"One thing, promise me." He grips her hand tighter. "Bring my little girl home."

"Yes, Raymond."

"You bring her home, promise?" His voice is stronger.

Rosamund reaches up and smooths his hair back from

his damp forehead. "I promise, Raymond. We'll find her. We'll raise her out here."

"Good." He lets his breath out in a sigh.

It's quiet, but I hear his breath still fighting in his chest.

"Open the window, Rose?" he asks. "I want to feel the wind on my face."

Quietly, Rosamund stands up and goes to the window, moving aside the curtain, letting the sunshine fall across the room, across the bed. She pushes the window open, letting in the fresh Western Territory air.

It's a beautiful day.

He closes his eyes, and I really do think he was waiting for her, because a few moments later, he's gone.

Rosamund presses his hand to her lips and begins to sob silently. Archer puts his hand on her shoulder.

Blue and Lesley Gable are in the doorway, heads bowed, hats off, and Jesse is weeping, tears streaming down his face.

The air smells so wild and strong, it's almost calling me. Sunbeams pour across the room of mourning, so bright it feels wrong.

The world shouldn't be this blazing alive with him gone.

# ROSAMUND

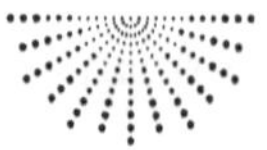

HE'S IN HIS OFFICE, WORKING AGAIN. DESPITE THE boarded up-window, despite the scrubbed boards still stained with blood.

It's just like the early days.

The thought feels like jagged glass in my heart. Those days are past, and they took the best and brightest with them.

He glances up and sees me.

"Rosamund." He smiles and gestures for me to come over. "Watch your step, the boys are still cleaning all this up."

I come over and sit down beside him.

He takes my hand in his free one. "Did you need something?"

"Just you."

He squeezes my hand and keeps writing.

"I was talking with Jesse," I begin, giving him time to

acknowledge me. "He might be willing to go East with me and see a doctor there, while I look for Ida."

"Really?" Archer looks at me, his eyebrows raised. "I'd never have thought it of him."

"Well, you are going to be busy here, cleaning up." I lean my head against his shoulder. "And I want to take care of my promise as soon as possible. Poor girl—"

I can't go on unless I want to cry again. I've been crying constantly, it seems.

"What would you think if I came with you?"

"Really?" I sit up, my heart lifting.

He meets my eyes, a question in them. "I won't make the decision for certain until you tell me what you think, but—I want to resign. Blue's getting sworn in as marshal tomorrow, and with Maria gone and things settling down as they are, I think this place can get along just fine without me."

Now I am crying. We could be together, for real, out on our land.

All the other dreams—of glory, of being history, of children and a large happy family—I cannot control those. But I can love what I have, and he's right here in front of me.

"I've already put in an order of lumber to be delivered to Jesse's—I mean, our ranch. Is that all right?"

I nod briskly through the tears.

"I know you enjoy life in town here more than I do, and the ranch is pretty far from all this. There'd be little reason to come back. Supplies now and then, maybe." He seems hesitant.

I twine my fingers into his and look him in the eye through my drying tears. "Those things don't matter anymore. I want to see purple sunsets with you on our front porch and wake to the sounds of birds among the sagebrush. I want to live where your heart is, not just visit it. That's the land you used to write me about."

"I did."

He leans over and kisses me, and for the brief space of that kiss, all the hurt in the world is washed away.

"I should tell Jesse you are coming East with me," I say. "I hope he doesn't change his mind."

"I won't let him." There's a twinkle in Archer's eyes. "I'll be home in an hour."

I smile and step out onto the porch. The wind blows, picking up the afternoon dust and swirling it in the street. The street is quieter than usual, but when I first came to live out here, we would have called it bustling.

This town has found its feet, thanks to Archer. Thanks to Raymond and the men who rode with him. We made history after all, though not the history I imagined, and certainly not the history Mortimer dreamed of on those hot, wild plains.

And I do not mind saying goodbye.

## THATCHER

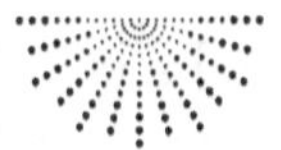

THEY SAY LIGHTNING NEVER STRIKES TWICE IN THE same place, but whoever said that has never lived out here, in the Western Territory.

It feels like a dream I'm dreaming again, but this time, I cannot find Raymond's tall frame in the crowd.

It's the same picture. Pale blue sky, green valley spread around us—a sea of black. The wind blowing our hair, the jackets of our suits, the skirts and veils of the women.

There were many for Irene Lacey's funeral. There are too many to count for Raymond's.

And even with all these people, it is quiet.

I'm beside Archer, Rosamund on his other side. There were remembrances earlier, most of us who knew him— myself, Jem, Kate, Lesley Gable, a dozen more—all sharing pieces of the man we'd come to say goodbye to.

But now, at the graveside, Archer clears his throat to

speak. He's wearing the suit he normally hates, with his graying hair brushed back and his collar uncomfortably high.

But now it seems to fit him.

He clears his throat, thanking everyone for coming.

"This territory knew Raymond Lacey for only a short time. Less than it has most of us." Archer clears his throat again and raises his voice to be heard better. "Yet the mark he has left on it will last long after we're all gone. He was a great man, and he's left a great hole behind him."

Rosamund stands solemn and dignified beside her brother's grave, roses in her hands.

The men who had carried him out, the men who'd rode with him over half this territory, bringing peace, step up to lower him in.

Rosamund steps forward alone and bends down to her brother's casket. Gently, she plants a kiss in the roses and lays them on the fresh pine wood.

She doesn't cry as he goes into the ground.

The wind seems to do it for her, picking up, whipping through the grass, blowing the black of our mourning clothes like flags.

Tears fill my eyes and blur the landscape.

It's not fair. A man as tough as Raymond Lacey doesn't die. His kind rides off into the horizon. He shouldn't have been the one to die fighting arrogant ambition.

Rosamund begins to sing.

The wind cuts her voice in and out, but it is steady and beautiful. It's the song of the hopefuls, the one sung by a thousand voices, most in graves by now. It is picked up now by a hundred voices, sweet and reverent.

But I can still hear hers most of all, tender and for one person alone.

*Let us go to the fields and be merry.*
*Do not cry, do not be afraid;*
*For we shall be glad in the abundance of the earth,*
*And we shall dance together in fields of plenty.*

It doesn't feel true, this mourning, even as my throat chokes and tears roll down my face. I reach up and wipe them briefly with one knuckle.

It just ain't right.

THERE'S a big meal at the house. With so many people traveling days, even weeks, to get here, some even from out East, a meal is warranted.

But the food sticks in my throat. I can't hardly eat more than two bites. I find myself wandering outside, into their picket-fenced yard.

It's like he could just come riding right over that hill to join us.

I keep thinking of things I want to tell him. Who came to honor him, a fine thing someone said about him.

It's like my heart just can't understand he's gone.

"Jesse." Rosamund comes down from the porch and crosses the grass to me. "How are you?"

"I should be asking you that." I hold out my hand and she takes it.

"He's at rest and—I think that will become a comfort, eventually." Tears fill her eyes.

I hug her gently as she wipes her eyes with a handkerchief, composing herself as neatly as the handkerchief she folds.

"You're a fine man, Jesse," she says with a little smile. "Raymond thought the world of you, he really did."

"Thanks." My blasted voice is going to fail me.

She heads back up the lane to greet another guest, and I shake my head. Everyone's got their failings, sure, but Rosamund Scott is strong.

I look out at the land one more time, imagine how it must have looked when he first clapped eyes on it, untouched and open.

No, he's not gone. Not entirely. While the wind is still here, blowing dust and combing through the green grasses he walked in, while the morning sun still washes over these boards and windows he put in himself, while this territory stands strong on the foundation he built—he won't be gone.

I stick my hands in my pockets and turn back towards the house.

# CARNEGIE

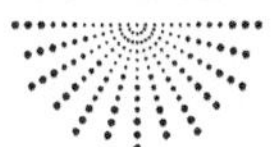

I PAUSE ON THE STEPS OF THE MARSHAL'S OFFICE, almost not wanting to go in, to break the spell and know that it has changed.

It feels like an eternity has passed since I asked Archer for my favor. And now the man I shot carrying tin for Raymond Lacey is wearing the marshal's tin.

I take a deep breath, raise my chin, and go inside.

"Good morning, Kate," greets Blue, setting down his newspaper. "You heading out at last?"

"Yes."

"Can't say I'm not sorry to see you go. You were a good deputy."

"Thank you. I am sure that you will have everything well in hand without me. You make a good marshal."

"I'm obliged."

The paper he was reading is a feature on Raymond

Lacey, hailing him as a hero, talking of the exploits done under his leadership.

Talking about us.

We're just words on the page to them. That's all we'll ever be. They won't know how our hearts beat strong in our chests, how we wept over each other's graves, how we bled into the dust of the earth.

"Archer said you have the guns he used to have in his office?" I ask, looking down at Blue, who is eating an apple now.

"Right, yes. He sent them over, said you might want them."

He takes a key out of his pocket and unlocks a drawer in a desk along the back wall. I slide it open, look at the pearl-hilted pistol, the one with the bullet scar on the barrel. Four of them.

I take them out, one by one and put them into my satchel.

"I see you're still carrying my .45," says Blue with a smile, pointing to my holster.

"I'll give it to you as a going away gift," I offer.

"Nah, you go show her the world."

I laugh.

"Well, goodbye Kate." He stands up and holds out his hand. I shake it.

I always figured this moment would come with me shaking Marshal Lacey's hand.

"I'll see you," I reply.

I step out onto the porch and then down to the hitching rail where my pinto is tied. I fasten the satchel up behind the saddle and then untie my mare, mounting up.

It's strange, riding out of town for the last time. Seeing Trasker's mercantile still standing, even through fights and fires and bad men, see the stage office where Sam and Barnes will be coming in, later in the day. Pass Carson's saloon, and for even that, I feel a stab of longing. Longing and pride for the girl who scrubbed her white hands red, dreaming of the day she could go join the wild spaces and watched those she admired ride out into them.

The wild spaces that are now haunted with their memory. The dust their boots tread whispers with their presence, as if you could turn around and they'd be here, standing before you.

Peter is waiting for me at the edge of town. I don't know how he knew I'd be coming this way, but I am glad.

I rein in and dismount.

"Goodbye, Peter."

"Bye, Kate." He gives me a little smile.

"There's room for two on this trip," I offer. "I could wait for you." It's spur of the moment, but I feel I can't leave it unsaid either.

"No. I'm going to stay here. Glory Mesa needs someone to look out for it who remembers the people who used to live here."

"I'll miss you."

"I will too."

"I won't forget you, Peter, not ever."

He thrusts his hands into his pockets. "Neither will I, Kate."

I reach out and catch him into a tight hug. He's too old for those. I realize in a flash that he's a man now and I missed entirely that stage where he was in-between. Maybe he never had it.

"You take care of yourself, hear?"

"Oh, I will," he says, carelessly. "It's you who should be careful, riding into the wild lands."

"As if Glory Mesa hasn't had its share of dangers," I tease.

"It'll be safe. I'll be watching it. Who knows, maybe I'll even be sheriff one day."

"I wouldn't be surprised."

"Well," he says, holding out his hand, "goodbye."

I grasp it firmly, then swing up into the saddle.

Peter starts back up the street, but he calls again. "Goodbye, Kate!"

I turn around in the saddle and I wave. He's a tall, lone figure standing in the street, waving his goodbye.

And somehow in my heart I know I'm never coming back.

I trot out to the old oak tree where the men used to gather for the posses. Still standing. Almost unchanged.

I stop the horse. This feeling inside me is so powerful I can barely move. I wouldn't trade the years here for anything. The people, this place we built. Archer told us we would build this territory with our own hands. And we did.

But it's been done, and it's time to move on. I have a future, and it's westward, on and on, into the setting sun.

Peter's gone, just the dust kicked up by the wind in his place. A tear drops so swiftly it misses my cheek altogether. I'm not sad—not exactly. The weight of what we were, what was and isn't now, is stronger than joy or grief.

I turn and face west. The sun's in the east right now, at my back. I whistle sharp and touch my pinto with the spurs.

I'll race it to the horizon.

The settlement is half in shadow, half in strong golden light from the setting sun. The houses are spread out by a mile or more each, well-built, standing on good earth, with creeks running and wells standing by sturdy fences. Fences that surround rich, dark earth, plowed up and sown with seed.

Smoke rises from chimneys, promising warmth and food and safety. This is what a home should look like.

I'm walking my horse. He took a little lame a week back and has been favoring his leg, so I've walked.

But what do I care if it takes me a week, a month, a year? We thought we'd never have this.

Good news can keep.

At a water stop earlier in the day, I asked after a White family, a father and daughter. They told me they were living down the river ten or fifteen miles, on a spread staked large enough for two farms.

My heart filled near to bursting when I heard that.

It's been twelve miles now, and I see a house, small but solid, the sort a man builds to stay in while he spends a couple years raising the big house where he wants to live the rest of his life.

A light shines inside already, but clothes are still hung out on a line in the fading light, and a woman is taking them down.

She sees me and goes inside. My heart is in my throat. I'm not afraid, but still my palms sweat.

I hear a laugh and stop short.

"It's just a traveler, father. His horse is lame." And she steps out onto the porch.

It's her, with her proud chin and determined nose, her hair pinned up high on her head.

She freezes, her fingers resting on the door handle. "Jack." It's just a whisper.

I leave my horse and walk slowly to the foot of the porch. "Beatrice. If you'll still have me—I am here."

Her eyebrows draw in with surprise. "What kind of a question is that?"

She runs down the porch stairs and throws herself into my arms with a sobbing laugh. "You made it, Jack. I was so afraid you wouldn't."

I put my arms gently around her. My heart's been afraid

to be glad until this moment. But now it bursts. Tears fill my eyes, stream down my face, and I'm laughing with her.

"Jack, what's wrong?" She pulls away just enough to look into my face.

"Nothing is wrong." I grip her hands tightly. I'm looking into her earnest green eyes, and I've never seen anything so beautiful. "Nothing at all."

She reaches up, her fingers touching the scar on my cheek, then my hair, her eyes searching mine as if she's looking for something.

"You look worn," she says, solemnly.

"Old sorrows," I say, taking her hand and kissing it. "All in the past."

"I want to show you our land, but not until you've rested. You're too thin, too."

"I've lived in the wilds for years, Beatrice. It's how I am now."

"A little more won't hurt you. I want to take care of you now." She pauses. "You aren't against farming?"

"No, not at all."

A little belonging—putting down roots—is exactly what my heart yearns for.

Gently I take her in my arms, put my arm around her shoulder where it belongs. The sunset is blazing like fire over the wide, wide horizon, and for the first time in years, my heart beats like it wants to live.

She turns in my arms, leans her head back against my shoulder. We're watching the setting sun together.

Then she laughs a little under her breath.

"What is it?"

She unclasps her necklace and slips my mother's ring back on her finger.

"I'll get down on my knee again if you like," I say.

"Tomorrow, perhaps." She leans her head back against me.

She cranes her neck around again as if she's just thought of something, and she looks up at me, eyes twinkling. "What if we just have the preacher come round tomorrow instead? He's a circuit preacher. If we don't have him tomorrow, we'll have to wait a month."

"I think I've kept you waiting long enough."

"My dress won't be white," she murmurs to herself, amused.

96

# NEWTON

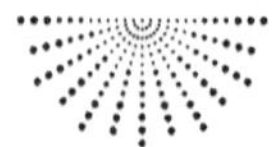

EVERY YEAR, I TAKE CHRIS TO VISIT HIS FATHER. HE'S laid to rest up on the piney cliffs overlooking his land. From up here I can see the fields that burned the week we were married, and I miss even that—the soot, the choking air, weeping in his arms.

At least we had each other.

I lay a bouquet of pale mountain wildflowers on the pine-strewn sand in front of his headstone and read the inscription, as I do every time I come.

Cristobal Newton. His dates, a mere thirty-one years. Husband, father, and friend.

I wish that I had been brave and told him that night what I suspected but didn't know for sure. At least he could have hoped for it a little.

"Give your flowers to Papa," I urge, crouching down beside him to help his little fingers lay his flowers down.

He's got his daddy's black hair and blue eyes, the same solemn expression.

The wind brings me the sound of slow hoofbeats. Someone is riding up the mountain.

It's a tall man, wearing a duster and smoking a cigarette. I haven't seen him more than once or twice since Chris died, but I know it's Harrison. You cannot mistake those eyes, no matter how weathered or weary the face is.

He comes over, not seeing us right away, then slows as he sees us by the grave.

"It's all right, you can come."

He trudges up, taking his cigarette out of his mouth.

"Sorry, ma'am." Harrison drops his smoke into the dust and grinds it out with his heel.

For a few minutes we stand in silence, regarding the stone and the land around it. The birds are singing peacefully in the trees. They are rarely disturbed by our presence up here.

"Do you come here often?" I ask.

"Yes, ma'am. I know you were here during a bad time between your husband and I, but he was one of the truest friends I ever had."

"He spoke of you highly when I first came out West. He really did."

He just swallows and gives a little grunt of assent.

"This your son?"

"Chris."

"Pleasure," he says, extending his hand and crouching down to be on the boy's level.

Solemnly, Chris holds out his hand and shakes Harrison's. "Pleasure," he echoes.

Harrison smiles at him slightly and straightens.

"I hear you've done your best by the place."

"I've done my best. I've tried to make the right decisions, if I can."

He smiles and looks at the ground, an ironic expression on his face. "Let me rephrase that. I've heard what you've done with the place. And you've done good. They're decisions Chris would have made, I'm sure of it."

My heart warms as I thought it no longer could.

"Thank you." I extend my hand and he grasps it politely.

"Well, I should be going. Like I said, I just—come up here from time to time." Harrison looks down at my boy. "Your father would have been real proud of you, kid."

He tips his hat to us both and collects his horse. I listen to the wind in the trees until the sound of the hoofbeats are swallowed up in it.

# 97

# THATCHER

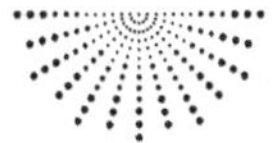

PPEOPLE PASSING THROUGH OFTEN ASK IF IT'S TRUE THAT my cousin was the first Territorial Governor of this here land.

I tell them he was.

Legends sprang up around Glory Mesa and its first governor quicker than a brushfire after he left town, and especially when he never went back.

Let me tell you, those stories range from beautiful to downright hair-raising.

I listen to them all, smiling and agreeing, glad for a break from work.

Some think he's dead. Others think he packed up and left for the far west, discontent with the civilization that came about after his resignation. Still others claim he's gone to the hills to sleep, to wake if ever the territory should find itself in danger again.

I don't correct them. When pressed, I don't tell.

But of a quiet day, I saddle my horse and ride down below the mesas, through the pine forests, and out to the gentle hills scattered far and wide with purple sagebrush and blooming cactus.

There, miles from anything but the beautiful land, stands a tall house and a barn and a corral of horses.

There's a garden with a white fence around it, and the house is painted with a neat blue trim, the very picture of beauty and contentment.

And if I'm lucky, as I often am, I'll see a tall familiar figure chopping wood for a supper I'm likely to dream of for the next week, the smell of fresh bread already on the air.

And in the yard, humming a sweet song to herself as she dances in sunbeams, is a tall young girl with flaxen hair.

9 8

PETER

No one alive remembers the people of Glory Mesa and the Western Territory as they were. Except for me, and I am now old.

Harrison Terhune never married and he died without family. On his death, it was found that he had left his ranch to young Cristobal Newton, and the boy, twenty-five and newly married, became the richest man in the territory.

Since, he's served a term as governor, though he admits to me that it only served to sharpen his desire to return to his own spread.

He's too modest. People said he was the best governor we've had since Archer Scott.

Every so often, he comes back with his children and grandchildren to visit. He does so more now that his mother, long-lived and well provided-for, has passed.

One of Jem Swift's sons runs the Swift ranch now. Jem

rebuilt the house with his own hands, and after a few years, Max came home and they grew the place to be twice the ranch it had been before.

Both were loved and great pillars of the territory when their times came.

As for me, I became Glory Mesa's sheriff and I held the position for forty-three years. But even after that, I couldn't bring myself to leave, though I live a little ways out of town now, away from the noise.

I GO OUT into the hills sometimes and just listen to the wind blowing. I do it more and more now.

Some days I think perhaps I will come over a hill to find Doctor Sikes, standing there in his black coat. I am not convinced the old man is entirely gone.

In the thunder, when it rolls off the hills, sometimes I still think I hear his voice.

When the herds of wild horses cross the plains, their hoofbeats drumming like the storm rains in summer, I think of the posse that followed Marshal Lacey, when they were stronger than an army. When the sky is hot and bright and the ever-thinning *isarks* pass the sun, I think of the rifleman Selby, who was worthier than many other men with cleaner hands. And when dawn rises, gold and pure over the eastern range, I think of Alan Swift, whose resting place sees the morning sun first of us all.

Our land is free and does not remember the curse. The

storm is over, and we survived it. All we know now is peace and the abundance of the earth. We benefit from the warmth of the sun and the watering of the rain. Our fields are full of ripe grain, our cattle graze on good land, our rivers are strong and clear.

All because of those whose tears and blood came before and made this place a good place to live.

No other man alive remembers them, for I am the last.

But the land remembers them. And the land will never forget.

# ACKNOWLEDGMENTS

When I come to the end of a journey like this, I'm not even sure what to say. After three books in the same world, on the same land, with the same people, you don't just get attached —you come out a slightly different person. Even when I move on to other stories, there will always be a piece of this one in my heart.

Thank you to my loyal readers who have taken this journey with me. Thank you for the love you have freely bestowed on these beautiful ones. And thank you for letting my show you the West as it is in my heart.

To Callie Sioux, for her generous insights, and to the memory of her friends, who helped bring me to a decision I didn't have the strength to make alone.

To my street team, who are really the coolest set of individuals...thanks for your input, for your support, and for spreading the word.

To James Egan, for the absolute ringer of a cover. Thank you for making my book look as cool as House Atreides sounds.

To my "coffee squad," especially Hannah, my dad, and my own real life Peter.

To The Inkwell, for being there for me. You are my squad, and I am a much saner and happier author for having you all in my life. And to The Storyteller's Hall and other individuals who kept me afloat with sprints and encouragement, much thanks.

To Cindy, Katie, Lydia, Hannah, Amy, Claire, Mollie, and every other friend who spoke truth and life to this tired author. You already know words have power, but these you gave me...they were extra special.

To my proofreaders, thank you, thank you, thank you. Jellybeans are on the house.

To Elisabeth, my editor, for the work that makes these books shine. From the days of 1 a.m. bao to the days we faced down the impossible, you're my SC.

To those whose collaboration made all these amazing characters come to life, your contributions were invaluable. I won't forget these hours. I had the time of my life fighting dragons with you.

Praise God from whom all blessings flow. You gave me this gift, and you have seen me through. I don't always know the next step, but I know who is leading me. Thank you.

EMILY HAYSE is a lover of log cabins, strong coffee, NASCAR, and the smell of old books. Her writing is fueled by good characters and a lifelong passion for storytelling. When she is not busy turning words into worlds, she can often be found baking, singing, or caring for one of the many dogs and horses in her life. She lives with her family in Michigan.

ALSO BY EMILY HAYSE

Crowning Heaven

Seventh City

The Last Atlantean

The Rivers Lead Home

These War-Torn Hands

The Beautiful Ones